Other Books by Emilee Hines

Fiction
Voting for Love
The Christmas dance
The Proposal
Callie's Choice
A Place to Love
Burnt Station
Shadows on a White Wall

Nonfiction
It Happened in Virginia
Til Death Do Us Part
East African Odyssey
Virginia's Remarkable Women
Virginia Myths and Legends
Speaking Ill of the Dead: Jerks in Washington DC

The Prince
and
the Passion

by
Emilee Hines

The Prince and the Passion
Copyright © 2017 Emilee Hines Cantieri
Cover and interior design by Joe Perrone Jr.

Published by Escarpment Press

ISBN-13: 978-0692976470 (Escarpment Press)
ISBN-10: 0692976477

First Edition
ALL RIGHTS RESERVED
10 9 8 7 6 5 4 3 2 1

Cover illustration copyright Catmando/Shutterstock.com
Sword illustration copyright Graphics RF/Shutterstock.com
Viking ship icon copyright Kurbanov/Shutterstock.com

In Appreciation

I wish to express my appreciation to Michael Myatt and Janice Liedl-Myatt for their help with the history of this period; to Barbara Liedl, who verifies facts swiftly; to Corinne Shane, my travel buddy when we explored Kiev and Kherson; and to Joe Perrone Jr for designing this book.

Chapter 1

The Forest of Kievan Russia, 988 AD

Talia pushed open the door of the log house and gazed out at the snow that fell so thickly she could see no farther than the third house away. Beyond lay forest and beyond that the unknown, still and frozen.

Fire smoldered in the center of the room, sending an acrid wisp of smoke upward through the hole in the roof. Their last log was burning, already turning to gray ash at the edges.

Beside the fire on a bed of pine boughs her mother lay, wrapped in bearskins, Talia bent, took her mother's thin, icy hand and said, "It's still snowing, Mother. I can't wait any longer going for firewood. Will you be all right?"

There was a slight nod. Then, "Tell your father . . ." Her voice faded.

"He'll be back soon," Talia said with more assurance than she felt. The hunters should have returned days ago. The food supply was dwindling, and the village would be almost helpless if raiders came. Only the very old men, lame Sasha, and young boys remained as protectors.

Talia could not meet her mother's eyes. They both knew the truth about their situation, but did not speak of it. "You can tell Father yourself when he comes, Mother."

"I won't be here."

"Don't say that." She squeezed her mother's hand and tucked it underneath the bearskin wrap, then went to pull on her boots. She fastened her fur cloak tightly about her and put on fur mittens. Picking up the ax, she went out. The snowflakes had turned into icy pellets that stung her face. She longed to stay inside by the fire, warm and protected, but that could not be. There was no warmth or safety. Unless she found fuel, they would both freeze to death.

The village was quiet and still, waiting. No deep, masculine voices or children's laughter broke the silence. Everyone huddled inside by the fire.

Talia's breath steamed the air as she floundered through the deepening snow, and when she inhaled deeply, her nostrils crinkled with frost.

Not far off the trail she found a suitable tree, and swung the ax at its base. As the blade bit into the tree trunk, wedge-shaped chips sprayed the snow around her. Cutting wood was satisfying. It was something she could do for her mother, something she did well. Lacking a son, her father had taught her to handle manly tasks.

She liked the smell of fresh-cut wood and the pull of her muscles as she swung the ax, the sharp crack as the last blow was struck and the tree surrendered.

The tree swayed for a moment before crashing onto the forest floor in a cascade of snow. She lopped off a large branch and began dragging it toward the village. Later she could cut it into smaller sections and come back for the main body of the tree. For now, this would warm her mother through another night. Perhaps if her mother were really warm, she wouldn't cough, that rasping cough that sometimes-signaled death.

As she emerged from the forest, she saw horsemen far down the trail. Her father and the others were coming home at last! She was about to wave and call out a greeting when she saw they were strangers. She hadn't heard them, for the snow muffled the sound of their approach. They rode slowly, silently, in single file. The horses plodded toward her, little puffs of steam coming from their nostrils. Leading the riders was a giant red-bearded man swathed in fur. He lifted his hand, and the caravan behind him halted.

No one moved. Even the horses were still, only snorting quietly. The leader swept his hood back with one hand, revealing a mane of red hair, and slowly swiveled his head to study his surroundings.

Talia sucked in her breath. How handsome he was! She felt her mouth shaping a smile of welcome, but her instinct told her to flee. He was a stranger, coming to the village at a time when no outsiders came. When the village was unprotected.

Had he seen her? Talia dared not move, sure the stranger's eagle eyes had found her, his prey. Perhaps her breath made giveaway puffs of steam, like the horses' breaths. Placing a hand over her mouth and nose, she stepped back carefully, only to trip over the tree branch she'd cut, tumbling backward into the snow.

The leader half-turned and gestured in her direction. A man behind him slid down from his horse and ran toward her. "She's mine!" he shouted.

"No!" the red-haired one commanded. "Bring her to me."

Talia stared at him for a moment, transfixed. But she had to escape, to warn the village! She scrambled to her feet and tried to run. She fell again, managed to pull herself up, and plunged on a few more desperate steps before the pursuer grabbed her.

His breath was hot and wet on her face as he pushed her into the snow and fell atop her. Holding her down with one hand, he began to grapple at her legs, trying to lift her fur tunic.

"No! Leave me alone!" Talia screamed. Her voice caught in her throat. Twisting her body, she struggled to free herself, but he was stronger and heavier. Her efforts only burrowed them deeper into the snow. She tried to think. She must save herself. The ax! Where had she dropped it? Her fingers touched its handle and she grasped it and swung it upward against her torturer.

She struck a glancing blow, hitting him not with the sharpened blade, but with the flat of the ax. Still, it stunned him into relaxing his hold on her for a moment, long enough for her to roll out from under him and pull herself to her feet.

He cursed and came at her again, but this time Talia was ready. With legs braced, she gripped the ax in both hands and swung. He grabbed for the ax, but the momentum of her blow knocked him off balance. She felt the blade bite into him. There was a sharp crack, and Talia knew with a thrill of satisfaction that she'd broken a bone in his arm. A red stain appeared on his fur-clad arm where she'd cut through his tunic.

Gasping in ragged breaths of the cold air, Talia turned to run for the village, but her attacker was not finished with her. "She-Wolf!" he cried, lunging for her. He caught the back of her cloak with his good hand.

"That's enough, Rognol!" the leader commanded.

The one called Rognol loosed his hold on her, but stayed so close she still feared him. She could feel the heat of his body and smell his stinking breath. She raised her gaze to her savior, the red-bearded leader of the group. He dismounted unsheathed his sword, pressing its point against the neck of her attacker.

Flakes of snow clung to his red-gold hair. His eyes, she saw, were not a raptor's, but regarded her with something akin to interest.

"Thank you," she whispered.

"Are you all right?" he asked, pulling her out of Rognol's reach.

Talia nodded, disconcerted by his presence. For a moment she clung to him gratefully, feeling safe in the circle of his arm. Then he released her.

Talia stepped back and looked up at him. His glance swept over her, judging her, and she felt herself flushing before the force of it. She couldn't move away or speak.

With his gloved hand he swept back the hood of her cloak, exposing her face to the stinging needles of snow. Taking her chin in his hand, he turned her head gently from side to side. "As beautiful as she is brave," he said. "She will fetch a good price."

"Kill her, Andrei," her attacker demanded. "Or let me. You see what she did to me." He pressed his hand against the blood seeping through his sleeve

4

"You deserved it," Andrei said. "Another minute and you'd have destroyed her value. There'll be time enough to slake your lust on the way to Byzantium. But not with this one. This brave little Slav is mine."

Talia heard admiration in his voice, but the rest of what he said puzzled and frightened her. Where was this Byzantium, and what did he mean about her "price"?

He turned the sword on her. "You. Walk ahead of us."

Talia felt numb with fear and cold. What would Andrei, the red-bearded one, do with her? He had saved her from ravishment and possible death—for she'd have killed herself if Rognol had taken her in lust. But for what? What was to happen to her? She made her feet move, one sluggish step ahead of the other, back to the trail where the other horsemen waited.

Andrei mounted his horse in a smooth motion and turned back to Talia. "Are you alone?"

She nodded, unable to speak. In spite of his calming voice, he frightened her almost as much as the one called Rognol did, but she made herself meet his gaze, and kept her hands tight on the ax handle to still their shaking.

"What were you doing out here?"

"Gathering wood." Couldn't he see? She pointed to the branch she'd cut. "May I bring this? My mother is ill and the house grows cold."

"Have you no father?"

"He is away." Did they know that the village was defenseless? Attackers, like traders, usually came in the spring, when the snow had gone and travel was easier and when there were skins to trade. There was little in the village now that would interest these armed intruders. So why had they come?

Andrei shrugged as if it didn't matter and gestured to another horseman, who rode up beside him. "Bring the branch." He held out his hand to Talia. "I'll take the ax."

"I have need for it." She glanced at the one called Rognol.

"I'll protect you and see that Rognol is punished."

"Rewarded, more likely," she returned.

He ignored her remark. "You have no choice now. Later, if you need the ax, I'll return it."

Their gazes met and held in a challenge of wills, then reluctantly she passed him her only weapon.

The young horseman dismounted and pulled the branch, with one hand, while he led his horse with the other. Talia trudged ahead of the group as Andrei instructed.

He signaled his troop to move. "We've lost the possibility of surprise. Her scream no doubt alerted the village, thanks to you, Rognol."

The trail broadened and became the snow-covered meadow with clusters of houses. People were outside, drawn by her scream as Andrei had predicted. Talia glanced at the third house on the right, where her mother lay ill.

Before Andrei could stop her, she plunged toward it, screaming, "Mother!" She heard hoof beats behind her, then beside her, before she flung herself to the side, against a protecting tree. The horseman thundered past and jerked his horse around, ready for another attack.

All around her women and children ran in panic. The curiosity that had brought them out into the snow was their undoing. Too late they realized they were the prey of the intruders. The horsemen spurred forward, shouting with blood-curdling frenzy as they rode right into the midst of the villagers.

"We don't want to kill you!" Andrei shouted. "Stand where you are and save yourselves." Few heard or heeded him. Mothers shielded their children behind them, or urged their young to run while they stood resolutely facing the horsemen. Talia saw one old man tottering blindly from his house out into the middle of the street. Before she could scream a warning, he was crushed underneath horses' hooves. Another man managed to send an arrow toward the attackers before he was cut down. She saw that it was Sasha. His lame body crumpled into the snow, and his blood dyed it crimson.

"Run! Run!" she screamed, but knew that her voice was lost in the din. She couldn't help her neighbors, but maybe she could save her mother. She thrust open the door and went in, seeking her mother in the dimness.

"Mother, we must go!"

Her mother said nothing. "Mother, wake up!" Talia urged. Could she carry her mother outside and slip away into the woods?

She gathered her mother's limp body into her arms and stood, uncertain what to do next. The acrid odor of smoke pouring through the door opening made her choice. The whole village was ablaze. Flames licked over the log houses with an audible crackle, and sparks danced in the air, red and gold amid the white snowflakes.

The roof above her caught fire, the curls of bark like tinder to the flames. A section fell onto the sleeping area where her mother had lain, and the pine boughs caught fire with a great whoosh.

Andrei was suddenly there in front of her, wheeling his horse before the log house. "Get out!" he shouted. "Do you want to burn?"

"Help me carry my mother."

Dismounting, he took the older woman and flung her over his shoulder as easily as he would have flung on a fur cloak. "Gather up what you can and get out," he commanded.

Making her way through the thick smoke, Talia found her mother's carved wooden chest. Whatever happened to them, her mother would want that. Tears stung Talia's eyes and she coughed, choking on the smoke. She shoved the little chest out into the snow and grabbed the fur bed coverings, escaping just as the entire house exploded in flames.

"Over there," Andrei ordered, pointing to a sheltering fir tree away from the flames. Talia stumbled after him, carrying the small chest and the furs. She looked back over her shoulder at the burning village, at the bodies that littered the clearing. Snow could not fall fast enough to cover the spreading red stains.

Andrei walked ahead of her to the edge of the forest and dropped his burden in the snow at Talia's feet.

"What are you doing?" Talia gasped. "You'll hurt her."

"Not anymore. She's dead. You might as well have let her burn. That's the best way to dispose of the dead." He strode away, walking among the corpses. "Fools! Why did they let themselves be killed? What a waste. I didn't want them dead."

Talia dropped to her knees and cradled her mother's head against her breast. "Mother, Mother," she keened. "If only I hadn't left you. If only Father were here." Tears spilled from her eyes and turned icy on her face. Gently she pressed closed her mother's unseeing eyes and drew the fur mantle over the beloved face, as if her mother might still feel the cold. Snowflakes and ash fell around Talia and on her, but she was insensible to them both.

Gradually she became aware that the flames were subsiding, that no horsemen were shouting. The only sounds were sobs, her own and others'. Her village was a blackened mass of partially burned logs that hissed as snow touched the hot coals. A choking cloud of smoke hung over everything. In the center of the road the horsemen had surrounded a shivering group of young women and children. Mothers pressed their young families against them, shielding their eyes from the horror.

Talia recognized her friend Olga, though Olga's hair had been burned away and her clothing hung in dark tatters. Olga gripped the hand of her little brother Grigor. Her eyes had the glazed look of someone staring into another world.

The child sniffed and a great shuddering sob shook his body. At his feet lay his beloved dog, a bloody mass trampled beneath the invaders' horses. Grigor broke away from his sister and lunged at the nearest horsemen. "Why did you have to kill him? Wasn't it enough you killed my mother?"

"Grigor, don't!" Olga begged, pulling him back.

"Keep him quiet, or we'll kill him too," the horseman ordered. Talia recognized the voice, and saw that it was Rognol, one arm hanging bloody and limp. Hatred burned in his eyes—hatred for her, and for her whole village—for what she had done to him in fighting back. A shiver of fear wracked her body at the sight of him.

She forced herself to look away, naming silently the fallen villagers whose corpses were being covered in cold, white mantles. What was the purpose of this raid? What had the horsemen gained by destroying a village? There was little enough to steal, only the furs that covered them and the scant food they'd stored for the winter. A few people owned bits of amber and lumps of ambergris, or even a handful of jewels, but all that treasure had gone up in flames or was buried beneath ash and smoldering logs.

Andrei strode back into the clearing, herding three dazed little girls ahead of him.

"Search the bodies of the dead, strip them and leave them for the birds," he ordered.

Cruel! Talia thought. *Barbarous!* Her mother was fortunate to have died of her illness, asleep and unknowing of this atrocity. At least she didn't have to see her friends murdered and her home turned to ashes.

Andrei's men moved through the corpses, stripping off furs and metal jewelry. The survivors stared numbly, unable to believe the horror before them.

Talia realized that Andrei stood before her and had said something.

"We are going," he repeated.

"What about my mother?"

"Leave her. The ravens will pick her corpse clean in the spring. It's the way your people deal with corpses, is it not?"

"She was not of that belief," Talia said, her hand still resting on the curve of her mother's head. "She was a Christian."

"Oh, one of the new sect." He thrust his sword into its scabbard and reached for her hand to help her up.

"She must be buried," she said, ignoring his outstretched hand. Even as she said the words, she knew how difficult that would be. Beneath the snow the ground was stone hard.

"We can't spare the time. We must reach camp before daylight fades."

"I can't just leave her here. I will stay with her."

"And do what? Fight off the hungry animals that come to feed on corpses? Starve? Or freeze? Look around you." With a gesture he indicated the ruined village.

Talia closed her eyes, refusing to look at the village or at him, the destroyer. She half expected to hear the swish of a sword pulled free, to feel its bite against her neck—and then nothing. Why had he spared her when others had been killed? Earlier she had thought him handsome and had been grateful to him. Now she could only envision his cruelty.

"Oh, very well," he said unexpectedly. "We'll bury your mother in the Christian way. I won't leave you here to die." His voice sounded different, more subdued, and weary.

Talia stood and threw a quick glance at his face, not comprehending why he had suddenly agreed to her request. Did he feel any pity for her in her grief, or any shame for the wanton killing?

He called out to several men, and soon had them hacking away at the ground with axes and swords, scooping out a shallow indentation. Talia watched, oblivious to the cold. As they prepared to roll the body in, Andrei said, "Take off the cloak."

"No! Don't leave her naked," Talia begged.

"She has no further need of clothing, but you do," he said. "Heat and cold are the same for her now. Take it off."

Talia knelt, undid the fastening of the fur cloak and pulled it free. Her mother's arms and legs emerged sickly pale and thin, but Talia was relieved to see that underneath the cloak her mother had worn a coarse woven shift. Almost as if she had known her cloak would be taken away.

Talia turned aside as the men scraped and kicked frozen clods of dirt and small stones over the body and finally piled rocks atop it. Bowing her head as she'd seen her mother do, Talia tried to form her thoughts into a prayer. She regretted she had never accepted her mother's belief while it might have meant something, but it was too late now. Her God must be powerless anyway. Otherwise all this horror never would have happened. Still, she must honor her mother's wishes. From the blackened remains of their house, Talia found two sticks and laid one across the other over her mother's grave, forming a simple cross. When her father came back, he would recognize the symbol, and know that his wife lay there. But what would he know about his daughter's fate? Could she leave him a message? But she didn't know where she was going.

"Let's go," Andrei said, breaking into her thoughts. He held his horse's reins with one hand and with the other he brushed the snow from her hair and lifted the hood of her cloak. Talia reached up to fasten it in place and her hand brushed his.

"I don't want you to die of cold," he said. "Though I've heard it said that it is a peaceful way to die."

"How does anyone know?" Talia said. "The dead can't tell us anything."

He nodded agreement, then mounted his horse and dug his heels into its side, turning it southward. "Put on your mother's cloak," he ordered Talia.

"No. Olga needs it more," she said, passing it to her ragged neighbor. Olga pulled it around her and lifted the hood to hide her blackened scalp. Talia picked up the chest and the fur bed coverings.

"When my father returns with the other men, how will he know where to find us? I must stay and tell them what happened."

"We came upon a group of hunters —"

"You killed them!" she cried. "Not just my village." Tears sprang anew to her eyes

"They were already dead and had been robbed."

"I don't believe you."

"Whether you believe or not changes nothing. I have no time to argue with you." He wheeled his horse around and shouted commands, and his men quickly formed a column.

Each horseman was lifting a child or a young woman onto his horse. Rognol rode toward her. "Climb up here," he ordered.

Talia stood, unmoving, clutching the small wooden chest, the bearskin over her shoulder. "No. Kill me here," she said.

Andrei charged between them and reached for her, hoisting her up onto the horse ahead of him as easily as if she had been a child. One strong arm remained around her waist, holding her close against him.

Talia's heart hammered painfully against her chest and her hands shook so she almost dropped the chest and furs. She looked down in terror. The distance from the horse's back to the ground was immense, and she'd seen the damage those hooves could do. What if she fell off? That didn't seem likely, as Andrei had her in his grip and the horse's back was solid and warm.

A moment before she'd been ready to die, but now she'd had a reprieve. Once more Andrei had rescued her from Rognol. Why? Where were they going, and what would become of her?

As the horse began to move, Talia stared back through thick-falling snow at the smoldering ruins of the only home she'd ever known. She could not stay, waiting for her father's return, even if Andrei had lied to her, even if he released his hold on her. The food was burned, the animals killed or tied to horses, the mother she loved lying beneath a heap of stones. Everything she valued was gone. Her present and future loomed equally bleak. Her last view of the village was dark smoking shapes half-obscured by falling snow. Then the trail turned, and even that image was lost.

She was riding away, in the warm, firm grip of a murderer. "What do you gain attacking villages of old people and children?" she demanded.

"I am following the commands of my lord Prince Vladimir. Even the old and weak can cause him trouble. Your tribe has not accepted his rule and must be subjugated."

"What could your lord Vladimir offer us if we accept him?" she blurted, amazed at her own temerity.

"His protection against warring hordes from the East."

"But nothing protects us from you, his soldiers. You are all killers, even the prince himself. He killed his own brother."

"He did not actually perform the killing," Andrei said. After a moment he conceded, "But he saw it done."

When he spoke, his breath was disturbingly warm against Talia's neck. Her hood had slipped down. She managed to tug it up over her hair, putting the fur between them. "How can you defend your prince?" she asked. "Killing seems common in his family. The brother he killed had killed another brother."

"I see that bad news spreads, even in the forest and villages of far Russia," he said. He shifted slightly behind her, pulling her more closely against his hard, muscular body.

She realized it was futile to struggle against him. "What is my purpose? What am I to do for your lord Vladimir?"

"Whatever I order you to do," Andrei returned. "You are my slave."

Chapter 2

As the horsemen moved southward, leaving the village behind, Talia made no further effort to look back. What was there to see? Blackened ruins and still, white shapes in the snow. And her mother's grave, which would soon be indistinguishable from other slight mounds in the forest floor.

Would she ever return? Was there any reason to return? She could still hear in her mind the crackling flames, the screams and the soft thunking sound when a weapon struck flesh.

She couldn't think beyond the present moment. The easy rocking motion of the horse lulled her into a dazed state between asleep and awake. She was conscious only of the bearded man's arm around her waist, supporting her, the fur robe around her and the little wooden chest she clutched against her. When she shifted her position to ease the numbness in her legs, the man tightened his grip on her.

"Have you ever been on a horse before?" His voice was low, concerned.

"No."

"Then I think I should continue to hold you. If you fall off, you might be injured, or trampled by the horses behind us."

"And would that be worse than being your slave?"

"Most people would think so. Are you Slavs so different?"

His tone was mocking, and she could think of no answer. Was she different? She had nothing to compare herself with, never having seen anyone beyond the next village. Those people were very much like her own neighbors, growing cabbages, onions and wheat and using the forests for fuel and building, hunting the fur-bearing animals. They worshipped the same gods: Svarog, the father; Perun, god of thunder and lightning; Strigog, who controlled the winds. A few, like her mother, had been converted by wandering priests who came in the spring along with the traders, but most still followed the old ways.

What had happened to the people in that next village? Had they also been captured? And what of her father and Oleg, the man she was promised to? Had they been killed as her captor said?

Snow soon stopped falling and the sky grew lighter. How long have we been riding? Talia wondered. Time was meaningless without a destination or a purpose.

"Have you a name?" the man asked, breaking the silence.

Of course she did. "Talia Militskaya."

He repeated it, and when she said nothing, he added, "My name is Andrei Ivanovich."

She didn't repeat his name. It meant nothing to her, though the proud way he said it indicated that he thought she might recognize its significance. What had he done that would make his name known in her part of the great forest?

After another long silence, she asked, "Where are we going?"

"To our camp at Kiev. It lies by the great river."

"How far away is it?"

"Perhaps another two hours of riding."

"What will happen to me then?"

"It depends on many things. You may receive food and some mead to drink if you give me no trouble in the meantime."

Again, Talia lapsed into silence. What kind of trouble could she give him? She couldn't run away even if the horse stopped and Andrei released her. She'd be lost in the wilderness, and would quickly freeze. Her feet felt numb in her soft leather boots, even though she had stuffed moss into them before she went out for wood. She wriggled her toes as much as she could inside the boots. Her thighs ached from being stretched across the broad back of the horse, and from the weight of the horrible one, Rognol, when he'd thrown himself on her in the forest. She was glad she'd broken his arm, but she wished she'd killed him. He was alive, and simmering with hatred for her.

What had happened to her neighbors? She leaned out to the side, trying to peer around Andrei but his body blocked her view. It mattered not. There was nothing she could do to improve their condition any more than her own. Her concern must be holding onto the horse, and she must not anger the red-bearded giant who held her destiny in his grasp.

They stopped.

Talia's eyes flew open and she looked around at the strange village. Children ran out to greet the caravan, dogs racing beside them. From holes in the earth men gathered, laughing and slapping their palms against the horses' rumps, and then against her legs.

Talia shrank from their touch. They seemed to be assessing her like an animal for slaughter. Andrei kept a tight hold on her and turned the horse, moving her away from the grasping hands.

Stranger than the people were the homes they came from, almost like caves cut into the side of a hill. Smoke curled from several holes in the snow–covered roofs. Small, low doorways were outlined with wooden poles.

But there were larger structures too, not made of logs but of stone, and as she looked back, she saw an enormous wooden gate being closed, shutting them in.

Andrei released her and swung off the horse, then lifted her to the ground with a single, smooth motion.

Talia crumpled onto the snow, her legs too numb to support her. The little wooden chest dropped from her grasp.

"Massage your legs," Andrei commanded. "The feeling will return." As if she didn't understand, he squatted beside her, shoved her fur leggings up to expose her skin, and began to rub her ankles.

His bare hands were strong and warm, dispelling the cold. He pressed gently, then encircled her right leg and moved his hands upward.

Talia's eyes widened. What was he doing? He released the leg and grasped the left one. Talia felt her face growing warm along with her legs. She drew away, confused. She should not be feeling pleasure at the touch of this man, this murderer. "I can stand now," she said.

He released her. "Then go in there." Pointing to one of the earthen hovels, he stood, offering her his hand. Talia ignored the offer and pushed herself up. The wooden chest lay only a few feet in front of her, but he made no move to touch it. She picked it up and walked toward the doorway, conscious of him beside her. She heard his low chuckle as he muttered something about proud Slav women.

"Our houses are better than these holes in the earth," she said scornfully.

"At least they don't burn," he answered

"Ours didn't until you came." The bitter memory returned, and she wouldn't look at him.

He turned from her, and she heard the jingling of harnesses as the horses were led away.

She felt oddly bereft without him, though a moment before she'd seethed with hatred for him. But she wasn't alone here. Eighteen of her neighbors had survived including Olga, who was soon to give birth. How had she managed the ride? She was bent over, moaning in pain.

"Olga, can I help you?"

"I think my babe will come tonight."

"It's too soon."

"I know." She gripped Talia's outstretched hand so tightly Talia winced. She managed to get Olga's arm over her shoulder and the two staggered toward the doorway. The group was being split: women in one house, children in another. Children wailed in terror as they were led away from their mothers by strange women.

Moving with slow dragging steps, Talia reached the shelter with her burden. She bent low to get through the door opening and pulled Olga into the house after her. It was surprisingly warm and neat inside. A fire burning within a circle of big stones in the center furnished the heat and the only light. An iron pot was swung over the fire on three metal poles, joined at the top. Something meaty simmered there, emitting a tantalizing aroma that made Talia's stomach rumble with hunger. Around the edges of the dugout, skins lay on low wooden platforms for sleeping.

A woman with long braided hair motioned them to stand in a circle and then walked around the dazed prisoners. She paused in front of Olga, poked her finger into the distended belly and said, "Soon you will be screaming like a mare." With unexpected kindness, she led Olga to one of the platforms and then went to the fire and dipped out a gourd full of the steaming broth. "You eat," she commanded. Olga took a few sips and turned away, curling herself into a ball.

Before the woman approached anyone else to offer food, Andrei came into the dugout, stooping low for the doorway, his great bulk filling the house. The woman in charge looked shocked at his sudden appearance, but made no effort to stop him.

"Talia Militskaya, do you know how to care for wounds?"

"Somewhat," she answered.

"It is our custom that the one who causes an injury should try to heal it. Since you broke Rognol's arm, you shall come with me to tend him."

Talia started to protest, but the way he had spoken told her protesting would be useless. She followed him silently out into the cold. He stopped before the doorway of one of the stone structures and opened its wooden door, gesturing for her to enter.

"Are you coming too?" she asked, surprised. In all the dugouts so far men and women seemed to be separate.

"Of course. I don't want you to kill one of my warriors. You would like to, wouldn't you?"

"Yes," Talia admitted. "I wish I had done so earlier."

"He was foolish, but you acted rashly. I would not have let him rape you."

"Nor would I," she said.

"So, I will watch, and help if it is necessary." His voice was low and menacing, adding depth to his threat. He would protect her from Rognol, but he would also protect Rognol from her. "And there are other men here who might do you harm to slake their lust."

Talia nodded, and went ahead of him into the building.

Rognol lay on a fur-draped platform, his damaged arm dangling over the side toward the fire. When he saw Talia he cursed and struggled to sit up. He was naked from the waist up, and the firelight gleamed off his sweat-slick torso. His rank odor made her stomach turn. She tried to take shallow breaths, but the stench was still there.

Andrei pushed Rognol back down. "She'll set your broken arm. I'll watch to see that's all she does."

Rognol cursed again and cut his eyes threateningly at Talia. She shivered at the hate she saw there, but made herself step forward and touch the arm. The bleeding had long since stopped. Her cut had been superficial. The real damage was to the bone. A jagged bit of white showed through the swollen flesh.

Bile rushed to her throat and she feared for a moment that she would be sick. She swallowed twice and bit down on her lip, determined not to show any weakness to her captors.

"Hold him down," she commanded quietly. "I must pull the arm until the two ends of bone are in place."

"I don't think you can," Andrei said. "Fyodor will help." He indicated a young man standing to one side whom she hadn't noticed. Looking down as if he too might be queasy, the young man approached, but still kept his distance from her.

"He's not used to women," Andrei explained. "Especially Slavs."

There it was again, his slighting mention of Slavs. "Are we Slavs really so different from other women? Are our parts not in the same place?" she demanded.

"I have no doubt they are, but this is not the time for me to investigate." He grinned, and in the firelight Talia saw the flash of white teeth in his sun-tanned face.

She felt her face grow hot with embarrassment, and regretted her outburst. This was not the time to challenge him. She must force herself to be submissive, but also wary. For now, she wanted only to attend Rognol's arm and escape from his odious presence.

"Ready?" She took Rognol's hand in hers and pulled while Andrei pressed down on the great hairy chest.

Fyodor did nothing until Andrei commanded, "Get over there and help her!"

Before Fyodor could touch the injured man, Talia pulled harder, and as Rognol let out a bellow of pain, she felt the bone slip into place.

Fyodor had flinched and looked as if he might vomit. Andrei laughed. "It's over, boy. Hand me those leather strips. You can do that, can't you?"

Fyodor passed him the bundle of animal skin strips and fled outside.

"He won't make much of a warrior," Andrei commented. "Or a doctor either." While Talia held the arm steady, Andrei whipped leather strips around it, over and over, until Rognol's arm was encased from elbow to shoulder.

He lay so still Talia thought he might be dead, until Andrei said, "The mead was a long time taking effect. I thought it would have knocked him out long ago. God, but he has a stomach for it! It took twice as much to dull his pain as it would for most men. He'll have a sore head tomorrow as well as a sore arm, but he'll recover."

He straightened from his task, and Talia laid the bandaged arm over Rognol's belly. He was already snoring.

"You did well, Talia Militskaya. Many men could not have done as well, like our Fyodor."

"He is young," she said. "And perhaps he has not seen blood before, as I have."

She waited a moment to see if Andrei had further need of her, and then turned toward the door.

"Wait," he said. "I'll walk you to the slave women's house. Some of my men may be wandering around outside."

"Do you think I haven't seen what men can do?"

"I have no doubt you've seen many sights, and after what you witnessed today, I'm sure nothing else could shock you. I have another motive. I wouldn't want you to break another arm. I can't spare any more men." He laughed and took her arm, guiding her in the growing twilight.

Talia was puzzled at the swift-changing moods of this red-bearded giant. He felt sympathy for the death of her mother, he'd helped bury her instead of leaving the body, he understood the horror she'd gone through—and yet he'd caused it. Taunting her one moment, at the next he eased her anger with a laugh. He was a cruel killer, but his hands had been gentle when he massaged her ankle.

With the coming of darkness the air had grown cold, and the snow crunched under their feet. A watchman guarded the horses, which were tethered in a rude shelter, and a fire glowed nearby.

"What will happen to me tomorrow?' she asked.

"Who knows what will happen to any of us?"

Chapter 3

Andrei stood a moment in the snow and watched Talia walk away from him and bend to enter the women's house. Most women would have stooped or squatted, but with one swift, graceful move Talia was down and inside, out of his sight.

She intrigued him. She was different from most Slavs. Where had that strength and spirit come from? She'd risked her life going into the burning cabin and if he hadn't stopped her, she'd have killed Rognol. She was not only strong, but also so beautiful she set him aflame with lust.

He 'd like to keep her for himself, and that surprised him. Ordinarily when he rounded up Slavs he considered them no more attractive than his herd of horses—and some even less so—but this Talia Militskaya seemed almost another breed.

He couldn't have her. He knew that. She would fetch a high price in Byzantium. Emperor Basil was said to be especially fond of red-haired virgins, though rumor had it that his Christian faith meant he had forsworn women other than his wife. That brought up another question about the Slav woman. Was she a virgin? Or had she already lain with some man? The emperor's eunuchs would examine her to make sure. If she had been penetrated, her price would drop, but he felt sure that even so she would still be desirable enough to please some wealthy Byzantine.

There was no profit in thinking of her. Whatever her fate at the end of the journey—if she and her kin even survived all that lay ahead—she would not belong to him. Prince Vladimir forbade his men to trifle with the captives. The booty, including the captured people, belonged equally to all his nobles, and only some special service rendered to Prince Vladimir would earn a larger share, or the attentions of a particular woman. There were always women available to satisfy the warriors' needs, but none that he wanted, except this one that he couldn't have.

His men were so tired from the raid that she would be safe with the women for tonight, but tomorrow he'd have to move her into his house, and when Rognol recovered there would be hell to pay. He knew Rognol well enough to know that he neither forgave nor forgot. The Slav woman had brought trouble on herself, but she had unknowingly kept her value high. And Rognol should have been in better control of himself. He knew the rules concerning captives.

Andrei turned sharply at a sound behind him. He'd been lax, inattentive. Failing to know what—or who—was nearby could get a man killed. But it was only a boy, the one whose dog had been killed. The boy huddled against the side of the women's house, snuffling.

"Here, what's the matter?" Andrei demanded.

The boy cowered, cringing at Andrei's voice. If he'd been a dog, his belly would have dragged the ground, Andrei thought. "What's the matter?" he repeated.

"I'm cold and hungry. And frightened." The words came out slowly, barely more than a whisper.

"Why don't you go inside? The women will give you some food. There's a pot of stew."

"Not any more. There wasn't enough to go around, and besides, they told me to come out here. My sister may have her baby tonight, and it's not something for me to see."

"Come with me, then." Andrei pulled the boy to his feet, noticing how thin his hand and wrist were. In the light from the dying campfire, he studied the boy's gaunt face. The whole village must have been on the verge of starvation, waiting for the hunters who would never return. The raid may have saved these people's lives. But for what? He wouldn't let himself think about what awaited a frail, almost pretty boy like this at the hands of some

23

perverted buyer. Many children died on the journey south to Byzantium, and they might be the lucky ones.

"We'll find you some food in my quarters, and a place to sleep tonight." He put his hand on the boy's shoulder. "Would you like to be a warrior like me and like the Prince Vladimir?"

"No. I want to catch fish and hunt big animals. And grow things. I like to grow plants."

Andrei sighed. The boy had about as much chance to be a farmer or a hunter as he did to become Prince of Kiev. In Byzantium he'd be put to work scrubbing floors or cleaning cesspits. Or, if he attracted the attention of some powerful slave buyer, he'd be used sexually. But tonight, he was just a frightened, hungry child. Fear and hunger Andrei could remedy, at least temporarily, but he couldn't change the future.

Chapter 4

In the women's quarters, Talia ate the small bowl of meat stew that was handed to her. She passed the bowl back and started toward Olga's bed, but strong hands pushed her aside. She couldn't help Olga, no matter what they did to the moaning woman. Talia heard Grigor crying outside and went to the door just as Andrei led him away. That too was beyond her control. The god Svarog had abandoned them all, and the god her mother worshipped had not intervened either. Tears of helplessness slid down her face. So much for faith in the gods, for praying. She had nothing left but life itself. Giving up, going to sleep and never awakening, beckoned as the easy thing to do, yet she didn't want to die.

All she had of the past was her mother's treasure chest. It lay against the wall, and Talia curved herself about it, hugging it against her waist. It was hard and angular, its sharp corners pressing into her flesh, but it was comforting too. Tomorrow she'd open it, see what it held. Her mother had showed it to her years before, saying that one day it would belong to Talia, would be her wedding gift. Now there would be no wedding, no gifts or celebrations—and no mother to advise her and prepare her for marriage.

The fire in the center of the room sent dancing shadows across the earthen walls. It gave off a familiar, homelike fragrance in the midst of so much strangeness. But fire was the enemy too, burning cabins, burning bodies.

Andrei had saved her, protected her—for what purpose? "The little Slav is mine," he'd said. She pulled her fur cloak tightly about her, as if that might save her from harm. Remembering Andrei's arm clasped about her waist, holding her safely onto the great dark horse, she shivered in spite of her warm cloak.

Finally, she slept.

It was still dark inside the shelter when Talia awoke, and for a moment she couldn't fathom where she was. The surface beneath her was hard and unfamiliar, and there were other people all around.

Then memories came flooding back. She closed her eyes to shut out the present, then opened them again. Around the edge of the door a strip of pale gray light signaled the coming of dawn, and her stomach rumbled with hunger.

In spite of everything, a new day was beginning and her body still functioned. She sat up, pushing back the skins that covered her and massaged her stiff legs. She eased her feet over the side of the bed, pulled on her boots, and tiptoed toward the door. Snoring and sighing came from various places on the board beds, but in the darkness she couldn't distinguish one person from another.

She looked out into a still, beautiful world. The snow had ceased, and the sky glowed pink. She could see now that the settlement was much larger than she'd thought. The sod houses formed a half circle on the side of a hill and the cluster of stone buildings faced them across a broad clearing. Farther up the hill, at the crest, she could see several tall statues, silhouetted against the early morning daylight. Surrounding it all was a high wall made of sand colored blocks. In the clearing a sentry slept, slumped beside the ashes of last night's campfire.

Some guard he was! she thought. *I could slip away and he'd never notice.*

But where? She wasn't sure which direction they'd taken to arrive here, and she didn't even know where *here* was. Falling snow had obscured any landmarks, and she'd slept part of the way.

Pulling her cloak tighter about her, she started walking downhill toward the gate.

The gate towered above her, twice as high as she was tall. Its great, carved wooden arms were fastened together with a huge latch just out of her reach. She jumped and touched it, but it didn't move, not even slightly.

"Are you trying to escape?"

She whirled at the sound of Andrei's voice. "No. I- I just wanted to see what's outside."

"You can't escape. If a mere slave could open the gate, there'd be no keeping any of you here, and we'd be vulnerable to attacks by every marauder that decided to come our way." He pushed against the gate. "You see how sturdy it is?"

Talia nodded. "Even if I could open it, I wouldn't know where to go. I have no home anymore."

"Do you know which direction we came in?"

"No."

"I'll take you outside and you can see what lies around us." He reached above her and lifted the latch, then threw his weight against the gate. Slowly the two sections parted and creaked open.

"You'll note that the gate opens outward so that we can attack, but our enemies can't push against it and force it open." He called to the sentry, who leaped up from his sleep and came toward them. "We won't be gone long," Andrei told him. "Stay here on guard and let us back in—or it will cost you." He didn't say what the cost might be, and the sentry didn't ask. He nodded and rubbed his hand across his eyes, yawning.

"And stay awake!" Andrei ordered, leading Talia outside the walls and into a forest.

"Did you sleep well, Talia Militskaya?"

"Why do you care?"

"Whatever happens later, a good night's sleep will stand you in good stead," he said. "I didn't sleep as well as usual, since I had an unhappy child in my quarters. It took some time to ease his fear, and I left him asleep when I heard you outside."

"You heard me? But I was being so careful! And I didn't hear you come up behind me."

"I didn't mean you to hear me. A warrior develops a keen sense of hearing and must be able to approach his enemy silently. Otherwise, he will be overtaken and killed."

As they made their way through the dense woods, Andrei kept a tight grip on her arm.

"I'm not going to run away," she protested, trying to shrug out of his grasp.

"I know, but you might fall."

As he spoke, they came out of the woods at a point where the ground dropped steeply toward the river. Talia gasped and clung to him. One false step and she'd slip in the snow and slide downward to the ice-covered water. What if Andrei decided to push her into the water? No one had seen her leave, so no one would have come to rescue her. But he wasn't pushing her, and he'd released his grip on her arm.

She took a step away from him. He trusted her not to run. No, he knew she would get lost and try to find her way back to him. Even though he was her enemy, he was her safety too.

The river marked a divider between two very different kinds of world, almost as if the earth had cracked and a part of it dropped away. On this side of the river the ground sloped sharply upward and was tree-covered. On the other side, to the east, the earth was flat and treeless, stretching out in a snow-clad plain as far as she could see.

Talia shivered in the cold and crossed her arms, thrusting her hands into her armpits for warmth. She watched the sky change color, from grayish pink to pale gold, with a sheen of lavender. Threads of cloud were strung along the horizon. They stood silently, watching the sunrise turn the snow pink and gold. And then the sun broke free from the clouds, and it was fully day.

Talia turned back toward the camp, right against the solid chest of Andrei. He wrapped his arms around her, stopping her progress.

She tried to pull away from him, but he held her firmly against him. Her heart thudded, and she was sure he could feel the frantic beats. "Ready to go back?" he asked.

"I can find my way back."

"It isn't safe for you here alone."

"Rusalka will look after me."

"Oh, you still believe in the forest spirits?" His tone was light, mocking.

"Yes. And Perun will save me from you." She struggled against him, but his arms were as strong as the leather straps that held sledges together.

He dropped one arm from around her, allowing her to move slightly back from him. "Are you afraid of me?"

She lifted her chin and looked up at him, right into his icy blue eyes. "Should I be afraid of you? Are you going to kill me?" She tried to speak firmly, but her voice quavered, and she couldn't stop herself from trembling.

"No, I'm not going to kill you or even rape you," he said. "You're too valuable."

"You're going to sell me, then?"

"Very likely."

When she made no response, he asked, "Were you planning how you might cross the river and escape?"

"No. What's the use? Where would I go? I don't even know where I am."

"A wise woman. This is Kiev. The river is dangerous, and so is the land beyond. You don't know which villagers can be trusted. Very likely none of them would help you, and neither would your gods. You might have been savaged by wild bears or captured by raiders from the east."

"Just as you have already done."

"Have I harmed you?"

"Not yet," she admitted. "But you have destroyed everything I had."

29

"You won't be harmed unless you do something foolish to cause it. Time to go back."

"What is there for me to go back to?"

"Food, and your friend who may be having her baby."

"I tried to help her, but the women pushed me away."

"Our women have been giving birth and assisting at births as long as your women have. Your friend will be well cared-for, but she may want to see a familiar face. And after that, a bath."

"For her?"

"The women will take care of her bath. I meant you. How long since you had a bath?"

Talia stopped walking and turned to face him. "Why? Do I smell bad?"

"You smell like smoke," he said, "and—other odors."

Talia cringed. Even as a slave she wasn't clean enough to suit him! "What if I don't want a bath?"

"Why wouldn't you? It's invigorating. But whether you consent or not, you will have a bath today. Lord Vladimir should arrive soon, and he insists on cleanliness. In everyone."

"He kills people, even his own kin, but wants his captives clean!" Talia spat. "He must be a madman."

"Whatever you think of him, you'd be wise to hold your tongue around him. He is the most powerful man in all of Rus."

"What more can he do to me? I have already lost my parents and my home, and I'm a slave." Talia felt cold tears slide down her cheeks.

"You could be given to the troops, to use for their pleasure."

"You can't let them take me," she begged, reaching for his hand. She felt faint at the possibilities of being given over to the crude, rough troops. Especially Rognol.

"So you don't think Perun will save you from the prince? And you need the help of an ordinary mortal? Don't worry. I'll look after you," he promised, holding onto her hand.

"And you can protect me from your own men?"

"I can and I will. Remember that. Now, let's hasten back to camp, or the food will all be eaten."

They were silent as they made their way through the forest. As they approached the big gates, Andrei called out and stepped back. In a moment the gates swung outward, each side pushed by a warrior. As they entered, the gates swung shut behind them.

The camp was astir. A fire crackled in the clearing, where a haunch of meat hung on a metal rod. Grease dripped into the flames, sizzling and flaming.

Talia started toward the meat, but Andrei held her back. "It isn't ready yet. It's just begun to cook. You have time now to see your friend if you wish."

"Yes," she said, and started toward the women's hut.

"That way," Andrei pointed. "She's been taken to the birthing hut, so she wouldn't disturb the other women and the children."

Talia went where he pointed, and cautiously pushed open the door. It took a moment for her eyes to adjust to the semi-darkness before she could make out Olga's still form. She lay on a white cloth spread over a heap of evergreen boughs. Her eyes were closed, and the skin beneath them was slack and bluish. Beside her lay her baby, swaddled in coarse white fabric up to its armpits. Its scrawny arms flailed the air, and a faint mewling sound came from its mouth.

Talia touched the infant's hand, and felt its thin fingers close feebly around hers. The tiny mouth made a sucking sound, and the child tried to put Talia's finger to its mouth. It was hungry, she thought. Anybody could see that. Why wasn't it being fed? Why wasn't Olga nursing it? Or was she dead? She wasn't moving.

Talia touched Olga's cheek with her free hand. Olga's skin felt warm, and her eyelids fluttered.

"Talia," Olga whispered. "It's too soon. My baby—"

"I know your babe came too soon, but it lives."

"Is it a son?"

31

"I'll see." Talia uncurled the tiny fingers from hers and unwound the swaddling at the bottom. She nodded. "It's a son."

"Rozhanitsy be praised! Sons may prosper. Girls suffer too much. Tomorrow you must make an offering to Rozhanitsky, Talia, if my son and I survive."

"You will," Talia said, with more assurance than she felt. "And somehow I'll get the food for the offering."

"How is Grigor?"

"I haven't seen him this morning," Talia admitted, "but Andrei told me he took care of him."

"Andrei?"

"Andrei, the leader."

Olga nodded as if she understood everything. "If I die, I want you to take care of my son."

"You won't die," Talia assured her, though the pallor of Olga's skin frightened her. "Can you nurse the baby?"

"My milk won't come in."

"I'll tell the women, and I'll get you something to eat."

"They know. They are kind, Talia. I didn't expect it. Ask the gods to help me." Her voice drifted off and her eyes closed.

Talia looked for the woman in charge of births and saw her already coming toward Olga's bed, carrying a bowl of steaming, fragrant broth. A small girl followed, carrying another bowl. Talia watched as the woman lifted Olga to a sitting position and began feeding her, coaxing a few spoonsful into Olga's mouth. The girl dipped her finger into the small bowl and let the baby suck on it.

Talia came out of the birthing quarters right into a large, maimed man. He had been peering in through the slit at the side of the door.

"Why are you here?" Talia demanded, forgetting that she was a slave and he one of her masters. Men were forbidden to attend births or to have anything to do with women for many days after childbirth. At least that was true in her village, she thought. But whatever the rule, this man was not the father of Olga's child and

32

had no reason to be here. He was grotesque: missing an eye and two fingers of his right hand. The empty eye socket was overgrown with twisted red flesh, and a scar ran from its corner down his cheek to his jawbone. Talia couldn't stop herself from cringing at the sight of him.

"I'm here for her," he said, pointing toward the door. "Your friend, she lives?"

Talia nodded, puzzled. Had Andrei sent him?

"She rode on my horse," he explained. "She was in pain, and I could not help. So beautiful and so brave."

Talia stared at him, open-mouthed and uncomprehending. This raider, killer, destroyer of homes and of lives, was concerned about one of his captives. And he thought Olga, swollen with pregnancy and bald with a burned scalp, was beautiful.

"And does her baby live?"

"Yes," she said, and added, "It's a son."

He nodded, and then smiled. His twisted face for a moment looked almost normal, and Talia felt her own lips lift in a smile. There had been too few smiles here at Kiev, and too many tears.

Without saying another word, the man turned and hobbled away. Talia watched him, even more puzzled. How could a man so wounded have joined in a raid? He would have lifted Olga, heavy with child, onto his horse with one hand, while somehow controlling the horse. Why had Andrei included him in the raid?

"He lost his eye and his fingers in a raid, and he deserves his share of booty," Andrei said, appearing beside her.

Talia gasped. Had she spoken aloud, or could he read her thoughts?

"Time for our bath, my little Slav."

"Our bath? You'll be with me?"

"The entire time." His voice held the light, mocking tone she was becoming accustomed to. Would he really share a bath with her, or was he joking?

Chapter 5

"Will you enter the women's quarters with me?" she asked, puzzled. She'd seen no women bathing there.

"Of course not. We'll go to the heat lodge together. This way." With his hand at her back, he guided her toward a small earthen hut and nudged her forward.

Talia bent to enter, and straightened in the hot space. A torch thrust into an aperture in the wall gave off a flickering, fragrant light. Against the back wall of the tiny structure was a seating space, and in front, a bed of hot coals glowed.

"Undress," Andrei ordered.

When Talia was slow to obey, he stepped close to her. "Here. I'll do it."

"No, I can." As she bent to pull off a boot, her hair fell across her face, and she was glad he couldn't see how embarrassed she was. She removed her boots and held them uncertainly.

Andrei took the boots from her and tossed them through the opening out into the snow. He threw off his robe and Talia saw that he wore nothing underneath. His naked body gleamed taut and pale by the torchlight. "Look all you like," he said. "Is this not a fine warrior's body?"

Talia tried not to look, but her gaze seemed drawn to his body. She stared at the muscular arms that had held her, and at the sculpted chest. She forced her gaze upward, not down. She would not look down. The air was stifling. She drew in ragged, hot breaths.

"Undress," he repeated. "Or shall I take off your clothes?" He stretched out his hand to the neck of her robe, and the touch of his fingertips against her skin stirred an unwelcome flutter of desire.

She raised her hand and pushed his away. "I'll remove them."

He stepped back and let his hand drop to his side, never taking his eyes off her.

With stiff, unwilling fingers, Talia began to untie the lacings of her garments. She could delay no longer. She undid the fastenings and let her robe drop to her feet. How could she be baring her body to this stranger? The honor of seeing her thus should have gone to Oleg her intended husband, and not until they were wed. She closed her eyes against the shame of it and stood unmoving, letting her captor look. Perhaps in the uncertain light he couldn't see her clearly. But that couldn't be, for she could see him. If she opened her eyes. She clenched them tightly so that she wouldn't see Andrei's nakedness.

Andrei stared at her, drinking in the curves and hollows of her body. She was magnificent! He'd had no idea how beautiful she was when she'd been swaddled in furs. She was meant to be seen, admired, desired, dressed in finery or bare of clothing. The torchlight flickered, making shadows beneath her breasts and turning her hair to golden flames.

He lifted a lock of her hair and let it slither through his fingers, imagining it brushing his shoulder as she knelt over him.

She stood unmoving, letting him touch her without flinching, but he could feel her quiver as he lifted her chin with the other hand. Her eyes were closed, as if she would shut out the sight of him. She probably was a virgin, unused to seeing unclothed men. He couldn't blame her, but he wanted her to look at him.

He dropped his hands to her shoulders and then slowly slid them down to the tips of her breasts. She gasped, and her eyes flew open. He could feel the nipples tighten under his palms. Andrei cupped and lifted her breasts for a moment, then let his hands slide down her sides, over the curve of her hips and down the length of her thighs. He tortured himself by imagining the eunuchs of Byzantium examining her, even more thoroughly than he was

35

doing. They would be checking her as if she were a prized racehorse.

And what was he doing? Letting his hands drop from her body, he stepped closer to the glowing coals. It had become so hot in the heat lodge he could hardly breathe. Her body glistened with perspiration, and he knew his own did as well. The fire was doing its work, driving out bodily poisons.

"Sit down" he said, indicating the earthen bench. As Talia eased onto the seat, Andrei grabbed up the wooden pail of water and splashed it onto the stones. The coals hissed and steam gushed up, filling the enclosure, so densely he could barely see Talia.

"Time to go out," he said when the steam cleared. He pulled her to her feet and led her out into the cold morning air. Taking up a pail of water set beside the heat lodge, he poured it over her, soaking the red-gold hair and sending rivulets down both breasts.

Talia gasped at the shock of the cold water on her hot body. Then, before she could adjust to the chill, Andrei was swatting at her with evergreen boughs.

"What are you doing?" she demanded.

"It's part of the cleansing. It warms the skin after the cold rinse. Here, thrash me."

He handed her a bough and Talia accepted it, though it felt awkward in her hand. She hesitated, uncertain about hitting him. Did she dare? What would he do to her?

After a few ineffectual swipes at his arms and shoulders, she stopped and let the bough droop beside her.

He struck her again, a sweep across her breasts. "Go ahead," he commanded. As he turned his back to her, a crowd gathered, warriors jeering and pointing at Talia.

So, Andrei was not just reveling in the sight of her nakedness himself, he had exposed her to all those leering eyes! She started to turn her back on them, to shield herself with the bough, and run. She glanced around for her clothing, but it had been taken away. Furious and helpless, she ran toward the men, slashing back and forth with the bough, and had the satisfaction of bringing a quick spurt of blood from one face. Another man put up his hands to protect his face only to have the force of her blow scrape the skin off his knuckles.

The men cursed and began to back away from her, stunned at her fury.

When Andrei turned, Talia attacked him. For the jeering men, for kidnapping her, for destroying her village, for stopping her from killing Rognol, for her grief and helplessness. Avenging the wrongs he'd done her, she struck and struck, putting all her strength into each blow. Hitting him didn't bring back the dead or make her situation better, but at least she expressed her anger. The impact of the blows radiated up her arm, spurring her on to greater strength and frenzy.

Andrei stood stunned at her onslaught, then he put out his hand to ward off her blows. When she kept on beating at him, he grabbed the bough and jerked hard, throwing Talia off her feet. She fell to the snow-covered ground and then scrambled up and ran.

He caught up with her in two strides and whipped his arm around her neck, grabbing her arms with his other hand. He marched her ahead of him, half stumbling, jerked open the door of a stone houses and thrust her inside.

"This is not the women's quarters," she whimpered.

"No. 'Tis mine. You'll stay here from now on." He reached into a corner of the room and tossed a blanket to her. "Cover yourself with this."

It was thin and tattered, but it would cover her nakedness. She wrapped it around her and tucked in the loose edge between her breasts. "What are you going to do to me?"

"Nothing. I've told you, I will protect you. Even against my own anger. What did you think you were doing in striking me?"

"Avenging myself. You beat me and humiliated me."

"You'd better not try anything like that again, no matter what your reason is. The cold water and swatting with pine boughs is part of cleansing." He touched his chest and she saw that not only was he still naked, but he was bleeding in several places.

She felt a quick satisfaction at having hurt him, even slightly.

He threw a fur over his shoulder and arranged it to cover him to his knees, then went to the door and spoke to someone outside.

"Where are my clothes?"

"They are being cleaned. Or perhaps burned. In either case, something will be found for you to wear. Sit down." He pointed to a wooden bench that stood before a low wooden table. A long cushion covered the seat.

Talia sat. Her skin tingled pleasantly, and now that her anger had abated, she felt relaxed and content. She closed her eyes, partly in drowsiness, partly to shut out the sight of Andrei. She didn't want to see his bloody wounds, though she felt he'd deserved them.

A woman entered, and stopped abruptly at the sight of Talia. Her eyes narrowed and her hands tightened on the basin she carried. She wore a loose garment of gray wool with an attached hood that had fallen off her pale hair.

"I'll tend your wounds," Talia offered. "After all, I caused them."

"That is my job," the woman said. "I will care for him." Turning her back on Talia, she dipped a cloth into the basin, squeezed it lightly and laid it on Andrei's chest, pushing him onto a cushioned bench opposite Talia.

Talia saw him wince as the cloth touched his abraded skin. The woman murmured something soothing, and threw an accusing glance at Talia. She dipped the cloth twice more and had Andrei roll over so that she could swab the cuts on his back. Finishing her task, she, pushed her hair back from her forehead with the back of her hand. "I will bring you food," she said.

"Bring some for her also," Andrei said, indicating Talia.

"Of course," the woman said. Her voice was flat and expressionless, but Talia saw barely controlled anger in the woman's eyes.

Talia knew instinctively that this woman had lain with Andrei in times past and she was now Talia's enemy. First Rognol, now this strange, possessive woman hated her. And she had to be wary of Andrei himself, but for different reasons. With so many enemies, where could she find a friend? Olga, of course, but Olga was lying half-dead and in need of help herself.

The woman returned, bearing two bowls of a steamy stew, set on a wooden tray. She handed one of the bowls toward Andrei.

He sat up, but did not take the bowl. "Give to Talia first," he said.

The woman set his bowl back on the tray and picked up the second bowl.

Why? Talia wondered. *Is my food not as good as his, or is there some worse reason?* As the woman came close, Talia thrust out her foot and shifted slightly so that the woman half-stumbled and spilled most of the stew on the stone floor. She cursed at Talia and handed her the almost-empty bowl.

Talia set it on the table in front of her but made no move to eat.

"You must be more careful, Marya," Andrei said. "But don't worry about bringing more. I can share my food with Talia. My bowl is very full, and it smells delicious." He stepped to the doorway and whistled. "One of the dogs will be glad to have a meal of meat."

"I can clean it up," Marya said, and began picking up pieces of meat from the floor.

"You don't need to do that." Andrei pulled her to her feet and led her to the door.

Marya tried to pick up another piece of meat just as a scrawny dog ran in and began to wolf down the meat scraps, even licking the floor to get up the broth. As Marya scurried out, the dog suddenly retched and spewed out the half-chewed meat. It slunk out of the house, whimpering.

"If I'd eaten that, I might have been sick by now too," Talia said.

"You tripped Marya, didn't you?"

Talia nodded, unashamed. "I was right to do so."

"So it seems. I don't think she wanted to kill you, only to frighten you."

"She succeeded. I am frightened. You could have killed me yesterday and I would almost have welcomed it. Today I want to live."

"And I want you to live," he said, meeting her gaze. "Come, share my food. I'll eat first and you can watch me to make sure no harm comes to me before you eat your share."

"You've said you'll protect me. You must tell your troops and servants—and your other women." She gestured toward the door where Marya had fled. "She has been your woman, hasn't she?"

He paused in eating and nodded.

"You must tell her that I am not your woman, and never will be."

"You can't be sure of that," he said.

Chapter 6

"I'll bring some clothes for you," Andrei offered after they'd finished eating. "I assume you don't want to go outside as you are." He started for the door.

"Are you going to leave me here alone?"

"I don't think Marya will come back any time soon, and the men you struck will hesitate before approaching you."

From the corner he picked up his sword and a round shield, painted red and black, and held them out to Talia. "Use these if you need to protect yourself."

Talia reached for the shield, and its weight almost brought her to her knees. "It won't be much help if I can't lift it," she said, passing it back to him.

He took it from her and set it aside, leaning it against the wall. "The sword, then."

Talia grasped its hilt with both hands and swung it.

He ducked to avoid the blow and caught her, breaking the momentum that almost brought her down against the bench. His arms were strong around her, and she could feel his heartbeat, racing almost as rapidly as hers.

Talia sucked in a shuddering breath. Her shoulders and neck were bare, and she clutched at the blanket that had slipped when she swung the sword. Andrei's breath was warm on her bared skin. For a moment neither spoke, then he said in a strained voice, "I think you'll be all right, but remember, you don't have to protect yourself from me."

"I'll remember if you will," she said, setting aside the sword and tugging at the blanket, which seemed to be caught in a tangle. He reached for the edge of it, his fingertips brushing her bare skin.

Talia flinched away from his touch. Each time he came close to her, her body thrilled with an unwanted desire. She could not let herself surrender to him, or even let him know how he affected her.

Andrei smiled slightly, shrugged, and stepped back. "You have privacy here. You don't need to cover yourself—unless you're cold."

Cold? No, she felt heat rising within her, the furthest thing from cold,

"Anything else besides clothing?" he asked. "More food?"

As he started out, she said, "Please bring back my box, if it's still there in the women's quarters. I left it on the sleeping platform."

"What's in it?"

"I don't know," Talia admitted. "It was my mother's, to be given to me and opened on my wedding day. I haven't looked in it."

"So you won't know if anything has been stolen?"

"I'll know if the seal has been broken."

After he left, Talia picked up the sword again and examined it. It was so heavy she could barely lift it, and was double edged, both edges faced with a shiny metal that was different from the main body of the weapon. She ran her finger lightly down one edge and drew a drop of blood. Some kind of ivory colored bone or tusk formed the hilt, which had been carved into a series of interlocking lines, like a snake curled back onto itself. Words or symbols were cut into the surface as well, but worn down so Talia couldn't decipher them. She traced them with her fingertip, wondering what they meant.

She hefted the sword once more and was about to set it aside when she saw the door pushed open. Stepping quickly to one side, she lifted the sword to shoulder height and was about to bring it down and crush the intruder when she saw it was Andrei.

"Oh!" she said, and let the sword drop to the floor with a clatter.

He tossed a bundle of clothing and her boots onto the sleeping area and picked up the sword with one hand, setting it carefully against the shield. In his other hand he held Talia's wooden chest. "Were you going to kill me?"

"Yes, if you had been someone else, or if you'd tried to kill me."

He set the chest down on the bench and grasped her shoulders, forcing her to face him. "Try to get it into your head that I am not going to kill you. I am what is standing between you and death or despoliation at the hands of my men." His gaze was commanding, and his breath fanned hot against her face. Talia could feel his searing touch even through the blanket.

Then, as if he managed to control himself, Andrei dropped his hands and stepped back. "Put on some clothes," he ordered.

"I will, now that you've brought them. Look away," Talia said.

"Oh, by the gods on high! I've seen you unclothed in the sauna."

"I didn't like the way you looked at me and touched me then," Talia said. "And that was a public place. This is your private quarters, and no one would think it amiss if you ravished me—just as you did with Marya." She didn't know why she added the last few words, and regretted them the moment they left her lips.

"I did not ravish Marya. She came to me willingly, and would again if I wanted her. You may come to me willingly someday as well."

"Never. I was taught to save myself for my husband."

"And he who would marry you is now dead."

Talia nodded and felt tears spring to her eyes and slide down her cheeks. She brushed them aside with the back of her hand.

"You may have a rich man for a husband in Byzantium, perhaps even a sultan or an emperor. Or if not a husband, then a richer master than I, someone who will gird you in silk and deck you in jewels, in return for your willing, loving caresses."

"How can I give loving caresses to someone I don't love?"

"You'll learn. Either that or you'll be treated no better than an animal. That would be a real loss for everyone." He lifted a lock of her hair and let it drop. It had dried from the earlier drenching, and felt as fine and shimmery as the silk she might soon be decked in. He longed to bury his face in her hair. It would smell of fresh pine boughs, as would the rest of her, but he knew he must control himself, for his own good as well as hers. Talia was not flinching from his touch, but neither was she responding. She stood as still as a fearful animal startled by the huntsman, just before it bolts and runs.

"Your glorious red hair, your fair skin and your body will make you very desirable to the wealthy men of Byzantium." As he spoke, his fingertip traced her lips and the faint crease at the corner. It would deepen when she smiled. He realized he had never seen her smile, and wondered how magical it might be. Such fantasies were madness. Why should he care whether she smiled or was happy? His responsibility was to keep her from being ravished until she could be presented in Byzantium as unblemished trade goods. "You'll fetch a high price," he concluded.

As he stepped back, he saw the muscles of her neck move slightly, as if she choked back angry words. Or tears. "I'll leave you to dress, then," he said. "When you are finished, come outside."

"What am I to come out for? More beatings with evergreen boughs?"

"You need to change the dressings on Rognol's arm, and swab it with some healing herbs. He must be able to travel when we begin our journey southward."

"Why must I tend him? Can't Marya do that?"

"Marya didn't cause the injury. You did."

He stepped outside, ignoring Talia's angry glare.

As soon as he was gone, Talia picked up the little chest and found the wax that sealed it intact. For whatever reason, it was safe. She smelled the aromatic fragrance that reminded her of home. Should she open it now? There might never be a wedding day for her, at least not the kind that her mother had hoped for and planned for. *I'll decide later*, Talia thought, setting the box aside to dress.

Her own boots had been cleaned and returned, but the clothing was unfamiliar. She lifted it item by item: woolen stockings, a shift of some filmy material, a long gown of dark green wool with fur trim about the neck and wrists, and a strange scarf stitched up in back. Whose clothing was this? Marya's? *No, she would never have given it up for me. Then whose? Who had owned and worn these clothes and given them away?*

Whose ever they had been, Andrei had meant her to wear these garments, and so she would. She slid her arms into the shift and let it settle over her body. The stockings were next, warm and welcome. She pushed her feet into the boots and tied the leather laces securely, then put on the dress. It fell in soft folds, its hemline touching the tops of her boots, the fur-trimmed sleeves just the right length, almost as if the dress had been made for her. Talia stroked the fur-trimmed neckline, reveling in its luxury.

She knew her hair was tangled, but had no comb to unsnarl it. Threading her fingers through her hair, she smoothed it as best she could, and covered it with the scarf, putting the seam at the back of her head so that it formed a cap.

Andrei turned with a start when she came outside to where he stood waiting. "The dress becomes you," he said, his gaze moving over her, down to her boots and back to her face. "I thought you would be about her size."

"Whose clothes are these?"

"They were my wife's."

"You have a wife?"

"I had a wife. She died giving birth to our child, and the babe died as well." His voice was low, and as dead as his words.

"I'm sorry," she said. "So you know how it feels to lose someone."

He nodded, never taking his eyes off her.

"How long ago?" Talia asked.

"Two years."

"And since you have lain with Marya." Talia knew her voice sounded accusing, and knew too that it was none of her business and that it would only anger him. But perversely. She wanted to know, even if it hurt her as well.

"Men have needs. Marya satisfied some of those needs—for a time." He reached for the ends of the scarf and wrapped them about her neck, the back of his hands brushing her cheeks. He dropped his hands abruptly, as if they'd been burned by touching her. "Despite the melting snow, it's still cold. You'll need your cloak."

"I don't have it. It wasn't returned to me, and you brought me none—of hers."

"The blanket then. That will be good at any rate, in case Rognol's wound festers. The dress should not be soiled." He stepped back into the house and returned with the ragged blanket. He held it out and was about to engulf her in it but instead moved a step away, leaving Talia to fling the blanket about herself as best she could. Without waiting for her, he strode off, and Talia ran after him, her boots squishing in the melting snow.

Rognol lay on the same platform where she'd left him, in the dimly lit quarters. Before she touched his arm, Talia knew from the odor that his wound was infected. She held back, half-shielded by Andrei, reluctant to approach Rognol, though she knew she'd have to tend him. When he saw her, he roared a curse and pulled himself to a sitting position.

"Will you protect me from him while I inspect the wound?"

Andrei nodded, and nudged her forward. "Hold him, Nicolai," he commanded a man who stood beside Rognol.

Talia saw that it was the man with the scarred face, the man who'd asked after Olga. He held down the angry Rognol while she cleansed and bound up the wound f, holding her breath against the stench as long as she could. When it was done, she staggered outside. Andrei followed.

"How much longer must I continue caring for him?" she asked.

"Until he recovers or dies, or until we leave for Byzantium"

"And how will I spend my days, other than that?"

"However you wish. You may console your friend, use the heat lodge, or do nothing at all. You can't leave."

"I know that."

"You should be grateful you don't have to work as some of the slaves do, but you may before we go downriver. There are times when everyone works, especially slaves, at disagreeable tasks."

"More disagreeable than caring for Rognol?"

"Probably no more disagreeable, but caring for him only lasts a short time each day. Tanning hides or loading boats goes on for many days."

She took off the blanket and handed it to him. "It may have blood and pus on it."

"No need to wash it until you've finished using it," he said, draping it over his arm. "In the meantime, you may wear the clothing you have on until something suitable can be made for you, and tonight you'll continue to sleep in the slave quarters." He laughed. "You will appear overdressed there, but it can't be helped."

Chapter 7

Talia was awakened by the feeble crying of the baby, and murmuring women's voices. She sat up and glanced down in surprise at the luxurious gown she wore. It took a moment to remember that Andrei had given her the soft, fur-trimmed garment.

No, he hadn't said he was giving it only that she could wear it. Wearing the clothing would make her beholden to him, and she didn't want to be in his debt. Not for anything, except her protection, and that she couldn't change. But clothing was another matter. Why did he even want her to wear his wife's gown? As soon as her own clothing was cleaned, she'd take off this borrowed finery and hand it back to Andrei.

Something was wrong with Olga's baby. The crying wasn't normal. Talia went toward Olga's bed, close enough to see the tiny infant was shuddering with each breath. "Olga," she asked, "can I do anything to help you? Or the babe?"

Olga was crying, silent sobs that shook her body. "He is dying," she said. "He came too soon."

"He has not died, not yet, but he suffers," one of the guardian women said. "He can't take the breast. He is too weak to suckle." She laid the baby against her shoulder and began to stroke his back. His shuddering lessened, but he continued to cry feebly, soft, mewing sounds. The other woman touched Olga's bare breast. "Your milk is not coming in as it should, and he is too weak to pull it out." She squeezed on the nipple several times, and a drop of milk appeared. She dipped her finger in it and thrust it into the baby's open mouth. She squeezed the other breast and presented a second drop of milk, then left the sleeping quarters and returned a moment later with another woman. "She has had a babe and can spare some milk."

The newly arrived woman opened her gown, took the baby, and expertly squirted milk onto his mouth. After a startled look, the baby swallowed, its tiny throat moving convulsively. The woman fed him several more swallows from both breasts and he settled contentedly against her.

The guardian woman handed him to Olga. "You must continue to squeeze and to put his mouth to the breast, or your milk will dry up."

Olga nodded and took her son. She held him close and tried to squeeze milk from her breasts.

"He has had enough now, and you should practice before he cries with hunger again." She indicated the newcomer. "Irina will help you. Just ask me when you need her." The women left Talia with Olga and her child.

Olga smiled. "I have hope now that he will live, so I can name him."

"Will you name him for his father?"

Tears filled Olga's eyes. She nodded. "I think so, after I am sure the child will live. I may never see Oleg again, but his son will carry his name."

"We won't see any of our men again," Talia said brutally, instantly regretting her words. Olga might benefit from a bit of hope, but it was too late to call back the words.

"How do you know?"

"They are all dead. Andrei told me they came upon a group of hunters' bodies."

"So much death, so much sadness, How much more?" Olga said. Tears slid down her face and fell onto the soft face of her sleeping child.

Talia took her friend's hand. "I don't know what will happen to us, and whatever it is, will be. I can't change anything, for you or me or your babe. I feel helpless."

"We all are," Olga said. "I can endure anything if only my baby is safe. And Grigor."

"Andrei looked after him the first night and possibly last night as well, but as soon as the evil Rognol recovers, I'll have to sleep in Andrei's quarters to be safe. Then Grigor may be sent to the children's quarters."

"Andrei has quarters of his own?"

"Yes. He's a leader."

"Then he should keep you safe."

But safe for what? Talia wondered. She said nothing but only nodded. "I will make the offering to the gods for you this morning, as I promised."

Olga ran her fingers over the fur trim on Talia's sleeve. "Where did you get such a fine garment?"

"Andrei. They belonged to his wife."

"Her cast-offs?"

"She is dead."

"So much death," Olga repeated.

As Talia left she saw Andrei coming across the clearing, a bundle of clothing slung over his arm. "Here," he said, thrusting the clothing toward her. "Put this on."

Talia took it, her fingers rebelling at its coarse texture after the softness of the borrowed gown. "I will be prompt," she promised. She started into the women's quarters and turned back to ask, "May I keep the undergarments?"

He shrugged. "Until we can acquire others for you."

So they were on loan as well. She went into the women's quarters and lifted the gown over her head, enjoying for a moment the brush of fur against her face. Folding it carefully, she laid it to the side and took up her own rough gown. She'd never noticed before how coarse and scratchy the fabric was, but now that she'd experienced the lush softness of that other gown, her own was almost unbearable. She flung on her cloak and when she came outside again, Andrei was still standing in the clearing, and Nicolai had joined him.

All around the settlement the sounds of activity rang out: the blows of hammers on metal, ax on wood, voices issuing work commands and the neighing of horses being shod. Something unusual was happening. The very air prickled her skin differently.

Nicolai held out a handful of grain. "You will need this for the offering."

"Thank you."

"And is your friend Olga well?"

"She is recovering. And the babe will live."

Nicolai touched his forehead, his abdomen and both sides of his chest in a gesture Talia didn't understand. "God be thanked," he said. And then, "I would like to go with you." Instead of going toward the river, he started walking uphill.

Andrei fell into step beside them, the gown slung over one arm, his sword bouncing lightly against his thigh. She made no comment, but walked silently between the two warriors. The sun had risen, throwing pink streams of light through the trees. Most of the snow had melted, leaving small patches of white against the gray and brown fallen leaves, and the air had a new freshness.

As they reached the clearing at the crest of the hill, Talia stared up at the tall, fearsome images of Svarog and Perun. Their eyes were glittering stones or bits of glass set into the wood, and both images seemed to glare at her with evil intent. She looked away, down at the ground, where a small cross had been thrust into the ground.

"I put it there," Nicolai said, following her gaze. "I am a Christian, but your friend wants to make a sacrifice to the pagan gods, so we will." With a stick he drew a circle in the earth, laid other sticks into a star-pattern, and sprinkled the handful of grain into the center. "I hope that will satisfy the gods, even the god of childbirth, who must be watching her. I have no animals to sacrifice."

"I only have my clothing and furs for the bed," she said.

"You have whatever is in your box," Andrei said, "but I won't let you throw it away in some foolish pagan ritual."

"Pagan?" she repeated. "Then you are one of the believers, a Christian?"

"I believe in nothing except the sharpness of my sword, the strength of my arms and the power of Prince Vladimir." He stood apart from them, his hand lightly on the hilt of his sword.

Nicolai had dropped to his knees, heedless of the muddy ground. Looking to the sky, he prayed, "Heavenly Father, thank you for bringing Olga and her son back from the valley of the dead. Continue to care for them, as you have cared for me. In the name of the Father, the Son and the Holy Spirit. Amen." He made the same four-point gesture again, and stood.

"You think some god healed you?" Andrei scoffed. "And that same god let you get injured in the first place. Where's the logic in that?"

"Believing is not logic," Nicolai admitted. "But there is a purpose to everything. We were created for a reason. That I believe." His voice rang with sincerity and conviction, and as a shaft of sunlight fell across him, Talia saw him as strong and vibrant, not a maimed man.

"But you still kill," Andrei pointed out. "Thor and Svarog would approve, but how does your god feel about killing?"

"I will fight if I must, but I will kill no innocents."

"Then you won't be of much use to Prince Vladimir," Andrei scoffed.

"Perhaps not," Nicolai conceded. "And I'm sure you will serve him and be well rewarded."

Talia stared from man to man. Had the death of Andrei's wife and child taken away all his belief in a god? She longed to ask him, but the cold set of his features stopped her. What did she herself believe? If Nicolai was right, was there some purpose for her? Something to look forward to?

She had not accepted her mother's belief, Nicolai's belief, but she could not empty her mind of all belief in gods as Andrei had done. It was too much risk. Surely there must be something to believe it, but all the gods she knew had deserted her. She looked at the design Nicolai had drawn in the dirt and up again at the fearsome features of Svarog and Perun. Did they mean her good or evil?

Both men ended their argument unresolved by falling silent and starting back downhill. Talia looked toward the river and saw a group of large boats coming toward them. "Look!"

Andrei and Nicolai turned to look. "Prince Vladimir!" Andrei exclaimed. "We must return quickly and prepare the fortress to welcome him."

Talia stood transfixed, unable to tear her gaze away from the oncoming craft. There were five boats, each one bigger than all the dugouts put together that she'd seen at the village. Their sails hung limply, but they glided downstream quietly, carried by the current. The front of each one was carved like a dragon, its shape rising above the boat's deck as tall as a house. Parts of the boats were painted in something that glittered in the morning sunlight.

"Come on!" Andrei grabbed her arm and turned her away from the spectacle.

Lookouts on the wall of the fortress had already sighted Prince Vladimir's flotilla. The great gate creaked open, pushed by half a dozen brawny men. Women ran back and forth, picking up stray bits of debris and shepherding errant children before them, into huts. Men tending or shoeing horses hastily completed their work and led the mounts away. Nicolai went toward the women's quarters where Olga and her baby lay.

To Talia's astonishment, Andrei dragged her into his house and stood guard by the door. "Don't try to escape," he said, his voice low and threatening. He seemed to realize that he still carried the fur-trimmed gown, and tossed it onto the bench where she'd sat the previous day.

Talia stared at him. "Why would I do that? Where would I go? You warned me already." Talia's heart thudded. Something had changed, but she didn't know what. What had she done wrong? Inexplicably she yearned for him to hold her close. Instead, he was scolding her.

"Listen carefully. What you do, how you act around Prince Vladimir can change what happens to you. Even whether you live or die. You must not anger the prince, or attract attention to yourself."

"Do you mean he'd kill me? He's a Christian, isn't he? Is this the way Christians act? Nicolai doesn't."

"Princes don't have to do as others do, but I don't think he'd kill you. And he's not a Christian yet. He is going to meet with the Emperor Basil and decide if he wants to become Christian." He shook his head as if to clear away a thought. "That doesn't matter right now. Don't argue." He lifted her chin and made her look at him.

Talia met his gaze, unflinching but half fearful. She clasped her hands behind her so that he couldn't see their trembling. Or know how much she longed to touch him. She needed to take strength from him, but if Andrei, the strong warrior, the leader, was afraid of what this Prince Vladimir might do, the prince must be very powerful. And cruel, worse than she'd heard told of him.

Could Andrei protect her, or would he surrender her to his prince? She made herself listen to his instructions.

"You are a slave. You must behave as one."

"How can I forget what I am—what you and your warriors have made me?" She tried to keep the anger and bitterness out of her voice, and failed.

"We could have killed you, but I saved your life."

"Do you regret it?"

"No. Do you?"

"How can I know? There are worse things than death."

He nodded. "But I want to protect you from those things. So listen, and heed. You must bow before the prince."

"Bow to a killer?"

"Yes. Bend your proud neck and do not meet his gaze—as you meet mine."

Talia felt the anger seep out of her as she gazed into his eyes and saw reflected there her own desire. So, he wanted her, wanted to lie with her as he had with his wife. *And with Marya, but I must not think of her.* "What else?" she asked, her voice barely above a whisper.

He lifted a lock of her hair and let it slither through his fingers. Talia thought he held it a moment longer than he should have, but he finally let it drop. "Cover your hair. Prince Vladimir will notice such tresses. He admires bright colored hair like yours, especially surrounding a comely face and atop a beautiful body. And he enjoys virgins, so you must not let him know that you are a virgin. You are, aren't you?"

Talia nodded, her face heating with embarrassment as she remembered the many hours she had spent in Oleg's arms, wanting him, knowing that he wanted her, but that they must both wait until after the wedding. Now that wedding would never happen. She might be forced to give up her virginity to the cruel prince who was approaching the Kiev fortress. Or even to Andrei. That possibility was not as awful, but it would still be a violation of her very being. She was his slave, and helpless. He or Prince Vladimir could take her whenever he decided to.

She realized that Andrei was still speaking, giving her more instructions.

"You aren't listening," he charged. "Don't you care what happens to you?"

"Do you?"

"Yes, that's why I'm trying to protect you," he said with some irritation. "So, you must wear your own coarse clothing and leave off your fur cloak. Cover yourself with the blanket, and tuck part of it about your head. Look to the ground and don't speak. If he asks you a question, pretend you don't understand, and I'll answer for you. Can you remember to do all that?"

Talia nodded and reached for the faded blanket. She wrapped it about her and looked down, as he had instructed her.

Andrei laughed. "And what is your name, slave?"

Talia said nothing.

"If you do as I instructed you, you may avoid the prince's attention." He opened the door and stepped outside, leaving her to trail after him.

Chapter 8

The courtyard seethed with movement. From all directions people poured out: workmen carrying their tools, women leading children by the hand, warriors bearing before them hastily grasped swords and shields. All eyes were trained toward the big wooden gate.

A deep note from a horn sent shivers down Talia's back, and in the silence that followed it, Prince Vladimir and his retinue rode through the gateway.

There was no mistaking that he was the prince. Talia allowed herself a quick look before dropping her gaze as Andrei had instructed, but that first image would be forever after imprinted in her mind.

The prince rode slowly, sitting high in the saddle of a shining black horse. He needed no crown to signify that he was ruler of all he surveyed. His fair hair fell loosely to the shoulders of his fur cloak, and he wore long gloves on hands that held the reins with careless abandon. Behind him rode a phalanx of warriors, their swords clanking, their armor creaking. Following the horsemen marched men in armor that glittered when the morning sun struck their breastplates.

Prince Vladimir halted in the center of the courtyard, raising his hand to signal his oncoming attendants. His horse pranced from left to right, then reared into the air, front hooves thrashing. The prince held his seat in the saddle, and Talia realized this maneuver was planned and well-executed, impressing onlookers with the prince's horsemanship. As the horse's front hoofs came down and struck the ground, the prince slid off the animal's back and tossed the reins to a youth who ran to take them. Then with a careless gesture the prince undid his long fur cloak and tossed it onto the back of the departing mount. The other riders also dismounted, freed their horses to the stable hands' care, and stood in silent attention to their lord.

"Bow," Andrei commanded Talia, his voice low. His hand rested on her shoulder, pressing down, insuring her obedience.

A quick glance around told her that the other slaves were kneeling in the mud, and she knelt too, glad at least that the beautiful gown she'd been wearing was spared the filth. Through half-lowered lashes she saw that a stream of others who followed the prince through the gate had also fallen to their knees. So they were slaves as well as she. Some were tied together, wrist to wrist. However cruel Andrei had been, he'd spared her and her villagers that indignity, and she resolved to thank him. *If I am spared and allowed to ever talk with him again.*

The prince gestured and the assembled warriors behind him closed ranks and stood at attention, awaiting his command. It came with another gesture. As a man, they relaxed, lowering their shields and placing their swords beside them, points down, but no one spoke or moved away.

Prince Vladimir began his inspection of the Kievan assembly, walking slowly around the circle of silent subjects. Talia had admired Andrei's height and breadth, had thought him majestic, but the prince loomed taller and broader than Andrei. And more majestic.

The ruler paused before Talia. She dared not look up, but focused on his huge boots, his sturdy legs incased in woolen trousers. He so overwhelmed her, without speaking a word, that she thought she might faint. .

"Stand up," he commanded.

Instinctively, Talia tried to obey, but Andrei's hand biting into her shoulder kept her down.

"She does not understand you, my lord," Andrei said.

The prince grunted and moved on. Talia felt Andrei's hand press her shoulder in approval, and then release her. What reason would Andrei have given if the prince had asked further? Would he have said that she was deaf, or an imbecile, or merely that she spoke some strange language?

Across the cleared space Talia saw Rognol, who stood with a group of warriors, his bandaged arm in a sling. He had been looking at her, she realized, but he now shifted his attention to Prince Vladimir. Would he speak of her to the prince?

She lifted her head slightly so that she could look around the courtyard, but her gaze kept coming back to the prince. He was talking with Rognol. Then he strode slowly back toward Andrei, toward her. As all the assembly watched, he stopped before her. With a swift gesture he swept the blanket back from her head, allowing her hair to tumble to her shoulders. He lifted a lock of it, just as Andrei had done.

Talia dared not look up, but felt the weight of his hand on her neck before he let go of her hair and stepped back.

"Send her to me," he said, and without waiting for Andrei's consent, turned and walked away. Andrei pulled the blanket back over her hair.

Only when the prince led his retinue away, to a large stone building farther up the hill, did Andrei help her to her feet. Talia rose stiffly, her muscles aching from unaccustomed kneeling, her heart thudding with fear. What would happen to her now?

Andrei grasped her hand and walked swiftly toward his quarters, dragging her with him. Twice Talia stumbled and half-fell, but he kept walking, not pausing for her discomfort.

Once in his house, Andrei led her up some steps to a loft where she saw a broad bed. "Take off your clothing," he commanded, and began to strip off his own. When Talia only stared at him, he said, "Undress. Quickly."

With fumbling fingers Talia obeyed, letting the blanket drop, and lifting her woolen gown over her head. She stood shivering in the silken undergarments Andrei had allowed her to wear. Was he about to dress her again in the finery to send her to the prince? Or did he want her to return the undergarments?

"Everything off," Andrei said, and when she looked at him she saw that he was naked. If he wanted her to change clothing, why had he also undressed? Still looking at him, she took off the shift and handed it to him, then stepped out of the silken trousers and handed them to him as well. He tossed them aside and pushed her backward onto the bed.

For a moment he stood over her, gazing down at her nakedness. Talia sucked in her breath and stared up at him, quivering with half dread, half anticipation. Before she could speak, he threw himself down beside her and cupped her breast with one hand, squeezing gently at the nipple.

"What are you —"

He put his other hand over her mouth. "Don't scream or cry out. I'll try not to hurt you."

Talia bit at his hand, but he scarcely noticed. His voice was low and soothing. "I hadn't meant it to happen this way, but it has to be." He flung his leg across her, pinning her down. She put her hands on his chest and pushed, but couldn't budge him. He was bigger, stronger, and determined to subdue her. Talia didn't know what he would do next, but his hard penis thrusting against her thigh was unmistakable.

Andrei lifted his hand from her mouth and brought his lips down on hers. At the same time, he caressed her breasts. Despite her resistance to him, her hatred of what he had done to her village, her breasts tingled and hardened at his touch. He slid his hands down her body, encasing her waist, flattening against her abdomen, moving lower, lower. Where his fingers touched, heat rose to her skin. She shuddered at the unaccustomed feel. He kept his mouth tight on hers, shutting off any protest, but Talia was beyond protesting. When his fingers parted the soft skin of her private place, her arms came up to clasp him to her.

In a swift motion, Andrei thrust inside her, hurting her, but she couldn't cry out. He paused, raised his head, and said, "It's done now. Shall I stop?"

Talia was too stunned to answer, and he took her silence for agreement or desire, and began to move in and out. It continued to hurt her, but not as much, and then not at all. Talia's whole body seemed to be heating, spiraling, fitting herself to him.

Just when she thought she could not endure another moment of it, he moved faster and then stopped with a groan. He clasped her tightly, shuddered, and went slack atop her before he rolled to one side and stood. "You'll want to clean yourself up," he said. "I hope I didn't hurt you too much. Are you bleeding?" He bent to examine her. "No, I don't think so. Virgins do sometime. I'm sorry it had to be like this, but I had to protect you."

"What do you mean?" Talia sat up, touched her lower body. It didn't look any different, but she knew that everything about her had changed in the past few moments with Andrei.

He was pulling on trousers, and paused to answer her. "I made sure Prince Vladimir would not have you sent to him. You are no longer a virgin."

"You kept me from being one of his chosen women? I might have become a princess."

"Don't be a fool!" He tied the belt of his trousers and looked at her squarely. "The only women who will become Vladimir's princesses are those he marries for political reasons. What would you bring to him—a country? Gold? A valuable ally?"

Talia shook her head. "None of those." She stared at Andrei's naked chest, full-muscled, glistening with perspiration. In spite of what he had just done to her, or maybe because of it, she longed to touch his chest, to lay her head against his shoulder.

"He has his pick of women, and after he has used them for a night's pleasure—maybe two nights if they are especially beautiful or interesting—he gives them to his men for sport. Rognol asked for you." He pulled on his shirt. "Would you like that?"

She shuddered at the thought of being touched by Rognol and for a moment could not speak. Then she shook her head. "Not that! So, what will become of me now?"

"I will try to keep you for myself."

"And I have no choice in the matter," she said.

"No. I told you the first day that you're my slave. I will treat you well, and I promise not to turn you over to Rognol. Beyond that, who can say what will happen?" He shrugged. "You can trust Svarog, or look to the new god, this Jesus Christ, but from what I know of life, neither of those, or any other god, cares a damn about mortals. If sacrificing and praying succeeded, then my wife and son would be alive, and I would be living on an estate, in a comfortable house, instead of this." He swept his hand around. "And you would be back in your village, waiting for your men to return. Do you think your god Svarog intended for them all to die? If you think he caused their death, then he is cruel, or they had done something that deserved punishment. If you think Svarog did not mean them to die, but was unable to save them, then he is weak and helpless. Who needs such a god? Of what use is he?"

He turned toward the door. "You see why I scoff at gods."

"May I wear the fine underclothing again?"

"Yes. It is of no use to me. You may consider it a small payment for the pleasure you have given me."

Talia picked up the filmy garments, considering them now tainted. Andrei had not said he wanted her to have them, but that he owed them to her. For them she had lost her virginity, and Andrei would have disposed of them sometime anyway. "Why didn't you give the garments to Marya?"

"That was a different experience, a different transaction. She offered herself to me for nothing, whereas I took you without your consent. So, please wear the garments if they please you, and think no more of it."

Think no more of it? Talia could think of nothing else. Her life had changed and there was no turning back, no undoing what had happened.

When she stood, Talia felt something trickling down her legs.

Without speaking, Andrei handed her a rough cloth and moistened it with water from the pail in the corner, then turned his back on her.

Talia wiped herself clean and handed back the cloth. Then, with numb hands she pulled on the garments. She smoothed the silken fabric before once again covering the precious undergarments with her own rough outer clothing.

Andrei watched her as she pulled on her boots. "I must go to drill with the other warriors," he said.

"What if Rognol comes here for me? Or the prince?"

"Go to the women's quarters. You'll be safe with the guardian women, and they'll have work for you. Every hand will be needed to prepare for the journey down river."

Talia nodded and pulled her cloak around her. The day was warm, but she felt strangely chilled.

"Cover your hair," he commanded, "so you don't attract undue attention. I'll come for you later."

He went down the steps and waited below for her to follow. After a moment she joined him. He spoke quietly, so she could barely hear: "Remember, do not answer the prince. Pretend you don't understand."

I don't understand any of this, Talia thought, but she believed Andrei that her very existence depended on doing what he asked of her. Her destiny was linked to him. It had been from the moment he and his warriors had seen her in the snowy forest.

Chapter 9

Inside the women's quarters, she went to Olga's bed and knelt beside her friend, finally letting her tears flow.

"Talia, what is it?" Olga looked from the infant she nestled in her arms to her weeping friend. "Has something dreadful happened?"

Talia nodded, bringing her head down onto Olga's shoulder. "Andrei took me in lust."

"Did he hurt you?"

"A little. He said he would try not to hurt me." She paused, gave a jerky little sob and went on," He said he did it for me."

"Men!" Olga scoffed. "Always giving some absurd reason for doing what they want to do. Why did he say it was for you?"

"The prince asked for me and Andrei said after the prince had had his fun, he'd turn me over to Rognol. But the prince only wants virgins, so Andrei made sure I'm not a virgin anymore."

Olga reached her free hand to lift Talia's chin so Talia was forced to meet her friend's probing gaze. "He may indeed have done this for you, but I have no doubt he enjoyed it too. I'm just sorry your first time had to be like this."

"First?" Talia repeated. "You mean there may be more such times?"

Olga laughed lightly. "Probably. Oleg and I did it often, and my babe was conceived in love and pleasure on one of those occasions." She ran her finger gently along the baby's downy cheek and smiled when the child sighed and snuggled closer.

Talia drew back, startled. "What if he has got me with child? Without love or pleasure?"

"It could happen—could have happened—but let's hope not."

"If I have to bear his child, I'll kill myself."

"I won't let you do that, Talia! We must pray that you are not with child."

Talia recalled Andrei's words about the uselessness of praying to either Svarog or the Christian god. "It won't help," she said.

"Yes, praying does help, Talia, and making sacrifices does too. Consider my babe. You prayed to Svarog and made an offering, to the gods and just look at him. He's changed, he was near death for coming too soon, but now he's going to live."

"Nicolai prayed to the Christian god for you," Talia said.

"I didn't know. That was kind of him."

"My mother was a believer in the Christian god, but she died. All our men prayed to Svarog, and they are dead too."

"Perhaps they are living well in the afterlife."

"I don't want to be in the afterlife!" Talia declared. "I want to live well here."

Olga bursts into laughter. "Ah, Talia! A moment ago, you were saying you'd kill yourself and now you want to live." She squeezed her friend's hand. "I want you to live. You are strong and full of life, and if anything happens to me, I would want you to take my babe and bring him up. And if you have a babe of your own, it will be strong and healthy and you'll love it, no matter who the father is. That's the way we women are made."

"How many times does it take to create a baby?"

"No one knows. For some people, only once. For others, many times. And for a few, it never happens. We are helpless before what must be, Talia."

"And is it intended by some god that I should belong to Andrei? I don't like being a slave!"

"No one does, but you are fortunate you are slave to Andrei and not Rognol, or someone else who would beat you or treat you badly."

Talia had a fleeting image of Andrei's bare, glistening chest, and recalled the feel of his body entwined with hers. "It could be worse," she admitted. "But all the same, I don't want to bear his child."

She noticed that Olga's eyelids were drooping. "You must sleep, and not concern yourself with my problems," she said. "And I must find the women who have work for me. Work may take my thoughts off what has happened."

As Talia approached the work area, a strong odor assailed her nostrils. Women were swirling clumps of sheep's wool in pots of urine. Talia squinted as the smell made her eyes water.

One of the women laughed. "It's a good thing we don't need any more help with softening the fleeces," she said. She pointed farther along. "I think they can use some help tanning the hides."

Talia walked on, and saw with a sinking feeling that these women too were poking something in pots of brown liquid. But this at least didn't stink.

"Here's a hide for you," a woman said, using a long stick to fish an animal skin from the pot and fling it onto the ground at Talia's feet. "You know what to do with this, don't you?"

Talia nodded and picked up the wet animal skin. "Do I take it outside?"

"Suit yourself. Most of us work outside, chilly as it is. There's scrapers outside for cleaning the skins. You'll probably want to leave your cloak with your friend and find a bit of cord to tie back your hair. Loose hair might hamper your work, and you wouldn't want it to get wet with the oak bark tea."

Talia readied herself, and spent the next few hours on hands and knees, scraping with a sharpened piece of bone at the surface of the animal skin. As much flesh as possible had been cut away when the animal was first slain and skinned, but there were always bits that adhered and had to be removed before the final tanning to keep the furs and leather from rotting. As soon as she finished a skin, it was taken away and another dropped into its place. By late afternoon her knees ached from kneeling, and her hands were cramped from holding the scraper.

But at least she was safe. The men were drilling off in the distance, including Rognol and Andrei. She could hear the beat of feet marching, running, and the clank of metal as sword struck shield. Her work and the men's drilling seemed to go on forever. Then, just as she thought she couldn't endure another body-cramping moment, the woman in charge said, "It will soon be too dark to see our work any longer. Time to give it up for tonight. There'll be plenty left to do tomorrow."

Talia pulled herself to her feet, feeling weak and dizzy. For a moment the world spun about her, and she saw a row of men coming toward her. They all looked like Andrei, and then the image cleared and she saw that it was Andrei, only one Andrei.

She wiped her damp hands down the side of her dress and started toward him, but he reminded her in a low voice, "Your cloak. It's growing chill with nightfall."

"Yes," Talia stumbled back into the longhouse for her cloak. Tonight's food was already simmering in pots not far from the pots of urine, their odors mingling. Her stomach clenched and for a moment she thought she'd vomit from the smell. She bit her bottom lip, grabbed up her cloak and tossed it about her shoulders How did these women bear the odors?

Andrei said nothing more until they were back in his quarters. It was growing dark outside, and lighted torches had been thrust into sconces along the wall. A fire burned in the fireplace, sending out welcome warmth. She went to stand before the fire and extended her hands toward the flames.

Andrei set his sword and shield against the wall and came toward Talia. "How do you feel?" he asked, reaching to unfasten her cloak. The hood fell back, exposing Talia's face and hair.

She flinched at his touch. "I ache all over, and I must look dreadful," she said, though she couldn't explain even to herself why it mattered how she looked. She was a slave, performing a slave's duty. Beauty would bring trouble.

"You ache all over?" he repeated, his voice barely concealing a laugh. "Then I must have been rougher with you than I intended."

"That's not what I was referring to," Talia retorted. "I've been scraping hides and my knees and back are cramped and my hands are shriveled and brown." She held them out so he could see. "Bits of animal flesh are clinging to my hair and my clothing."

"If I'd known how an afternoon of work would ruin your looks, I might have spared myself my earlier effort to render you unappealing to the prince." Crinkles appeared at the edges of his eyes, and he grinned, unmistakably making fun of hr.

"Your effort! You know you enjoyed it."

"Of course I did. I always enjoy pleasuring myself with a lovely young woman. I just meant that Prince Vladimir would not find you so comely if he could see you now." He pulled the cord that bound her hair, letting it fall free. "That's a bit better." He ran his fingers through her hair. "There's nothing clinging to your hair, as far as I can tell. Binding it out of the way was wise. Hair such as this cries out for flowers and jewels to bedeck it, but for now we must hide it from admiring eyes."

"Even yours?" she asked.

A fleeting smile touched his lips. "So you think I admire your beauty? You are right, and I own it. You belong to me, all of you: your hair, your body, your labor."

Talia did not speak. She licked her dry lips and looked at Andrei. What else did he plan to do to her?

He took one of her hands in his and studied it. "I'm afraid we can't do much to improve the looks of your hands. Oak tea stains them beyond remedy. They will be brown for some days, but that too may be an advantage in warding off unwanted attentions."

The whole time he was talking, Andrei watched her, and Talia knew her face was flushed at his attention. She snatched her hand from his grasp. His touch, on her hair, even on her hand, stirred unwanted feelings.

Andrei folded her cloak and laid it on the bench, then placed his round shield before the door. "That will give us some privacy. Not enough, but at least we will be warned by the falling shield if anyone enters."

"Who would come? Marya?"

"No, the prince's men." Then, as if his statement were inconsequential, he led the way up the steps and indicated a basin of water. "Would you like to bathe first?"

"You'll watch me?"

"Yes. I have that right, and I have seen you naked twice before: here today and earlier in the sauna."

"And when you beat me with the branches," Talia added.

"As I recall, you gave more beating than you got."

Taking as much time as she dared, Talia pulled off her boots and bent to place them carefully against the wall before she slid the silken undergarments off and laid them aside. She luxuriated in the way they felt against her skin, but they were a reminder of what Andrei had done to her.

Keeping her back to Andrei, she could feel his eyes boring into her as she soaped up her body, shivering slightly in the chill of the room.

Andrei tried to look away, but his gaze kept swinging back to Talia. The flaring torch at the wall threw shadows across her body so that he could see her only in silhouette, but his memory furnished the details. As her hand holding the warm, damp cloth moved down her body, he could imagine his own hand tracing those movements: around the fullness of her breasts, down the curve of her abdomen, between her thighs and up into the hot center of her. It was all he could do to stay seated and not leap up to claim her. The tightness of his arousal pressed against his trousers. She was the cause of it, a Slav. He could have used Marya to slake his desire, but ever since he had captured the Slav he had coveted her. He knew she didn't desire him. She feared him, hated him, and he shouldn't care that he stirred no desire in her. What did it matter?

She was a slave, and from now on he could have her as often as he wanted. He had claimed her, made sure he was her first. Now no other man could break her virginity.

But perversely, he wanted her to want him. He wanted to hurry her, to get through the bath quickly, but at the same time he savored the sight of her shining, naked body.

She stood on one foot, balancing like a dancer, or a graceful bird, while she washed the other foot.

She turned, and for a moment he was struck dumb at the sight of her. Light from the torch shone on her naked, glistening skin, and cast an erotic shadow pattern against the far wall of breasts, arms and long, lithe body.

"Shall I pour the water outside?" she asked.

"I'll do it."

"But I'm the slave."

"You are, and if you were clothed there would be no question you'd be attending to your bath water and mine as well, but I don't want anyone to see you without clothing." He took the basin, pushed aside the shield that blocked the door and dashed the water outside without looking where it went. There was an exclamation of anger. "Someone's spying on us," he whispered, returning to her side.

"Why?"

"If you had stepped outside, you might have been set upon. Now they know that we know they're out there."

"What do we do?"

"I'm going to have my bath." He began stripping off his clothing. He kicked his boots aside, dropped his trousers and stepped out of them and turned so that she could see him. She sucked in her breath and looked away. She started to don the undergarments, but he said, "Leave them off. I'll be quick with my bath."

She sat down on the bed and held the garments in front of her, shielding her breasts. Andrei bathed quickly, aware that she was watching him, wanting her to watch him. It took only a few minutes to wipe off the grime and sweat from the afternoon's drilling and run the coarse towel over his body. At another time he might have taken a woman without bothering to bathe, and he recalled the leisurely baths he'd taken with his wife, soaping her body, sliding his hands over her and into her. This business with the Slav was different from both those occasions. Vladimir's men— or, the gods forbid, Rognol—waited out there. For what? At some signal to come in and take the woman?

He dared not linger. Any moment they might tire of waiting, and burst into the house. He finished bathing and dashed the second basin of water in the direction he'd heard the earlier exclamation. There was a grunt, perhaps from spattering of water, but the predators had obviously shifted their location. He seized the torch and flung it toward the place the grunt had come from, and was rewarded by a cry. Good!

The house was plunged into darkness, and the light from outside would show up anyone breaking in on them. Andrei knew he'd have a moment's advantage, but only a moment. He felt for his sword, grasped the hilt, and brought it close to where he could reach it quickly. Then he pushed Talia onto the bed and lay beside her, holding her down with one hand, the other clasping her mouth closed so she couldn't cry out.

"Make no sound," he whispered. "Put your arms around me." Changing position, he straddled her. Talia's arms came up, above his back, but did not touch him.

"Do it!" he commanded, and as she brought her arms down to encircle him, two men burst in. Only momentarily stopped, by the falling shield, they lifted their torches to expose Andrei straddling Talia.

Andrei grabbed up the sword as he swung his feet over the side of the bed, pulling away from Talia. He made no move to cover himself or her. "What are you doing in my quarters?" he demanded, though he knew well enough why they were there.

71

"The prince wants the woman with red hair," one said, pointing at Talia.

"She's not a virgin, so the prince wouldn't want her," Andrei said, speaking as carelessly as if it scarcely mattered, though his heart hammered painfully at the thought of Talia being used by the prince and raped by the soldiers. "You have just seen with your own eyes that we have mated."

The men stood awkwardly for a moment, the light from their torches casting highlights and shadows on the glistening naked bodies of Talia and Andrei. They stared at Talia, their gazes raking over her, drool stringing from their mouths at the sight of her. One swiped the back of his hand across his mouth to wipe the saliva away, and then both men dropped their torches and departed without another word.

Andrei extinguished one torch and set the other into the wall sconce. He went to the door to make sure the men had gone, and then returned back to Talia. "We have been witnessed. We may as well complete our union." He sat down beside her and touched her breast. The sight of her curved, clean body, her skin glistening stirred his desire.

Talia shrank from him. "No! You have humiliated me and exposed me to those strangers. Isn't that enough?"

"We had to be seen joined together by the prince's representatives. If you had been taken, you would have been examined to determine if you are a virgin. It would have been more humiliating than what just happened."

Talia twisted to one side and tore the skin of his back with her fingernails.

Andrei grabbed both her hands and held them together by the wrists above her head, while with the other he made sure she could not pull away from his penetration. It was over quickly. Andrei loosened his hold on her and rolled to one side, sated but ashamed. He hadn't meant to be so brutal. She was probably tender from their earlier joining, and his treatment would have brought her no pleasure.

Talia sobbed quietly and curled into a ball, as far away on the bed as she could get from him.

Andrei covered her with a fur and pulled another over himself. He was grateful that a few embers still glowed in the fireplace. Tonight would be cold, and Talia would accept no comforting warmth from him this night, he was sure. Not tonight.

Chapter 10

Talia awoke stiff and cold. The fur robe had slid off onto the floor, leaving her naked to the chill air, and the fire in the fireplace had gone out. Her skin prickled with goose bumps. For a moment she thought she was back in the village, awakening in the log cabin, and needing to see to the fire. But as she reached for the fur cover, she saw Andrei sleeping on the bed beside her, and the truth of the present came flooding over her.

His fur robe was displaced too, in a provocative way, as if he'd purposely arranged the disarray. His shoulders and upper arms were exposed, and his feet protruded from the other end of his fur robe. The middle of his body was covered, but Talia recalled vividly how it looked: taut with muscles, glistening with sweat as he lay with her. In the dim early morning light she could barely make out his face, but she remembered that too, looming over her as he took her in lust.

She wrapped the fur robe tightly around her and leaned back against the wall, studying Andrei's sleeping form. Her fingers itched to touch him, to feel the ridges of muscles across his chest. She'd never explored a man's naked body, not even Oleg's. *Oleg!* The man she'd thought to marry had respected her. He would never have treated her as Andrei had.

How could she even consider touching Andrei? She jerked her hand back just as Andrei opened his eyes—eyes as blue as the sky on a clear winter day—and gazed at her.

"I've been awake for some time," he said. "Don't be shy. Come closer and touch me. We can mate as often as we want to from now onward." He grasped her wrist, trapping her.

Talia pulled back, but resisting him was useless. She let her arm go limp, but kept her body rigid, and with the other hand clasped the fur robe about her. "I'm not shy. I hate you."

"That is to be expected," he said, unconcerned by her outburst. "It's in the very nature of slavery that slaves hate their masters. If I were you, I wouldn't want to be my slave either."

Talia stared at him. She'd expected anger and yet had dared to express her feelings. He didn't seem to care.

"As your master, I have total control over you. I could beat you, use you nightly to slake my lust, sell you, give you away. I could even have you killed."

"Do you want to kill me?"

"Of course not. I would no more have you killed than I would shoot a healthy horse."

"I am just a horse to you?" Talia burst out.

"I was making a comparison," he said, "to indicate that you have value to me."

"Do you plan to sell me?"

"Only if I am offered a very high price. Otherwise, I'll keep you for myself. If the prince allows it, that is."

"But you made sure the prince doesn't want me."

"Not as a mistress, but he decides which of the warriors get what booty—here, on the way, and in Byzantium."

Talia stared at him, wide-eyed in horror. Moments before, she'd been angry at him. Now she feared she might be taken from him by someone more repugnant. "How will he decide?" she asked.

"It's based on our service. The best warriors get their choice of slaves as well as a share of whatever riches we find along the way. If two warriors want the same slave, then they may have to give up a share of riches, or fight each other."

"You would fight for me?"

"It probably won't come to that," he said, without admitting or denying his actions. "It will all be decided before we leave for Byzantium."

"When are we going?"

"In a few days. The weather is warm enough for travel, and the prince's troops have gathered in all the booty this area has to offer. It's time for trade downriver."

"Is the prince going?"

Andrei nodded. "He doesn't usually make the journey, but sends his warriors and tradesmen. This trip is special. He wants to see for himself what the Christianity of Byzantium is like."

"Why is he interested in Christianity? Doesn't he believe in Svarog and our other gods?"

"His kingdom is surrounded by religions that are expanding, making converts. He wants to control which religion his kingdom follows. He sent emissaries in all directions to study the beliefs of the religions. To Kazakhstan to investigate the Jewish faith, to the Arab lands where the people follow the teachings of Mohammed, called Muslims. The prince was favorably inclined to the Muslims, as they can have more than one wife, but the strictness of their beliefs and the bleakness of it didn't appeal to him. He is most inclined to Christianity, since it combines the teachings of the Jewish faith as well as that of Jesus, but he has learned that not all Christians believe the same thing. There has been a split in their great church. To the west are the Germanic Christians. Their worship struck him as plain and austere. His messengers have reported that in Byzantium there are beautiful churches, special music, and jeweled garments for the priests."

"Those things shouldn't matter," Talia objected. "Only the power of the god himself. Isn't Svarog powerful enough for the prince?"

"The prince wants Kiev to be more modern. Svarog and all the other gods his subjects worship he considers part of the ignorant past. He wants his people to move ahead, to become the equal of the countries around us. The prince controls a vast territory, but it's backward and its people full of superstitions. Why do you care?

You are a slave and always will be, even if you become a part of some pasha's harem."

"What's a harem?"

"A group of women kept by some powerful man for his pleasure. You would have good food and beautiful clothing, and you would not have to do hard work, but you could never leave the harem."

"Am I not already in your harem?"

He laughed, the first time she'd heard him laugh: a deep, rich sound that made her want to join him in merriment. "Since I have only you as my slave at present, it can't be said that I have a harem. Moreover, that applies only to Muslims, who live near Byzantium. You could be considered my concubine."

"And what is that?"

"It's a long word for a slave, but a special kind of slave. A concubine is a woman who tends to the sexual needs of a powerful man. He doesn't marry her, but he protects her when she becomes old and unable to please him. Then he chooses a new concubine, younger and more pleasing, and he gives the older woman easy duties to perform as long as she is able."

Talia pondered the possibilities. She imagined herself like Marya, cooking and taking care of others, no longer desired by Andrei. But Marya wasn't old. What if Andrei or the prince sold her to become part of a harem? She'd spend her time pleasing some man, living with other women who didn't speak her language, and she could never return home. None of these futures appealed to her. But she had no choice anyway. She'd have to do whatever Andrei decreed.

As if he could read her thoughts, Andrei said, "You could make your lot easier by trying to please me."

"How would I do that—by submitting to you whenever you want me?"

"That would be one way, but that's not all. What did you do to please the man you were to marry?"

"I didn't have to do anything to please him. We were betrothed, and until we were actually wed, we would never have spent time together without clothing."

"A pity," he said. "So, I must train you. You can start by rubbing my back." He released her hand and turned away from her.

Talia leaned forward and brushed her hand down his back, from the neck to the point where the fur robe began.

He sat up and let the robe drop lower. "Not like that! Must I teach you everything, even something so simple? Lie down on your face and I'll show you how it's to be done." He pulled the cover off her despite her clutching fingers and pushed her down onto the hard bed.

"This is not comfortable," she protested.

"No, I suppose it's not," he said. "Sit up and let me put the fur beneath you."

"And I'm cold."

He sighed heavily and stood, tossing her fur robe over her. He put on his own robe. "I'll tend the fire, but from now on it will be your job. You do know that."

He squatted before the fireplace, blowing on the gray ashes until a few glowing embers were exposed. He added dried grass, and slivers of wood, then larger pieces of wood as flames appeared. His robe had fallen open, and Talia stared in embarrassment at his bare thighs—and at what hung at their joining. She felt her face—and her entire body—go hot, but she could not stop looking at him.

When the fire was burning steadily, Andrei glanced up and caught her gaze. He grinned and as he stood, the fur dropped back into place, cutting off her view.

"Fire's taken care of, so you should soon be warm, though I'll wager from the looks of your face that you're already getting heated."

Talia couldn't speak, but closed her eyes and cut off the sight of him.

"Come now, it's all right to look." He whipped off the fur robe and flung it aside. "I should also like to look—and admire." He tore Talia's robe from her grasp. Her eyes flew open in astonishment.

"Now, where were we?" Andrei mused. "Oh, yes. I was attempting to show you how to rub someone's back satisfactorily. Would you like to lie on the fur robe?

When she still didn't speak, he spread the fur robe on the bed and pushed her down onto it. "It will be more comfortable if you turn your head to the side."

She did as he suggested. "You must have rubbed the back of many women."

"Not many. Not enough, at any rate. Women are usually rubbing my back—as I shall expect you to do regularly, as soon as you learn how. Now lie still." He knelt, straddling her, and brought his hands to her shoulders.

Talia lay stiffly, trying not to flinch at his touch. His thumbs were pressing into her neck. "That's not my back," she protested.

"It's where your back begins. You're as stiff as a corpse on a battlefield—though they usually wear clothing."

Talia laughed.

"That's it. When you laughed it relaxed your shoulders a bit." He eased the pressure on her neck and ran his hands down her back, so gently she could barely feel the path he followed. Then he increased the pressure, massaging her back and waist, with smooth, circular motions.

Talia sighed, relaxed, and yet was vibrantly aware of him. His knees pressed against her thighs, clasping her so she couldn't move, even if she'd wanted to. Her heartbeat thrummed to the rhythm of his movements. The massaging slowed as he bent lower over her, and then stopped altogether. Talia dared not move or speak. In the stillness she awaited his next move.

He lifted her hair, wrapped it about his hand, then uncurled it slowly to one side and kissed her neck, a kiss as light as a butterfly poised on a flower.

But that changed with a swiftness that astonished her. He dropped to one side beside her and rolled her over onto her back.

"Is it my turn now? I don't think I can rub quite the way you did," Talia said, her breath coming in quick little gasps.

"No, we're doing something else. Touch me here." He grasped her hand and forced it against his penis. She stretched out her finger to touch it, then drew back. She knew now what he intended. "No. You tricked me."

But she was unable to stop him from doing what he wanted. It was over quickly and roughly.

He seemed to be satisfied, but she wasn't. "Did I please you?"

"Yes, you did."

"You didn't ask if you pleased me. Well, you didn't. And you lied. You said it was to protect me from being used by the prince's men, but you're using me yourself."

"It's my right."

"You feel nothing for me any more than you did with Marya. What if I am with child? Olga says it can happen any time."

"If you are with child, I will take care of you—and the child."

"Would my child also be your slave?"

"If it is a girl, yes. If it's a son, he could become a warrior, and my heir, to replace my son who died." He spoke as if he had thought the matter through beforehand.

"Would I replace your wife who died?"

"No, you couldn't. She came of my class, of a good family. Marrying her brought me a large tract of land. You would bring me nothing."

"Except pleasure," she said, reaching for her clothing. "You are no better than the prince."

He shrugged and began to get dressed. "As long as you please me, I won't sell you or beat you or turn you out of my quarters."

"I might be better off if you sell me to someone's harem," she said. "At least then I'd have lovely clothes and good food, as you said." She pulled on her clothing and started for the door.

"Where are you going?"

"To bring some food. That's what slave women are supposed to do, isn't it? I may even have to cook for you."

"Can you cook game meat and not just gruel?"

"I can skin, gut, and cut up all kinds of birds and animals. I can even kill them, if I have to."

"And I know you can hew the wood for the fire, if need be," he said. "I've seen you at that."

"And I'll find a way to change my situation, even if it means using an ax again," she said. "So you might think about pleasing me."

"Masters don't have to please slaves."

"I was not a slave until you made me one. I was free, and respected, and I will be again. I don't know how it will happen, but it will happen somehow."

She picked up the wooden eating bowl and went out. The courtyard was quiet and dark, except for a large fire burning near the women's quarters. A woman stood beside a pot, stirring gruel with a wooden paddle. It was Marya.

Talia felt some compassion for her. Marya too had been used by Andrei and known his scorn. "Can you spare some gruel for Andrei?" she asked, holding out the bowl.

"This for Andrei," Marya said, and spat into the bowl. "And this for you." She spat onto Talia's face. "Go cook something for him yourself."

Talia stepped back and wiped her hand across the spittle that ran down her cheek. So much for compassion. Without speaking, she walked toward the women's quarters. She didn't want to awaken Olga and the baby, but there must be someone else awake there who could give her some grain and water to make gruel, and she could cook it back in Andrei's house. He'd made the fire to warm her, but it could also be a cooking fire.

Two days later her bleeding time came. So, there would be no child, not this time. And she would see to it that there was no other opportunity for a child. She wanted love and respect, not having to please Andrei just to save her life.

Chapter 11

For the next week Talia was doubly safe from Andrei. She knew he wouldn't touch her as long as her bleeding lasted, but she didn't need that as a reason to avoid him.

He paid little attention to her. He was totally occupied with military drilling as Prince Vladimir directed for all the warriors, He didn't even notice that when she dressed she tied a moss-filled cloth between her thighs. He made no objection or any comment at all when she turned her back to him on the bed.

All he asked of her was to bring him food in the early morning and at the end of the day's drill. He left the house as soon as it was light in the morning and she would hear the door closing behind him. She seldom saw him again until he came in at night, ate quickly and dropped into bed unwashed and exhausted.

Talia's bleeding time was no excuse to avoid work. She was instructed to continue scraping the hides being tanned. At other times was put to cutting up meat and cooking it along with dried vegetables and spices to make the stew that was the steady diet at the fortress city. Cutting the meat was a smelly, slimy enterprise, that kept her hands sticky, but cooking the stew was a pleasure. She could be outside in the fresh air, away from the temptation or danger of Andrei, and the wooden stirring paddle would be a useful weapon in case any of the other men approached.

"I came to help you," she heard one evening as she stirred the stew, and turned to see Grigor standing nearby, looking down at the ground.

"That's good of you, Grigor," she said. "Here, you can stir this." She handed him the stirring paddle and stepped to the side.

She didn't really need his help, but he needed something to occupy him.

"It wasn't my choice," he admitted. "I want to be a warrior, and Nicolai said I could try, but the other warriors said I couldn't."

"Nicolai wants to keep you safe."

"It's not fair!" He stirred so vigorously that a bit of stew flew out of the pot, and sizzled in the fire, sending up a smoky, meaty fragrance. "They sent me away from the drilling and told me to learn how to cook and tan hides. That's woman's work."

"It's hard work, and important," she said, justifying it to herself as much as to him. "The warriors need food to stay strong, and the hides are valuable for trading. And when you have grown tall and strong you can be a warrior."

"No matter how tall and strong I become, I can't be one of the prince's warriors."

"Why do you want to be one?"

"I want to be powerful and important, and that's the only way," he admitted, pausing in the stirring. "But I can't be anything, because I'm a slave."

"I know, Grigor. I'm a slave too, and so is your sister." She touched his shoulder. He went on as if she had not touched him. She let her hand drop. "We're all slaves."

"But we weren't before, before they destroyed our village and captured us."

"That's true, Grigor, but there's no going back to the way things were. All we have is now." She clasped and unclasped her hands, having no work at the moment to occupy them.

"What can we do, Talia?" he asked. "My sister can't run away—not very far, anyway—with a baby, and I won't go without her. She's given up everything except taking care of the baby, and she won't even let me talk to her about running away."

"It's different with women, Grigor."

"So you're like my sister, even though you don't have a baby. You're afraid to take a chance," he charged.

"I'm not afraid," she said. "I just see things as they are. There's nothing to go back to, even if we knew how to find our village and had food to sustain us while we traveled. Our men are dead."

"That's what Olga says too! But it can't be true. Our men wouldn't let themselves be killed."

"I don't know how it happened, but they are dead."

"How do you know?"

"Andrei told me."

"And you believe him? He is our enemy."

She nodded. "He's our enemy, but I believe him. Deep down I knew it even before our village was attacked." She saw tears slipping down his face. He too knew the truth, but didn't want to accept it. "We would have starved if the attackers hadn't come."

When Grigor said nothing, Talia asked, "Has anyone beaten you?"

He shook his head, spilling tears. "They make jokes and shove me around and call me bad names, and I can't fight back. Sometimes I want to kill them, and sometimes I want to die."

"Don't do either," she said. "I thought that way too for a while, but things have gotten better." As she spoke, she realized she was not just consoling a frightened boy, but she was speaking the truth about herself.

"What's going to happen to us, Talia?" he asked.

"I don't know," she admitted. "But I think we'll find out soon."

They did find out, the very next day.

Dawn was just breaking when Talia brought in the morning's food. She saw that Andrei had not girded himself for military drills.

"Set the food aside," he said.

Talia did, and stepped back just out of his reach. Was he about to mate with her again?

He laughed, as if he knew her thoughts. "We must both go to the sauna," he said. "I've scarcely cleaned myself for days, and you must want to be cleansed. If we go now, we can avoid the others."

"Are you going naked?" she asked, staring at him.

"Yes. Anyone who wishes to see me naked is welcome to do so."

"I want to be covered, at least outside."

"I thought you might. Go as you are, or get the blanket."

"Aren't you cold?" she asked, wrapping herself in the blanket.

"No, I'm never cold. Hot blood courses through my veins." He touched her cheek. "Your face feels warm. I shall have to warm the rest of you."

Talia whirled away from him and plunged out into the chilly dawn. She walked ahead of Andrei, conscious of his footsteps behind her, of his even breathing as he leaned over her to open the entry to the sauna. It was dark inside the enclosure, lit only by the glowing coals in the center fire pit. She made her way to the seating space and didn't flinch away when Andrei sat beside her. As her eyes became accustomed to the darkness, she turned to Andrei at the same moment that he turned toward her. His body glistened with sweat. The heat was bringing out the impurities in her body too, and beads of perspiration appeared on her neck and trickled down between her breasts. Andrei ran his hand down her sweat-slicked arm and then, to her astonishment, leaned over and touched his tongue to her breast.

Talia jerked back.

He laughed. "Don't worry. I could take you, with pleasure, if I so desired, but I won't. The prince forbids us to lie with women until the voyage is well under way and we are safely past the Pechenegs. He thinks we lose our energy and our will to fight if we spill our juices into women."

Talia was silent, trying to make sense of what he was saying. Finally she asked, "When are you going on the voyage?"

"*We* are going. Perhaps today, certainly by tomorrow."

"Who are the Pechenegs?" She stumbled over the unfamiliar name.

"Our enemies at the falls. We may not encounter them, but we must be prepared. They kill without mercy, and use the skulls of their dead victims for drinking cups."

Talia gasped and shuddered. "Are you torturing me with imaginary attacks?"

"Why would I do that? I only wish I were inventing enemies." He stood and pulled her to her feet. "Time to go outside."

Just outside the door stood pails of water. Talia shrieked as the cold water Andrei sluiced her with hit her hot body. He slapped his hand over her mouth. "Do you want to awaken the whole camp so they come running to see why you're screaming?"

Talia shook her head and stood a moment while the water trickled down her abdomen and legs. Andrei handed her a pail of water and she dashed it over him. Then he bundled her into the blanket and guided her back to the house.

When Talia had finished her bath and dressed, she saw that Andrei had donned his military uniform. "Why are we making a special effort to bathe and dress today?" she asked.

"It may be our last chance for a very long time. The prince never wants us to be caught off guard, wet and naked, if we are attacked. And there are no saunas, or soap on the journey. The terrain is wild, with few still pools. And no privacy," he concluded.

"Why are we leaving Kiev to go into such a place?"

"We have to get through the wild country to reach Byzantium. There it will be warm and you can surely have a bath as often as you wish. There are actually public baths."

"So I am going on the journey?"

"Yes, unless the prince decides otherwise."

She paused, one boot on, the other in her hand. "He still wants me?"

"Or someone else wants you. It will be decided."

By the time they'd finished eating and left the house, a crowd had gathered in the center clearing. Some warriors stood together, shoulder to shoulder, while others stood behind their women, in the same way

Andrei took up his position behind Talia and bade her kneel. The women she'd worked with came from the women's quarters, drying their hands on their skirts, brushing hair back from their faces. Some took their places beside or in front of men, while others stood in a cluster near the fire, holding their hands out for warmth.

The sun had come up and the air was growing warm, but Talia still shivered. What was about to happen? She looked across the gathering to see Olga, standing shakily, leaning on Grigor. Tall Nicolai stood beside them, holding Olga's baby. Talia smiled and gave a surreptitious wave. Olga smiled back, but made no move.

A horn sounded and Prince Vladimir stepped into the circle. Everyone bowed to him. Talia had no choice, as Andrei pressed her head downward, forcing her to bow. As others straightened from their bows, he released the pressure so that Talia too could look up at the prince.

The prince's glance swept the crowd. "Who will speak first?" he demanded.

People shuffled, coughed, looked around at each other. Then Nicolai stepped forward. "Sire," he said, "I am willing to stay behind and guard the fort."

The prince turned his gaze on the scarred warrior. Talia thought Nicolai might be embarrassed to have his sovereign and his colleagues stare at him, but he seemed untouched by the scrutiny of the crowd. His arm hung at an awkward angle and the jagged scar that marked his face stood out lividly. There was something noble about him, like a proud, injured god. *That's how Svarog might look if he'd been injured*, Talia thought.

"And why are you willing to do this?" the prince inquired.

Nicolai shrugged and held up his maimed hand. "I am not the warrior I once was, and I might prove a hindrance in battle. But I can train young warriors. I have not forgotten my lessons learned from you, Sire."

The prince nodded approvingly. "You fought well and in incurring your injuries you saved the lives of others. We owe you a debt of gratitude."

"Thank you, Sire," Nicolai said.

"Staying here will earn you no glory, and you realize that you forfeit your portion of the booty we may win in battle."

"I agree to forfeit the booty of battle, but I ask a boon of you instead."

"What might it be?"

"Grant me the slave Olga and her baby."

From across the crowd Talia saw Olga's mouth drop open in shock, and she stared up at the gentle, maimed giant beside her.

When the prince didn't speak, Nicolai went on, "The baby is small and weak, and the woman has not recovered from giving birth. They might both die on the journey, and at the least, they would hold back the progress of the warriors."

"Well said," the prince stated. "So you are willing to care for these feeble slaves?"

Nicolai nodded.

"Granted. Is that all you require?"

"No, Sire. I would also ask for the boy Grigor. He is brother to the slave Olga. He too is weak and sickly." He pointed at Grigor, who appeared to Talia even thinner than when she'd last seen him. "If he stays here, he can help with the work at the same time that I begin teaching him to fight."

"The boy is also granted to you, as a slave. From the looks of him, it's doubtful he will become a fighter," the prince said, with a dismissive wave of his hand.

"We shall see, Sire," Nicolai said. "In time I may be granting him back to you as a warrior, to replace me."

"He may become a warrior, but not to replace you. You gave of yourself in my service, as few have done. Are you sure about your choices? You can change if you wish."

"One more thing, Sire."

The prince looked surprised. Few dared to ask for more than one boon. He nodded.

"I request permission to marry the lady Olga, if she will have me," Nicolai concluded.

A murmur of surprise ran through the crowd. People muttered to each other and stared at Nicolai. Olga's face turned ashen as she gasped and looked as if she might faint.

"Marry? A slave? You don't need to do that. You already own her, by my wish."

"I am a Christian, and I want to marry her, after a suitable time."

"I don't pretend to understand your reasoning," the prince said. "She brings no treasure to you, and doesn't even appear strong enough to serve you as a slave should. But perhaps after we have studied this Christian faith more thoroughly in Byzantium, we shall come to your way of thinking. That, after all, is one of the purposes of this journey: not just to trade and capture slaves and territory, but to choose a faith suitable for my kingdom."

The assembled group waited silently for the prince to finish speaking. Some stared still at Nicolai, and shook their heads in disbelief. *Marry a slave! Why, when you could get children on her with no responsibility? And calling her a lady, too! Nicolai has lost his senses to this strange new religion.*

"Who is next?" the prince asked. Both Andrei and Rognol stepped forward.

"I want her!" Rognol declared, pointing at Talia with his injured arm.

"She is mine, Prince," Andrei said. He threw his arm around Talia, shielding her from Rognol.

"She is the cause of this injury," Rognol declared, indicating his injured arm. "I want my revenge!"

"Revenge is not a valid reason for my assigning her to you," the prince announced. "Slaves are valuable, and if you kill or injure a slave, you have destroyed a valuable asset. And how was she responsible for your injury? Were you defending her?"

"Just the opposite," Andrei said. "He was attempting to rape her, and she fought back."

The prince did not look at Andrei but bore down on Rognol. "Is this true?"

Rognol nodded. "But she is only a Slav, no better than my horse."

"Then you should bugger your horse!" another man shouted. Others snickered or laughed aloud.

"Silence." The single word from the prince was sufficient. After a moment he asked, "Are you willing to forfeit the rewards of our journey if I grant you the woman?"

Rognol stared at Talia, a look that chilled her as if a cold wind had blown in from the river.

Before Rognol could answer, Andrei said, "I claim this woman. I have lain with her and she may already be carrying my child."

Talia knew this couldn't be true, and so did the women she had worked with. She had a momentary fear that one of them might speak up, but the moment for disclosure passed. Talia herself dared not speak up. If the truth came out, the prince might award her to someone else, and she wanted to belong to Andrei.

When the prince hesitated over his decision, Andrei went on, "There are witnesses to my debauchery of her. I ask for her not for revenge, but to protect her, to make up for my unbridled lust."

"You took her before witnesses?" the prince asked.

"We were interrupted in the act," Andrei said, "by your Highness's own messengers."

The prince nodded, recalling. "I grant you possession of this slave woman, Andrei Ivanovich. Do you plan to marry her?"

"No, Sire."

The prince looked from Andrei to Nicolai. "So Nicolai wants to marry a woman who has borne another man's child and take on the care of her family, while you, Andrei Ivanovich, do not plan to marry the mother of your own child. Truly this Christian faith makes men do unusual things." He turned back to Rognol. "Do you wish to say anything more? You can fight Andrei for the woman. That is permitted."

Rognol shook his head and cursed. He again lifted his injured arm. "How could it be a fair fight?"

"Then perhaps we should let the slave herself decide," the prince suggested.

"A slave decide? But slaves have no rights," Rognold protested.

"I can give slaves rights if I so choose. Do you question my power to do so?"

"Of course not, Sire."

The prince walked over to where Talia knelt fearfully in front of Andrei. "Stand up, slave," he commanded.

Talia rose to her feet, hardly able to stand.

"What is your name, slave?"

"Talia Militskaya," she whispered.

"What would you say if I had granted you to the warrior Rognol?"

"I would kill him! Or myself."

"A slave with spirit," he mused. "Perhaps we should give you a sword and shield and train you as a warrior." The prince laughed. "Except that I think even I might fear you. So, do you agree to belong to Andrei Ivanovich?"

Talia nodded, managed to say, "Yes, Sire."

He turned abruptly back to Rognol. "What shall we do about you? You have served me for many years—with certain regrettable lapses. Would you like to stay here in Kiev until you recover?'

"No! I want to go to Byzantium."

"Shall I assign you a slave woman? Not Talia Militskaya." He walked slowly around the group until he stood before Marya. "You!" He tapped her on the shoulder. "You shall belong to the warrior Rognol."

"No!" Marya cried.

"So, being awarded to Rognol is worse than the prospect of being sold in Byzantium, or taken captive by the Pechenegs?"

"I want to belong to Andrei Ivanovich."

The prince's eyebrows rose in surprise. "Rognol Petrovich, I wish that you might strike as much fear and dread into the hearts of the Pechenegs as you do to these slave women." He turned back to Andrei. "And I might come to you for lessons in how to attract women. I know why women are attracted to me, but you lack my power, my height, my strength and my proud features."

Andrei chuckled, not offended by the prince's boastful comparison. "As you say, Sire. I can't compare to you. My attraction is a mystery to me as well as to you. Of course, the choice was between Rognol and me, not between your Highness and me."

"True," the prince said, and clapped Andrei on the shoulder.

The remainder of the prince's assignments were handled quickly. Talia paid little attention. Her breathing returned to normal and she realized she had been clenching her teeth in dread. It was done, at least for a while. She had been granted to Andrei, not Rognol. But she could still be sold in Byzantium. Andrei had said so. It could happen if she did not please him, or if he got a high offer, one too high to refuse, or if Andrei were killed. Then what would happen to her? Her mind closed off the possibilities, as the courtyard whirled about her and blackness took over. She heard through a fog Andrei's voice asking, "What's wrong with you?" and then nothing more as she toppled to the ground.

Chapter 12

When she was next aware of her surroundings, she was lying on the bed, back in Andrei's house. A damp cloth lay on her forehead, and someone's hand was slapping her cheeks. A strange woman's face appeared, the eyes studying her closely. "I think she'll be all right," the woman said. "I'll go now. There's much work to do today, and she should be helping with it."

"I'll make sure she's fit to work before I send her to you" Andrei said.

"If I didn't know better, I'd say she might be with child," the woman said. "But it isn't that. She just had the bleeding. She may be faking sickness to get out of working. She didn't much take to the work we assigned her, always complaining how tanning hides ruined the looks of her hands. As if anybody cares how a slave's hands look!"

"Thank you, Anna," Andrei said, and Talia could hear the annoyance in his voice. "I'll look after Talia Militskaya. I think she is faint from not eating today."

"So you want me to bring food?"

"No, I'll see to it. You've done enough for her. I don't want to keep you from your tasks." He stepped closer to the bed. The woman nodded curtly and left.

Andrei sat down beside Talia, took the cloth from her forehead, and turned her face to look at him. "Can you tell me why you fainted? Anna may think you faked your collapse, but I know better. What is it?"

"It never ends," she said. "I thought after the prince said I belong to you, it would be over, but it isn't. Rognol wants to kill you, or kill me, and he'll grow stronger as his arm heals."

"Even at his best, Rognol can't out-fight me," Andrei stated. "And I mean to protect you. You're valuable."

"But you could be killed, and Rognol or someone else could claim me."

"Life is unsure. You above all should know that. I'll do everything in my power to protect you and to keep myself alive. As to whether I sell you, that depends on how valuable to me you become." He took her hand and pulled her to her feet. "You are able to walk now, aren't you? And to work? The ships must be loaded today. Come. I'll walk with you to the women's quarters."

The courtyard teemed with people, walking toward the river carrying loads: wooden chests full of dried fish, barrels that sloshed with ale at each step of the carrier, and bundles of hides and furs, tied with leather strings.

Andrei pulled Talia out of the way of a man staggering under the weight of a clay urn, its neck sealed with beeswax.

"Will you sell all this?" she asked.

"The hides and furs we'll sell, and as many urns of honey as are left. The ale we'll drink on the way, and the grain and beans are for all of us to eat, including you."

"What's in the small boxes with metal bands?"

"Amber. The ladies of Byzantium like it for jewelry. In return we get silver and gold coins which our ladies like for jewelry." He stopped walking and turned to face her. "What is in that decorated wooden chest of yours?"

"I haven't opened it."

"What are you planning to do with it? If you take it along, it may get lost or dropped in the river, or be stolen."

"I hadn't thought of that. I'll leave it with Olga."

"Do you trust her?"

"Of course."

"Wouldn't you like to know what you're leaving with your friend?"

"It's for my wedding day. If I am sold in Byzantium, there will be no wedding—or not one that my mother would bless. Olga may be having a wedding with Nicolai. If I return, she can give it back to me."

Without waiting for his permission, Talia ran back to the house and retrieved the box. She brought it to her face, breathing in the familiar smoky, spicy smell of the wood. Her fingers lingered on the clasp. Would it be wrong to open it before her wedding day? What if she gave it away and never saw it again, never knew what lay inside? A vow is a vow, she reminded herself. If I opened it and saw what was inside, I might want to keep it with me, wherever I am going.

"Talia, gather up your things. The loading is finished and some of the ships are ready to leave," Andrei said, coming into the house. He picked up his sword and shield and turned to go out.

"That's all you're taking?"

"Yes. I'm coming back here."

"But you're preparing for battle. Otherwise, you wouldn't need that shield," she pointed out. "It's big and heavy."

"We may well be attacked," he said. He drew a small dagger from his belt and handed it to her. "I probably shouldn't give you this, but you may need it. Women get attacked too. There is no honor in battle. If you can't defend yourself, you can at least end your life swiftly and avoid rape and torture." At Talia's stunned look, he said, "Take it."

She did, feeling the metal still warm from his body. Holding it awkwardly for a moment, she finally thrust it into her pocket, still holding the chest with her other hand.

"Get your belongings, and hurry," Andrei said.

"The box and the clothes I'm wearing are all I have. You know that."

"You can take a comb, a towel and the washbasin and soap. There should be room for those things, but you may have to use the dagger to keep them away from the other slaves. Most won't have such luxuries."

Talia gathered up the items, rolled them into a ball and after a swift glance around at the room, followed him out. It might be the last time she'd ever see this place. She'd hated it, hated him, but it had come to seem familiar and comfortable to her, and Andrei had treated her kindly. *With certain exceptions,* she thought, and those exceptions wouldn't be repeated on the voyage.

As she pressed the box into Olga's hands, Talia felt tears spring to her eyes and slide down her cheeks, and she saw tears in Olga's eyes too. "I'll keep this safely for you, Talia."

"Andrei says he will return here. If I don't come back with him, open the box. Whatever is inside will be yours. It can be for your wedding."

Olga's hand shook as she took the box. "How can I marry him, Talia?"

"Better to marry him than any of the other men here," Talia said. "Of course you don't love him, and he's not handsome like Andrei or the Prince, but Nicolai is a good man."

Olga laughed, the first time Talia had heard her laugh since their capture. "So, you think Andrei and the Prince are handsome?"

Talia nodded. "But looks don't matter as much as how someone treats us. Nicolai will care for you and the babe and Grigor. Give him a chance, Olga."

"I have to," she said. "I've been given to him." She touched Talia's shoulder. "I wish you were staying here with me, Talia. I need you. I need your strength."

"I wish I were staying too. At least you know what your future will be like. I don't." Talia gripped Olga's hand so tightly she heard the joints crack. She let go. "I'm sorry."

"Time to go." Andrei came up behind her, leading a horse. Over its saddle hung a silvery coat of arms and a leather pouch, filled to roundness.

"Oh." She stood still, unable to move.

"Say farewell," he said. "The ships are ready."

"Farewell, Olga." Talia said, giving Olga a quick hug. "I treasure our friendship."

"Svarog be with you," Olga said. "I'll pray and make offerings so the gods will protect you."

Talia walked away quickly before she cried, running to catch up to Andrei. "I haven't seen your armor before," she said as she came even with him.

"I had no need of it in Kiev. A warm woolen cloak was more appropriate. But for the open battlefield, this will protect me."

They joined the throng passing through the great city gate and moving down the hill toward the waiting ships. Talia looked back and saw Olga, standing solitary. *Is this the last time I'll see her, see this place?* Talia wondered, and couldn't bring her hand up to wave. She swiped her fingers across her face, wiping away tears. *I'll miss it all, even the sheep and the dogs and the pigeons.*

Andrei took her hand and pulled her forward, She'd been so intent on looking back that she had not seen the fleet of boats that waited, hundreds of them. They clogged the river, moving slightly in the current like brightly colored birds alight on the water. People swarmed over them, laden down with bundles and boxes. Shuffling into several of the boats were rows of women, their hands bound with chains.

She looked back over her shoulder at Andrei, who had paused at the wooden pier.

He nodded in answer to her unspoken question. "They are slaves, just as you are. I could have chained you, and perhaps I still could, but I don't think you'll make any effort to escape, will you?"

Talia shook her head. "No, master."

"You may call me Andrei, unless others are around, including the prince. But remember that if you don't please me, I can always have you put in chains like the others. So far, I think I have treated you well."

"You have—Andrei," Talia said. She had thought of him that way, but she had not been accustomed to calling him by any name, and the word felt strange on her lips. But a name didn't change anything. She was leaving everything familiar and she was even to be separated from Andrei. Who would protect her?

"Go aboard," Andrei commanded.

"Where will you be?" Once she'd hated him. Now she wanted to be near him.

"With other men, and with my horse."

"The horse is going on the boats too?" The boats were hollowed out logs, with boards attached to the sides. Despite their length, they looked too small to carry people and cargo, much less horses.

"Where the trail is close to the river, or where we need protection from attack, we will ride them"

"What about me?"

"You will stay on the boat during the day, unless we need you for labor. When we push the ships, you may have to help."

"Push them?"

"At the falls we'll push the ships over land. On our return we'll use sails and oars, or, do without boats altogether, and walk along the river bank. You may not be returning. And I may not either. Now, no more questions. Go aboard. And stay on deck as much as you can. It's much more pleasant there than below."

Talia touched his sleeve, feeling the warm, muscular flesh beneath. Then, when there was no answering touch from him, she let her hand drop and stumbled along the boards onto the boat She'd never been on a boat this big, never even seen one. It was strange, and foreboding. She teetered as she stepped from the creaking boards onto the boat itself, and someone reached a hand to steady her.

Where was she supposed to go? Women in chains stood in clusters, anxiety clear on their faces. No one seemed to know any more than she did where they were to sleep, what they were to do with their scant belongings. And how would they wash or do other necessary things with their hands chained? she wondered. Andrei had told her to watch and learn. The other slaves stared at her, their faces twisted with envy at her freedom from chains. *But I'm a slave too*, she wanted to say, but no one spoke to her.

She turned to look back at Andrei, but he had gone.

Chapter 13

Andrei wanted to run after her, to reassure her. But reassure her of what? He couldn't tell her that everything would be all right, because it might not. Regardless of how he felt about her, she was still a slave and he, her owner and master. He could keep her or sell her, but he couldn't protect her from danger on the voyage. For a moment he watched her, then turned resolutely along the riverbank to the pier where warriors and their horses were being loaded.

He thought of her body in the bed next to his, warm and soft. His fingers tingled at the memory of touching her silken hair. *Fool! You've already lowered her trade value with your lust. It wasn't just to keep her from the prince. You lied about that. The prince might have taken her for one of his concubines. He has at least a hundred concubines, and will undoubtedly have more whenever he wants them. But you want Talia for yourself.*

Resolutely he jerked his thoughts back to the voyage. He couldn't let himself be distracted from his duty or his surroundings. A distracted warrior could easily become a dead warrior.

He was glad to be leaving Kiev, going into a new situation. His fortunes could improve with trade, or he could be injured or killed or taken captive. This voyage was unlikely to be the disaster of the previous excursion, when he'd left behind his young pregnant wife and returned to find her and the babe both dead.

He'd had no part in killing Prince Vladimir's half-brother, Iaropolk, but he'd sworn loyalty to Vladimir, recognizing him as sovereign even though the prince's mother had been a servant. "What is, is" was the rule of his life.

Andrei stood beside his horse, steadying himself and the mount against the expected movement of the boat. It shifted each time another horse or warrior came aboard, and then righted itself. The boat was new, and the boards that formed its side panels smelled of the pine forests of the northland. Only a few days before the boat makers had brought this year's newly built boats, their tribute to Prince Vladimir.

Almost overwhelming the fragrance of pine was the ripe odor of panicked, penned sheep and goats, and caged pigeons trained to carry messages. His horse snorted and shuffled nervously. Andrei patted it absently, his thoughts on other matters. The last few animals were led on board other boats and tethered securely. The first boat in the procession had already cast off its mooring lines and begun its journey downriver, down toward the Great City, Constantinople.

Townspeople had gathered along the river's edge, waving farewell to the departing fleet. Dogs ran back and forth along the riverbank, barking. Up the hill, beyond the great gates, Andrei glimpsed the rooftop of his house. No smoke rose from his chimney. For a moment he wished he were back in his house, with Talia. They would be safe, from Rognol, from the Pechenegs, from attacks by Greek ships. He could have stayed in Kiev, but his ambition, his pride, had urged him to go. Nicolai, equally courageous in battle, had chosen to remain behind, and Andrei almost envied him. Almost.

He saw the rope uncoiled and tossed onto the deck. The line of oars dipped into the water, shoving the boat out into mid-stream. It lurched, and Andrei braced himself against the sideboards. Common sense would have told him to sit, but he wanted the last look at Kiev before the boat rounded a bend in the river and the fortress was lost from sight. He couldn't see the boat Talia was on, and hoped that she was safe.

Was Marya on the same boat? She'd insisted on coming along, as had Rognol. They both meant danger to Talia, and at this point he was helpless to protect her from them.

Talia held onto the sides of her boat, standing on tiptoe to see over the boards for a last look at Kiev. She dared not let go of the boards, or of her cloak, for fear she would fall or her cloak would be swept off. She saw one tiny corner of Andrei's house before the sight of Kiev faded into the distance. Still she clung to the boards, her feet wide apart to adjust to the rocking of the boat.

The odor of the penned animals in an adjoining boat stung her nostrils, and she could only imagine how much worse it would get as the trip wore on. Someone would have to clean up after animals. Would it be assigned to her? There were men slaves on board, and in the village they'd have been the ones to clean up after animals, but the male slaves were rowing the boat. Someone would also have to cook and tend anyone who was sick or injured. She could do that, but it wasn't her decision. Would Andrei decide? There was no use wondering about such things. It would become clear soon enough.

Along the riverbank she noticed the coming of early spring. Small clumps of grass grew down almost to the water, and up on the hills a few wildflowers grew in sunny spots. The sky was a clear blue, with puffy clouds drifting past. As the hours passed, she grew tired of standing, and her hands were cramped from gripping the rail. She wasn't going to fall into the river and drown, she told herself, and it seemed she was not going to be attacked by the other slave women—at least, not so far, not in daylight. The sun was warm. She took off her fur cloak, folded it carefully onto the deck and sat on it, leaning back against the rail.

Talia fell asleep, and was awakened by the bump of the boat against the shore. She pulled herself up and peered over the rail. The boat was turning now, oars splashing in the water, as the bow pointed outward, the stern toward the riverbank. All along the bank men were jumping from boats, catching ropes and guiding boats into mooring. The sun had sunk low in the sky, and they were stopping for the night.

She watched as a section at the back of the boat was removed and turned into a makeshift pier. People and animals began to walk across, and she realized it was her turn. The oars had been stilled and pulled into the boat. Women in chains filed off, and Talia followed them. As soon as her feet touched solid ground, she looked around for Andrei. Where was he? He could be in any of the boats that were being moored, tied to stakes driven into the earth. Sheep and goats were led ashore, and tied to other, smaller stakes.

As she started up the hill, Talia felt something bump against her. She looked around and saw Marya, her feet slipped on the moist earth and she went tumbling, too startled to scream. The world whirled about her and she scrabbled for something to grasp, but there was only dirt, hand-packed and bare of grass or shrubs.

An oarsman stepped into her path, keeping her from falling into the water. He extended a gnarled, calloused hand, and Talia took it gratefully. With her free hand she shook her cloak, trying to dislodge the mud that adhered to it. "Thank you," she said, letting go of the hand of her rescuer. Slave women in chains trudged past, eyes downcast, avoiding her. They couldn't have helped her with their wrists shackled, but Talia sensed that they wouldn't have even if they could. They resented her. She had two known enemies on the voyage—Marya and Rognol—and only one friend, Andrei.

"What happened?" Andrei asked, appearing from behind a flock of goats. "Did you lose your footing? Sometimes it feels strange to walk on solid ground after being on a boat."

"Marya pushed me."

Andrei looked around, but Marya was nowhere to be seen. She had disappeared into the swarm of people and animals making their way uphill.

"Try to keep out of her way," Andrei said.

Talia didn't answer. Of course she'd try to stay away from her enemies. She touched her belt, where Andrei's small dagger was hidden. Would she dare use it? Only if she had no other choice, she decided. She wanted Anicdrei to hold her, to comfort her, but that wasn't possible. Masters didn't touch their slaves in public except in punishment.

Andrei strode ahead, leading his horse, and Talia struggled to keep up with him. When he stopped for his horse to crop grass and then to urinate, she caught up and asked, "What am I to do? Where am I to go?"

"You stay close to me and do whatever I ask."

"And what would that be?"

"You can either fetch water or hold my horse while I do. I suggest you hold the horse. He won't move more than a few arms' lengths, in search of grass." He handed her the reins. The horse shied and eyed her, snorting uneasily. Talia god a good grip on the reins and moved to stand beside the tall mount.

"If he escapes, he won't go far. He's trained to come back to me," Andrei said over his shoulder as he walked away.

He returned in a few moments with a wooden pail of water and set it down before the horse.

"You're letting him drink ahead of us?" Talia demanded.

"We don't drink river water. We'll have mead. It's good with roasted meat."

Talia put her hands over her ears to shut out the terrified screams of animals being slaughtered. The doomed sheep scuffled briefly against their fate, then lay still, their fleece matted with blood. In a trice men had stripped off the skin, gutted the bodies and thrown the entrails to waiting, hungry dogs. She vowed to herself that she wouldn't be able to eat any of the meat. Fires were kindled and the carcasses spitted over the coals. Soon the aroma of roasting meat wafted through the air, and Talia changed her mind. She was hungry.

Andrei borrowed the dagger to cut meat for the two of them, and they ate it with their hands, washing it down with mead drunk from leathern flagons. Then men brought boards from the boats and laid them on the ground in clusters. "You may want to go into the woods to take care of your needs," Andrei said. "It will soon be too dark to see our way."

"Our?"

"I'm coming with you. There could be any number of dangers out there, and you won't be showing me anything I haven't already seen and touched."

Talia could feel her face growing hot at the memory of Andrei's hands touching her, and was glad of the growing dusk that hid her embarrassment from him. She started walking toward the forest, seeing others walking that way. Andrei took her arm and didn't release her until they were inside the shielding darkness of the forest. He turned his back while she squatted quickly and lifted her skirts.

Light from the glowing cooking fires led them back. People settled on the boards and pulled their cloaks to cover themselves. Talia lay down and felt Andrei drop down beside her. She turned her back and moved as far away from him as she could on their boards, but he pulled her close to him.

"People will see and hear us," she objected.

"See and hear what? I'm just trying to keep you warm. The air may seem warm now, but by morning you'll think it's still winter."

"Oh," she said, and tried to will herself to sleep. Andrei's great bulk curved around her, his legs against the back of hers, one arm slung across her shoulder. *I won't think about him, about what he could be doing to me,* she vowed. She could tell by Andrei's breathing that he was still awake, and she knew if she moved slightly, if she encouraged him, all her vows would be for naught.

Andrei's horse, and other horses, snorted and stamped nearby. Dogs snarled at each other, fighting over the bones from the roasted meat. The river lapped softly and occasionally moored boats bumped each other. There was a murmur of voices, and other sounds that told her some couples were giving in to their urges.

Finally she fell asleep.

Chapter 14

That day set the pattern for the next ten days. A few more boats, with warriors, horses, and trade goods, joined them at a settlement downriver. Talia felt safe and comfortable, even though she was still separated from Andrei, still among chained women who resented her.

On the tenth day, Andrei warned her that they were approaching the first rapids, Essupi.

"It has a name?"

"They all do. Essupi means 'Do not sleep,' so we always approach the rapids by daylight."

Talia was standing in the bow of the boat when she heard the roar of the rapids. Boats were being rowed ashore and moored. As soon as the passengers disembarked, the cargo and animals were unloaded.

The roar of the water swirling around the giant rocks in the middle of the river terrified her. How would they get past? She watched as the first boat was untied and guided towards the falls by men stripped naked, wading in chest-high water.

Andrei was one of these. The river beat against the rocks, the boat, and the men as they towed and pushed the craft past jagged outcroppings. Finally it was below the rapids and into stiller water. The men tied up the boat and walked back upstream to guide the next boat. Others carried cargo and led animals to reload the boats.

Talia watched Andrei as he walked toward her, his powerful body naked and glistening with beads of water in the morning sunlight. To her embarrassment, he stopped within arm's reach of her, so there was no avoiding him, no avoiding looking at him. She met his gaze, but before she could bring herself to speak, he smiled, turned and walked away to guide another boat.

At a signal, Talia picked up Andrei's discarded clothing and joined the other women heading downstream to where boats were waiting. She breathed easier, enjoying the warm spring air, the ordinary noises about her, the tiny yellow wildflowers carpeting a nearby hillside. The first rapids weren't as bad as she'd feared. She sat down on the cool earth and sniffed Andrei's shirt, inhaling his familiar smell. Aghast at herself, she put it aside just as he walked up and said, "You can go on board now."

That night as she lay beside Andrei, he pushed close to her and whispered, "Did you like what you saw today?"

"Do you mean the way you and the others maneuvered the boats down the rapids?"

"That too. The cold water shriveled my lust — or at least, my ability to do anything to slake it. However, that's no longer true."

"I can tell," she said. "Is slaking your lust on the journey the way I am to please you so you won't chain me or sell me?"

"Is that the only reason you'd accept me?" His breath was warm against her neck and the whole length of his body was hot against hers.

"I have no choice but to *accept* you," she said, "but if you want me to participate willingly, then you must persuade me."

He drew back from her. "By the gods! *Persuade you*? You're a slave."

"Then you must take me as a slave and not as a woman you care for. I will submit if I must." She chose her words carefully, not daring to anger him. He could always chain her like the other women. "Do you want to get me with child, or keep my value high for a sale?"

"I haven't decided," he muttered. "And talking about the matter has taken away my desire. Which is probably a good thing. I need to get some rest ready for the next waterfall. Good night, Talia."

"Good night, master," she murmured.

She thought she heard him say, "Damn you," but she wasn't sure.

The fleet maneuvered past the second waterfall, Ulvorsi, with no trouble, and Talia grew more comfortable, almost complacent, with the idea of waterfalls. As they approached the third, she was standing in the bow of the boat, peering over the boards to watch the men strip and begin guiding a boat over the rapids.

Something was wrong. Her boat, turning its stern toward the riverbank, had instead gotten caught in the current. It was being carried toward the opposite side of the river, toward rocks. Below her she could see oars being frantically dug into the water, but to little effect. Talia screamed, her voice lost in other screams. She saw Andrei and other men turn toward the runaway boat, and flounder a few steps in shoulder-deep water toward her. But they couldn't reach the boat that was heading toward the rocks, or abandon the one they were guiding downward.

"Jump!" someone screamed. But she knew it was too late to jump. She'd be dashed against the rocks if she did.

Talia's boat turned and turned and turned, bobbing helplessly on the unforgiving current. Oarsmen tried to control the direction, but the top-heavy craft had a will of its own. It banged against a rock, close beside where Talia stood gripping the rail. Boards splintered, and water gushed in through the opening. She was thrown back onto the hard boards, and as she regained her footing, slave women ran to the bow, tipping it downward just as the boat reached the point of no return.

Striking another rock, the boat was swept downward, water pouring over its bow. It went down and down, bouncing, tearing itself apart before it plunged into a whirlpool at the bottom of the rapids.

Water closed over Talia, cold and dark. She bobbed to the surface, choking and gasping. Something grabbed her arm, pulling her down. She tore free and swam a few strokes away. A slave woman was going down, weighted by the chains and unable to swim because her hands were shackled together. Talia grabbed the woman's arm and dragged the two of them ashore. She looked back. There were others kicking and struggling helplessly in the river. Talia went back into deeper water and pulled another to safety.

Then the river was full of rescuers, all naked: the men who had brought a boat over the rapid were now trying to rescue the passengers of the destroyed boat. They tore at the boards still remaining on the craft, which was filling with water, drowning the oarsmen.

Andrei swam toward Talia, reached her, and pulled her toward him. "You're safe!" he said. "Svarog be thanked."

"I'm safe," she gasped. "Help the others." She wasn't sure he heard her above the screaming of the trapped people, the bleating and kicking of penned animals trying to free themselves, and the insistent pounding of the water on rocks above. But he swam away, and Talia reached for a young slave woman floating near her.

As she pulled the woman from the water onto the riverbank, floundering in deep water, she realized this woman was not resisting her or clutching at her. As she laid the inert form on the ground, Talia saw that her help had come too late. The woman was dead, her eyes wide and staring with fear, her hands still manacled. Talia closed the frightened eyes with her fingertips and went back into the water.

Andrei and other men managed to pull a few oarsmen to safety, but then had to jump from the remains of the battered boat. It had been wedged against a rock, but as weight was removed from it, it floated higher and suddenly yawed, broke free from the rock and was carried off downstream.

Talia stood in shallow water at the river's edge, staring at the devastation around her. There were no more survivors to rescue. Anyone who might still be alive on the boat was too far downstream to be saved. The animals that had freed themselves were either struggling ashore, or floating farther downstream, out of reach. She heard women crying, and realized she was one of them. Sobs shook her body, and she shivered uncontrollably from the cold. The remains of her clothing were sodden, and clung to her body, outlining her for all to see, but it didn't matter. No one would notice her amidst the tragedy.

Andrei did. When he paused to survey the horrific scene, he saw her standing alone, crying. He made his way toward her through the shallow water, and put his arms around her. She turned to stare at him with a dazed expression, as if she didn't recognize him, and then fell against him, still sobbing.

"It's over," he said. "You were very brave, and you're alive and safe now."

"But all those others," she whimpered.

"It's the will of Svarog," he said. "He controls life and death."

"Was it Swarog's will that people were chained and animals trapped in pens? That's why they died. I'm alive because I had no chains to hold me down."

"And I'll see that you never do. You've proved to me that you won't run away. Some of the chained ones had tried to escape."

"Their owners won't have to worry about their escaping now," she said.

"And they have lost their slaves' value."

He could see the revulsion in her face as she turned away from him. "They were people," she said.

"It's done. We can't do anything for them now, except collect their bodies for the ravens." He dropped his arms from her, and turned back upstream. "Go join the passengers from the other boats. There will be a lot of work for all of us."

For the rest of the day men kept guiding boats over the rapids, while others gathered the bodies of the dead and boards from the shattered boat. Still others made their way downstream from the site of the wreck and herded sheep and goats ashore or dragged carcasses out of the water to be skinned. Talia had to look away from the platform that was being hammered together for the dead who could be found.

As the sun warmed her and dried her clothing, Talia could finally make herself join in the work of skinning and dressing out the drowned sheep and goats. There would be feasting, as the meat had to be consumed before it spoiled. These animals would have been slaughtered and eaten eventually, just not so many so soon.

By nightfall the last of the boats and all five ships were safely past the rapids, and the dead lay on platforms waiting to be devoured by ravens. Cooking fires were burning on the shore below the falls. It was almost as if nothing terrible had happened, Talia thought. It was so normal to be sitting on the ground beside Andrei, waiting to eat the meat that gave off such a tantalizing odor. When she bit into her portion of roasted meat, tears sprang to her eyes. This animal had wanted to live, just as the dead and the survivors had. Did the gods really control things? If they did, how had they decided which person or animal would live and which would die on this day? Could human beings change what the gods had decided? What had the gods decided for her? Why had she lived? Because Andrei had not chained her, she reasoned. That was Andrei's decision, not the gods'.

She passed the roasted meat to Andrei.

"Is something wrong with it?"

"I'm not hungry," she lied.

"You must drink some mead," he said, passing the flagon to her.

Talia took a mouthful, swallowed, drank more before her stomach rebelled. She ran for a patch of weeds and vomited, casting out the mead and the water she'd swallowed from the river. Empty, she staggered to the sleeping boards.

He came soon after and lay beside her for a few moments without speaking. Then he said, "Talia, I'm grateful to the gods for saving your life."

"I'm angry at the gods for taking the lives of so many others. I was so helpless to do anything."

"I felt helpless when I saw your boat going toward the rapids. I said a prayer that you would live."

"Thank you. But I thought you didn't believe in the power of the gods."

"Old habits die hard," he said. "In a crisis, most of us cry out to some god."

She closed her eyes and tried to sleep, but over and over she felt the boat going over the falls, saw the bodies tossed into the water, the dead, staring eyes of the drowned woman.

"Wake up, Talia!" Andrei was shaking her. "You're having a nightmare." He held her close, his face against her hair, his voice as calm and comforting as her mother's had once been. "It's over. You're safe. I'm here with you."

Gradually her terror subsided, and exhausted, she slept.

When she awoke, for a moment she forgot what had happened. It was a beautiful sunny morning, and people were stirring around her. Men were arguing, Andrei among them, about how the survivors of the destroyed boat were to be situated. Talia closed her eyes and tried not to listen. Nothing she said would change what they decided. Slaves had no part in decision-making.

When the time came for boarding, Talia drew back, terrified. "I can't!"

"You must. We can't leave you here. You'd be captured or killed before we pass the next rapid."

"There are more?"

"Yes, but we will all walk past the great waterfall, carrying the boats and the trade goods. You'll have to carry a load like all the others."

"Like all the other slaves, you mean?"

"Everybody will be carrying something. You'll be on my boat. We'll be crowded, but grateful to Svarog that so many survived. Come." He took her hand and swung her around so that she had no choice but to walk ahead of him, up the boards and onto the boat. His horse was already there, tethered and shifting uneasily. A pile of chains lay on the deck at her feet and she looked back ashore at the platforms where the dead lay. In death they had finally been freed from their chains.

There was no safe place to look. She couldn't bear the sight of all those dead, bodies, stripped bare, awaiting the devouring ravens. She didn't want to look at the water, for it was dangerous. It could kill. Looking at Andrei was dangerous in another way. She closed her eyes and leaned against Andrei's horse, feeling its shoulder quiver at her unexpected touch and unfamiliar smell.

When she opened her eyes, the ropes securing the boat had been tossed onto the deck, the stern closed, and the boat was being rowed out into the current.

Chapter 15

All day she saw debris from the wrecked boat. Sometimes it was only a piece of wood bobbing on the surface of the river. Twice boats steered toward the river bank to rescue stray animals that had somehow survived, once to pluck from an overhanging tree branch an oarsman, half-crazed and babbling incoherently. Farther downstream they passed bodies caught by tree limbs or sandbars.

"Aren't we going to stop?" Talia demanded. "What if they're still alive?"

"They're not," he said. "They're already bloated and turning dark. What can we do for them? We have no space for bodies and no way to burn them or build platforms."

She turned away, unwilling to admit that he was right. Some of them may have been Christians, as her mother had been, and would have needed burying. But who knew what their faith was? Neither Svarog nor the Christ had protected them, and they were now beyond anything mortals could do for them.

Around mid-day they came upon the final remains of the battered boat, caught against an earthen bank in a bend of the river. The boat ahead of theirs put to shore beside the wreck and brave men made their way with axes to break up the derelict craft. As their blows broke through the crushed deck boards, a cry went up: four oarsmen had miraculously survived, and were pulled from the wreckage to safety. The men with axes shook their heads, signaling that there were no more alive below deck. Pulled onto already crowded boats, the survivors begged for water through swollen lips, and shook uncontrollably, still fearing death. The hulk of the boat, with its dead cargo, was set afire, and the fleet continued southward.

When the fleet approached the biggest cataract, which Andrei said was called "insatiable," all the boats were steered ashore some distance above the falls and tethered to stakes driven into the ground.

The riverbank was soon piled with heaps of goods: bundles of hides and furs, earthen jugs filled with mead, sacks of grain, chests of amber and honey. Terrified animals were being unloaded, defecating and urinating as they were herded together, bleating their fear. Men trudged back and forth between the boats and the shore, balancing goods on their heads or tied to their backs, sometimes slipping in the animal droppings. Slave women stood in a cluster, their hands shackled, awaiting their fate.

And above the noise of humans and animals the cataract roared, a dangerous presence that reminded the travelers of their frailty against nature. The water gained speed as it neared the precipice, before plunging downward, sending spray high into the air. A rainbow arched above the falls, sparkling in the morning sunlight.

Andrei led his horse up beside Talia. "This is where we portage the boats. Do you want to carry a load, or would you prefer to be chained like the other slaves are?" He held one of the shackles that had been worn by a drowned slave.

Talia looked at the shackle in his hand and at the group of shackled women, who were being tied together with ropes. "I'll carry a load."

"Before the day is over you may wish you'd chosen differently."

"What are you carrying?"

"I'm not. I'll be guarding you and all the others. You may see me from time to time as you walk."

"You're guarding the slaves so they won't run away?"

"No. They might be killed by the Pechenegs, and so might you. As long as we're on the river we're relatively safe, but when we're ashore, especially carrying burdens, we're at their mercy."

He tossed the shackle aside and brought a leather harness like the ones being fitted onto the shoulders of others, almost all of them men. She and Marya and a few others were the only women not shackled. She stood straighter. She'd show Andrei she was strong and useful, a woman to be kept, not sold.

He tied a bag of grain to each end of Talia's yoke, and she almost fell to her knees from the unaccustomed weight. The harness went across her back, with straps over her shoulders that cut into the soft flesh on both sides of her breasts. She struggled to stand upright.

Andrei gathered his weapons and mounted his horse. He held the reins lightly with one hand, and in the other carried a spear. A bow hung across his chest, a quiver of arrows at his back, and the hilt of his sword glittered at his thigh. Talia watched as he rode away, handsome and powerful.

She soon realized that Andrei had been correct that everyone must work—except the chained slaves. They were marched overland in a column, their hands shackled and a rope connecting one to the other. When one stumbled and fell, the walkers ahead of her and behind also went down, impeding the progress of the entire group. After it happened several times, Talia suspected the women were falling on purpose. If she'd been shackled, would she have done the same?

All day the procession moved along the shoreline. Boats were emptied, stripped of their heaviest fittings, and upended to be carried southward on the shoulders of men. Other men carried bundles of furs and hides, or tools, lumber and the assorted belongings of a mass of people on the move. The luckiest ones drove the livestock, occasionally having to run after a stray and bring it back into the fold. Talia realized then that she could have asked Andrei for a lighter load, or even volunteered to look after the animals, but it was too late. Somehow she'd carry her load past the roaring waterfall. She would not beg Andrei for mercy, or even let him see how close to collapse she was.

Andrei rode back and forth, facing away from the river and the struggling walkers, looking always toward the wooded hillside.

Talia walked behind the line of chained and roped slaves, her back bent and aching, her legs quivering from exertion. Sweat trickled down her face, but she didn't bother to wipe it away. There would just be more. Her dress clung to her sweaty body. How much longer? She couldn't spare breath to ask, and the straggling group probably didn't know anyway.

In the group of chained slaves Talia recognized the young woman she'd rescued from the boat wreckage, the woman who'd struggled against her so fiercely. Her pale hair hung lank and tangled, and her eyes had a half-crazed glint. She didn't return Talia's smile.

Talia waited a moment for a sign of recognition. To her surprise, the woman said, "You shouldn't have rescued me."

"Why not? You would have died." Talia's words came out faint and raspy. Talking was difficult.

"I want to die. The captors chain us up so we won't run away. I wouldn't run. I'd drown myself if I had a chance. It would be an easy way to escape from our misery."

Talia didn't answer. Was she miserable? Yes, at the moment. Her clothing was sweat-drenched and foul smelling. Her hair clung damply to her head and neck, wet with sweat and with the ever-present mist from the churning rapids. Her back ached with a pain she'd never known before.

"What do we have to look forward to?" the woman asked. "We'll either spend the rest of our lives working or be sold to some old man who will put his filthy stick into us whenever he wants to. But maybe a rich man will buy you. You're pretty."

"Pretty?" Talia didn't feel pretty. She'd almost forgotten what it felt like to be clean and attractive.

"Move faster! No talking!" Rognol had ridden up beside the column, and slashed out at Talia.

She screamed with pain as the whip struck her lower back, ripping through her flimsy dress.

Andrei whirled his horse around to face Rognol. "What are you doing?"

"Making sure the loads get moved."

"It's not your job or mine," Andrei said, letting go of his horse's reins to grab the whip. He jerked, and Rognol tumbled to the ground, still holding the reins. His horse reared, and Rognol was dragged along the rocky earth before he could let go. When he did, the horse reared again, its hooves coming down just a hand span from his head. He rolled over, whimpering.

"Get up!" Andrei ordered.

Rognol got to his feet and reached for his horse's reins, but the animal bolted, escaping his grasp, and ran off into the woods.

"Take her load," Andrei commanded.

"You can't order me," Rognol said. "Only Prince Vladimir can do that." His hand reached for his sword, but that was the arm Talia had injured. He would be no match for Andrei in battle, and both men knew it. He let his hand drop to his side.

"With your whip and my weapons I can command anyone, and I have every intention of reporting your actions to the prince when we are less occupied."

Talia looked from one man to the other, from Andrei's handsome beloved face to Rognol's, twisted with hate and anger.

"Take her load," Andrei repeated.

Rognol came toward Talia. She made herself stand very still as he lifted the harness and the two bags from her, even though the pressure of his hand against her skin was repellent, almost sickening.

"You have no right to make me carry loads like a slave," Rognol declared, bent under the load.

"If you have broken the skin of this woman, you've lowered her value. The prince will take that into consideration."

Talia had been so relieved, so grateful to Andrei for protecting her, but now it was obvious that his interest was not in her as a woman, but in her as a sale item. "What shall I do now?" she asked, watching the procession move on downstream.

"Walk back to the mooring point and get another load. Someone will help you with the harness."

"But not you?"

"I must continue guarding. Fortunately for you I came along as Rognol did."

"Yes, fortunately for me," she said. "I get to carry another load."

"You would have in any case. There's enough daylight this time of year for everyone to make at least two trips. You'll be able to end your second trip early, thanks to Rognol's attack."

"Do you want to examine my back to see if he damaged me?" She touched her back, which still ached from walking bent over, and smarted from Rognol's whip.

"I couldn't very well do that without your lifting your clothing, and I don't think you'd want me to do that here. There will be time enough later."

"Can I ride Rognol's horse?" she asked, though it was nowhere to be seen.

"Our horses eventually return, but it will very likely show up at the loading point." He wheeled his horse around, facing into the trees, and rode off at a steady pace, leaving her standing, bereft. She had no choice but to walk back for another load, as he had instructed her. What would he do if she instead walked on downstream, without a load? Shackle her, probably. Worse, Rognol was there, even more angry and vengeful now that he had been again publicly humiliated on her behalf. She dared not get near him without Andrei to protect her.

Talia trudged back northward, glad to be able at least to walk upright. People passed her in both directions, the walkers going south struggling with loads, those going north moving briskly, urged to make another trip while daylight held.

When the boat carriers reached a relatively level area, they set down their burden and rolled the boat on a series of round logs, running to place the rear logs in front of the advancing boat.

Talia wasn't sure how long the trail around the cataract was, only that she lost count of her steps after five thousand and gave up counting. It didn't matter anyway. She'd have to keep carrying loads and returning for more until darkness fell or all the cargo was transported, whichever came first.

Finally all the people, the animals and the cargo and equipment were deposited below the cataract, and the shackled women were unfastened to prepare the evening meal and lay out the bedding for the exhausted workers. The fading sunlight sparkled off the mist from the river, creating rainbows that hung above the water. It was beautiful, but Talia knew she would never again see a rainbow without thinking of the danger from the rapids

Andrei walked over to where she stood. His horse roamed free with the others, nickering softly, browsing on the spring grass, or drinking from leathern water containers.

"Shall I go fetch food?" she asked.

"You've carried burdens today while I've only ridden. Just this once, I'll go for food while you rest—and prepare for bed."

"You'll make the other women hate me even more if you treat me well."

"I won't let it become a habit. You've worked well today, better than I expected."

"What if I had not worked all day?"

"Then I'd have chained you like the others." Without looking back at her, he walked away. He returned with two bowls of cooked grain. "Marya cooked this," he said, "but I don't think she'd try again to poison you. Anyway, she doesn't know which bowl you'll eat from."

"Do you?" Talia took a bowl from him and sniffed at it suspiciously.

"No. I think it's safe, even if it doesn't taste very good. Marya was never a good cook." He dipped into the bowl, took a spoonful. "Ugh! She still isn't. Fortunately for her, she has other talents. Which Rognol is undoubtedly enjoying to the best of his ability."

"Where was she today?"

"Shackled like the other slave women—all but you. Rognol isn't taking any chances she'll run away, or attack him."

"Would she attack him?"

"Why wouldn't she? You did."

"I had a good reason. I was protecting myself."

"She may have as good a reason as you did. One of these days Rognol will go too far, and someone will kill him."

"I wish I had."

"I stopped him to save you both."

"You saved his life and now he hates you anyway."

"I saved your life. Do you hate me?"

"Not anymore."

"Good."

She stood and dropped the bowl at his feet. "You're impossible to reason with."

"Even so, you should eat the rest of your food."

"The grain is bland and lumpy. I'd as soon eat grass with the horses."

"I hope it won't come to that," he said. "I agree with you about the food. Still, we must all eat enough to sustain us until we get to Byzantium. Then you'll learn what good food really tastes like. We'll fatten you up then. The emirs like their women plump."

The emirs were fools, he thought. *Why would any man prefer a fat woman with great pillowy breasts and bulging thighs to a slim, muscular woman like Talia?* And yet they must. The buyers in Byzantium always bid the highest prices for the fattest slaves and said they could double their money when they sold the women to some potentate's harem.

Andrei studied Talia, her body outlined by the fading daylight against the clusters of cooking fires spotted along the shoreline. Even in bedraggled clothing, with her hair unkempt and straggling from her kerchief, she was still beautiful and desirable. He felt his desire grow at the memory of her body beneath his, her arms coming up to touch his back. He held the bowl in front of him so she wouldn't notice, but she seemed oblivious to his lust.

Men lie with their slaves all the time, he knew, both male and female. He could take her legally any time he wanted her and no one would criticize him. And she would have no alternative but to submit. But he had known the joy of sharing his body with a woman who wanted him, who gave herself freely, out of love and not force. A quick poke with a slave was no substitute. It merely gave a man a physical release, but no lasting satisfaction. If only Talia weren't a slave. As long as he could command her very existence, he'd never know whether she came to him willingly or only because she had no choice.

She was rubbing her lower back and moving her shoulders up and down. "You must be stiff and sore from today," he said.

"Of course I am! I walked all day and carried a load. You rode."

He chuckled. "You're right. Come here and let me massage your back." He set the bowl down and reached for her hand.

She sat on the sleeping board beside him, her back to him.

"Lie down and roll over."

After a moment's hesitation, she obeyed.

He felt her muscles tense as he straddled her and brought his hands down onto her back. Running his thumbs along her spine, he could have counted her vertebrae. He hadn't realized she was so thin. Had she eaten so sparsely because she feared being poisoned? Was she sick? For whatever reason, she was anything but the plump-bodied woman the slave buyers would look for.

Making small, gentle circles with his fingertips, he caressed her back, moving up to her shoulders. To relax her muscles, he'd have to knead more forcefully. He pressed down, then released.

"You're hurting me," Talia protested.

"It will hurt for a few moments, but then the pain will go away and you'll feel so much better you'll want to kiss me."

"Don't wager on that," she murmured, but she lay still and let him go on massaging her. As his hands moved down to her hips, he felt the knife. "You're still carrying the knife I gave you. You could have stopped me, or Rognol, at any time today."

"Yes, I could have," she said, "but fortunately for both of you, I didn't need to. You came to my rescue when Rognol was beating me, and you've always told me I don't need to fear you. Is that still true?"

"It is." He touched the spot on her buttocks where he thought Rognol's whip had cut her skin. "Does that hurt?"

"A bit. I think it bled, but it stopped. It will heal."

He heard her sigh when she was fully relaxed, and when he turned her over, she was asleep.

He wasn't surprised. She'd been exhausted. And despite his lust, he was glad. This wasn't the time or the place to test her desire for him. He promised himself that once they reached Byzantium, he'd see to it that she had a bath and was suitably dressed in a silken garment. Then he would caress her until she was delirious with longing. He'd claim her just once more before he showed her to buyer.

Chapter 16

Andrei awoke just before daylight to screams coming from every direction. The Pechenegs!

He leapt up, buckled on his sword, and grabbed his spear instinctively. When he looked down for his bow and quiver of arrows, he saw Talia, still asleep. He jabbed at her with the tip of his boot. "Get up!"

She rolled over, looked at him sleepily, and then sat up with a start. "What's happening?"

"The Pechenegs are attacking. Get up!" He pulled her to her feet, glad that they'd slept in their clothes and shoes. "Can you use your knife?"

"Yes!" She slid her hand into the slit in her skirt where she had the knife hidden.

"Good, because you may have to. I've got to go and fight with the warriors, but if some Pechenegs break through our line, they'll go for the female slaves. At least you're all unshackled."

When Talia still looked stunned and dazed, he handed her his bow and arrows. "Here. I can't manage all three weapons and my shield. Have you ever shot a bow?"

"No."

"Well, leave it then. It's too late to learn today. Try to keep out of danger." He grabbed up his leathern helmet and secured it on his head, picked up his shield and ran, leaving her staring after him. He looked for his horse, and was relieved not to see it. If the Pechenegs captured it, his faithful steed would be ridden to a haggard skeleton, or be turned into roasted meat. He wanted to fight on foot. He knew he was a better warrior than any Pecheneg and they would be on foot, having set their horses loose.

The attackers had chosen the perfect time to attack. The slaves had been unshackled, but were awakening sleepily, or returning from urinating in the woods, adjusting skirts or trousers. Fires banked for the night were being kindled, goats milked, water brought from the river. The ships and boats were unready for escape, their oars lying on the ground beside the crafts. Animals ran in frightened circles, in and out among the bundles and chests, looking for safety that didn't exist.

Who had been on duty? Andrei wondered. Whoever it was had fallen asleep—or been killed from behind—and had left the fleet defenseless.

No, by the gods, he wasn't defenseless! He walked faster, looking for Prince Vladimir. The prince's father had been killed by the Pechenegs on just such a mission as this. Rumors said that the Pecheneg chieftain used his slain enemies' skulls for drinking cups. The image enraged Andrei. He hoped he'd find some skulls that had belonged to Kievans. He'd make sure they were treated with respect and taken back to Kiev for a proper ceremony.

An arrow flew past his right ear, and he was glad he was wearing his helmet. He felt a momentary regret at leaving Talia unprotected, without helmet or shield or spear. But his first duty was to the prince. Slaves could be bought and sold, but the future of the empire itself rested with Prince Vladimir. Andrei broke into a trot when he saw the prince. Men were lining up, all equipped as he was.

He regretted leaving his bow and arrows. The spear could only be thrown once, and if it struck its target, he'd have to get in close and pull the blade from its victim. If he missed, the Pechenegs could hurl his spear back at him or at some other warrior. He'd made a mistake. Svarog willing, it would not be a fatal one.

Another arrow whizzed past, then another. The Pechenegs were too far away to shoot accurately, but it was only a matter of moments before they came into better range. The next arrow thudded into the ground at his feet.

The battle horn blew, and the prince's crack troops turned smartly and started marching away from the river and the camp, toward the hillside where the Pechenegs were dug in.

Behind him he heard screams, as some of the arrows struck a target, but he dared not look back. He kept walking, parrying arrows with his shield. He heard cries from the camp too. Was one of them Talia?

Before he was ready for the onslaught, Pechenegs poured down the hill from the forest, screaming for blood. He had only a heartbeat of time to respond as a bearded man ran straight toward him. Andrei threw the spear and saw it pierce the belly of his enemy. The man dropped his weapons as he clutched his middle, trying to pull the spear out. Then with an agonized scream, he fell forward, almost onto Andrei. Andrei thrust the dying man away from him, tossing him onto his back. Blood poured from the wound. Andrei set his foot onto the man's chest and pulled the spear free, tearing flesh as he did so. The man stared up at Andrei with a frightened, unbelieving expression, and Andrei saw that he was little more than a boy. A boy, eager to prove himself in battle, running ahead of the others to his death. He was brave, but it was for naught.

Andrei regretted killing him, but only for a moment. If he hadn't thrown the spear and stopped the enemy boy, he might now be the one lying on the grass, trying to hold his intestines in his torn abdomen.

Andrei dropped the spear. It was useless now, for men were swarming all around him. He grabbed up the fallen warrior's sword, not stopping to unsheathe his own, and slashed out right and left. The sword was so heavy that the momentum of his swing almost threw him off balance, but he managed to retain his footing, and felt the jarring impact of the sword on a shield. His own shield protected him, but a blow onto its surface ran a quiver of pain up his arm. He got in a good swing at his opponent, and felt the sword bite into soft, unprotected flesh. Andrei's sword caught the

Pecheneg on the side, and went deep into his body just below the ribs.

When the man dropped his shield, Andrei went in for the kill. He swung high, clashing first with the opponent's sword, but the next blow cut into the other's arm, and blood spurted out, glistening and sliming the sword. The sword hand wavered, and in that instant, Andrei stabbed into the enemy's throat, stepped back to avoid the spray of hot blood, and swung again. This lopped off the enemy's head. It fell at Andrei's feet, eyes still staring at him. The body amazingly stood upright for a few moments before crumpling at Andrei's feet.

He'd have liked to take the head along as a trophy, to make his own skull drinking cup, or to at least display the head on a pike or nailed to the deck of the ship. If it was still there when the battle was over and he was still alive, he'd collect it, he decided.

But for now, he had more Pechenegs to fight, more trophies to collect. Or to become one himself.

Talia watched as the army formed and moved uphill to meet the Pechenegs. Would the prince's men defeat the attackers or would the enemy come roaring down the hill and destroy the camp as her village, had been. Destroyed? Then she had struck in self-defense, and she would again. She had nothing but the bow and arrows he'd left and her own dagger.

All up and down the riverbank people and animals were running, some actually jumping into the water. But others were seeking safety behind bales of hides, or underneath the empty boats. That was far wiser than standing in the open. There was nothing on the sleeping boards that needed protecting, she decided, only herself.

Without thinking any further, she grabbed up Andrei's bow and quiver of arrows, and ran for the nearest boat. As she crawled underneath it, she bumped into something warm, something living, and gasped with shock. Who? Or what? A goat had taken cover under the boat. Talia laughed at her fear. The goat had more intelligence than some of the people. It knew to hide.

An arrow thudded against the wood. The Pechenegs must be getting closer. Andrei and the warriors weren't holding them back. Whatever her future with Andrei, it would be worse to be captured by the Pechenegs. If she couldn't protect herself, she'd kill herself. The slave woman who'd talked of misery waiting for them might be right. A quick death would be better than torture. But she didn't want either, not if she could prevent it.

Through the opening at the back of the boat she peered out at the melee around her. More people were getting under boats, and right in front of her she saw an arrow strike a woman, who fell to the earth and lay still. Another woman ran into Talia's view and stopped, staring around wildly. It was the woman Talia had rescued from drowning, the woman who'd called Talia pretty. She'd said she wanted to die, and standing out in plain sight, in daylight, was one way to do it.

But what if she really wanted to live?

Talia crawled out and grabbed hold of the woman, dragging her back toward the boat. "Come under here. We'll be safe. They won't see us," she said, but she wasn't sure the other woman understood her words, or even heard her. Her body was rigid, her eyes unfocused.

Talia brought her foot to the back of the woman's knees, buckling her legs. As she crumpled to the ground, Talia shoved her under the boat.

When she touched the goat, the woman let out a little shriek. "He'll kill me!" she cried, and started crawling back outside.

"It's just a goat, and he's as frightened as you are," Talia said. "I just wish he didn't smell so bad, worse than they usually smell. He's let loose his bowels in fear. But why are you worried about being killed? You told me you wanted to die. Should I have left you outside for the Pechenegs?"

"No. I thought I was ready to die, but I'm not. I stood and waited and I thought if an arrow found me, it was meant to be, but the arrows missed me and you rescued me. That's twice you've saved me. You are my guardian angel."

"I'm not an angel, whatever that is," Talia said. "I'm a fighter. Can you use a bow? Or a knife?"

"I'll try," the woman answered, her voice faint with doubt.

"Since we seem to be joined by fate, we should know more about each other. I'm Talia, and I was seized by Andrei when my village was burned. My family and the man I was to marry were killed. Or so Andrei told me."

"I'm Inga. I come from the far north. My father was a chieftain. Prince Vladimir's men killed him and took me prisoner."

Another arrow thudded against the boat, cutting off her words. After a moment, when no more came, she went on, "I was supposed to become one of the prince's concubines, but I tried to kill him." She laughed shakily. "It sounds preposterous, doesn't it? A mere woman trying to kill a ruler? When I failed, I was thrown into prison and starved and beaten. I tried to kill myself, but I failed at that too. So, what do I have to live for?"

"I don't know," Talia answered. "But the will to live is strong. I always think that I can somehow make my life better."

"I hope you're right," Inga said.

Three arrows striking the side of the boat in quick succession silenced the women. Were the Pechenegs coming closer? Talia peered out from beneath the boat but could make out nothing of the battle, only the confusion and death nearby. Had Andrei been captured or killed? Talia tried to imagine life without him. He had treated her well, and without him to protect her, she might be captured by the Pechenegs or taken by Rognol. She shuddered at either possibility, but would not let herself believe that Andrei was dead.

The battle raged for hours. At times Andrei was conscious of the sound of the roaring cataract as well as the moans the wounded and dying, and the cries of fury as men set upon each other. At other times he forgot the cataract altogether, fighting hand to hand against Pechenegs. He was near to drop with exhaustion, and his hands were slippery on the hilt of the sword, from the blood of his enemies and from his own sweat and blood. He swung the sword he'd taken from the dead boy soldier against the sword of another Pecheneg, and felt it shatter. He flung aside the useless weapon and reached to draw his own, but was it too late? The enemy in front of him closed in and another was beside him.

Andrei jerked his sword from its scabbard and swung at the closest man, striking his shield. His own shield impeded his movements, and he'd long since left his spear behind, imbedded in the chest of a Pecheneg attacker.

This might be the end! How had he gotten into this mess? What could he do now? What would Talia do? Questions whirled through his mind unanswered while he struck again and again at the oncoming enemy, growing weaker with each blow.

Suddenly a spear flew through the air, just to his left, striking one of the Pechenegs in the abdomen. He fell back and his companion looked for the spear-thrower. In that instant, Andrei was able to stab him and protect himself.

Who was his savior? He was finally able to turn and thank the warrior who had saved his life.

"Thank you," he gasped. "Who are you and how did you come to be just where I needed you?"

"Anatoly. I've been fighting near you all morning. You've killed more than your share of Pechenegs, but even you can't be expected to fight two at once."

"Between us, we killed both of these," Andrei said, "and all the others have fled."

"We've won, then," Anatoly said.

"For the moment. They may attack again farther down the river. For now, it's time to gather our dead and tend wounds." His arm was bloody. He wasn't sure if it was his blood, or that of some

131

of the men he'd killed. He wasn't in pain, but he knew from past battles that the pain sometimes came a long time afterward.

"What do we do with these men?" Anatoly asked.

"Take their weapons and leave the bodies for the Pechenegs to collect and bury."

"Shall I cut off their heads?"

"You may if you wish. I don't want to," Andrei said.

As the two walked back to the encampment, Andrei saw the head of the Pecheneg he'd killed. How many hours had it been? It seemed a lifetime. Flies buzzed about the boy's head. The body lay nearby, bloating in the sun. "I killed this one and cut off his head," Andrei said. He touched the head with the tip of his sword. It rolled slightly.

"Are you going to take it along?" Anatoly asked. "The prince said the Pechenegs use our warriors' heads for drinking cups."

"I thought this morning I'd collect the head as a trophy, but I'm tired of killing. He was just a boy, told to attack us. Once I might have reveled in the triumph over our enemies. Now I just want to protect what is ours: our people, our slaves, our trade goods." He shrugged. "I can't speak for you. Take it if you want."

Anatoly had been staring at the young man's head. "I didn't kill him. By the standards of honor, he is yours."

"If you want to claim him, I won't tell anyone. After all, you saved my life. You could have taken the head of the warrior you killed."

"I'll be satisfied with the weapons." Anatoly hefted the sword he'd taken from the dead Pecheneg. "This is a good sword, better than mine."

"I fear you'll have other chances to kill and take heads. We're not anywhere near the end of our journey." Andrei clapped Anatoly on the shoulder. "Come on. The day is almost done. Let's see how many of ours we've lost."

As they approached the boats, Talia crawled out from beneath her hiding place when she saw Andrei, and ran toward him.

"You're alive!" she cried before she could stop herself. Then she realized that he was sticky with blood and that he was not alone. She stepped back, embarrassed at her own joy and concern for him.

"Yes, I'm alive, and I'm glad to see you are as well." He smiled. "Though you may wish I'd been killed. Then you'd have been free."

The enormity of that possibility swept over her. Free! But far from home and alone. Without Andrei.

"Who must be killed for me to become free?" Inga demanded, coming out from beneath the boat, followed by the goat. "The prince himself?"

"What slave is this?" Anatoly asked, turning to gaze at her. "You don't behave or talk like a slave."

"I was a chieftain's daughter, captured to become one of Prince Vladimir's whores," she said, standing straighter, head thrown back defiantly. "I tried to kill him."

"Kill the prince?" Anatoly stared at her.

"He killed my father and attacked me. I defended myself, but all the same, I was put in prison, in chains." She held out her hands so they could see the welts the chains had worn into her flesh.

Anatoly touched her wrist, but she jerked her hand back.

"Does it hurt?" he asked.

"Not any more. It did at first. Now I just have the scars."

"You weren't chosen by any warrior at Kiev?"

"No, slaves in chains are meant to be worked and used and then sold, not chosen by warriors. Besides, I'm not pretty." She brushed her lank hair back from her face.

"You could be," Anatoly said, and realized instantly by her expression that he'd said the wrong thing. "What if I asked for you?"

"Why would you do that?"

"What does it matter why? Wouldn't you like to be free of chains?"

"Would you beat me?"

"No. At least not unless you tried to kill me as you did the prince."

"I make no promises," Inga said, "except that I will do whatever I have to do to defend myself."

Talia looked from one to the other, aware that an important exchange was taking place. She hardly recognized the dejected girl who'd wanted to die in this suddenly spirited warrior woman.

"You know that slaves chosen by warriors can be sold in Byzantium if they don't please their masters," Anatoly said. "Are you still willing to become my slave?"

"I will be free of chains as your slave?"

He nodded.

"Then I accept. How will you get possession of me?"

"I'll have to prove to the prince that I deserve you." He turned to Andrei. "Can we go back and collect some enemy heads?" He dropped the seized weapons at the women's feet.

"It's almost dark, and your wounds need tending," Talia protested.

"We'll return as soon as we can," he said, ignoring her plea.

Talia watched helplessly as the two men trotted off, back into the wooded hillside. Andrei trailed behind the younger Anatoly, and she knew he had lost blood and needed care, but she was helpless to do anything unless it was what he also wanted. She turned to study the transformed, radiant face of Inga. "What if Anatoly mistreats you?" she asked.

Inga shrugged. "Will it be worse than what I have already endured? I don't think so. Did you see how he looked at me? I think I can control him—and please him."

And have I pleased Andrei? Talia wondered. *He never says. And what if I haven't? I am as helpless as Inga.* "We can begin to please our masters by preparing food ready for their return," she said. "Shall we kill and roast this goat?"

"No!" Inga objected. "It's brought me good luck." She bent to look underneath the goat. "I think it's a female. She may give us milk."

Talia laughed. "You're very practical. Anatoly will be foolish if he mistreats you or fails to respect you."

The men returned just before dark, bearing one severed head and two sets of enemy weapons. After one quick look at the head, Talia turned away. "He looks so young, and his eyes accuse us all. Can you put it where I can't see it?"

"We have to keep it near or scavengers will carry it away," Andrei said. "It will soon start to smell, but that can't be helped."

"Did you kill him?" Talia asked.

The two men exchanged a quick look. "Anatoly killed more than this one," Andrei said, "We could have brought the heads when we first returned, but we didn't know Anatoly would need any tribute to show the prince."

Talia realized that he had not answered her question, but he obviously wanted to help Anatoly, and she wouldn't pry into who killed the boy.

He set the bloody head down on the ground and laid two shields over it, crisscrossed. "I think the prince will accept one head and the weapons in return for a slave he has probably forgotten about. I'm surprised he didn't give her to Rognol if he wanted her punished and mistreated. He knows how Rognol treats women."

"Rognol only wants the women that you want," Talia said.

Inga stared at Talia. "You have broken the arm of a warrior, and yet you are not in chains?"

"Andrei saved me, so I try to please him," Talia said. "And now, master, I have water and soap and a cloth to clean and bind your wounds."

Andrei didn't resist, but sat down on the sleeping board and allowed her to sponge the dried blood off his chest and arm. She gasped when she cleared away the blood and saw the gaping flesh hanging loosely on his arm. "I must stitch this closed," she said, threading a thin bone needle with a bit of thread raveled from the hem of her gown.

Andrei winced and bit his lip when she punctured the skin and brought the edges together. When she finished stitching, knotted the thread, and bit it off, her mouth was close enough to his arm that he could feel her warm breath against his skin. He clenched his teeth so that he would not give in to his urge to pull her into his arms. But what then would he do with her? he wondered. He was weak from fighting and loss of blood and what might be the beginning of fever, but his body reacted to other reasons. He touched her cheek. "Thank you," he whispered.

Talia straightened quickly from her work, knowing that if she stayed close to him she might give in to her desire to be held and comforted and caressed. "Tomorrow I must find willow bark and make a poultice for your wounds to take away the fever—if it is not already too late. For now, you must sleep, and help your body heal." She went to the edge of the encampment to throw out the bloody water, lest it attract vermin to the smell of human blood. It gave her a moment alone to calm down, to talk herself out of wanting Andrei. When she returned, he had fallen into an uneasy sleep. Anatoly and Inga were eating cooked grain, and Inga passed her a bowl. "I was about to give this to your master," she said, "but he suddenly fell asleep."

"He can eat tomorrow," Talia said. She ate because she knew she would need to be strong, but the food had little flavor, and she soon set it aside and lay beside Andrei, tense and worried. What else would happen to them, to her?

Chapter 17

When daylight came, Andrei and the other warriors scoured the battlefield for their fallen comrades, and for any overlooked enemy bodies that could be stripped of armaments.

Talia found willow trees and cut a few branches to brew for Andrei's wounds. He'd been pale and quiet as he led a group into the hills. *Why should I worry about him? Would he worry about me if I had been wounded?* She dared not answer her questions with honesty: she cared what happened to Andrei. She wanted him to return safely, to recover from his wounds, to be with her on the voyage.

Inga was put to work clearing up the area where the retinue had camped, and after the first boats were launched below the falls, to reloading cargo. Then she was put back into chains, screaming and protesting. "He said he would redeem me!" she cried.

"He will when he returns," Talia assured her. But what if Anatoly and Andrei encountered Pecheneg forces and were killed or captured? She stayed with the pile of weapons and the severed head. Flies buzzed about the head, and about the bodies of Kievans who had been struck down. How could Svarog have let this happen? Was praying to him useless? Nevertheless, she had to pray to some god, to ask for safety and blessings. *Just don't let Andrei be dead*, she prayed. *Even if he sells me, I want him to live.*

Before midday Vladimir's troops returned, bearing Kievan bodies, some of them headless. Platforms were hastily built with poles thrust into the soft earth, and the bodies of all the dead laid atop them for ravens to pick clean. Talia felt her stomach heave at the sight of mutilated bodies, stripped of weapons and even clothing by the Pechenegs, just as Vladimir's warriors had done to the enemy dead. At least Andrei was not among the dead!

"Where is she? Where is Inga?" Anatoly demanded.

Talia pointed. "Back in chains."

He kicked aside the crossed shields, picked up the enemy head by its hair, gathered up an armful of weapons, and stalked away in search of the prince.

Andrei unbuckled his sword and let it slide to the ground. Talia picked it up and laid it atop the shields and spears, and then turned to Andrei himself. The bandage she'd applied the night before was stained red with fresh blood, and Andrei's face was ashen. Using her dagger, she cut the bandage free and made herself look at the wound beneath. It was swollen and livid.

"Sit down," she said. Her stomach churned at the sight of the wound, the smell of dead bodies. She couldn't let herself be sick. She had to take care of him.

Andrei started to sit and then sagged against her, almost knocking her off her feet. She bore his weight to the ground, and reached for the basin of willow brew. She tipped up Andrei's chin and forced him to drink a bit of the brew. Talia laid him flat, dipped a cloth into the basin and dabbed at his wound and then poured the remaining few drops directly into the cut.

He winced and groaned. His eyes closed.

"Sleep," she said. "It's all I can do for you. The rest is in the hands of the gods." To herself she added silently, *The gods have not been kind to us on this trip. But at least he is still alive.*

By the time the last of the boats had been loaded and were ready for launching, Andrei had begun to mumble and rave in delirium. Talia sat by his side, helpless. She held his hand and stroked his forehead, which seemed to calm him at least for a while. She couldn't lift Andrei to a standing position, even if he could walk once he was upright. What would happen to them? Would the prince leave them behind for the Pechenegs and the animal scavengers and ravens?

Several boats had been launched and were already moving downstream, and she could see people going on board the last few craft. The shore was deserted, except for Andrei and her and the dead. "Help me!" she called, but no one turned back to help.

She gasped with relief when she saw Anatoly approach, leading Inga. She was unchained, but within his control.

"Help me move him," Talia implored.

"Of course. I never meant to abandon you or him, but I had to rescue Inga." He knelt, lifted Andrei onto his shoulder, and slowly straightened. "I can carry him if you and Inga can bring the weapons and our bundles." He started walking slowly toward a boat, and the women gathered up heavy loads and staggered after him.

He paused to rest and they caught up. "Prince Vladimir said that in consideration of my services I may have the services of the slave Inga, and keep her in the same boat with me, just as our leader Andrei has done with you."

Talia nodded and followed him onto the boat. It teetered beneath their weight and righted itself as Anatoly laid Andrei onto the wooden deck. Andrei murmured, "You can bring the head."

"He doesn't know what he's saying," Anatoly said.

"I know," Talia said. "He has been grievously wounded. I pray to Svarog that he recovers."

"Svarog?" Inga exclaimed. "I shall pray to the real god on his behalf."

"Svarog is real," Talia said. "I have seen statues of him, and seen how he works his power."

"The Christ is all-powerful," Inga said. "You may not believe, but I do, and I shall pray for Andrei."

"Where was your Christ when you almost drowned?" Talia asked.

"He sent you to me."

Talia said nothing more. This was the third person she'd known who believed in the Christian god: her mother, Nicolai and now Inga. She'd accept prayers to any god on earth or in heaven if it helped Andrei to recover.

She was hardly aware when the lines were cast off and the boat began to move downstream. The sun beat down and Andrei's face glistened with sweat. She had nothing to protect him with. The shields! she thought. She left Andrei's side for a moment, despite his mumbled protest, and picked up one of the heavy shields. It wasn't the one she remembered Andrei showing her how to use, and might even have belonged to a Pecheneg. It didn't matter.

She remembered the day Andrei had handed her his sword and shield and showed her how to use them, how she'd almost struck him by mistake. She hefted the shield and struggled with its weight but managed to get it across the deck to where he lay. No wonder he was wounded. How could he fight while carrying such a heavy shield?

She propped it up so that it cast them in shadow, shutting out the searing rays of sunlight. A few moments later she realized that the area around them was growing dark as a shadow moved across the deck. She peered out to see that the boat was moving between cliffs on each side of the river, so high that the sun was shut out.

In the next instant an arrow struck the deck close beside her and embedded itself into the wood.

"Go below!" someone called out. Footsteps thudded past as passengers fled. Talia sat where she was. She wouldn't leave Andrei to be attacked, not after all he'd been through. If Svarog meant her to die, it would have already happened, the day her mother died. Andrei could have let Rognol kill her or take her for himself, but he had not. She would not desert him now. The god Svarog or Perun could have struck down Andrei, but he was still alive, and if she could do anything to keep him alive, she would. She pulled the shield as close to them as she could, and almost instantly heard an arrow thunk against it, and felt the shield quiver.

From other boats she heard screams of pain as arrows found their mark, and to her left she saw Anatoly grab up a bow, fit it with an arrow and launch it up to the attackers on the cliff. It found its mark. A man fell off the cliff into the water and sank near them. He surfaced briefly and then was swept away downstream.

Beside Anatoly stood Inga, also holding a bow with an arrow fixed against the taut string. She let go and the arrow whizzed past. It struck a man, who cried out and dropped to his knees, but didn't fall into the water.

Talia closed her eyes and said another prayer to Svarog. It was all she could do. She couldn't fight like Inga and Anatoly. She could only sit with Andrei behind the shield.

The boat passed beyond the cliffs and the attack ended as quickly as it had begun. The attackers had had the advantage while the boats passed below the cliffs, but as the river widened and spread out, the Pechenegs were vulnerable once more to attack, and they fled for safety.

Anatoly laid the bow and quiver of arrows beside the other weapons. "You're a brave, loyal slave," he told Talia. "I hope Inga will be as loyal to me."

"Andrei has treated me well," Talia said. "You must treat Inga well if you want her loyalty."

"If he does not, he may find himself struck with an arrow," Inga said, and all three laughed.

"You could have left Andrei and saved yourself," he said to Talia. "If he were killed, you'd be free."

Talia met his gaze but didn't answer. She'd never be free of Andrei.

Over the next few days Andrei was alternately burning up and sweating so that his clothing grew damp, or shivering with chill. Talia stayed by his side, seeing to his care when the boats were guided past two more waterfalls and were at last gliding smoothly downstream. The river had widened so that she could barely see the opposite shores, and the strong sunlight abated somewhat so she only needed the shield at intervals for shade. A breeze came up from the south, carrying with it an unfamiliar tang.

"We're almost to the sea," Anatoly commented, answering her unspoken question. "The air smells different, doesn't it?"

Almost as if the breeze stirred him, Andrei opened his eyes and sat up. With one hand he rubbed his eyes and with the other sought and found Talia's hand. "Where are we?"

"The island of St. George," Anatoly said.

"How did we get here so quickly?"

"We didn't, sir," Anatoly said. "You have been asleep for most of the journey since your injury. You do remember that, don't you?"

Andrei touched his injured arm and flexed it slightly. "I do remember being stabbed, and your saving my life," Andrei said. "Did I thank you?"

"Several times. Not only that, but you told the prince of my heroics and that was partly responsible for my being awarded Inga as a slave. So, I should thank you."

He turned to Talia. "You tended my wound?"

"Yes."

"Then you too have saved my life. I have no suitable reward for you."

Talia felt tears spring to her eyes. She let them slide unchecked down her cheeks. "You are alive. That's my reward. And now that you are healed, you can again be my protector."

"Has anyone harmed you?"

"No one would dare while Inga and I are present," Anatoly said.

Inga came up beside him. "I too owe my life to Talia. Without her, I might have given up and drowned myself."

"We must all join in the sacrifice of thanksgiving on the island," Anatoly said. He helped Talia and Andrei to their feet as the boat nudged in against the island. Talia staggered from the numbness in her feet and legs from sitting so long on the wooden deck. She caught herself against an upright beam and made her way slowly ashore, following Inga and Anatoly who held Andrei between them.

She stared about her at the sandy bit of land. "Is this Byzantium?"

Andrei laughed, which brought about a fit of weak coughing. When he could speak, he said, "Byzantium is vast and beautiful, and bustling with people. It's the grandest city in all the world. The streets are broad and the palaces and churches are roofed in gold. You'll know when we get there."

"How much longer will it be?"

"It depends."

"On what?" she asked.

"On the wind and waves and how soon we can persuade the nearby people to give us food and supplies. We still have to sail the great sea. It would be closer if we sailed across the center of the great sea, but it's more dangerous, so we go around the edge. It depends on the prince too."

"Doesn't he want to go?' Inga asked before Talia could speak. "Hasn't he planned this entire voyage? Doesn't he want to get to Byzantium and sell his slaves?" She reached across Andrei to touch Anatoly's arm. "He would have sold me."

"He plans to marry the Princess Anna, sister of the Emperor Basil," Andrei said. "She was promised to Prince Vladimir as a reward for defeating the emperor's enemies in an uprising last year. The emperor had sent to Kiev for help against the Bulgarians as well, and Prince Vladimir with six thousand troops saved Byzantium for Emperor Basil." He paused, drew in several ragged breaths, and continued more slowly. "If Princess Anna and her retinue are already on this side of the great sea, or arrive soon, he will marry her here. Otherwise, we will go on to Byzantium and the ceremony will be held there."

"But he already has wives," Talia objected.

Before Andrei could say anything more, a priest in white robes walked into the midst of the group and held up one hand for silence. In the other, he held a chicken by its feet. Its wings had been bound close to its body so it could not flap or struggle. Talia saw that a fire had been laid on the sand and smoke began to arise from the burning wood, twisting and curling in the breeze so that sometimes it blew straight to her, then veered away. The acrid smell stung her nostrils and eyes, but she made no attempt to elude it. She stared at the priest, the flames, and the fowl. And at the pile of rocks atop which stood a wooden carving of the face of Svarog.

The crowd grew silent and the priest began to pray: "Lord Svarog, god of all gods, creator, supreme over us, we give you thanks that you have seen fit to bring us safely past the rapids in the great river and past the swords and spears and arrows of those who wished to kill us. We offer you the life of this fowl as a symbol of our own lives that we are willing to sacrifice for you if you so need."

A youth approached, handed the priest a knife, and knelt a moment on the sand.

The priest struck off the head of the fowl with a single sweep of the knife. The body jerked in the priest's hands as its lifeblood gushed out onto the sand, soaking it in crimson. A few drops came fell near the tips of Talia's shoes, and she stepped back in revulsion.

She felt her stomach lurch. Hadn't they seen enough blood shed? Worthwhile humans had been killed on this journey, but at least most of them had chosen to fight. This chicken had not. Somehow seeing the hapless fowl slaughtered needlessly was harder to witness than the severed head of the Pecheneg that had lain at her feet. She shook her head to fling away tears as the body of the chicken was cast into the fire, and the smell of burning feathers and flesh polluted the air.

"How soon can we go back onto the boat?" she asked.

"As soon as the priest and the prince leave," Andrei said. "I need to lie down again. Or at least sit."

Just as the priest turned toward the waiting boats, a man ran toward the group, bowed before the prince, and handed him a rolled paper.

The prince unrolled the missive. As he read, his features stilled, his face darkened. He turned, and with an imperious gesture to his closest warriors, he stalked off.

"What's happening?" Talia asked.

"I don't know, but Anatoly can find out and tell us. By the look of the prince's face, it's bad news. Whatever it is, it's out of our control," Andrei said.

A sense of dread swept over Talia. If whatever happened was beyond Andrei's control, then she had even less ability to affect anything. All she could do now was to tend Andrei's injured arm and try to avoid Rognol. He could now fight and Andrei couldn't. She was in a precarious situation.

Anatoly came back with news. "The prince has been betrayed. The emperor had promised his sister in marriage, and my Lord Vladimir had even been baptized as a Christian to make the marriage acceptable to the princess and the emperor. But she has not been sent here for the ceremony."

"He already has seven wives," Talia said. "He doesn't need any others, and he has enough sons to rule after he dies."

The two men stared at her for a moment before Anatoly said, "It's a matter of power and respect. Prince Vladimir can't let the matter go as if it's unimportant. He must do something to even the score with Emperor Basil, or other rulers will take away Vladimir's kingdom."

"So what does he plan to do?" Andrei asked.

"We'll attack Kherson. It controls the river, and it belongs to Emperor Basil."

"It might be difficult," Andrei said. "It's well fortified."

"Will you take those people slaves?" Talia asked.

"No. We can't sell them in Byzantium, since they're part of Basil's empire. He wouldn't buy his own citizens. We might take a few captives as an example to the others, though, and parade them before Basil in chains," Andrei said.

"You're very sure of winning," Talia observed. Andrei seemed to have gained strength as he talked eagerly of a coming battle. His face had its normal ruddy color and his eyes sparkled.

"We almost always win the ones we plan. It's the unexpected attacks on us that we can't control. The attacker always has the advantage," Andrei explained. "I wish I could take part in the attack." He flexed his injured arm, winced, and touched it lightly with the other hand. "My arm is almost healed, Talia, thanks to you. Perhaps if I hold my shield over it just right, I'd be able to fight."

"You'll have other opportunities," Anatoly said. "We're surrounded by enemies."

Prince Vladimir was quick to turn his decision to attack Kherson into action. Men were put to work attaching sails to the boats, and soon the craft were beating their way across the open sea to the settlement. It had been a town since ancient times, Andrei explained, settled by the Greeks before the time of Christ, and conquered over and over again by various warring tribes. As their boat approached Kherson, Talia could see fallen columns, the ruins of long-ago houses and temples, white in the spring sunlight, as Andrei pointed them out. He braced himself against the mast with his good arm, and despite the sunshine and the brisk wind, his face once more looked pale and strained. She was relieved Anatoly had talked him out of joining the attack.

When they anchored off Kherson, traders rushed to service the boats, unaware that this voyage was different. The prince did not reveal his intentions until after the tradesmen had brought out their products and his crew had exchanged a few furs and a barrel of honey for fish and fresh fruit.

Only then did he send a message to the town elders, demanding they surrender to him. The answer came back within minutes: No.

"Then be damned!" he roared. "We will attack."

"Those poor people," Talia said to Inga, though she knew Andrei was listening. "They have done us no wrong."

146

"Us? Then you have become part of Vladimir's forces," Inga said. "I don't care if the prince wins or not. I almost hope he loses. He deserves to lose, after all he has done to others."

"Bridle your tongue," Andrei advised. "The prince might kill you as a traitor. Or he might take you back from Anatoly and make you his own slave again, or have you flogged and sold in Byzantium."

Talia shuddered. The same thing could happen to her, except that the prince had never had a claim on her. Only Andrei had. She knew deep down that whatever the prince wanted, he would take, but he did seem to show some respect to his elite warriors in not seizing their women.

Her sympathies lay with the beleaguered residents of Kherson: the women and children and old people, the sick and lame, who had no part in making the decision to fight or not fight. *Just like my village.* She longed to call out to the inhabitants to flee, but no one would have heard her above the din of clanging weapons and the movement of soldiers and horses.

And there was nowhere to go. Whatever else she thought about Prince Vladimir, she acknowledged that he was a superb military strategist. From the boat she saw in the distance the prince's horsemen lined up in a semicircle around the land side of Kherson while the boats, even the very boat she stood on, formed a barricade by water.

"Why is he attacking these people instead of sailing right on to Byzantium and confronting the emperor?" she asked.

"Two reasons," Andrei answered. "The Greek Fire is one."

"What's that?"

"The Greeks throw a substance onto the water and it catches fire and burns our ships."

"How can something burn on the water?"

"I don't know. Their wise men invented it, and keep secret how it's made."

"What's the other reason?"

"Territory." He spread the palm of his left hand and pointed with his right index finger. "Pretend that we are here." He touched a spot near the hinge of his thumb, then traced an area toward the base of his fingers. "Kherson, Doras, Pullae, Sugdaea. All this belonged to Russia, but Svatoslav lost it. Prince Vladimir wants it back. And he's sure he'll get it. He's already sent a message saying so to Emperor Basil."

But over the next days the prince's victory seemed doubtful. The inhabitants of Kherson hurled as many spears and shot as many arrows as Vladimir's troops. The attackers and defenders were evenly matched and neither side was willing to surrender. Vladimir prepared for a long siege. He knew that the town had ample food supplies—supplies they had been ready to trade to the Russians—but eventually their supplies would give out. Eventually. Meanwhile, the sun beat down, baking the grass around the town and forcing his horsemen to go farther afield each day to find forage for their mounts. Vladimir's forces grew restive with inactivity, and fights broke out among them.

"How long can they hold out?" Talia asked Andrei, her hand shielding her face from the merciless sun. But it was this sun that had made possible the cherries and oranges she devoured, licking her fingers to rescue every drop of juice. Cherries would not ripen in Kiev for another month, and oranges never would

"They'll hold out as long as they have food and water. And so can we," he said, taking a section of orange from Talia.

The days wore on with no sign of change. Vladimir's troops marched back and forth in sight of the town's sentries. Fewer spears were hurled, fewer arrows fell. Talia stayed by Andrei's side, until the day came when he announced that he was ready for battle, and went to join the other warriors.

Talia watched him go, angry at the spring in his step, the eagerness with which he ran toward the enemy. Hadn't he taken enough chances with his life—and hers—already? When would this siege end so they could go on to Byzantium? Whatever awaited her there, she thought, was no worse than this stillness under a blistering sun and stifling heat. The townspeople weren't the only ones who would eventually exhaust their food. The prince had not planned on staying here, but instead had counted on getting fresh food and water and continuing across the great sea.

Inga joined her one day, equally impatient at Vladimir's stalemate. "Men!" she scoffed. "I wish I were in charge. I'd talk to the women. They'd persuade their men to surrender. No woman wants to see her child die of hunger or thirst, or be stabbed by a Russian sword. Men don't think like that. All they want to do is kill."

Talia nodded agreement. "And they keep on fighting and killing, even after they're wounded, as long as they can stand or stay seated on a horse." She pointed toward Andrei. She could always recognize him among the horde of troops. To her surprise she saw him wheel his horse and ride off to one side, dismount and pick up something from the ground. He rode back with it toward the prince, and as soon as the prince read the paper Andrei brought, he sent a detachment off, away from the main body of troops.

"What are they doing?" Talia asked aloud, but Inga had no more information than she did.

"We'll have to wait to find out," Inga said. "The prince isn't moving any other troops."

It took another day to find out what had happened. Anastasius, a Russian who lived in Kherson, had shot an arrow with a message telling Vladimir where the springs that supplied water to Kherson were located. Vladimir's men dug up the pipes and broke the connection, and within a few hours Kherson's elders signaled surrender.

Vladimir took a few captives and left a large contingent of his elite warriors to occupy the town. Boats were being loaded for the journey to Byzantium when a ship arrived carrying the Princess Anna. The boat was richly decorated, and banners that Talia took to be the royal standard flew from the masts, but the princess was nowhere to be seen.

Vladimir saw the boat's approach and stopped the loading of his own boats. He barked a command and his elite cadre of troops lined up in formation. They had been helping to load boats, and many had to scrabble for shirts to cover their sweaty chests. The prince himself was disheveled, and at a signal from him servants ran toward him with pails of water, drying cloths, a tent to shield him while he dressed, and a fresh uniform. After a few minutes the prince stepped out from behind the tent, resplendent in garb Talia had not seen him wear. Gone were the mailed vest, the bronze helmet, and the scuffed boots. He had donned white shirt and trousers and dark green suede boots. A red cape thrown over his shoulders was held closed at the neck with a huge gold circle pin. His red-blonde hair hung loosely, and broad gold bands encased his tanned forearms. He looked handsome and powerful, rightly a ruler.

"The princess can't fail to be impressed by our prince," Talia said.

"*Our* prince!" Inga scoffed. "I lay no claim to him."

Princess Anna's handmaidens stared at the prince, then scurried back into a curtained enclosure on the royal ship, and escorted the princess onto the deck.

She stood unmoving, giving all her future subjects and her future husband ample time to admire her.

Talia caught her breath at the beautiful clothing of the princess, and felt herself plain and poorly dressed. But then, she was not the sister of an emperor, born in a palace. She was a slave.

Beside her, Inga murmured, "I must find clothing such as that. No man can resist such beauty."

"Her face is covered by the veil."

"But the rest of her is not," Inga said. "Look how she stands. As stately as a statue. Compare her hands to ours."

Talia looked at the soft white hands of the princess that held an embroidered silk shawl lightly around her shoulders. Gold bracelets adorned both her wrists. Her long red silk tunic was embroidered in gold around the curved neckline, and belted with gold about her slim waist. Embroidered slippers peeked from beneath her white pleated underdress.

"Who can say what the shy princess looks like beneath the veil?" Inga mused. "She may have a long nose, or thin hair, or worse, hairs growing from her chin."

The Princess Anna nodded almost imperceptibly, and one of her handmaidens drew back the veil that hung from an embroidered cap. Her nose may have been a trifle too long, but the rest of her features were perfect. She had glossy black hair and dark lustrous eyes. Pearl earrings hung from each ear lobe, and more pearls encircled her neck. Her face was painted, Talia saw, so that her eyes seemed doubly dark against her pale skin, and her lips were outlined in vermilion.

The princess smiled and nodded at the prince, who rushed forward to help her down off the ship, then knelt at her feet and kissed the hand she extended. "Have you brought a priest so that we can be married immediately?" he asked.

"No, my brother didn't send a priest. We must find priests here, and sacred books and relics as well. As eager as my brother is to spread the Christian faith, he is showing his anger at you by withholding the means to establish churches. He won't send priests until you have sent him my bride-price."

"This conquered territory will be my bride price. I'll instruct my commander to tell your brother so. We shall find a priest here in Kherson to marry us, and perhaps persuade him to go with us to Kiev, and bring his church books and relics."

Only the small group of elite troops witnessed the wedding and joined the prince and princess's retinue that turned back northward. The remainder of the caravan loaded and victualed the boats and set off for Byzantium.

Chapter 18

For the first days of the sea voyage, the weather was fair and the warm wind belled the sails, pushing the boats onward across the smooth sea. Then a storm came, beating against the flimsy craft, tossing them like hurled stones, throwing people and animals alike against the boards. The livestock yowled their fear, and the humans lay flat on the wooden decks or clung to the sides of the boats, vomiting.

Andrei was not one of the sufferers. He was in high spirits. His wound had healed, and he'd gained back his feeling of self-worth by going out to fight at Kherson. He knelt beside Talia as she lay on the deck, wan and wasted. He held out a section of orange.

She turned away. "I don't want anything to eat."

"You'll feel better if you eat, even a small bit."

"It's no use eating. It just comes back up." She rolled onto her side and rubbed her aching belly. "It would have been easier to give up and drown at the rapids than to die like this."

"You're not going to die. These storms abate as quickly as they appear. Look!" He pointed toward the horizon. "I can see a bit of blue sky. The storm is almost over." He pushed her lank hair back from her face. "It's a good thing you'll be cleaned and dressed before the slave auction. The way you look now, you wouldn't bring many besants."

She stared at him, aghast. "You still mean to sell me? Have I not pleased you? I cared for your wounds and cooked for you. Does none of that matter? Are you abandoning me because I'm ill?"

"In truth, I haven't decided. My plan was always to sell you, though I will miss you a great deal. You should sell for many besants, and I'll have my share of the sale of the ordinary slaves as well. That should make up for some of my financial losses of the past few years. I admit I'm tempted to keep you and trust that the furs and other goods fetch a fair price."

"I hate you!" she moaned. "You let me think I meant something to you."

"At times you pleased me very much. I'll do everything I can to see that you are sold to a rich but kind man. Some slaves find that they become like members of their owner's family, and live in much finer style than they would have in a forest cabin, or even in Kiev. Byzantium is after all the center of the trading world, and a beautiful, cultured place. We call the city itself Miklagaard."

She turned her face away from him and didn't answer.

After a moment he walked away and would not let himself look back. Even ill and disheveled, Talia attracted him. It had been a terrible mistake to lie with her, to touch her even, and thanks be to the god Perun that he had not impregnated her. He could not marry her, for she was a Slav and could never rise to his class.

Soon he would have to marry again, to a woman with status equal to his and father a family. But how could he find someone who stirred his senses as Talia did? And how could he forget the touch and sight and smell of her? She would remain forever in his memory, and a memory was all he could keep of her. He must see to it that someone worthy of her purchased her, and when he next came to Byzantium to trade, he would ask of her, discover if she were being well- or ill-treated. If anyone dared to mistreat her, he'd—

Andrei halted, his thoughts churning. What could he do to protect Talia? He'd kept Rognol from raping her and later from claiming her as his slave, but Rognol was subject to the command of Prince Vladimir, while the Greeks of Byzantium and even more the slave buyers from Kazan and beyond were powerful, under the command of no one. And by the time he returned on another voyage, Talia might have been taken to a far off country beyond his reach, beyond even any communication.

But perhaps some good-hearted man, some Christian from Byzantium, would buy her. Why had he brought her along? He could have left her in Kiev to work as other slaves worked. If he had, Rognol would undoubtedly have chosen to stay behind as Nicolai had, and Talia would have been at Rognol's mercy. There was no good outcome, and had not been since the beginning. The best he could do for her was to make her hate him, so she would be glad to join the family of whoever bought her, or even be part of a harem. The way she'd looked at him, he was well on the way to earning her hate.

The storm abated as the fleet continued westward, almost always in sight of the shoreline. Talia stayed on deck, careful not to get too close to Andrei, denying to herself how much she wanted him to touch her, to kiss her. But she knew that she was unclean, wearing ragged garments, her face reddened by the sun. Why should he be attracted to her? She thought longingly of the beautiful fur-trimmed garment he'd let her wear that one time, the silken undergarments he'd given her. She wouldn't think of the circumstances of being allowed to wear such luxurious clothing, but she wished she had some way to make him think of her as a desirable woman again, not just as a slave.

As she looked shoreward, she saw horsemen riding along, keeping pace with the boats, and realized that they'd been following in just the same way for two days. "Who are those riders?" she asked Andrei. "Are we being escorted? Or are they spies?"

"Scavengers," he said. "They're watching to see if any of our boats stray too close to the shore and wreck, or if we anchor and go ashore to hunt. Then they'd board and plunder us, taking anything they could carry away, including slaves."

"Why don't you shoot them? You have arrows left. Or go ashore and fight them?"

"Why stir up trouble? As long as we stay out at sea they can't bother us. If we do have to go ashore, we'll be armed and do our best to protect the fleet."

Talia shivered in spite of the warm sunlight. Was there no end to the danger?

Then on the tenth day since they'd left Kherson, the fleet turned into a calm strait, which Andrei said was called the Bosporus. The shoreline was low and wooded, and the marauders ashore had disappeared. Then the boats came out again onto a broad sea, and in the distance Talia could see a towering gray wall. It grew closer as the fleet rounded a curving spit of land and began to anchor nearby. The harbor was crowded with all manner and sizes of ships and boats. Strange languages sounded from the ships, as loads were lowered onto the docks. Several of the ships had large metal tubes protruding from their sides. "What are those round tubes?" she asked Andrei.

"They throw the Greek Fire across the water to other ships. Those are the emperor's warships, protecting the harbor from attackers."

"They let us in. How do they know we are not enemies?"

"We have our certificates giving us the right to trade. And you see the gates are closed and locked. We won't be allowed to enter until the Varangian guards give us their permission."

Talia looked up at a huge bronze gate set into the stone wall. They had arrived at Miklagaard, the beautiful special city, but they were still outside.

Soon guards arrived, examined the papers Andrei presented as Vladimir's representative, and the gate swung open. Andrei gave instructions for unloading the boats and storing their contents in secure warehouses, and then sorted the people around him into groups.

"The prince's troops will stay in the quarters of the Varangian guards. Male slaves will follow this eunuch, female slaves that one.

You will all be allowed to use the public baths, and slaves will have a change of clothing brought to you by the eunuchs."

Talia stared at the eunuchs. Their faces were bare of whiskers, their bodies sleek and plump, and their skin as smooth as her own — nay, smoother, for they showed no sign of sunburn, and she did. These were strange, unusual men.

She realized that Inga was tugging at her to start walking, and Talia fell into step beside her friend. Out of the corner of her eye she saw Rognol looking at her, a look that made her shiver with dread, before he followed Andrei. Marya was there as well, staring after Andrei and Rognol before she too joined the other female slaves.

Talia longed to run after Andrei, to know when she would see him again, but he had gone without a backward glance at her.

Andrei shepherded the two chained men from Kherson toward the royal palace. It was doubtful he would actually get to see the emperor, but he would at least give the prince's message to someone who would see that it was delivered to the ruler.

Even though he had been to Miklagaard on previous trips, he was always awed by the beauty of the city, the crown glory of Byzantium, indeed of the entire world. He was escorted by two guards who made sure the prisoners didn't escape, as if they might run away dragging their clanking chains, so Andrei felt free to look about him. In every direction the domes of churches thrust up against the porcelain-blue sky, and from the Hippodrome he heard the sounds of chariot wheels striking stones, the slash of whips and the jeers and commands of drivers. Close by, fountains tinkled softly in the midst of peaceful gardens. This was indeed a beautiful city as well as the richest, and inhabitants had poured into the city from the four corners of the earth, eager to trade, to work, to grow wealthy. Some too came to steal and cheat, to kill if they must for the power they craved.

To his surprise, as soon as he gave his name and indicated that he represented the prince, he was escorted into the presence of the emperor. Basil II sat on a throne raised above his courtiers, so that Andrei had to bow low, touching his head to the floor, then rise and look up at the emperor. A woman played the harp and sang softly, but the emperor seemed to pay her little attention. In fact, he was playing with a mechanical bird that tweeted a melody of its own. He set it aside and signaled the harpist to cease before saying to Andrei, "I am told that you represent Vladimir, Prince of Russia."

"Yes, my lord. And he is now your sister's husband and controls Kherson, your town at the mouth of the river."

"So she married him? She seemed unwilling, but in the end agreed to marry for my sake and for her faith. I hope that he will treat her well and will forsake his other wives."

Andrei doubted that last wish.

As if understanding Andrei's thought, Basil went on, "He has become a Christian, as she is, and as all of my subjects here in Constantinople are. You have seen some of my churches?"

"Yes, my lord."

"Christians have only one wife, only one husband."

"I feel sure my Prince Vladimir will try to please your sister."

"So what other news have you for me?"

"I bring you these two representatives from Kherson. They surrendered to Prince Vladimir and his forces. He presents them to you, as well as returning Kherson to you as bride price in return for the Princess Anna."

"He gives me what was already mine?" Basil roared.

Andrei refrained from pointing out that Prince Vladimir might have taken the princess northward and given nothing in return. Without sending special forces to overtake Prince Vladimir and his bride, there was little Basil could do to change the situation.

The emperor seemed to realize the weakness of his position. He sighed. "I accept. May I see the message the fiend has sent?"

Andrei handed him the scroll and waited while it was read. There would be no return message for Prince Vladimir, but Andrei knew he was not to leave the emperor's presence until he had been dismissed.

"Hmm!" the emperor murmured, looking up from his reading to address Andrei. "The prince took special notice of your slave with the flaming hair. He urges me to bid you bring the woman forth, and I so bid you. He thinks she might be good breeding stock for one of my cousins." He looked squarely at Andrei, as if seeing him anew. "Why did the prince not claim her for himself?"

Andrei hesitated, uncertain whether to tell the truth about his perfidy. If he told Basil how he had defiled Talia to keep her from becoming one of Vladimir's concubines, it might also keep her from making a good marriage here. He had acted selfishly, wanting to keep her with him as long as possible, but did he have the right to hold her back in lowly slavery? "I had rendered the prince special service in battle, and he gave each of his druzhina the privilege of choosing a slave. I chose the woman Talia Militskaya, since I had taken her captive at the beginning."

He had no idea what else the prince might have written, and he couldn't determine if Emperor Basil believed him or not. The ruler's dark eyes regarded him as unflinchingly as a raptor gazing at his doomed prey, and Andrei dared not look away. To do so would signal his guilt.

After what seemed an eternity of time, Emperor Basil said, "So you own this woman." It was a statement, not really a question.

"Yes, my lord." Andrei berated himself for continuing to repeat the same phrase, but Basil expected no more elaborate answer.

"Then bring her to the races at the Hippodrome tomorrow, suitably dressed so that none at court will know that she is a slave." He gestured at Andrei. "You too should be more suitably dressed, as befits the escort of a beautiful woman."

"I apologize, my lord. I came straightaway from the fleet with the message for you." Andrei felt his face flaming in embarrassment, even as he defended himself, but knew that apologizing to an emperor changed nothing. "It seemed the most pressing of my many duties here in your city."

Emperor Basil gestured again, signaling that the interview was over. He picked up the mechanical bird. "This automata is very clever, is it not, and in many ways superior to a living bird. This one will not drop feathers or excrement, it will sing to me whenever I wish it to, and it will not fly away and desert the palace or the city. Nor will it grow old and frail or irritable. Would that all my subjects were as satisfactory as this toy." He set it chirruping, and as Andrei backed his way out of the emperor's presence, he saw that Basil's throne was being raised mechanically to a still higher position, so that the emperor looked down on all around him.

Andrei walked slowly back to the dock where the boats were being unloaded, not just the ones from Kiev, but also boats from far-flung places. Some cargo was destined for storage and other goods would be taken to the central marketplace for trading. He saw one of the Kievan slaves herding livestock off a boat. There was the goat Talia had protected, had refused to have slaughtered. He'd promised her he'd save the goat's life, but it would be trouble here. How could he protect it? No better than he could protect her, he reflected. He gave orders that the livestock was to be fed and penned up safely, and the brown goat was not to be killed. It ran toward him and he laughed. It must have remembered him. What had Talia called it? He couldn't recall, or even if she'd named it. He turned it back toward the livestock caretaker with instructions to milk it if necessary.

Ordinarily he would have enjoyed the medley of voices and languages, the enticing scents of spices and perfumes, the entreaties of the food vendors. At other times he might have paused to buy fruit or a flagon of wine, might have asked the news from across the sea. Today his thoughts were whirling. His logic told him that he must dress Talia in the best he could afford and have the attendants do everything possible to bring out her beauty so that she would appeal to the royal cousin and bring a high sale price. But his heart constricted in his chest at the thought of not having her with him.

Chapter 19

Talia couldn't stop turning to admire something new, something she'd never seen before. Everywhere she looked there was beauty. It was incredible, so different from Kiev and from her village. White carved pillars held up gold-domed rooftops, glittering against the clear blue sky. There was even beauty underfoot. "Look, Inga!" She bent to trace with her fingertip the face of a woman made of tiny bits of colored stone.

The eunuch, who had not spoken as he strode ahead of the slave women, turned at Talia's voice. "No talking!" he commanded. "Walk faster." His voice sounded high-pitched, unlike Andrei's or Anatoly's.

"That's the first thing he's said," Talia whispered after they'd run a few steps to catch up with the group of slaves. "I was beginning to think someone had cut out his tongue."

"I think they cut off something else," Inga whispered back. "He has no sex, so he is safe to escort us and look at us as we bathe."

"No talking!" the eunuch repeated. "I can have you flogged if you continue to disobey me."

The women followed him meekly into a closed courtyard. There he took the women two at a time to small rooms. Each was furnished with two beds and a table on which stood a basin, a pitcher of water, and a stack of folded cloths. In one corner of the room there was an oval hole in the tile floor. To their astonishment, the eunuch hitched up his robe slightly, squatted over the hole, grunted, then stood and pulled a chain that hung from the wall. Water gushed into the hole, swirled around, and disappeared. "You understand its use?" the eunuch asked.

The two women nodded.

"Soon we go to baths," he said. He pointed to the stack of cloths. "Bring those." He pointed to himself. "Byzas, named for the founder of Byzantium."

Talia and Inga each pointed to themselves and repeated their names. Byzas nodded and went out.

"Before he comes back, I'm going to make use of our floor hole," Inga said, squatting to urinate. Talia followed, and the two women watched with satisfaction as the water carried away their urine.

"Andrei calls this city Miklagaard and some others call it Constantinople. Whichever, it's amazing," Talia said, "and beautiful. Much better than Kiev. I want to see it all. I might like to stay here, even as a slave. At least I wouldn't have to empty slop buckets and scrub them every morning."

"It has many interesting things," Inga conceded, "but I want to go home. Every day we came down the river brought me farther from my home. I don't like these bare stone floors and people everywhere. I hate having people like Byzas watching us all the time. I miss the birch trees and evergreen forests covered in snow. I want to be where I can breathe in cold, crisp air."

"What if Anatoly sells you?" Talia asked. Inwardly she wondered, *what if Andrei sells me?*

"He won't," Inga said confidently. "He wants to marry me, but I will only marry him if he becomes a Christian and goes with me to my home country. There with him at my side we can take back the power Vladimir took from me."

Talia stared at her friend and smiled. "And to think you once were ready to give up and die."

Inga nodded and clasped Talia's hand. "You saved my life. If you're ever in danger, I'll do everything I can to save you."

Byzas came then to take them to the public baths. It was the time of day when women were to bathe, he told them. He ushered them into a large room with tiled walls and a shallow pool in the center. The bottom and curved sides of the pool were covered in tiny pieces of stone and glass, in shades of blue and green that formed a picture of sea creatures. The walls had the same design. To Talia's surprise, Byzas didn't leave, but began to disrobe her. She pulled away, embarrassed at having a strange man see her naked.

Byzas laughed. "You are safe with me. I feel nothing when I look at your body, and not at the body of a boy either. Take off your clothes and get into the pool. I will burn your clothing, as I have been instructed."

"But what will we wear?" Inga asked.

"I will bring your new garments."

"What's wrong with ours?" Talia asked. "All they need is washing."

"They would probably fall to pieces," he said, "and in the meantime, they may harbor vermin."

Talia felt a prickle of shame. Her clothing was ragged and her body filthy with weeks of caked-on dirt. As long as she'd been traveling, with people in her same situation, she hadn't noticed, but now she looked at the women luxuriating in the pool, and at the colorful clothing hung over the backs of chairs nearby.

She slipped into the water and slid down its smooth sides as deeply as she could, until the water rose to cover her nipples. Inga lay beside her, also partially submerged. Other women Talia remembered from the voyage were also bathing, including Marya. In the days of battle, of caring for Andrei and of seasickness, she'd all but forgotten Marya, but it was clear from Marya's look that she well-remembered Talia. Her evil stare caught and held Talia's attention, so that she could not look away. Marya's body bore bruises, some yellowing with age, others fresh. Either she had been clumsy, or Rognol had beaten her. Marya slid into the water up to her neck, hiding her bruises. A eunuch stood at the edge of the pool, across from Talia and Inga.

It was disconcerting when Byzas left with their clothing and returned quickly to squat at the edge of the pool and begin soaping her back. His hands moved with soothing circular patterns, so soothing that Talia felt drowsy. It wasn't right somehow for any man save Andrei to see her. But then, Byzas wasn't really a man.

"How did you get to be like this?" she asked, and stopped, embarrassed. It wasn't right to ask a stranger a personal question.

He didn't seem to mind. Perhaps he was used to having people ask him, she thought. "It was done to me when I was a child, before I really had a choice. One of my older brothers became a soldier, but I am not large or strong enough for that career. Another is a trader, but I have no mind for figures, so that job was not suitable for me. My parents offered me to become a eunuch for a certain price paid them by a rich man, and besides serving the emperor, I sing in the churches. The surgery on me and the other boys in my age group kept our voices high." He paused in washing Talia and sang a few notes that echoed throughout the bathhouse, clear and pure. "If you attend church, especially at Hagia Sophia, you may hear me sing."

He resumed washing Talia, finished, and began soaping Inga. She jerked away, refusing his ministrations. He shrugged and turned back to Talia. "You have many questions. I can tell by your face."

She nodded. "Don't you miss the pleasures of a woman?"

"One can't miss what one has never had. I have compensations. People pay me for favors, so I can send money to my family. I have the ear of the emperor, and I have an ear to others as well. People go on as if I were one of their pet animals or even a mechanical toy, and say things they should be careful of. I report to the emperor if there is something I think he should hear, and he rewards me. Sometimes other people pay me not to tell what I've heard, or pay me to speak to the emperor on their behalf. Perhaps you may need my services."

"I have no money," Talia said.

"But you have beauty. I may be able to help you, and after you have achieved status, you can reward me."

"I don't think I can achieve any status except for being a slave," Talia said. "I am to be sold."

"I can enhance your beauty, so that you will be purchased by a very rich man. Or a powerful man. There are many of both here in Constantinople, even among the priests. Your present owner will be grateful, and you will be well treated and will eventually wheedle power of your own from the man who buys you. He may even marry you. It has happened."

"I can't understand all this," Talia said. "I only arrived this morning to this strange, beautiful city. I don't know anything of the ways of the people here. What you tell me sounds difficult to believe, and how do I know I can trust you?"

"You don't," he agreed with a chuckle. "As soon as I return you and your friend to your quarters and lock you in, for all you know I may go and chat with the emperor."

"The emperor would have no reason to be interested in anything you could tell him about me," she said.

"That's true now. You have committed to nothing and didn't even try to wheedle any special attention, but somewhere in your consciousness my words have taken root. We will talk more later. Now you and you friend must be dried off and dressed." He held out a large soft towel and enveloped Talia in it, patting her dry through the thickness of the fabric. Inga didn't wait for his assistance, but stepped from the pool bare and dripping, and grabbed up one of the towels to dry herself. Byzas didn't register any annoyance at Inga, but handed both women identical white gowns that draped around them and were fastened at the shoulder by a shiny metal clasp.

Across the pool the other eunuch gave a short command and a group of women scrambled out of the water, dried themselves and put on clothing from a stack he provided. Marya was among them, Talia noted. Only she and Inga had a eunuch of their own. Why had they been singled out for better treatment? Had Andrei ordered it, or Anatoly? Or someone else?

Byzas led the way to a commons area, across the paved courtyard. Inside, women slaves, all dressed in the same toga-like garments, lined up for a meal of fish, coarse bread and dried figs, with wine to drink.

Inga took a sip and grimaced. "How do people drink this? It's not nearly as good as our mead."

Talia sipped, swallowed. "We may have to get used to it." She tore off a chunk of bread and thrust it into her mouth, followed by one of the small fried fish and more wine. "It's better when you eat something with it," she concluded.

Byzas had stood nearby, watching impassively. As soon as they finished eating, he said, "Time to go."

Back at their quarters, Byzas lighted an oil lamp than hung from the ceiling, indicated a pile of bedding that had been laid on each bed, bowed slightly, and left. They heard the wooden bar drop into its slot. They were locked in. Others could open the door and come in, but they could not leave.

They spread the linens on the bed, Talia blew out the oil lamp, and they stretched out fully clothed. "I wonder when we'll get a change of clothing?" she asked in the darkness.

Her answer came in the morning. They were awakened by a tap on the door, which was opened almost instantly. Byzas entered carrying an armful of bright colored clothing, which he laid on Talia's bed. "Take care of your morning ablutions. Your master wants you to wear these garments. I will return with food and help you dress." He turned to go.

"What about me?" Inga demanded.

"Your master sent no message," he said.

Talia looked from her friend's crestfallen expression to the silken clothing. She was sorry for Inga, but triumphant that Andrei had remembered her, had not abandoned her. She lifted a length of red silk and let it slither through her hand and pool on the bed.

"There're three gowns here, Inga. You're welcome to wear one of them."

"No. Andrei chose those for you. Anatoly obviously doesn't care as much for me. You'd better do as Byzas says before he returns." She sat on her bed, not meeting Talia's eyes.

"I'll ask Andrei why Anatoly didn't buy new clothing for you?" Talia said, reaching to touch Inga on the shoulder.

"No!" Inga jerked away. "I'm humiliated."

"No one knows but Byzas."

"I know! Anatoly will be sorry he has mistreated me. I am a chieftain's daughter."

Talia said no more, but used the toilet, pulled the cord and washed her hands and face in the basin. She was still impressed at the water and sewage system of the city, so that even slaves could use them. It would be pleasant to go to the public baths again, but slaves probably didn't get that privilege every day. She certainly hadn't bathed every day in Kiev.

She chose a blue length of silk, and as she lifted it, she noted that Andrei had provided silk undergarments as well. She slipped them on, fastened the loops around the buttons, and turned to Inga. "Will you help me drape this silk, please? I'm not used to how the Greek women wear their clothing."

"Of course. I don't begrudge you your clothing and your happiness." She wrapped the length of silk deftly, and fastened it at the shoulder with the clasp Byzas had given them the night before. "Andrei should have sent some better ornaments than this," she said, "but at least he chose colors that will become you."

"Not the red," Talia said. "He may have meant that for you. Or Anatoly may have asked him to send it. It's obviously meant for you with your pale gold hair and not me."

Byzas returned then, without knocking. He bore a tray with fruit, cheese, a pot of coffee and two small cups. "Eat quickly," he said, setting the tray down on Talia's bed. "We have much to do to make you beautiful enough for the entertainment he has planned for today."

"What entertainment?" Talia asked.

"I can't say for certain, but I suspect it will be a brief walk around this part of the city and perhaps an exhibition at the Hippodrome." Byzas left, and returned quickly with a basket lumpy with its mysterious contents. He stood with his arms crossed, obviously impatient for Talia to finish eating breakfast.

She bit into a ripe pear, letting its sweet juice drip down her chin.

Byzas darted forward, dabbing at her chin with a cloth and taking the remaining pear away from her. "You must learn how to eat!" he said. "For now, it's enough to protect the silk garment." He handed her a triangle of cheese and a slice of bread. "Eat, and drink coffee."

Talia almost choked on the coffee. It was thick and bitter. "I'm glad I only need to drink a small cup of it," she said.

Inga laughed, and Byzas let a small smile creep across his face. "You will find this coffee offered everywhere you go, so you must get accustomed to it. You will add sugar and sip it slowly. Sometimes there will be tea. Both of these come from afar, and are considered special."

"What about mead?

"A drink of barbarians, not ladies." He took away the cup and plate. "Sir. We have work to do."

Talia sat patiently as he brushed her hair, starting at the tips of each strand, working out tangles, until her hair hung smooth and silken. Then to her surprise, he gathered handfuls of it, twisted and fastened it in a crown atop her head with pearl encrusted combs. "Now the face," he said.

Talia tried not to flinch as he spread fragrant oil on her arms, her hands, her face. She closed her eyes and tried to imagine that Andrei was touching her skin, but the touch was not the same. She made herself stay very still as Byzas bent to massage the oil onto her legs. "You have rough skin. I will do what I can, but it will take time to bring you up to what is expected."

"This is the way I am," Talia protested, jerking her eyes open. "Why should I change?"

"Don't you want to be more beautiful? Don't you want your master to be proud of you when he displays you?"

So this was the way Andrei wanted her, and he'd told her she needed to please him. She didn't cry out when her eyebrows were plucked and she didn't object when her lips were stained a vivid red and a black substance was spread on her eyelids.

Inga, who had thrown the offered red silk around herself, watched the beautifying procedure. "You look different, Talia. Not at all like the woman I met on the ship."

"Let me see," she commanded.

Byzas handed her a small mirror. She held it this way and that, hardly recognizing herself in the painted, primped image she saw.

"You are almost ready," Byzas pronounced. He produced a pair of sandals and placed them on her feet, winding the leather thongs about her ankle. "Now, hold out your arms," he commanded, and when she did so, he placed a broad metal bracelet on each arm.

"Ready?" Byzas asked.

Talia stood and nodded. She felt awkward in the strange shoes, and brazenly bare in the short blue garment that bared her arms and much of her legs. She took a few steps, adjusting to the feel of the sandals on her bare feet. She missed the leather boots, the moss stuffed in for softness, but Andrei must want her to dress like the women of this city, Miklagaard, he called it, Byzantium or Constantinople others called it. She would have to discover which name she was supposed to use.

She followed Byzas out of the shaded compound, through the gate and out into the brilliant morning sunshine. There stood Andrei, glorious and handsome as she'd never seen him before, in a bright red uniform glittering with gold trim. Perhaps he had sent the red silk toga so that they might be wearing the same color. She stopped, awestruck at the sight of him, unable to move. He smiled and held out his hand, and she walked forward to take it.

"You look beautiful, Talia," he said. "Everyone who sees you will be impressed."

"Who will see me? Where are we going?"

"You'll see."

Chapter 20

As Byzas turned back with a self-satisfied smile, Andrei led her along the paved street to stand for a moment in the shade of a tree. He let go of her hand and looked down at her face, scarcely recognizing her. "We are going to tour Miklagaard, the Great Town. It has more churches than I can name, all of them fine examples of architecture, and gardens everywhere. There are hospitals and orphanages to care for the less fortunate. I trust we will not need either of those. Byzas told me that you have already seen and used the public baths. What do you think of the city so far?"

"I can't say, master. All I have seen is our slaves' courtyard, the public baths and what little I saw of the city on our hurried walk from the port." She had been looking around at the city, up at towers, down at the patterned pavement beneath their feet. Now she made herself look at him, though when she did she could scarcely breathe.

"For today, you must not call me 'master,' but 'Andrei Ivanovich,' my full name. We will enter the Palace grounds. I have permission. On the way to the Hippodrome we will see the Pharos, a lighthouse that lets the emperor send signals to his ships and armies afar."

There was so much that she didn't understand in what he said. "The signals? That's how Prince Vladimir knew when the Princess Anna would arrive, and how his message got back to the emperor about Kherson?"

He nodded approvingly. "You're intelligent, Talia. You'll soon learn your way around the city. Let's walk on."

She had a multitude of questions, but she didn't want to annoy him by asking too many. Once they were inside the Palace compound, he pointed to the Pharos. She looked up and up, until her neck ached. At the very top she saw a man, looking no taller than her thumb. "How do they send signals?" she asked.

"At night they hold up lanterns, one or more, depending on the message, and black them out in a set pattern. We must walk around the city tonight as well as this morning, especially to the House of Lanterns, a shop that's lit up at night."

She looked down from the great lighthouse and back at Andrei, dazzled by him as much as by the exciting city around her. She longed to touch his face, run her fingers through his hair, go into the circle of his arms. But he was not holding out his arms, only his bent left arm. He took her hand and tucked it into the crook of his elbow so that they were walking side by side, and she could no longer look into his eyes. He pressed his arm against his side, and she could feel his body warm and firm, and the shape of his ribcage. What did he have in mind for her, and where were they going? She had to ask him more questions. "What is the Hippodrome?"

"A great stadium."

"What is that?"

He chuckled. "I forget that you've never been in such a city. It's a big open place like the city center in Kiev, only bigger. All around the sides are seats so people can watch races and games, and sometimes executions." At her stunned look, he regretted saying that.

"Why would anyone want to watch executions?" She stopped and pulled her hand free from him.

"There must be witnesses to see that justice is carried out. The families of the victims want to see it done, and some people just enjoy violence. They used to watch wild animals tear humans apart."

"Then this Miklagaard only *looks* beautiful," she said. She was aware that people around them had stopped to listen and stare.

"It's fortunate you don't speak Greek," he said, "or some of these people might commit violence against you for your criticism. Vikings and Russians can be violent too," he reminded her. "We'll tarry here for a while, just in case there are executions being carried out this morning. They're usually done early in the day. If the emperor passes this way, we'll know the executions are over. He doesn't like to watch them either. He's a Christian, and he's trying to change many things in his empire."

Almost as if Andrei had conjured up the procession, a trumpet sounded and uniformed guards strode ahead of the emperor's retinue and stood at intervals along both sides of the street, bows with arrows nocked and ready. Andrei pulled Talia back out of the way, into an alley, but close enough so that she could watch the spectacular procession. The emperor sat high and straight on a white horse that stepped briskly, prancing from left to right and back. Its saddle, bridle, and reins were all tipped in gold, glittering in the sunlight. The emperor wore a scarlet cloak over a white toga, and white leather boots trimmed in gold.

"He's not wearing a crown," Talia whispered.

Andrei signaled her to be silent until the procession had passed. "This is not a victory procession or a saint's feast day," he said. "The emperor is just going to watch the sports at the Hippodrome, and so shall we. We're almost there."

They moved along with the crowd, and entered through a stone archway. Talia stared around at the vast space. Life-size sculptures of horses standing on polished stone blocks adorned the Hippodrome. The crowd closed in on them, and then stopped, blocking their way, and Talia felt a moment of panic. All she could see was a mass of bodies, with their backs to her. What was happening? Andrei gripped her arm and pulled her close to his side, turning her face against his chest, but she had already seen the cause of the stopping: a head stood on a pike at each side of the entrance, the eyes staring, blood still dripping from each neck. This was almost as bad as being among the Pechenegs, she thought, but dared not say that to Andrei. At least here it was beautiful and clean. Some poor wretches had died here, but she was in no danger.

Talia reveled in the warm comfort of Andrei's chest, and of knowing that he wanted to shield her from something ugly, but they couldn't stand thus, blocking others who wanted to enter the Hippodrome. She lifted her head. "I'll be all right. I saw heads without bodies and bodies without heads when the Pechenegs attacked us. Do you remember the head Anatoly took to the prince? I hated seeing it, but it was there beside us and I didn't run from it. I just don't want to see the head being removed or hear the terror."

"I should have remembered that you and Inga were as calm as any of our warriors," he said.

"Whose heads do you think these are?"

"Corrupt officials, very likely. The emperor punishes cheats and thieves." When she nodded, he asked, "Shall we find our seats?"

Andrei took her hand to guide her toward the steps, and then went ahead, turning to make sure she could maneuver the high rising stone steps. Talia felt awkward in the strange sandals and the long flowing garments. For a moment she trod on the edge of the dress, and feared that she might fall forward against him, but his bulk shielded her and she recovered her balance.

They climbed upward until Talia was gasping for breath, and finally sat close beside the steps on the curving stone platform. Others moved over to make room.

"Did they want to sit here?" she whispered.

"Probably, but they recognize my rank and your clothing, and we have precedence." He indicated the medallion hanging around his neck by a heavy chain. "This trading medallion is our protection, and our badge to enter palaces and the Hippodrome."

Talia looked around her at the magnificent city. In one direction she saw a tall stone tower close to the harbor, and in the other direction an enormous building with many domes. Andrei looked where she pointed. "The tall structure that's pointed on top is the Tower of Galata," he said. "Watchmen man it all the time, making sure no enemy ships slip into the harbor of the Great Town. The big church is Hagia Sophia. It's more than four hundred years old." He pointed across the Hippodrome. "And there is the emperor's special seat. Now that he is seated, the spectacles will begin." He gestured and bowed at someone sitting near the emperor. The man gave a slight returning bow. Several people nearby turned to stare.

"Why are they looking at us?" Talia asked, glad that she was not speaking Greek, so no one would understand her words of embarrassment.

"They're staring because you are so beautiful," Andrei returned. "Also, as you may notice that most of the women—and the men too—have dark hair. They haven't seen anyone with stunning red hair like yours. Smile to let them know you accept their admiration."

Talia made herself smile. Something was still troubling her that had sunk into her thoughts earlier. "Why did you say I should not call you 'master' today?"

"Because you don't look like a slave today. I have had you dressed as a courtesan, a woman of the court."

"I thank you for the beautiful clothing." She ran her hand over the silken fabric of her dress, loving the brush of it against her skin. The wide bracelets on both her wrists glimmered in the sunlight. "May I keep this, or is it just for today, like the dress trimmed in fur that you once let me wear?

"This clothing is yours to keep, and we may buy you more garments, perhaps even more jewelry besides the bracelets, depending on what events you are invited to."

"I am to be invited somewhere?"

"We don't know yet, but considering how people look at you, and what a good job Byzas did preparing you, I suspect that a

175

certain highly placed nobleman may invite you to see more of the city."

"Will you also be invited? Will Inga?"

"I'll be with you to translate, but I'll keep back so that you'll have some time alone with the man in question. Inga? No."

"Why did Anatoly not send beautiful clothing for Inga?"

"Because he plans to marry her, so he has no need to show her off here. He will buy lengths of silk for the wedding "

Talia sucked in her breath, stunned, and felt her face flaming with shame and anger. Andrei had dressed her up to show off to some other man. He didn't want her himself! She leapt to her feet, ready to run back to the slave quarters. But which way to run?

Andrei guessed her intention and pulled her down. "This is not the time to fight or to act like a barbarian. Sit down." His voice was low, but his tone carried menace.

Talia sat. Tears slid down her cheeks. She'd been so pleased that Andrei was buying her things, and had wanted to look beautiful when he saw her. She'd looked forward to being with him, and now it was all like a rotten fruit—something that had seemed beautiful and good but was now distasteful. She'd felt sorry for Inga, when actually Inga was the lucky one. Anatoly loved her, planned to marry her, even if he didn't send her gifts. Andrei's gifts were a way to buy off his conscience, a way to make her attractive enough that some other man would want her—would even *buy* her and own her. And there was nothing she could do. If she ran away, she'd be found and returned. The Greeks respected slavery. Andrei had told her he'd keep her if she pleased him, and she'd tried, but it wasn't enough.

All she could do was try to get along with the 'highly born man' that Andrei had intended for her. She looked in the direction Andrei had looked, but she had no idea which man Andrei had bowed to. She'd been too consumed with wonder at her surroundings, with being with Andrei, to notice another man. Her body quivered with sobs.

"You may as well watch," Andrei said, not even pretending not to notice her distress. "We can't leave now."

Reluctantly, Talia nodded. She swiped the edge of her shawl across her eyes to wipe away her tears, and turned her attention to the spectacle that was beginning below.

Two figures came out onto the field near the emperor's box, and faced each other. Their bodies were fur-covered, horns protruded from their hair, and their faces were grotesque smiling masks with long teeth. But their arms were bare and their hands ended in long claws. "Are they animals or men?" Talia asked.

"Men dressed as animals. Long ago men fought lions and bears and bulls, and crowds watched as men were torn apart by claws and fangs. The Byzantines are more enlightened now. Men dress like animals and fight each other—not with swords as they used to do, but with their bare hands. This way they don't usually kill each other, but they can do some damage."

The two men, one garbed in gray fur, the other in brown, circled each other, arms up and bent, with clawed fists protecting their faces. Once in a while one or the other would lunge forward with clawed fingers outstretched, much as an animal would.

Talia's own nails dug into her fists as she watched the two figures slash at each other. The two seemed wild, savage. She knew rising excitement and a certain dread of what might come. When the brown one slashed across the gray facemask and tore it off, drawing blood, she sucked in her breath and closed her eyes. Why did men enjoy watching other men fight?

Then the gray-furred one struck back, ripping the brown fur off his opponent's arm with a blow so strong the sound of a bone snapping carried up into the stands. The crowd stood in mass and roared its approval, and Talia jumped to her feet as well.

Andrei pulled her down. "You must not behave so."

"But it was a fair fight. The injured one defended himself, just as I defended myself against Rognol." As she spoke the dreaded name, she wondered where he was, and where was Marya? She sat back onto the hard stone seat, and scanned the crowd.

"It's not a matter of what's happening on the field, it's how you behave. It's unseemly for women to cheer so fiercely, unless they are lower class."

"How could I be lower class? I am a slave, as you keep reminding me. Master."

"Keep your voice down, and cover your hair. We have attracted enough attention. Perhaps we should go. Or can you sit quietly and watch the clowns and the horse races like a well-brought-up young woman would?"

"I shall," Talia answered, her voice low and tinged with anger, as she pulled a bit of the blue silk up over her hair. "Why must I do this?"

"Look around you. The Byzantine women cover their hair and appear modest, though they are entitled to participate in public affairs and own property, and many have power in the government."

"Then their modesty is a pretense."

"And you would do well to learn pretense," he returned with a whisper.

"So I should smile and pretend to be happy that you are selling me after I have tried so hard to please you and have failed."

"You have pleased me, but buying and selling is a business matter. This is not the time or place to discuss it." He pointed toward the center of the field where three figures dressed in bright floppy suits ran out, turned somersault and cartwheeled their way across the space. They stood, bowed to slight applause. Then two stood side by side while the third jumped onto their shoulders, one foot on each man. After a spattering of applause, the top man turned and stood on the shoulders of one man, and bent to grab the hands of the other, pulling him up and up until all three stood like a tower. Talia clapped along with the crowd. Fighting she had seen all her life, but such leaping and balancing were new to her.

"That was amazing," she said.

Andrei grinned. "You may enjoy the horse races too."

"Do you still have your horse?"

"Of course. What is a warrior without a horse?"

"Will your horse be in the races?"

"No, he's trained for battle, not racing."

"Do you still have my goat? Mine and Inga's?"

He nodded. "I didn't let them kill it. It's been spared for a bit longer—at least until we decide what becomes of you. If the man who is interested in you meets my price, you will stay on here. Then Inga can decide if she wants to take the goat back with her, or perhaps kill it for her wedding feast."

"You are cruel! You discuss my goat and me as if we are both equal, and as if neither of us matters to you." She turned away from him, stung.

He was spared making an answer by trumpet sounds announcing the beginning of the races.

In spite of herself, Talia turned back to watch. "What kind of carts are those?" she asked, pointing to where the horses and drivers were lining up.

"They are chariots, fashioned after the Roman ones."

"Why are the drivers standing up? It can't be like our sledges, where standing up makes the front lift and go better over the snow."

"No, that's not it. The drivers have better control of the horses if they stand. Their long whips can reach the front-most horses."

At a signal the row of chariots raced forward, churning up a thick dust from the track. It swirled upward to cover the spectators at the lower rows of seats with a fine film, and even Talia felt grit in her teeth. The spinning wheels, the bright helmets of the drivers and the metal fittings on the horses glittered in the sunlight, forming a colorful collage through the dust. The crowd roared, almost drowning out the shouts of the drivers and the pounding of the horses' hooves. Despite her anger at Andrei, Talia was caught up in the excitement of the race. She clutched his arm and pointed to the black and gold chariot that was far out ahead of the others.

"That's the one I bet on," Andrei said, and roared his approval of the driver. Then he added, "But a fast start doesn't mean he will win. Anything can happen. A horse can go lame, a leather harness can break, especially if someone has cut it beforehand."

"Who would do that?"

"Many people. His personal enemies, someone who has bet against him, the grooms of the other drivers' horses. Sometimes horses are even poisoned."

"How cruel! The horses are beautiful, and look how they are panting and doing their best to win."

The chariots raced around the huge track, circling the statues of other horses, and were only tiny specks at the other end of the Hippodrome. Talia realized she'd been gripping Andrei's arm and let go. She strained to see which driver was ahead.

"They'll be back very quickly," Andrei assured her, and Talia saw the black chariot round the curve at the far end of the track and begin its return circuit.

As the chariots approached them, the driver of the red chariot lashed his horses to overtake the white one, but he misjudged and his chariot snagged the back wheel of the white one. The crowd grew suddenly silent, watching the disaster. Both chariots overturned, in a tangle of metal, splintered wood and struggling horses. The driver of the green chariot, which had been last in the race, swerved to avoid the crash, and began to overtake the black chariot. The last horse pulling the white chariot struggled to his feet and the team of four began to run, manes flying in the air, frightened, fleeing without their driver. He lay in the dust, and after a stunned moment managed to pull himself up and run after his horses. Far down the track others came out to intercept the runaway animals, and eventually caught their bridles and halted them.

"Does this happen all the time?" Talia asked, concerned about the horses pulling the red chariot, one of which had still not managed to right itself.

"Too often to suit me. I hate to see a horse injured. It means death to a noble animal, but this crowd loves it. They come to see accidents and death."

Talia shivered. "At least now your driver has a better chance to win." She scanned the track, looking for the two remaining chariots. They rounded the curve and at a signal, drew to a stop before the emperor's box. Men ran out onto the track to carry away the injured drivers of the red and the white chariots and to clear up the wreckage. Others came out to rake the track, readying it for another race.

"Who wins?" Talia asked.

"My driver," Andrei said. "He was ahead when the race was halted. Let's go collect my wager. As soon as the emperor leaves."

"Then everything is finished for today?"

"Yes and No. I want your likely buyer to meet you. The emperor requested that I bring you to the palace."

"The emperor is buying me?" Talia's eyes flew wide with astonishment.

"No, of course not. He has a wife, and you were not born of the purple. It is a distant cousin of the emperor, but you would from time to time be invited to the palace as the cousin's wife—or even as his concubine, so he wants to meet you and give his approval before the buyer and I discuss how many besants you are worth."

"And I have no choice—it is all between you and him?"

Andrei didn't answer, but Talia knew that if he had, his answer would have been, 'You are a slave.'

"I will go down first," Andrei said. "If you falter, I'll make sure you don't tumble. In any case, you are supposed to walk behind me."

Numbly, Talia followed him down the narrow stone steps and across the dusty racecourse, careful to keep her dress lifted above the dirt. A thin, dark-haired man in a white toga awaited them near the emperor's box.

"Hail, Sextus Demetrios," Andrei said, extending his hand and bowing slightly.

The other man bowed as well. "I believe I owe you some besants, Andrei Ivanovich," he said. "Your wager was a lucky guess."

"Perhaps," Andrei conceded. "Or perhaps I am a good judge of horseflesh, used as I am to riding in battle."

"It could not be foreseen that my chariot and driver would be overturned by another's carelessness."

"True," Andrei said. "There will be other races and other wagers. Did your horses suffer any injuries?"

"Fortunately, no."

When are they going to stop talking about horses? Talia wondered, studying the man called Sextus Demetrios. He had a neatly trimmed black beard and his hair had not begun to thin, so he was not very old, perhaps not much older than Andrei. He was dressed like many of the men she had seen on the street in the short walk, and at various places around the Hippodrome, in a white flowing garment clasped at the shoulder with a big metal ornament. His sandals were decorated with metal, and their leather straps wound around his ankles. Sneaking a look at his feet and legs as far up as she could see, to where the toga began, Talia noted that he had no masses of black hair growing on his legs. That was in his favor. Broad bracelets encased both his wrists, above clean hands. His face was bronzed, and bore no traces of anger or dissolution.

"Do you approve of what you see?" he asked. It needed no translation for her to guess what he'd said.

Talia blushed furiously, embarrassed at being caught staring at him. Andrei would be angry and reprove her for her lack of modesty. She managed to nod, and then looked down at the ground. Her hair covering had slipped, and she tugged it back into place.

"Don't cover your hair," he said, and Andrei translated. "It is a wondrous color, like sunrise on a spring morning." He turned to Andrei and said something Talia could not understand.

Andrei answered him at length, and Sextus Demetrios made a short remark. The two men shook hands and Andrei turned Talia away. As they walked back toward the slaves' quarters, Talia said, "I don't like people talking around me when I can't understand."

"You must become accustomed to it. It will be a spur to learning the language. For now, I will have to translate."

"What did he ask you?"

"He asked why I am willing to sell such a beautiful woman."

"And what did you say?"

"That because you are a Slav, I can't marry you, and yet I find you very attractive. I might father a child with you, and I would not want my child to be a bastard."

Talia's heart swelled as Andrei said that he was attracted to her, though she had known it from the first time he touched her, but her spirits sank at the rest of his words. She almost missed Andrei's statement: "Sextus Demetrios said that he had no such dilemma."

Chapter 21

Talia held her tears until Andrei had gone and Byzas was escorting her into the slaves' quarters. Once they were alone, out of earshot of Andrei and away from the listening ears of other slaves, Byzas asked, "Did your master not like the way you look in the clothing he chose?"

"He said I looked beautiful."

Byzas nodded and smiled. "Then he must have also approved of the way I fashioned your hair and adorned your face. So why are you crying?"

"He still plans to sell me, and I love him!" Talia burst out.

Byzas shook his head in disapproval. "Slave women cannot afford the luxury of loving someone who has power over them. Did he mention any potential buyers?"

Talia sniffed. From a fold in his toga, Byzas produced a handkerchief. "If you insist on crying, you must always have one of these in your possession. It will be useful also if you attend the races, to ward off dust."

"We did attend the races," Talia said. "We saw a fight, some men standing tall on each other's shoulders, and the races. Two carts overturned."

"Then you have been entertained. And what did you think of our wonderful city?"

"It's beautiful," Talia said. "But I want to go home to the north, to Kiev."

"We can't always live life as we would wish," Byzas said, with a tinge of sadness in his voice. "I would not have chosen to become a eunuch, but duty to my family required it. I have made the best of my situation. I live in luxury, I have a certain amount of power, and I can help my family. You may find that if you become the concubine or wife of a powerful man, your life can be pleasant indeed. Who is this buyer?"

"Andrei called him Sextus Demetrios."

Byzas stopped walking and turned in surprise. "You have been introduced very high into our society, from your first day. Did he approve of you?"

Talia nodded. "He asked my master why he was selling such a beautiful woman," she said, quoting what Andrei had told her. "He wants to show me something of the city tomorrow, and take me to the palace."

"And what did you think of him?" He shrugged and went on without waiting for her answer, "But it doesn't matter. We must prepare you especially for your tryst with him, and I will train you what to say so that he will choose you. Then you must keep me in mind and bring me into your household. I can be very useful."

Talia laughed in spite of her unhappiness. "You are very sure of me, and of yourself."

"It is always wise to plan ahead, and act accordingly. One never knows who may rise from the lowliest to high places, or who might fall from power." He turned again toward the slaves' quarters and thrust a key into the lock of the door. He stopped. It was already unlocked. He pushed it open and held it for Talia to enter.

Inga sat on her bed, dressed in new finery. She looked up with a radiant smile. "Anatoly sent me a dress to wear for shopping, and he will take me tomorrow to choose fabrics for my wedding dress. We will be married here. Then we can openly share quarters on our return home."

"That's wonderful, Inga!" Talia said, happy for her friend, but envious almost beyond bearing.

"And he will be baptized before our wedding, so that it can be performed in a church here."

Byzas held out his keys. "I won't lock you in this afternoon. You are free to walk in the courtyard. If you wish to go to the baths, send for me to escort you. Tonight I will regrettably lock you in once more—not to keep you from escaping, but for your protection against men who might harm you." He bowed and left.

Inga studied Talia's face. "What's wrong, Talia? I've been so busy babbling about my own happiness that I paid no attention to you."

"Andrei took me to the races, and that was exciting. Miklagaard is a beautiful city."

"But what happened? Didn't he like the way you were dressed?"

"Yes," Talia said bitterly. "He thought I looked beautiful enough to attract a highly placed buyer. He introduced me to the man."

"Oh, Talia, I'm sorry." Inga's smile faded and she touched Talia's hand with her own. "I know how you care for Andrei, and he's ten times a fool if he sells you, no matter who buys you or how much he pays for you. Can I do anything?" Her face brightened with an idea. "Perhaps if Anatoly told him how you feel, he might change his mind."

"Oh, no, don't! I don't think it would do any good anyway," Talia said. "The man he's chosen to sell me to is a cousin of the emperor. Andrei says I'll have a good life, and that he is doing what is best for me. He doesn't want me himself, and doesn't love me."

"He must!" Inga insisted. "I've seen the way he looks at you."

"He lusts after me, but he doesn't love me. He thinks of me only as a slave, a Slav, inferior to him. He told Sextus Demetrios he could never marry me, and doesn't want to take a chance on my having his bastard child."

"I never before thought Andrei was cruel, but he is!" Inga declared vehemently. "How could he speak so harshly about you? We must think of something."

But by morning they had not had any good ideas. When Byzas came in to dress Talia's hair, he brought plates of food and indicated that they were to eat while he worked. He paid little heed to Inga, but went straight to Talia and set down a tray of food before her. "While I prepare you, you must prepare yourself. Eat bread and meat so you will not be hungry when your buyer invites you to dine."

"But why not? Would it not be a compliment to enjoy the food he offers?"

Byzas shook his head. "Slaves are always hungry, courtesans are not. Eat a small bit of each dish and say how delicious it is. If it is something truly terrible, he will not think it amiss if you only eat a sample. You can always say that it is unfamiliar and must be an acquired taste. Eat a few grapes, and let just a tiny drop of juice escape. Then delicately lick it off your lips like this." He ran just the tip of his tongue across his bottom lip. "He will find it tantalizing, and will fantasize about his own tongue touching those lips."

Talia sat very still, her gaze locked on him. "I never thought to be taught to eat," she said.

"I am glad not to need such instructions," Inga added.

Byzas laughed lightly. "I am not teaching you to eat, I am training you in the ways of seducing powerful men, men who have perhaps lost a portion of their desire and need stimulation. I think you will be an excellent pupil. Now eat a grape and show me what you will do."

Talia reached for a single grape from the stem, bit into it and let juice moisten her lips, as he'd instructed. She ran her tongue across her lip, imagining Andrei's lips against hers.

"Now smile," Byzas instructed.

Talia did.

"With your eyes open. Smile, and then look down, as if you have been too brazen."

Talia almost laughed aloud. This training in seduction was ridiculous. Either Sextus Demetrios bought her or he didn't. She recalled the lusty way Andrei had taken her, his mouth on hers and on her breasts, making her body tingle all over. She'd needed no seduction to arouse him, and hadn't even intended to. It had just happened. Maybe Byzas was right, that her future owner had lost part of his desire and needed stimulation. "Is that all I must do?" she asked.

"That is only the beginning. When you walk, stand upright, proudly. Don't look down."

"But what if I stumble on a paving stone?"

"Then he will be embarrassed, for he will have led you onto an unsafe area. He will then be in your debt. A slight stumble might be good, for then he will take your arm to assist you in walking, and will make sure it does not happen again. But be assured it will only happen out in a public area. In his home the floors will be smooth polished marble. There will be no hazards for your feet." He smirked. "The other hazards will be to your honor. Are you a virgin?"

Talia hesitated. She knew Inga was listening as well as Byzas. She shook her head.

"Have you lain with many men?" Byzas asked.

"No! Only one. My owner."

"Buyers understand that, though every man wants to be the first to dip his beak into your sweet moisture. You must behave so that the question of your virginity never comes up until the final negotiations for your sale price. At that point, the buyer may insist on a physical examination of you to determine whether you are intact. It is your task to see that the buyer has become so besotted with you that he no longer cares that you have been claimed by another."

Talia stared at him. How could she manage flirtation? She had never had to do such a thing and didn't know how.

Byzas answered her unspoken question. "I will train you the best I know how. Shall we begin?"

Talia nodded. Inga watched, and in her peripheral vision Talia saw her friend shake her head in doubt. Inga had no need for such superficial tricks. Her future was secure, as long as Anatoly lived.

Byzas laid down the comb and let her hair fall loosely onto her shoulders. "We shall get back to the adornment, but the buyer has already seen you and admired you, so your beauty is established in his mind. How you behave will mean a great deal more from now on. So, pretend that I am the buyer. I take your hand." He tsk-tsked. "It's a pity that we don't have time to whiten and soften your hands. They are brown and hard from your journey, but then, so are the hands of most slaves. I bring your hand to my side. What do you do?"

"I don't know."

"You allow him to press your hand against him for a short time, and then you gently pull your hand back and look down. Do it."

Talia complied.

"Not bad. Now, pretend that the buyer has just paid you a compliment, which your owner has translated. What do you say?"

"I don't speak his language. Whatever I say must be translated by my master."

"True, but you must say something, and the tone of your voice will tell him much of what he wants to know. You have a loud voice, which you must learn to mitigate. Speak softly, smile. Practice on me." He took her hand and said, "Talia Militskaya, you are very beautiful."

"Thank you," Talia said in a low voice.

"Smile. Pretend I am the man you are trying to charm, the man who can make your life very pleasant, and who may become the father of your children."

Talia tried a smile, but she couldn't envision the stranger Andrei had introduced her to as the father of her children. That should be Andrei, she thought, or Oleg, a man like her, tall and stalwart, with red-gold tresses and a muscular body.

"Not like that!" Byzas scolded. "I realize that you find it difficult to consider me as a suitor. Close your eyes and imagine you are being led to the altar by your husband to be. You are happy, and grateful to him for rescuing you from slavery and raising you to a high position by giving you his name."

Talia closed her eyes obediently, but the only face that came to her mind was Andrei's, his blue eyes studying her, his lips parted slightly as he leaned in to kiss her. She raised her hand to touch his face, but her eyes flew open as she came out of her reverie and knew that Andrei was not with her.

"That was too much," Byzas chided. "Smile, but don't touch him. You have good teeth, unlike many of our women, so allow teeth to show. He may touch your hair or your cheek. Despite the days you have spent in the sunlight, your skin is not damaged, just darkened. That makes an interesting contrast with your bright hair." He sighed. "You will simply have to do the best you can. It's impossible for me to change your lifetime of behavior in one morning."

"What shall I do at the palace?" Talia asked.

"You are going to the palace? Why do you think that?"

"My master, Andrei, told me so."

Byzas threw up his hands helplessly. "You should have told me that first. All I can advise you at this point is to look around at other women and do as they do. One thing you must do is to bow low before the emperor if you are brought into his presence."

Inga snorted. "It's good that you are the one being introduced at the palace and not I," she said. "In my country I am like an emperor's daughter, and I have no wish to bow to the one who rules here. I want to go back to the northland as soon as we can."

"It is indeed fortunate," Byzas conceded, turning on Inga. "I doubt my ability to convert you into a courtesan." He picked up the comb again and deftly arranged Talia's hair, thrusting a jeweled pin into a coil atop her head. Over it he arranged a gauzy silk scarf, draping it about her shoulders so that the ends fell forward, camouflaging her breasts. "Modesty," he reminded her. He applied color to her lips and cheeks and pronounced her ready to go forth. Inga nodded her approval.

"What will you do today?" Talia asked Inga.

"Anatoly will come for me soon. We are going to church. He is trying to decide if he believes enough in the Christ as I do that he can be baptized. I already believe, but I want to see the magnificent Hagia Sofia."

Talia remembered hearing that name, but it brought forth no image. She didn't stop to answer the puzzle, but followed Byzas out to meet Andrei.

Chapter 22

When she saw Andrei waiting for her just outside her quarters, she wanted to run to him, but she forced herself to smile and to walk slowly with her head held high, as Byzas had said would appeal to a man. She could practice her wiles on Andrei until they reached the place where Sextus Demetrios was to meet them.

"Good morning, Andrei Ivanovich," she said, smiling at him as she extended her hand.

"Why are you so formal? This is not your usual behavior."

"Don't you like the way I look? You chose the garments and instructed Byzas the eunuch to dress and adorn me."

"Yes, you look beautiful. But you don't sound like yourself or walk the way you used to."

"Byzas said this would appeal to the buyer you have chosen to own me. Where are we meeting him?"

"At his house. This way." He walked off at a fast pace and she struggled to walk as Byzas had instructed, not looking down, just managing to keep up. "Please, Andrei, go slowly."

He paused to let her catch up. "We are late. That damned eunuch took too long getting you ready. He must think it makes you appealing if someone must wait for you."

Sextus Demetrios was standing by the doorway to his home. "I will offer coffee and the hospitality of my home later," he said, after greeting them. "Now I would like to attend a Christian service at Hagia Sofia. Will you join me?"

Andrei looked startled. "But we are not Christians."

Demetrios nodded. "I am aware of that, but we Christians are instructed to spread the good news to all who come our way, and if our negotiations succeed, Talia Militskaya will need to become a Christian so that we may be married at the Hagia Sofia."

Talia heard her name and asked Andrei, "What did he say about me?"

"We are going to church, to Hagia Sophia," he answered shortly and motioned her to walk beside Demetrios.

As they walked, Demetrios took her hand and tucked it into the crook of his arm. "I know some words of your language from trading, but I can't use them with you. Such words are not suitable for courtship."

Soon Talia was looking up at the grand church she'd seen from the Hippodrome. Its central dome rose above a circle of other domes, all topped by silvery rooftops. She was still staring upward when Demetrios said, "Inside. Upstairs for women." He pointed toward the rear of the church and opened a small door. Talia went in and climbed the narrow stone steps. She came out onto a darkened balcony and sat down beside two other shadowy forms.

What was she supposed to do next? She peered down through a wooden lattice to the floor below. It was fashioned of shining marble covered with flower-patterned carpets. Men stood in clusters, holding lighted candles. A shaft of light fell onto the center of the church, and Talia looked upward to see where it was coming from.

The domed ceiling stunned her with its beauty. Its entire surface was covered in tiny pieces of stone or glass—she couldn't tell which—forming scenes of people in bright clothing. Gold framed the heads of some of the figures. Below the dome there were more pictures on the walls, and in the smaller dome above where the women sat, other pictures entranced her. Who were these people in the pictures, and who had built this marvelous place? She could scarcely get her breath for the overwhelming magnificence of it all.

She turned to her right as someone else made her way onto the seat in the semi-darkness. Talia moved over to make room, and realized the newcomer was Inga. Her eyes had grown accustomed to the darkness, but Inga's had not, and she gasped at Talia's touch. "Shhh!" Talia said.

"Oh, Talia, I'm glad you're here," she whispered. "We can share all this. Isn't it beautiful?"

"I've never seen anything like it," Talia said. "Pictures made of little pieces of stone that look like real people."

"Our churches are so plain compared to this. It seems as if we can almost look right into heaven from here."

"Who are the people in the pictures?"

"I'm not sure about all of them, but whenever there is a picture of Jesus, he has a gold halo around his head." She kept her voice low, and pointed. "There he is as a baby, in his mother's arms. They both have halos, because he is the son of God, and his mother is holy too." She pointed again. "He was crucified."

Talia looked at the hideous picture of a man almost naked, hanging bleeding from two crossed pieces of wood. "But he died. What kind of god lets his son die like that?"

"Shhh! The service is about to begin. We'll talk later."

The clusters of men moved to each side as a procession came from the main door and made its way slowly toward the center of the church, singing as they came. The men wore long black robes and dark crowns on their heads. Their hair and beards were black, so that in all the mass of men she could pick out Andrei by his red-blonde hair. He was looking up to where she sat, and she longed to signal to him, to let him know how she felt about being in Hagia Sofia, but she dared not move.

The music swept over her, carrying her to an unknown state, the way she had felt sometimes as she emerged from a dream. Candle flames wavered hypnotically and made golden shimmering patterns on the big silver cross the first man of the procession carried. Another swung a metal lantern back and forth, and a smoky perfume rose into the air. Talia felt tears sliding down her face from all of it: the poor son of God suffering, the haunting music, the golden halos and brilliant colors. The voices blended, rose to the dome, and seemed to envelope all the worshipers. "Kyrie," was the sound Talia heard. She must remember to ask Inga, or perhaps Sextus Demetrios, what it meant. Inga was singing the word too, bowing her head over and over.

Was this the reason her mother had become a Christian? Had she ever heard such music, seen such a wondrous place? Or had she somehow believed without all this?

One of the priests went up into a little tower and began to speak, and when he paused, the people spoke, that same word, "Kyrie," and sometimes "Alleluia." Talia found herself joining in without knowing what she was saying, carried along by the majesty and the beauty of it all. She wanted the music to go on, and wanted to know what the words meant, and why this Jesus who died a horrible death had such power over people, even her own mother.

Talia was startled when Inga stood and the woman on the other side of her did as well. "Time to go," Inga said. "Our men will wait for us downstairs."

Talia followed Inga downstairs, hardly aware of the stone steps beneath her feet and of the women behind her. At the door she stopped and let other women pass so she could peer into the huge church and see paintings and mosaics hidden from her view above. Inga went off to join Anatoly. They wanted to talk to a priest about Anatoly's baptism and their wedding, Inga said. Andrei and Demetrios found Talia there, a rapt expression lighting her face as she looked about at the icons and up at the domes.

"What did you think?" Demetrios asked, breaking her trance.

"Svarog and Perun have no such altars," she said.

Andrei laughed. "Our gods need no such structures, though I admit I was moved by the words and music and the building itself."

Demetrios looked from one to another, until Andrei explained what they'd said.

"I didn't understand it," Talia said, hoping that he comprehended what she said. Andrei translated.

"I shall explain," Demetrios said, "as we dine. I too worshipped false gods until the spirit of the Christ touched my soul."

Andrei translated, and Talia asked, "The Christ?"

"Jesus Christ."

"Why do you worship someone who died?"

"Because he arose from the dead. He had a new life, and went to heaven."

They started walking, moving with the crowd that thinned out as they approached the home of Demetrios. A servant opened the door to his knock and he bowed to indicate that Talia and Andrei were welcome. He spoke briefly to Andrei, who translated to Talia: "Sextus Demetrios has asked if you would like to retire to the ladies' rooms." Talia understood that this was the way he referred to her need to relieve herself, and nodded. Demetrios tapped on a heavy metal circle suspended above the floor, and a woman servant appeared and led Talia to a private part of the house.

The toilet was of fine porcelain, much finer than the facility at the slave quarters, and the floor was shining marble, immaculate, with not a smudge or speck of dirt anywhere. The maid left while Talia used the toilet, then returned with a soft towel. She poured warm, perfumed water over Talia's hands, and handed her a bowl of soap. Talia blotted her hands on the towel and looked at herself in the tall mirror. She'd never seen herself entire all at once, for Andrei's house had had no mirror so large. A bowl of flowers beside the hand basin perfumed the room, and Talia bent to inhale the intoxicating odor. The servant plucked a blossom from the bouquet, snapped off its long stem, and thrust it into Talia's hair, tucking the veil back in place. Talia smiled her thanks and returned to the reception hall where the two men awaited her.

Andrei had watched her walk away, and watched her re-enter the room. He'd never imagined when he rescued her from Rognol in the snow, when she was cold-bitten, frightened, and furious, that she could look so beautiful, so ladylike, even queenly as she did today. He remembered too the way she'd looked after spending a day tanning hides for trade, her hands stained and reeking of the hides. The eunuch had done a good job, and Talia was very definitely a good pupil of his teachings. She walked gracefully, smiled at the right moment, and had lowered her voice to a seductive timbre that sent shivers of desire through him.

He could tell that Sextus Demetrios was falling under her spell. By another day of Talia's company, the Greek would be willing to pay a high price for her. He could hardly keep his eyes off her, and he was practically drooling with the desire to get his hands on her, and to claim her sexually. Andrei could read the man's desires and intentions in his face. He recognized the emotions, for they were the same as his.

Andrei knew he should be pleased that his plan and Byzas's training had been so successful, but he felt a sour taste in his mouth at the thought of another man lying with Talia. How would she react to Demetrios? Would she respond as she had to him, her body warm and lithe and giving? His hands ached to touch her.

He realized that his host had spoken and he had no idea what he'd said. He came out of his reverie with a start. "I'm sorry. I was thinking of something else," he lied.

"There is no problem," Demetrios said. "I merely indicated that it is time we went to partake of our mid-day meal. I have arranged for my servants to serve us on the stoa." He took Talia's arm and guided her toward the porch.

The trio were seated at a round table on the paved stoa, with a view out over the city and down to the harbor. When Demetrios lifted his hand, a servant came forward, set down glasses, and poured wine. "You may not be used to our wine instead of your mead," he said, looking steadily at Talia, "but this comes from my vineyard and I want you to try it."

Andrei translated and to his chagrin saw Talia smile at Demetrios, nod, and sip the wine. The tip of her tongue came out and flicked across her lip, licking away a drop of the wine. She smiled her pleasure, and no words were necessary. She took another sip, smiled again, and held the wineglass as if it were a casket of jewels. Andrei took a long drink of his own wine and set the glass down onto the marble-topped table with such force he thought for a moment that it might shatter. He'd have to get control of his behavior, he told himself. Later he could talk to Talia—and tell her what? She was behaving as a courtesan, just as he'd had her trained to do. How would she fare if Demetrios took her to the palace?

Demetrios leaned in close to Talia and lifted the edge of her veil to sniff the flower in her hair. "I see that you enjoy my flowers," he murmured. "This rose is one of my favorites, and one of the most fragrant. It came from a plant brought from Persia."

Andrei began to translate, but Talia broke in. "I like it, but I should not have disturbed the bouquet."

"I chose those roses especially for you. The color of that particular variety reminds me of your tresses, and I suggested that the servant offer you one if you admired it. You passed my test."

As Andrei translated, Talia flushed with embarrassment, and without meeting Andrei's gaze, she could feel his anger. She smiled at Demetrios, triumphant. He wanted to please her, as Andrei had not. But the day, the situation itself, was planned by Andrei. Let him see how well she could perform her role.

She looked about at Demetrios's house. Spiral-carved columns rose to the roof, each twined with grape vines and flowers, that formed a sun-dappled roof over the veranda. Clusters of ripening grapes hung within her reach, and she touched one with her fingertips. "May I have one of your grapes?" she asked.

"You may have as many as you wish," her host said.

Talia chose a large, perfect grape and bit into it, feeling the juice squirt. She'd let too much juice escape, but it was too late. She'd already used the seductive mood Byzas had told her to use, and she was trying to think what to do next when Demetrios himself reached across the table to wipe away the droplet with his fingertip and bring it to his mouth.

This was something Byzas hadn't prepared her for. She smiled at her host, plucked another grape, and held it out to him. He bit it, and let a bit of juice stain his lip. Talia brazenly swept up the escaped drop, her fingers brushing his dark, silken beard. She put her finger into her mouth and sucked the juice.

Demetrios laughed aloud at the gesture. No words were needed for this kind of communication. He signaled his servant for lunch to be brought, and served Talia's plate with a bit from each of the dishes before passing each on to Andrei. Andrei accepted servings without looking at what was being doled onto his plate, his gaze locked on Talia, watching her every move.

Talia looked from one man to the other. Andrei sat stiffly, his golden hair tumbling to the shoulders of his uniform, his blue eyes like cut stone. He gripped the stem of his wineglass so tightly that his knuckled were white against his tanned hand. Demetrios, on the other hand, lounged easily against his chair, his fingertips playing idly with his glass while his attention was totally on Talia. His dark hair was cut short, and his beard was neat and pointed. His eyes, as dark as obsidian, had crinkles at the corners, and the skin beneath his chin was creased in a circle. He was older than Andrei by years, Talia concluded, and his body lacked the muscular tautness of Andrei's, but this man so far had treated her kindly.

She realized that unlike meals in Kiev, the two men were waiting for her to begin eating. She was grateful Byzas had instructed her in the use of the eating instruments as she surveyed the array beside her plate. There would be no eating with her hands here. She picked up the fork and pierced a thin slice of meat that dangled toward the plate. Andrei shook his head almost imperceptibly. She picked up the knife with her other hand and saw him nod as she cut the meat into tiny bits and placed a forkful into her mouth. "Umm," she murmured, and noted that Demetrios smiled and began eating.

"The lamb is good," Andrei noted, so she knew the word for the meat she was eating.

She next scooped up a small bit of a pale greenish mass, thrust it into her mouth, and longed to spit it out, but that was impossibly rude. It tasted tart with the flavor of something fermented. Managing to chew and swallow what she had in her mouth, she murmured, "This must be an acquired taste."

Andrei laughed and translated, then said to her, "Cucumbers in a sauce of soured cream and milk. I don't like it either. Try the asparagus. You'll like that." He pointed at the long green spears that crisscrossed her plate, and picked up a spear from his own plate, dipped it into melted butter and bit off the tip.

Talia followed his instructions and example. It was the freshest, best-flavored vegetable she'd ever tasted, so much better than turnips, peas, or beans. It was like holding springtime in her mouth. She finished that spear and two more almost immediately, then stopped guiltily. Byzas had told her to only eat a tiny portion of each food offering, and that bit should be eaten slowly. She looked up to see Demetrios watching her and flushed in embarrassment.

Dimitrios said something and Andrei translated, though with obvious reluctance: "He said that he is pleased you enjoy the asparagus. It is the food of the gods, an aphrodisiac."

"What is that?" she asked.

He seemed even more reluctant to tell her, but said in a low voice, "It will make you more likely to want to make love with him."

"Oh!" And she had eaten three spears of the delicious vegetable!

Demetrios laughed when he saw that Andrei had correctly translated. "We are not sure it works. It is just a myth. Pleasing a woman takes skill and patience more than feeding her asparagus."

When that was translated, Talia was even more embarrassed. She didn't need Byzas's instruction to tell her to look down, not to meet those knowing dark eyes—or the mocking blue ones of Andrei. The two men went on eating. After a while Demetrios signaled again, and a servant came with a huge brass tray to collect the dishes and glasses, while a second man appeared with another tray carrying more food, tiny cups, and a pot.

Demetrios held out a plate with some fruit, sliced through to show a mass of pale pink seeds embedded in pink-purple flesh. As she took one of the sliced fruits, Demetrios said, "Figs," and added something more which Andrei translated, grinning as he did: "This is another food of love. The open fig is like a woman's womb. They have legends or myths about figs as well as asparagus and a few other foods and drinks, but you must not worry. Go ahead and eat it if you wish."

Talia feared her face must be as deep pink as the inside of the figs, but she ate another nevertheless, and sat back, waiting for whatever embarrassing thing might come afterward.

Demetrios offered them small golden pastries, shiny on the outside. "It is made with honey and nuts, in a thin crust," Andrei explained without waiting for Demetrios to speak. "You will like it, and it signifies nothing. Have some coffee with it."

Talia ate one of the pastries and put her hands in her lap to stop herself from reaching for another. The coffee was sweet, but bitter too, and she was grateful the cup was so small.

"Have another," Demetrios said, passing the plate of pastries to her. At a nod from Andrei, she took one, noting that it made her fingers sticky. What would she wipe them on? While she was trying to decide if she should discretely lick her fingertips or wipe them on her scarf, a servant appeared with tiny bowls of water with a slice of lemon floating in each. Demetrios dipped his fingers into one of the bowls and wiped them on a small napkin the servant held out. Relieved, Talia followed.

Demetrios rose. "Andrei, I'm sure you want to see my prize-winning horses. Would Talia Militskaya also be interested, or should we postpone our visit to the stables for another day?"

Talia heard her name and realized that some decision was being made that concerned her. Andrei said, looking at her, "I'm sure she wants to see the horses."

Talia nodded, and remembering Byzas's lessons, waited for one of the men to pull out her chair. Both men reached for the chair, both stepped back, and then Demetrios took control of the chair. As he assisted her to rise, his hand brushed her hair and her shoulder, lightly, but she was sure it was an intentional touch. She glanced up at him, smiled, and murmured her thanks for his assistance.

She followed the two men beyond the patio and through a lush garden toward where she heard horses nickering at the approach of their owner. She longed to linger in the garden, to smell each of the different fragrant blossoms, but the men were walking on ahead, and she ran a few steps to catch up.

Demetrios must have arranged it ahead of time, Talia decided, because as they reached the stable, dark-skinned young men led out three horses, saddled for riding.

"I thought this one would be appropriate for you," Demetrios said to Talia, reaching to rub the flank of a sleek white horse with long mane.

Talia touched the horse's muzzle. "Beautiful," she said.

Demetrios took her word as approval, the horse was led to a stone, mounting block and one of the young men and Demetrios boosted her up onto the horse's back. She almost tumbled off, but managed to right herself. She was expected to ride sidesaddle, with one leg bent beneath her. It was uncomfortable, but she didn't think Andrei or Byzas would want her to complain.

As Andrei and Demetrios mounted their own horses, Talia's mount suddenly reared, brought its hooves down, and ran for the opening in the stable grounds that led down toward the water. Talia screamed and grabbed at the horse's mane, holding on fast to the runaway animal.

Andrei wheeled his horse around and raced after her. As his horse came abreast of hers, he reached out and plucked her off the saddle and into his arms. Talia leaned into him, sobbing and shaken, and reveling in the strong warmth of his arms and chest.

She wished they could ride away together, all the way back to Kiev. All too soon Andrei slowed his horse and rode back to the mounting block where he dismounted, still holding Talia close. When they both stood on the stable grounds, he asked, "Are you all right?"

She nodded. "I am now. I was so frightened."

"What happened? You have ridden horses before."

"Not that kind of saddle, just astride behind you," she said. "And something made the horse rear up and try to throw me off. I could have been killed, dashed against the paving stones, or trampled by the horse if you hadn't saved me."

"I couldn't let you be killed or injured when we're so close to selling you. Demetrios is enchanted by you, and this will put him totally in your debt. He'll realize he almost lost you." As Demetrios dismounted from his own horse and walked toward them, Andrei whispered, "You're doing fine. Byzas is a good teacher, and you're a good learner. You'll impress the court."

"I am so sorry," Demetrios said. "That's never happened with my horses before. Something must have spooked it. Would you like to try riding another horse, or shall we discontinue the riding for today?"

"I think Talia Militskaya would prefer to rest," Andrei answered on her behalf. "She has been somewhat shaken by the experience."

"My humblest apologies," Demetrios said. "I shall attempt to determine what caused the horse's behavior, and if one of my grooms is at fault, I shall see to punishing the guilty one. Perhaps later we can arrange riding lessons so that she will feel more comfortable on my horses. I had hoped to show her some of Byzantium, even outside the city. Shall we count on going to visit the emperor tomorrow instead of this afternoon?"

"Yes," Andrei decided without consulting Talia. "Today has been very full already, with church, lunch, and getting to admire your horses. We have much to think on."

He didn't translate all Demetrios's remarks, but instead told Talia, "We will go now and visit the palace tomorrow. You must thank Sextus Demetrios for his hospitality, even if it turned out badly. It wasn't his fault that your horse bolted."

Talia nodded and bowed to Demetrios. Byzas had instructed her in a few polite phrases, including 'thank you.' "But I want to know what the priest said at the Hagia Sofia today, especially the part when people joined in."

"It was a good message for you, and I think you must have instinctively absorbed its message without knowing the actual words. It said that in Christ there is no male or female, no master or slave."

"I think I should like to become a Christian," Talia said. "Can it be arranged? What must I do?"

"We'll discuss that tomorrow. I'm pleased at your decision, and if you are baptized, it will be more appropriate for me to free you."

Andrei had been translating rapidly, and Talia saw the dismay in his face. She smiled at Demetrios and touched his hand. Let Andrei see that another man would accept her as an equal, would free her and lift her up in status. He would never make her feel as Andrei had done, but he would appreciate her as Andrei had not done.

Andrei said a few more words to Demetrios and led Talia toward the door. Demetrios stopped them. "Wait. Let my grooms bring the chair for Talia Militskaya. You can walk alongside."

Andrei started to protest that it was not necessary, but Talia thanked Demetrios and again smiled at him and touched his arm. Within moments the chair was brought, Talia got in, pulled the curtains closed and the two dark-skinned youths lifted the poles on their shoulders and went out at an easy jogging pace.

From inside Talia pulled the curtains partially back so that she could see the gleaming buildings of this Miklagaard, as Andrei called it, or Constantinople, as Demetrios called it. She could also spy on Andrei, who stalked along beside the chair, striking his fist into the opposite palm. His face was creased with tight, angry lines. She wondered why he was angry. Had she made some big mistake? She thought she'd done just what she was supposed to do, remembering all the words and gestures Byzas had taught her. Demetrios certainly seemed pleased at her behavior.

Andrei wanted to beat someone, something, anything. He couldn't blame Talia for today's events. She'd done as he'd told her. He'd even arranged to have the eunuch train her how to behave like a courtesan of Miklagaard instead of the illiterate slave she was. He'd wanted her to appear attractive and feminine so she would bring him many besants, and she'd succeeded. When she'd touched her lips with the tip of her tongue, he'd wanted to kiss those lips, feel her tongue in his mouth, crush her against him, but he'd had to sit watching and try to control his emotions so he didn't have an erection.

He couldn't blame Demetrios either. He had responded as any man would to a beautiful woman who smiled at him. Why had Talia smiled so much? Because she was pleased at Demetrios's home and hospitality, pleased to be complimented. She enjoyed wearing silks and jewelry, having someone bathe her, perfume her, feed her. He had done none of these things, he realized. He'd taken her as his right, since she was his slave.

All that had happened was his own fault. He'd tried pricking her horse so it would shy and she'd appear awkward as she tried to control it, but that too had backfired. She could have been thrown and injured, or killed. Then he'd have lost his entire sale—and Talia herself. That was stupid of him. He hoped no one had noticed. If either of Demetrios's grooms had noticed, they'd surely tell their owner. He could be in trouble with Demetrios, and Talia had already turned away from him.

Chapter 23

Byzas unlocked the door to the slave quarters and said, "Your companion is away."

It was an unnecessary remark, as Talia could easily see that the room was empty. She knew Byzas was eager to question her, and she said nothing.

"You have returned early," he said. "Did the luncheon not go well?" His voice had an edge of anxiety. "Did I not train you properly?"

"It was not your fault—or even mine," she said, and could sense that he relaxed as he waited for her to go on. "We attended church."

"That is a good sign."

"And had lunch at the home of Demetrios. I ate as you suggested, except that I ate all three of the asparagus spears. I smiled and Demetrios smiled. The trouble began when I was lifted onto the horse. It didn't like me, and reared up. I almost fell off, but my owner rescued me."

"Did Demetrios appear annoyed?"

"No, he apologized, and plans to take me to the palace tomorrow."

Byzas grinned in open pleasure. "Then we have another chance for tomorrow. You have not been rejected. You will impress him and we will move you to his home. Then after a suitable time you can reward me by bringing me into your household." He rubbed his hands together, gleeful at the prospect.

Talia looked around at the slave quarters, seeing it afresh. When she and Inga had been first brought here, it had seemed comfortable and even spacious after the cramped space of the riverboats and unsteady ship in which they'd made the journey across the sea. Now she'd seen the home of Demetrios, plush with marble floors, elegant furnishings, comfortable cushions, and gracious service. All that could be hers, if she continued to smile at Demetrios and make him want to buy her.

She took off her bracelets and the jeweled pin Byzas had thrust into her hair, and placed them on the shelf beside her bed. Next she took off the shawl and folded it, followed by the silken gown. She donned the simple white toga Byzas had given her to replace her ragged garments from the river journey. The fabric of the toga felt rough against her skin compared to the silk. If Demetrios bought her, she'd wear silk and beautiful jewelry ever after—if she pleased him. But how could she be sure she would please him? She hadn't pleased Andrei enough to make him want to keep her.

Before she could consider the problem further, Inga strode in, walking proudly ahead of Byzas, who backed out and locked the door behind him.

Inga was smiling and her eyes were shining. "Anatoly was baptized today," she announced, "and we will be married in two more days. Will you come and stand with me?"

"Of course."

"You can't be a legal witness and sign the church book, because you are still a slave, but I want you with me. I owe you so much. If you had not talked to me and made me reconsider, I might have drowned myself. I didn't fear death, as there is a life hereafter for me, and that would have been better than living as a slave. But now I have a chance for a good life on earth, with a Christian husband, and there is still a life hereafter waiting for us."

"How can you be sure of all this?" Talia asked, envious of Inga beyond anything she'd felt before.

At the sight of Talia's expression, Inga said, "Oh, I didn't mean to mention that you are still a slave. Did things not go well today?"

"That isn't what I meant," Talia said. "I meant the certainty about a life hereafter."

"If you believe in Christ and live your life according to the Commandments, you can be forgiven for your sins and look forward to a life hereafter with those you love."

It was a huge set of ideas all at once. "What are the Commandments?"

"There are ten. We can go over them one by one."

"What are my sins?"

"Everyone commits sins, some big and some small. We lie, we steal, we hate, we lose faith. That was one of my sins that I confessed to. And we must forgive others who sin against us. That's sometimes the most difficult part. I've worked hard to forgive Prince Vladimir for killing my father, kidnapping me, and mistreating me, but more and more I am seeing that it was God's will. I was meant to suffer so that I might appreciate Anatoly and that I might win him to Christianity. And, Talia, I think God meant you to come to comfort me, and in turn I am meant to win you to Christ as well."

She paused and took Talia's hand, her face shining with happiness.

"How will I come to believe?" Talia asked.

"I can't say for sure, but it will happen if you want it to."

"I would like to see my mother in the life hereafter. She was a Christian. But what about people I loved who are not?"

"That's complicated. If they never had the opportunity to hear about Christ, but they lived a good life, then they too may be in heaven with you. If they hear but reject, then they will not have everlasting life."

Talia was silent, contemplating all Inga had said. "I must think of this," she said.

Inga too was silent. After a moment she said, "Tell me what happened to you today. You look unhappy."

Talia told her, describing the house, the food, the horse, Andrei's attitude, and finally the news that she was to be taken to the palace the next morning. "And if Sextus Demetrios chooses to buy me, then I will be baptized as a Christian. Is this what is meant to be my future? I feel nothing when I look at him or touch his hand, but when I touch Andrei, I feel desire even though he doesn't care for me. Is this a sin?"

"Loving someone is not a sin, but just as I had to suffer at the hands of Prince Vladimir and forgive him to find happiness, you may have to turn your back on Andrei and accept Sextus Demetrios. He is a Christian and you may come to love him."

The next morning Talia was carefully bathed, perfumed and dressed ready for her presentation to the court. "Remember," Byzas reminded her as Andrei and the sedan chair arrived for her, "today you have a chance to rise from slavery to one of the highest positions in all of Byzantium. The gift of your beauty has brought this about. See that you use it well."

Andrei was waiting just outside the slave quarters, standing beside the sedan chair. He bowed without speaking and helped her into the chair. Talia thrilled at the touch of his hand, and smiled at him, but got no response. As the two carriers lifted the chair to their shoulders, Talia peeked out between the curtains of the chair to watch Andrei. He walked beside her, looking down, hands clasped behind him. His uniform was freshly pressed and his boots polished. He'd had his hair trimmed and his beard shaved cleanly. Talia could have reached through the curtains and touched the top of his head, but she wouldn't allow herself to do so. Andrei had made it clear that he wished no contact with her. She let the curtain drop and sat still, little caring where the chair was being carried. It rocked gently with the steps of the carriers and she sat back against the cushions and adjusted to the motion.

Just as it was set down, she heard Sextus Demetrios's voice speaking to Andrei, and then the curtain was swished aside and Demetrios reached in to help her alight. "Good morning, Talia Militskaya. You look beautiful today," he said, and she understood his meaning without Andrei's translating. He took her hand, brought it against his side, and turned her toward the paved forum area. Andrei moved to her other side and the trio made their way past a crowd of noisy citizens in the square.

"Why are they meeting?" she asked, and Demetrios answered, understanding her question: "Who knows? The citizens of Constantinople often gather here to air their grievances against the emperor or against an unpopular citizen, even a losing horse." He laughed. "It is their right, and it helps to keep the peace. If they couldn't shout out their displeasure, they might take up swords against us."

Andrei was paying scant attention until Talia asked him to translate.

Guards stopped them at the palace gate until Sextus Demetrios introduced himself. The head guard bowed, apologized, and stepped back to let them enter. Talia remembered Byzas's lessons and walked proudly, Andrei on her left, Sextus Demetrios holding her hand against his side on her right.

As they approached the main entry to the palace, a roar split the air, followed by another. Talia jumped. Where were the animals that roared? Demetrios laughed, understanding why she was startled, and pointed to the huge metal lions. As she stared, the metal creatures turned heads, flexed claws, and opened their giant mouths to show menacing teeth.

Talia laughed shakily. "They sound so real."

"You will see more such marvels inside the palace," Andrei told her. "The emperor has hired the most talented craftsmen to make animated objects for his entertainment."

Fulfilling his words, the emperor bade them approach with a gesture of his right hand. Perched on his left hand was a bird, its feathers blue, yellow, and green. A merry tune trilled from its beak.

"May I touch it, or will it fly away?" Talia asked.

Andrei translated, and both Demetrios and the emperor laughed. "It can't fly," Andrei said. "It's not a real bird."

"It has feathers and it sings," Talia protested, unbelieving.

"Very clever," Demetrios said. "It has a mechanism that makes it sing a few tunes, and a mechanism that allows it to flap its wings, but it can't fly away, so there is no need of a cage. The emperor is to be commended for finding such talented makers of mechanisms."

The emperor smiled and invited them to walk in the garden. This time it was he and not Demetrios who extended his arm to Talia to escort her. She glanced at Andrei, who nodded, and at Demetrios, who smiled back, obviously pleased at the honor she'd received.

Fountains misted the morning air, and sunlight brought out the fragrance of roses and gardenias. A pebbled pathway led between flowerbeds and gracefully trimmed shade trees. A lovely woman sat on a bench in the shade. Her fingers flew nimbly back and forth as she embroidered a length of damask fabric. "My wife, the empress, is making altar cloths for the Hagia Sofia. You have been there?" the emperor inquired of Talia. When Andrei translated, Talia nodded, and bowed to the empress.

She patted the seat beside her, and Andrei indicated that Talia should accept and sit. Though she could not converse with the empress, she could sit and rest, and enjoy the garden. As Talia sat, the empress put aside her needlework and lifted off the veil that covered Talia's hair. "She is as lovely as you said, Sextus Demetrios," she said.

Andrei translated, and Talia said, "Thank you," a phrase Byzas had just taught her, anticipating that she would need to respond to compliments, real and superficial.

Talia studied the empress: her dark silky hair that was pulled up on top of her head, encircled with a gold ornament, and fell about her face in soft ringlets. Her porcelain skin, her serene expression and her light fragrance made Talia feel plain and awkward, with hair too bright, shoulders too broad, clothing too bright. The pale delicate hands made Talia want to thrust her own tanned ones behind her. Byzas had done what he could to beautify her, to make her presentable to Sextus Demetrios, but a few days of

211

primping and instruction couldn't make up for a lifetime's hard work and exposure to sun and wind and strong soap. Was her future to turn on whether the empress approved of her? What could she do or say to earn the approval of the highborn lady?

The needlework lay on the seat between them, the portion the empress had been working on encircled by thin wooden hoops that held the fabric taut. Talia touched it with the tip of her finger. "It's very beautiful," she said, lightly tracing a golden thread that formed the beginning of a cross.

The empress didn't wait for a translation. The tone of Talia's voice spoke her admiration. "Do you do needlework?"

Before Andrei finished translating, Talia flushed and shook her head, remembering the crude sewing she had done, stitching together the edges of furs to make cloaks or coverlets, turning coarse woolen into trousers and long skirts. "I have sewed, but nothing so fancy as this," she said.

Andrei translated, and the empress smiled. "Perhaps you will find the time to learn and join me in making sacred vestments and altar cloths. I know at first you will be far too busy, acquainting yourself with the routine of your husband's household, attending church services, and even taking lessons in dancing and singing. And of course you will find time to attend events at the Hippodrome, and receptions at court."

As Andrei translated, Talia's head spun with the knowledge of all that was expected of her. She would be transformed into a different person—if she could manage it all. She looked up imploringly at Sextus Demetrios as the empress signaled a servant to bring her lyre.

He patted her hand and smiled, a reassuring smile. "You will not have to do all this at once," he said. "And not at all if you don't want to, though I am hoping to show you off to the court and to all who matter in the city."

She didn't look to Andrei for translation. She understood enough from Sextus Demetrios's tone to comprehend that he was encouraging her, and managed a weak smile in reply. Andrei said nothing, but scowled at her as if she'd done or said something wrong.

The empress accepted the proffered lyre and began to strum softly, her fingers moving gracefully over the strings.

Talia listened, enthralled, and she could hardly breathe when the empress began to sing, her clear, crystalline voice following the notes she played. She bent so that the dark curls of hair fell forward over her forehead. She seemed to be playing not for Talia and the two men, but for herself, or for some unseen listener. Talia strained in vain to pick out familiar words. This was a stately song, not one that would be danced to.

For a few moments after the empress finished her song, there was silence. Then Sextus Demetrios said a single word: "Marvelous," and made the sign of the cross in the air.

"What is the song?" Talia asked. Andrei translated, waited for the empress to answer, and said, "It is a psalm of praise to God. The empress heard it sung in Hagia Sofia and taught herself to sing it."

Talia sat transfixed, wanting to hear it again, but not daring to ask such a favor.

Sextus Demetrios took the hand of the empress and brought it to his lips. "Thank you, my Lady."

The empress smiled and nodded her appreciation to him and then to Andrei. Talia looked quickly at Andrei for instruction. Should she also kiss the hand of the empress? He shook his head. She stopped her hand in mid-air, but the empress clasped Talia's hand in both of hers and said, "You must come and see me again, Talia Militskaya. If you wish, I shall teach you to sing and play and do fine embroidery."

As Andrei translated, Talia felt tears spring to her eyes. If only she could speak to the empress without the need of translation! She could never hope to be as beautiful or as accomplished as the empress, but she could at least learn to speak as the Byzantines did.

That is, if Sextus Demetrios bought her. He and Andrei must come to some agreement soon, or Andrei would offer her to someone else. That someone else might not be as rich or as kind as Sextus Demetrios, who wanted her for a wife, not a slave. And someone else might not be as handsome as Andrei. She stopped herself from thinking of Andrei. It did no good. It was only torture to recall lying with him, having his hands caress her, his mouth claim hers, his fingers touch her so expertly that she felt herself soaring. There would never be another lover like Andrei, but he would never be her lover again. Sextus Demetrios would be patient with her, she could tell by the way he smiled at her and touched her hand, the concern he showed when her horse bolted. In time she might come to love him, love the children she would bear him. She would accept his gifts and compliments and learn to listen to his words in his strange language. She would wear silks and fine linen, and from being a slave she would have slaves to tend to her needs. She would be welcome to visit with the empress. But she would never again know the all-encompassing rapture of Andrei.

As they walked away, the empress picked up the lyre and began once more to strum it and to sing. The haunting music followed them out of the garden and ceased only when the heavy doors of the palace swung closed behind them. Talia looked back once, hoping to see an encouraging smile from the empress, but she was lost in her song and gave Talia no notice.

Andrei did notice her. The graceful sway of her hips as she walked beside Sextus Demetrios brought an uncomfortable tightness to his chest—and to his groin. Why hadn't he noticed long ago how beautiful she was, how womanly and seductive?

Sextus Demetrios too was aware of her attraction, and slipped his hand first about her waist and then let it drop lower and snake around the curve of her hip. He saw Talia's back stiffen as she flinched away from the unaccustomed touch.

Sextus Demetrios murmured something that Andrei could not catch, some remark that he knew Talia would not understand, whatever it was. Damn the man! Andrei thought. Couldn't he even wait until the deal had been concluded, the money changed hands, before he took control of Talia?

Andrei imagined the pudgy Byzantine stripping off Talia's clothing, pressing his slack lips against hers and touching her body. He could envision those fingers, dark with hair, roving over Talia's body. The more he thought about the buyer claiming Talia, sowing his seeds in her body, the more angry Andrei became. What was he letting Talia in for? She seemed to enjoy all that Sextus Demetrios had to offer, and why not? What slave woman wouldn't enjoy being the mistress, being pampered, ordering others to do her bidding? Would she enjoy the physical attentions of the Byzantine? Was she pretending to be charmed, or did she realize it was the price she must pay for the luxury and position to be granted her?

He was hardly aware that they had left the palace and were almost at the door of Sextus Demetrios's house.

"We must conclude our deal, Andrei. I am a good judge of horseflesh and of women, and I am satisfied with Talia Militskaya. I think she will serve me well, and will fit into my life. And I will make sure no one again pricks her horse when she rides with me. I want to keep her safe and healthy so that she can give me many sons."

Andrei felt his face flame. So, Sextus Demetrios knew that he had pricked the horse. But that was nothing compared to the rest of his words. He placed Talia in the same category as his horses, to serve his needs and to breed healthy offspring.

"Let us come inside out of the heat of this day," Demetrios said, opening the door and stepping back to let Talia and Andrei enter. He waved them to sit at a round marble table. "May I offer you something to drink?" he asked.

"No, thank you." Andrei gestured dismissively, though the day was hot and steamy and he could see beads of perspiration on Talia's face. He didn't want to delay this matter a moment longer than was absolutely necessary. It was a dirty business, and best gotten over with quickly. Talia would remain behind, and she could ask for her own drink. After one fleeting glance at him when they first entered, she had looked down at her hands, refusing to meet his gaze. Was she pleased or sad at being sold to such a rich influential man? He had a momentary image of how difficult it might be for her in this house trying to get food and drink and to administer the household without him to translate. Sextus Demetrios would be patient for a time, but eventually he would become irritated at her inability to handle things. Then what?

And what would he do without her back in Kiev?

Sextus Demetrios brought out a bag of coins, spilled them onto the table, and began to count out the besants. "I believe this is what we agreed on," he said.

'No." Andrei shoved the stack of besants back across the table.

"Have I counted wrong? Or are you raising her price?"

"Neither. I don't want to sell her." Andrei was surprised at the startled look of joy on Talia's face. Her head came up and her eyes flew open as she half-stood.

"Do you think you will get a better offer?"

"No."

"Then you must think that I would mistreat her. You misjudge me."

"No, it isn't that."

"Then you want to keep her for yourself. I can understand why you would. Has this only occurred to you lately, perhaps seeing her in favorable settings I have provided?"

Andrei nodded.

Sextus laughed. "Then I have done myself an ill turn. If you change your mind, bring her back and we will negotiate once more. If you wait too long, though, I may find someone else. After all, I need a wife and a mother to my children. I doubt I could find another as beautiful, but I may find someone almost as lovely." He lifted a lock of Talia's hair and let it slide through his fingers and drop back in place.

Talia looked from one to another, half comprehending what was happening. She was only sure when Andrei stood and reached for her hand. Sextus scraped the coins back into his moneybag and stood, bowing slightly to her. "Farewell, Talia Militskaya. Perhaps we shall meet again sometime. You would have fared well with me. I hope that this man who owns you will treat you well."

Talia said nothing. She could ask Andrei later what had been said. She only knew that Andrei was not selling her—at least not today.

As she and Andrei left, Talia looked back at the opulent home she might have had: the fragrant garden, the tinkling fountain, delicious food prepared just for her. She'd had no say in her future; the two men had made the agreement and broken it without consulting her. What if she'd had a choice? Would she have chosen Byzantium and the nobleman who wanted to marry her? What if she broke free of Andrei's handclasp and turned back now? She knew that the time might come someday when she would regret giving up luxury and status to return to Kiev, to hard work and an uncertain future, but for this moment she exulted that Andrei wanted her, that he had refused a good deal of money for her.

The air was hot and humid, and Talia wanted to stop and rest, and speak to Andrei. He walked swiftly, pulling her along. "Please, may we stop?"

"Do you want to go back to him?" He stopped at a bench in the shade of a tree and made space for her to sit down beside him.

"No, but what if I did? You gave me no chance to choose."

"Very well, I will give you that chance now. You are not in chains, and dressed as you are, you could walk the streets of the city and no one would take you for a slave and arrest you. Do you want to go back?"

"No," she said. "But what is to become of me if I don't? Will you sell me to someone else?"

"No. I'll take you back to Kiev with me."

"As your slave still?"

"No, I'll free you. Then I won't be tempted to sell you, no matter what is offered."

Talia smiled, unbelieving. She was to be free and to be with Andrei. What would become of her after that? It didn't do to think far ahead. So much could happen, had happened. Perun and Svarog could bring disaster or joy to anyone's life. And perhaps this Jesus had some say in her future as well. Inga could tell her.

"Where am I to go now? If I am free I shouldn't be in the slaves' quarters."

"That's true." He stood and took her hand to help her rise. "I must make arrangements. I'll come for you later."

"When?"

"As soon as I can."

She held onto his hand all the way back to the slave quarters and only let go when he opened the door to the quarters and turned away.

Chapter 24

Inga leapt up to greet Talia. "You're back! I didn't know if I'd ever see you again. Did you come to get your things? When will you wed?"

Talia shook her head. "I'm not marrying Sextus Demetrios. Andrei refused to sell me."

"Why not?"

"He said he wants to keep me, and he'll free me!"

"Then we can go back to the northland together." Inga hugged Talia. "And if he frees you right away, you can be an official witness at our marriage. Andrei can too, even though he is not a Christian."

Before Talia could respond, Byzas came in and went straight to Talia. "Tell me everything that happened while we gather your things. Did you meet the empress?"

Talia nodded.

"Did she like you?" His eyes shone with curiosity.

"She seemed to. She played the lyre and sang for us, and said she would teach me to sing and play and do embroidery as she does."

"Oh, that is *so* promising! This means you will be going often to the Palace. And you will take me into your household where I can serve you and other ladies of the court."

"No," Talia said.

"You won't take me with you?" he demanded, his face darkening. "After all I have done to prepare you for this day?"

"I'm grateful, and I think Andrei Ivanovich paid you, didn't he?"

"A pittance."

"I'll see that he rewards you a bit more," Talia said, puzzled at his anger.

"I don't want his 'small bit more,' I was counting on changing my position in life, and you are ungrateful and refusing to help me."

"I would, except that I'm not going to marry Sextus Demetrios."

"What did you do to offend him?" he demanded.

"Nothing. My master refused to sell me, and I'm so pleased. I'll be going back home," she said, and realized that she now thought of Kiev as home. She'd be glad to get away from the stifling heat and dust of Miklagaard, back to cool days and even snow, when she could lie close to Andrei under a thick fur coverlet. She'd miss the flowers and fruit, but there were berries to enjoy that only grew in the colder places. But most of all, she would be with Andrei.

"You fool! You have let him throw away your chance to move up in life, and my chances with it."

"There will be other slaves who can help you," she said.

He said nothing, but gathered up the combs and brushes, the creams and perfumes he'd used on Talia and stormed out, slamming the door behind him.

"He's really angry," Inga said. "I hope he doesn't do anything to harm us."

"If he tries, he might lose his position here," Talia said. "Or Andrei could protect us."

"Andrei is a foreigner here," Inga pointed out. "And so is Anatoly, and so are both of us."

But Talia refused to worry about something that might not happen. Soon Andrei would make arrangements to take her away from the slave quarters, and later they would leave Byzantium altogether.

It was almost dark when Byzas came back in and said, "Talia Militskaya, I am to take you to your Andrei."

"Then I'll need to gather up my things. I'll be quick."

Byzas seemed about to speak, but kept silent, waiting, but not offering to help.

Talia was still wearing the finery Byzas had dressed her in for the visit to the Palace, and she didn't take time to change. She gathered her few garments into a bundle, and thrust the dagger Andrei had given her into the belt at her waist. "I'm ready. How far is it?"

"Not far at all."

"Why didn't he come himself?" Inga demanded.

"He—he is making the place ready," Byzas said, not looking at her as he answered.

As he opened the door and Talia followed, Inga said, "I'll go too. I want to see Anatoly, and they will be somewhere close together. Anatoly told me where they are staying. Is it near there?"

"No," Byzas said, walking fast. Talia trotted to keep up.

"Talia, wait!" Inga called.

Talia turned.

"Don't go with him!" Inga cried out. "Something is wrong."

Byzas grabbed Talia's hand, pulled open another door in the slave quarters, and with a shove against her back thrust her inside. Inga heard Talia scream before the door was slammed shut. Without a backward glance, Byzas walked away rapidly. Inga beat on the door twice, and then ran.

The force of his shove threw Talia to the stone floor. She looked up into the eyes of Marya and Rognol. "Oh!" she gasped. She attempted to stand, but Rognol put his foot on her abdomen and held her down.

"You're at my mercy now," he snarled, "and this time you don't have an ax to strike me."

Talia fumbled for the knife at her belt, but he had seen it. "Take the knife," he commanded Marya.

The slave woman reached for it without speaking. Talia saw that her face was purpled with bruises, one eye was swollen almost shut, and a crust of dried blood clung to her lip. She'd fallen, or more likely, been beaten by Rognol. *She must hate Rognol,* Talia thought, *but she hates me too. If I die, she'll go for Andrei again—if Rognol gives her up. She has no reason to help me. I've got to help myself, or I'll be killed.*

While still holding Talia down with his foot, Rognol jerked the chiffon scarf from her hair and tossed it onto the small table that stood beside the single bed. "That will do for tying you up," he said. "Fitting that you should be bound with a piece of the beautiful clothing that you could be wearing now in safety. But you scorned it for Andrei. A bad choice. A fatal one, in fact, but it played right into my plans."

Talia's mind worked frantically, trying to think how she might escape. She'd heard Inga knocking and then giving up and leaving. If only Inga had gone for help! And if help came in time, before Rognol raped her or killed her. She had no doubt that was what he intended, what he'd intended as revenge ever since that first day in the snow at her village. He stood with one foot on her, staring down at her, enjoying her helplessness. His eyes gleamed with hatred, and he licked his lips as if he saw something appetizing.

Talia tried to roll to the side, but he only increased the pressure on her. She could hardly breathe, and she forced herself to breathe slowly, not panicking at the lack of air. Her hands were still free, and she brought one up to touch a wet spot on her face. Her fingers came away stained with her blood.

"It's just blood," he said. "It's not a broken arm. That comes later. Don't you wish you were back at the house of Sextus Demetrios?"

"How do you know I scorned the marriage Andrei arranged for me?"

"It's interesting what can be learned from eunuchs for a small payment," Rognol said. "I approached him some time ago, but he turned me down. Then today he came to me of his own accord, ready to deliver you into my hands."

"But he liked me."

"He, like almost everyone, looks out for his own self-interest. He cares nothing for you nor for me, only for money and manipulation. I daresay I could have paid him to kill you, but I want that pleasure for myself, and I want to enjoy it for a long time span."

He's crazy! Talia thought desperately. *He's not just vengeful, he's crazy. There's no way I can persuade him to let me go.* She turned her head so that she could see Marya. For a moment Marya met her gaze, and then dropped her eyes, avoiding contact. Talia saw her touch her bruised face with her fingertips, touching the spot of dried blood. She held the knife loosely in the other hand. *Drop the knife. Help me. He'll kill you too,* Talia concentrated on projecting her thoughts to Marya, imploring, pleading for her to understand and help. Marya stared at her, unblinking, and lifted her hand to touch her swollen eye. It was bloodshot and the other was dark and unrevealing.

Talia grabbed at Rognol's leg, digging her nails into the flesh above the boot. He cursed and jerked his foot back, then brought it sharply against her ribs. She gasped with pain, and knew from the crack that he'd broken one of her ribs. He kicked her again, knocking the breath from her, paralyzing her for a moment. In that moment he rolled her onto her face, grabbed her hands and whipped the scarf around them, trussing her like a chicken ready for market. Talia felt her face ground against the dirty stone floor. Her skin stung, but that was minor. She had much worse to fear, and she knew she had to keep her wits about her. Her chances of escaping had just diminished hugely.

Marya stood impassively as Rognol rolled Talia onto her back, her bound hands trapped beneath her. Talia knew she could stand and kick if the opportunity came, but doing either one would be futile at the moment. It would only work if Rognol could be distracted. And then, could she get the door open?

"Let's see what Andrei thought was valuable enough to give up a big profit," Rognol said. He reached down and grasped the neckline of her dress, jerking so that her head was lifted from the floor and dropped back before the fabric tore with a rasping sound. Talia felt cool air on her skin as the dress ripped down to the hemline. She was exposed from her neck to her shoes, and with her hands tied there was no way to pull the remaining fabric over her nakedness.

He ran his rough hand over her right breast, and squeezed the nipple until Talia cried out in pain.

He laughed, and let his hand trail down her bare abdomen, pinching one thigh so hard that Talia knew there would be a bruise. But what would a bruise matter? She'd be dead.

He pulled off his shirt and tossed it to one side and began to untie the drawstring of his trousers. "Marya, look at her. Now do you see why Andrei chose to keep her? She's beautiful, but by the time he sees her again she'll be dead, and looking ugly. He'll only have a quick look at her before I kill him." He let his gaze rove over Talia and she knew he was planning to rape her.

"Should I have my pleasure now and leave her naked so he'll know what happened? Or should I wait until he comes for her and kill him first? Then he can see her beaten and be helpless to do anything, and she can see me kill him and be helpless. Yes, I think I'll kill him first. What do you think, Marya?"

With a high-pitched cry, Marya dodged around the table, around Talia, and reached for the door.

Rognol grabbed her by the hair and jerked her back. "Do you think I'd let you out to warn Andrei? I want you to watch him die too."

Marya still held Talia's knife. She spun around and stabbed Rognol just below the ribs. He gasped in surprise and looked down at where the haft of the knife protruded from his gut. With an angry roar he pulled the knife free and tossed it aside, then reached for his own larger knife and swung it at Marya, almost severing her head.

She crumpled to the floor without a sound, blood spurting from her slashed arteries, pooling on the floor beneath her. She fell so that her swollen eye was obscured, and her good eye remained open, staring unseeing at the ceiling.

Marya risked her life and lost it because of Andrei, Talia realized. *She really cared for him.* And Rognol had killed Marya because of Andrei, when he could have sold her for a good price. She felt tears gather in her eyes and spill down both sides of her face at the hopelessness of her situation and grief for Marya. She hadn't deserved the ill treatment or death at Rognol's hands. *And I don't either! Svarog and Perun, if you have any power, help me and help Andrei.* She blinked, and the tears spread. She saw through a blur that Rognol had pulled off his boots, and she heard them thud against the wall. He paused in removing his trousers to examine the oozing stab wound. He kicked angrily at Marya's body, pushing it partially under the bed, making a broad red smear where it moved across the stone floor.

Talia knew how an animal must feel, trapped, tied, helpless, staring into the face of its executioner. She was glad she'd saved the goat, had Andrei protect it. She'd at least done some good for another creature. She tried to think of anything else she might have done that would persuade the gods to save her. *Jesus, if you have power, save Andrei, and save me. I believe.* She closed her eyes to shut out the sight of Rognol. Whatever he might do to her she couldn't stop him, but she didn't want to look into his evil face.

She felt him touch her hair, and her eyes flew open. He had a knife, and was sawing at a lock of her hair. "I'll take this with me," he said, "as a reminder of my revenge."

Out of the corner of her eye Talia could see the knife moving back and forth, and then the release when he finished cutting. He held up the lock of hair where she could see it before he laid it carefully on the table. If only that were the worst he did! But she knew more was to come. He was cruel and wouldn't stop until he had sated his lust and hatred.

Chapter 25

As she felt his weight bearing down on her, and his breath, hot and stinking, she heard footsteps outside. Intent on taking her, Rognol missed the first sounds, but then leaped up toward the door. As he threw himself to block the door, Talia kicked out and he stumbled and caught himself on the table. It was enough time for Andrei and Anatoly to break in.

Andrei didn't hesitate, but went straight for Rognol with his sword, slashing out wildly. The blow caught Rognol's bare arm and severed muscle and blood vessel. Rognol backed away, panting, holding his bleeding arm with the other hand. His eyes flicked back and forth, seeking the knife he'd used to cut Talia's hair. "Would you strike an unarmed man?" he whined.

"It looks as if you've attacked two unarmed women, and killed one of them," Andrei said. "And if your nakedness is evidence, you were about to ravish Talia."

Rognol said nothing, but reached around to the table where the knife was. Anatoly called, "Watch out, Andrei!"

"I see. You're no longer unarmed, Rognol, so I can kill you in a fair fight."

"And if he doesn't, I will," Anatoly said.

Instead of striking out with the knife, Rognol picked up the lamp and hurled it at Andrei. Andrei dodged to the side and the lamp exploded against the stone wall, pouring flaming liquid onto the floor. "Get her out!" Andrei commanded, and Talia felt Anatoly lifting her and dragging her through the doorway and out into the humid night.

"Help Andrei," she begged, as Anatoly rolled her over and cut her hands free. Inga ran forward, taking off her shawl, and spreading it over Talia to cover her nakedness.

"Andrei doesn't need help, or want it," Anatoly said. "This is his fight. He's been blaming himself all the way here for having abandoned you tonight. He wants to kill Rognol, and it's his right to do so."

"They'll burn!" she protested.

"Andrei won't, but he'd better finish the job and get out, before people come running to put out the fire."

As he spoke, Andrei plunged from the flaming room, closed the door behind him, and picked up Talia as easily as if she were a child. He set off at a trot, Anatoly and Inga beside them. "We've got to get away," Anatoly said. "The fire will burn itself out, but there are two dead bodies inside."

"Foreigners, one a slave," Andrei said, too out of breath to say more.

"Dead bodies, all the same," Anatoly said. "The Byzantines don't like unexplained murders."

"I could be a witness," Talia said, lifting her head from Andrei's chest.

"You're a slave," Andrei said, "God help me. Anatoly's right. We've got to sail at first light."

Behind them in the darkness she heard voices and running feet as eunuchs and guards ran toward the smoldering quarters.

They came out of the darkened quarters into the well-lighted section of the city. On each side of the street torches in glass globes burned, lighting the way. Andrei set her down, but held her close to him. "Can you walk, Talia?"

"Yes. You must be tired," she said.

"We must appear to be ordinary citizens, two couples walking home after a night of revelry," Anatoly explained in a low voice. He took Inga's hand and brought her close to him.

Talia longed to run, to escape from the horror behind them, but she forced herself to breathe normally. She pulled the skimpy shawl around her, sure that every passer-by was staring at her near-nakedness. Her hair was uncovered and tangled, and the outer garment, which had fallen open when she lay on her back, was stained with Marya's blood. Rognol had torn the inner garment asunder, with only bits of its back and sleeves clinging to her. She clung close to Andrei, sheltered by his bulk, and glanced furtively at other walkers in the square. No one seemed to care that she was bloody and disheveled. They were intent on their own errands, their own companions, and were heedless of anyone else. Talia had begun to breathe normally and feel safe when they left the lighted area and plunged into a dark alley.

They went downhill toward the water, half running, half stumbling, not stopping until they reached a storage warehouse. Andrei set her against a column, and said to the trio, "Wait here for me."

Talia grabbed his sleeve. "Don't leave me!"

"Anatoly and Inga will take care of you," he said. "And I'll be back as soon as I can." He took her hand, brought it quickly to his lips, and then dropped it. He stepped into the darkness and was gone.

Talia leaned her face against the stone column, feeling its coolness against her ravaged skin. She sobbed with relief and shock, and bit her knuckle so no one could hear her cry. Inga held her close, trying to calm her shuddering body, her hands gentle on Talia's head. Her fingers stopped. "What happened to your hair?" she whispered.

"He cut it off. He was going to kill all of us and leave, and he wanted my hair to remember."

"If Andrei hadn't killed him, I'd have killed him myself," Inga whispered back. "And I could. I've killed men who attacked me."

Anatoly laughed, a strange sound in the midst of horror. "I must remember that."

Inga whispered something to him, and Talia envied them their easy familiarity with each other. Andrei had kept her for himself, had saved her from Rognol, but he didn't love her, and it made all the difference.

After what seemed hours, Andrei returned. "Quickly," he said. "Down this way. We have to go carefully. The darkness is a help and a danger. I think I know a way through the city wall, but we have to get through before the guard changes." He clasped Talia's hand and walked swiftly but carefully. Once he made a misstep, half-stumbled, and cursed in the darkness. Behind them he heard Anatoly also curse, though there had been no sound except for a squish.

Finally they reached one of the gates in the fortified wall and were halted by a guard. Andrei spoke a few words and handed the man a coin. Without speaking he opened the gate, let them through and closed it quickly behind them. As the bars dropped back into place with a grating sound, Talia knew they were locked out henceforth from Miklagaard.

They stood on the edge of the harbor. The slap and smell of water made Talia want to cry with relief. "Are we free?" she asked.

"Almost. Knowing a few words of the language is a big help," Andrei said.

"And so is a bribe," Anatoly added.

Andrei whistled a three-note tune, and after a moment they heard an echoing whistle, and then the lap-lap of a boat being rowed toward them. Other craft bobbed in the water, and Talia couldn't make out which boat was their rescue, but one came closer. Then there was a soft thump and the rower said something Talia didn't understand. Andrei answered, and helped Talia wade a few feet into the water and climb into the boat. He squeezed in beside her, solid and comforting and safe. She leaned against him as Inga and Anatoly joined them and the boat was pushed off from the shore.

The lights from the city sent flickering patterns across the water. Ahead she saw a dark looming shape and after a few minutes their boat bumped into the hull of a ship. Anatoly and Andrei between them boosted Inga and Talia aboard, climbing a swaying network of ropes. In the darkness they found places on the deck, and Andrei covered Talia with a coarse length of cloth.

"Andrei," Talia whispered.

"Sleep, Talia. We'll talk tomorrow, and begin our journey home."

"Home," she murmured.

"I wish we could go sooner, but we dare not set sail until daylight."

Talia wanted to talk, to tell him all that happened, but her eyelids closed and she slept.

Chapter 26

She awoke to the sound of a creaking windlass and sails flapping above her. It took a moment to realize where she was: on the deck of a ship that was moving. She sat up and peered through the heavy fog that enveloped everything, shrouding the city of Miklagaard. She searched in vain for familiar buildings, but the city was obscured. Somewhere out there was the home of Sextus Demetrios, where servants would be preparing fruit and pots of hot tea and baking fresh bread. Beyond it lay the Palace where the empress might be arising and being dressed for her duties of the day. There too would be the Hippodrome and beneath the streets the amazing cistern that held enough water for the thousands who lived in the lovely city. She'd never see any of it again, she was sure, but she had seen it and now she was going home with Andrei.

Andrei? Where was he? Had the authorities discovered the bodies of Marya and Rognol and somehow come for Andrei? Was he sending her north across the sea to safety and staying behind to accept punishment for killing her attacker? As she turned back from the ship's rail, something soft brushed her face. She whirled, right into the face of the goat she and Inga had saved. Inga was right behind the goat, holding it by a rope about its neck, and laughing. "Look who else is on board," she said.

Talia reached up to nuzzle the soft furry nose of the animal, which burped, bleated, and backed off. Then it reconsidered and rubbed against her.

"It remembers who saved it," Inga said. "We must name it."

Talia was uninterested in the naming. "Where is Andrei?"

"He's below, checking our cargo, securing it for the storms." As she led the goat away, she said, "There's food. I've already eaten."

Andrei mustn't see me like this! Talia thought, bringing her hands up to touch her ravaged face and the stubble where her hair had been. She brought them down and looked at them. Her hands were encrusted with dried blood and three nails were broken and bloody where she'd clawed at Rognol's leg. She stared at her fingers. There might even be bits of his flesh embedded beneath the nails. She pulled herself up, shuddering at the pain in her rib cage. The cloth she remembered Andrei covering her with fell away, and she saw bruises on her breast, her thigh and in the two places where Rognol had kicked her. She pulled the edges of her cloak together and fumbled for the medallion on her shoulder that had amazingly survived. She managed to secure the two sides together. Her shoes were damp and misshapen from wading to the boat. "Inga, I need some water and a comb. I don't want Andrei to see me until I'm cleaned up."

"I'll see to it, but Andrei doesn't care how you look."

Does he care at all? she wondered. *If he doesn't, why did he keep me? He could have sold me for many coins, and he wouldn't have killed Rognol. We'd all be safe, not fleeing from Miklagaard.*

When Inga returned with a basin of water and a soft cloth, Talia said, "You were to be married today, and now there can't be a ceremony. I'm sorry."

"It isn't your fault." Inga dipped the cloth into the water and began gently bathing Talia's face, pausing when Talia winced with pain.

"Don't stop," Talia commanded. "I must get used to the pain. It will heal. And all this is my fault in a way. Mine and Andrei's."

"How can you say that?"

"If Andrei had sold me, then I would be living in a fine house and Sextus Demetrios would have married me in church and I could have been witness to your ceremony."

"You still can be our witness, sometime. Andrei will free you and we will marry back in our own country. We'll find a priest." She took Talia's hand in hers and began washing away the blood and grime. "We couldn't leave you to die. Do you wish you were back in Miklagaard with the rich Byzantine?"

Talia looked around at the crowded, uncomfortable deck and recalled her seasickness from the earlier voyage that was sure to return. In the home of Sextus Demetrios she would have had her own perfumed bath, fresh clothing, a servant massaging her aching body, and a husband hovering nearby to pamper her. But would it all have happened the way it had been promised? How long would it have lasted? Would she ever have come to love him, to lust after him the way she did for Andrei? Or would she have been repelled, and come to hate her Byzantine husband? She'd never know, and there was no going back to the serenity of that house or the glitter of the palace. This rocking ship, these friends, the journey northward to Kiev was reality. "I will miss the figs and oranges," she said after a moment.

Inga laughed. "Oh, Talia! You will be my friend forever, beside me to cheer me up when I start complaining of Anatoly, or of life itself."

"Why would you be complaining about me?" Anatoly asked, coming up behind her.

"I said *if* I started complaining," Inga said. "You must try to make sure there is no reason for me to complain." She dashed the water over the edge of the ship and stood, leaning against Anatoly. He pulled her close to him and bent to kiss her.

As they moved away, Talia saw Andrei coming toward her. She brought her hand up to cover her trembling lips. He mustn't see her cry when she saw his reaction to her ravaged looks. He'd shed his soiled, bloody uniform, and had bathed and dressed in loose trousers and shirt. He carried a bowl in one hand and a cup in the other. He set them down on the deck beside her, and she saw that the bowl contained three large, ripe figs. She burst into tears.

"What's wrong? Did I bring the wrong food? Does this remind you of what you could have had?"

"It's the right food," she said. "I just hate you to see me like this." She touched the stubble on the side of her head.

"Hair will grow back," he said. "Is that all Rognol took from you?"

She nodded, understanding the meaning beneath his question. "He touched me and kicked me and stood with his foot on me. I couldn't escape. Marya tried to run, to warn you that he was going to kill you, and he killed her. I would have been next, but I prayed and Jesus saved me."

"Jesus? Didn't you pray to Svarog or Perun?"

"Yes, but nothing happened. And then when I prayed to Jesus you came to save me."

"Inga brought us, not Jesus."

"Jesus made it happen at the right time," she insisted. "Otherwise, I would have been killed."

He shrugged. "Believe what you want. I'm just grateful that your god or mine held Rognol off until we arrived—if that's what happened. Your Christian god says it's wrong to kill, but I'm glad I killed Rognol. I wish I'd killed him back in Kiev. He was unworthy to be a Kievan warrior."

"That's how you think of him still—as a warrior, one of your class?"

"He was born that," he said, "but he broke the oath he took as a warrior. The prince had doubts about him because of his behavior on earlier attacks, and we should have left him back in Kiev."

"Then Marya would still be alive. He chose her as his servant because she cared for you."

"Cared for me? But she was a slave."

"And so am I," she said quietly, not adding, *And I care for you.*

"I'll free you. I promised, and I will."

She said nothing. She was conscious of the hard deck beneath her, the cooling sea air that belled the sails. She wasn't free, but she was alive. Andrei still controlled her and she would remain a slave until he saw fit to change her status. Finally she asked, "How were you able to get a ship so quickly?"

He leaned back against the rail, close to her but not touching her. "I sold all my trade goods the first day and bought what I needed for the return. You were my last property to dispose of. I was prepared to sail as soon as I turned you over to Sextus Demetrios. I didn't want to stay on in Miklagaard afterward and see you with him."

Talia bristled at his calling her *property*, and was about to protest, but he'd said he didn't want to see her with her new owner. That meant Andrei cared. Perhaps.

"Then, after I reneged on the sale, I still planned to sail today from Miklagaard with you. There was no more reason to stay. If we had lingered, you might have begged me to take you back to his house or the palace. You know what we left in Miklagaard is far better than what we're going home to. And better than this ship." He waved his hand to indicate the cramped, uncomfortable space. He waited for Talia to speak.

"I didn't want to stay with Sextus Demetrios," she said. "But I liked the way I was treated. And I liked wearing nice clothes."

"I bought bolts of silk to sell in Kiev. I'll arrange for some dresses to be made once we get back. For now, can you or Inga see to mending what you've got?"

"Mending?" She lifted the torn edge of her inner garment. "This is beyond mending. We may be able to sew the two sides of the tunic together and I'll wear that. But it's bloody and dirty, especially in the back." She waited for him to say he'd give her a bolt of silk, or buy her clothing at Kerson, but he didn't. "You only wanted me to wear nice garments when I was being displayed!" she charged. She stood, clutched her soiled clothing about her, and fled.

She had no idea where on the ship to go. Where was she to sleep? It didn't matter where she went, just away from Andrei.

She'd said she didn't want to be with Sextus Demetrios but Andrei hadn't responded at all to what was as close as she could get to saying she loved him. He wasn't going to treat her any better than he had before. In his mind she was still inferior. He'd free her, but always think of her as a servant, not entitled to fine clothing or good food or compliments. Even Byzas had treated her well—as long as he thought he would profit from it. Andrei was no better. He gave her beautiful clothing, saw to it that she was bathed and groomed, and took her to places to be admired—as long as there was to be profit for him.

"Wait! Where are you going?" Andrei called.

"What do you care?" She didn't look back, or down, and stubbed her foot on a raised threshold and almost fell, right into Inga's arms. She'd bite her tongue before she ever told Andrei she loved him. And maybe she didn't love him after all. She'd thought she did, and had been almost delirious with joy when Andrei decided to keep her instead of selling her. But what future did she have with him?

Inga caught her. "Talia, where are you going? What's wrong?"

"Away from Andrei."

"What's he done? I'll ask Anatoly to speak to him."

"No! It's not what he's done. It's everything. He just thinks of me as a servant. I should have stayed with Sextus Demetrios. He was kind and rich. But I didn't have that choice. Andrei never asked me what I wanted. He just said he wasn't selling me."

"But he must care for you, at least a little, Talia, or he would have sold you. He was asking a high price for you, Anatoly said, higher than any other slave had sold for." She put her arms around Talia and pulled her close. "If it's the will of Christ, Andrei will realize how much he cares for you."

"He doesn't believe in Christ."

"Jesus Christ was a living being, as well as a god. Someday Andrei must believe too. He's intelligent. Don't give up, Talia.

Now let me show you where you'll be sleeping." She led the way down a narrow corridor and pushed open a door so low she and Talia had to stoop to enter. Two wooden bunks were attached to opposite walls. "This is for you and Andrei. Anatoly and I are in the next cabin."

"It's tiny," Talia said, envisioning being in such a cramped space with Andrei so close she could reach out and touch him.

"It's the best space on the ship. You don't want to see where the crew stays. You'll manage. Now, let's see what we can do about your clothing. That looks dreadful."

Talia laughed. "You've changed so much from the woman who didn't want to live. Now you're in command, arranging things and telling people what to do."

"I didn't want to live as Vladimir's slave," Inga said. "Now I'm free and I'm going to marry an honorable man and return to take back my father's country. And things will change for you when Andrei frees you." She lifted the edge of Talia's garment. "Take this filthy thing off and let me wash it before we even start working on repairing it." Before Talia could protest, Inga lifted the garment over her head. She handed Talia the cloth Andrei had covered her with on deck, and left with the dirty clothing.

Talia was huddled on the bunk when Andrei pushed open the cabin door and came in without knocking. "I'm sorry," he said.

"For what?"

"For how I've treated you."

Talia felt her face heating. "Did Anatoly speak to you about me?"

"No."

"Then Inga must have." When he didn't deny it, she said, "I didn't want her to talk to you. I wanted you to change because you thought it was the right thing to do. What did she say?"

He laughed. "She'll be a strong ruler. I only hope Kiev stays at peace with her. She said if I didn't treat you better she'd turn me into a eunuch, toss me and my genitals overboard, and turn the ship around to take you back to someone who *would* treat you well. Is that what you want? Do you want to go back?"

"No. I already told you that."

"You must have told Inga more than you told me. Women talk among themselves about things men don't care about, don't they?"

"Sometimes."

"How do you want me to treat you?" He touched the stubble where the lock of hair had been cut off, and then ran his fingers across the side of her face and let her hair slide through his fingers. "Like this? Gently?"

"With respect. The way Sextus Demetrios treated me."

"But he planned to marry you. He wanted to impress you."

Talia stared at him in disbelief. He didn't even realize how hurtful and insulting he was. "It's how you think of me, not what you do to me." She tried to move past him, but his bulk blocked the doorway. She waited, unmoving.

After a moment he said, "When you come out onto the deck, I have something for you." He bent and exited the low doorway.

Outside, he stood against the rail, the sunlight glinting off the sea and the breeze lifting his hair and molding his shirt against his muscular torso. Talia approached warily, tucking the cloth about her so the breeze wouldn't lift it and expose her nakedness.

He turned and held out the plate of figs that he'd offered her earlier, their purple skins just cracked with ripeness. "I was planning a special feast for us when Inga came for me last night. Saving you was more important than food so I had to leave the feast behind. These we had on the ship. I wanted you to enjoy them as we crossed the great sea."

"Thank you," she said. She reached for one of the succulent fruits and bit into it, letting a drop of the juice slide unchecked down her chin.

"I noticed how much you liked figs that the Byzantine gave you." Just as Sextus Demetrios had done, Andrei touched her chin with his fingertip, dipping into the juice and bringing his finger to his mouth. "And I can see why." He took another fig from the dish and held it out to her. "These are all for you, and all I could procure in my haste."

"It was kind of you," she said.

"Figs are supposed to be an aphrodisiac," he said over his shoulder, walking away down the deck.

"What's that?"

"The food of love. Or so the legends say. Didn't I translate it before?" He continued walking.

Chapter 27

By late afternoon a storm arose. The sky darkened, the wind roared, and the sea pitched huge waves over the deck of the boat. The tiny craft bucked its way up to the crest of each wave then dropped into the valley beyond, shaking and quivering so it felt as if it would be torn asunder. Talia stayed on deck as long as she dared, but eventually couldn't bear to watch the storm. She fled to the cabin and threw herself down onto the hard wooden bunk. She'd been dreading the sea crossing, and this was worse than the earlier one. Before noon she'd eaten the figs Andrei had given her, and some bread and cheese along with Inga, Anatoly, and Andrei, but as the air grew heavy and humid, she knew eating anything more would be a mistake.

Her stomach churned, and she closed her eyes so she wouldn't see the oscillating, swinging lantern hanging from the ceiling. The ship rocked, almost throwing her from the bunk and an occasional roar of thunder signaled the anger of the sea god. She put her hands over her ears to shut out the claps of thunder, but the memory remained, and dread of what was to come. She had lost track of how long the storm had lasted when the door creaked open and Andrei came in.

"Are you all right?"

"No. I'm sick and frightened," she admitted.

"I can't do anything about the sickness, but I'll stay here with you if you want me to."

"Yes, please." Then she added, "If you want to."

"The storm is blowing itself out. It won't go on much longer, and I think the ship is sturdy enough to stand the pounding." He sat down on the bunk beside her, his thigh pressed against hers in the cramped space, and took her hand in both of his. "I can't think of anything to say or do to change the world outside, but I'll be here to rescue you if we start to sink."

Talia didn't answer.

"Would it help if I put out the lantern?" he asked.

Talia opened her eyes and looked into his face. He seemed concerned about her. She wanted to keep on looking at him. He was solid and unmoving, and the warmth of his body beside her calmed her fears. But the motion of the lantern made her queasy. "Yes," she said.

He stood, pulled the lantern down, and blew out the flame. When he didn't sit back onto the bunk, she asked, "Are you leaving?"

"No, I'm taking off my clothes."

Talia sucked in her breath. It had been a long time since Andrei had lain beside her, had kissed her, or touched her. The cabin was cramped, with little space between the bunks. Maybe he was getting into his own bunk.

He wasn't. She heard the faint rustle of clothing dropping to the floor, and then he eased down beside her. He drew off her sandals and caressed her ankles, then the soft flesh underneath her instep, then her toes, one by one. Talia sighed, relaxed, forgetting the creaking of the wooden boat, the howl of the wind outside. She felt almost drowsy, as if the storm were a gentle breeze lulling her to sleep. Then she realized that Andrei's hands were on her calves, moving up and down along the muscles, then making light tracings on her thighs. She tried to sit up, to escape from his roving, knowing caresses, but there was no escape. With a smooth movement he flung himself down beside her, pinning her in the bunk.

The bunk was really too narrow for two people, but he slid his arm beneath her and drew her tightly against him, making space for himself. Her elbow was still pressed tightly against the cabin wall, but she was scarcely aware of the discomfort.

Andrei's hands slid beneath the cloth she had around her, and inflamed her bare skin like bringing a glowing ember to firewood. Talia quivered with the knowledge of how Andrei would make her feel, around her, inside her. He held her so closely that she couldn't move, but she didn't want to move, no matter what happened to the ship or its crew, or the howling storm.

Andrei unfastened the clasp of Talia's makeshift garment and flung the cloth onto the floor with his clothing. The metal clasp dropped to the floor with a sharp ting. The cool air struck Talia's skin and she momentarily regained her sense of where she was and what Andrei was doing and was about to do. "No," she murmured.

He put his hand lightly over her mouth and whispered, "You'll be all right."

Even his light constraining touch was too much for her, too much like being gagged and fondled by Rognol. She twisted her face away from Andrei's hand and her body stiffened in protest. "I can't—Rognol."

He guessed what was wrong. "I'm not Rognol," he said. "He's dead. He can't hurt you or anyone else ever again. And I won't hurt you either. Have I ever hurt you?"

"No," she admitted. "It's just so soon after—so awful." Even hours later, with an expanse of sea between her and the slave quarters of Byzantium, she didn't feel completely safe. Would she ever feel truly safe again, safe enough to trust? "Will they come after us?"

"They?"

"The authorities. Whoever punishes killers."

"We're not killers. At least, you're not."

"I wanted to kill him, and they may think so when they find two dead bodies."

"Who will care that two bodies are found in the slave quarters?"

She recoiled from his harshness. Slaves didn't matter to him. "I could have been one of them. Won't Byzas tell who they are? And tell that he took me there?"

"Not likely. He's probably taken whatever money Rognol gave him and gone back to the village he came from. And I'm sure he has money saved somewhere he can get at it in a hurry. The eunuchs all do. They know their income depends on connections, and once they fall under suspicion, the connections break. He'd talk if he could see some profit in it, but who's to pay him for the information about two foreigners? And if he told, he would be implicating himself. How else would he know who the people were?"

It all sounded logical when Andrei explained it, and she could feel some of her worry slipping away, but she remembered Byzas's smile, his assurances that she would rise to high places in Constantinople. "I trusted him. I thought he liked me." She knew her remark made her seem naïve and foolish, but his betrayal still rankled. It could have cost her her life. She'd been manipulated by his flattery and thought herself important, when she was really just Andrei's property, Sextus Demetrios's pretty companion, and Byzas's pawn. Sextus Demetrios at least was willing to pay well for her, but to Byzas she was of little consequence. Whatever Rognol paid him was what she was worth to Byzas, no more. When she was no longer to be married to Sextus Demetrios, her value fell to the cost of a small bribe. And to Andrei? He'd risked his life for her. She needed to think about that, later, when he was not beside her.

"Eunuchs have no loyalty, except to themselves," Andrei said, bringing her back to Byzas. "They revel in knowing secrets, influencing important men, mainly through flattering their consorts. Sometimes they even neglect their own families, and I could understand that. After all, it's the family that castrated the eunuch, ending his chance of ever having a wife and children. But let's say

243

no more about the traitor Byzas, wherever he is. You'll never see him again."

Talia shivered, imagining coming face to face with the betrayer, but Andrei's words had taken away some of her fear of Byzas.

"Byzas would be a fool to seek us, and I'm sure he knows it. After a time he may find employment with someone else and work his way back up. But I promise you if I ever see him again, I'll kill him and not think twice about it."

"You'd kill him for me?"

"Yes, just as I killed Rognol. I may yet have to report that death to Prince Vladimir. He never trusted Rognol, but he needed warriors who would not shrink from killing Pechenegs. "

"I had forgotten them," Talia said, remembering the battles along the river. "Will our return be as bad as the journey to Byzantium?"

"We won't know until we get there. The Pechenegs may be occupied with battles to the east, or bringing in their crops. I've passed that way several times, and I could have spared you that danger if I'd sold you to Sextus Demetrios."

"But you didn't," she said, wanting to hear him say he was glad he hadn't sold her, to explain why he refused a good offer.

"No, you have value for me," he said. "And we needn't worry about anyone from Constantinople coming after us. We'll soon reach the safety of the river, and we'll probably find some other traders who are ready to make the journey back to Kiev. And just listen. The storm is passing."

She realized that as Andrei had talked, she'd forgotten the storm. She listened now and noted that for the moment at least the wind had abated and the ship was rocking less.

Andrei lay beside her without moving, his body warn and comforting. For the moment he was not a lusty man trying to seduce her or conquer her, but only a bulwark against her falling from the bunk.

"Will you be all right?" he asked into the darkness.

"I think so," Talia said. "I must learn to be." A sudden whistle of wind swept away part of her answer, but Andrei seemed to hear and understand. He touched his lips to her cheek, felt a tear, and wiped it away with his fingertip.

"You've endured much, and you're brave, a fitting companion for a warrior."

A companion but not a wife. Never a beloved, Talia thought, but did not say it aloud. For now she would accept whatever he offered of himself—not love, but comfort and a kind of caring.

Chapter 28

She was both glad and sorry when she felt him leave her side. In a moment she heard the soft thud as he dropped onto his own bunk. He'd spread her loose garment over her, and she pulled it up to her chin, clutching it with both hands as if it might protect her. The ship rolled and lurched, and she braced herself so she wouldn't roll out. Andrei would rescue her, would lift her back into her bed, but she wanted him to minister to her because he wanted to, not because she was in danger. Gradually she became accustomed to the motion of the ship, and slept.

She awoke to the gray of daylight coming in through the open hatch. By the dim light she could see that Andrei was gone. She heard footsteps on the deck outside, and Inga's light laughter. The rumble of her stomach told her she was hungry, and no longer nauseated. She sat up and as her garment fell away, she saw that she was naked. She remembered Andrei tossing the clasp to her garment onto the floor, and her fingers found it. She fastened the cloth about her and ran her hand through her straggling hair. When she touched the stubble, the memory of Marya and Rognol and the slave quarters came rushing back. But Andrei had said she was not in any danger now. Her hair would grow back, but not soon, and Andrei would not find her beautiful. She didn't feel beautiful, as she had in Miklagaard, or Constantinople, as Sextus Demetrios called it.

"There she is!" Inga called cheerfully as Talia went up on deck. "Come and see if you like the new gown I've sewn for you." She held out a white silken garment, much like the ones Talia had worn in the slave quarters, except that the fabric was finer. And though it might remind her of that time, it was much better than the torn rag she was wearing. Talia ran her fingers across the silken surface. "Thank you," she said.

"Come, let's put it on you." From behind her Inga drew out another, smaller garment made of the same white silk. "You'll want these too, I think," she said. She led Talia back into the cabin, unfastened the clasp, and snatched off the old, tattered garment.

Talia crossed her arms over her bare breasts, embarrassed.

Inga laughed. "I know what breasts and all the rest of you look like. Put these on," she said, holding out the smaller garment.

Talia pulled on the underwear and tied the string about her waist. "When did you have time to sew?" she asked.

"These were mine, part of the clothing Anatoly bought me. I was on my way to meet him when Byzas took you away. Fortunately I had the presence of mind to hold onto my bundle."

"Thank you," Talia said. "Someday I'll find a way to repay you."

"You owe me nothing. Now, put on your sandals and let's go back outside. The storm is over and there's some bread and wine to be had and some crumbly kind of cheese that the Byzantines seem to like."

"What about my hair?"

Inga laughed. "Two days ago you were near death. Now you worry about your hair! Andrei doesn't care how you look."

And Talia feared that was true. If he cared for her, wanted her as a woman, then he'd notice how she looked, but he didn't.

The sun was shining, glinting off the water, making diamonds of the spray that occasionally tossed up onto the deck. The trio sat on the deck, backs to the rail, eating bread smeared with cheese, and sipping wine from earthenware bowls.

As Andrei strode toward them, the ship yawed and a giant wave broke over the side, splashing the three as they sat. Anatoly jumped up and took Inga's hand, pulling her up and away from the rail.

Talia half stood, then sat back, laughing and holding her bowl out for more wine as another wave drenched her. The seawater soaked her clothing, plastering the filmy garment against her body. Her hair hung in tendrils, damp and clinging to her scalp.

"Get up, Talia, or you'll be splashed again," Inga said.

"I'm already wet, The water's cold, but I needed a bath, and I'll dry in the sun. Give me some more wine to warm me."

Andrei couldn't stop looking at her. The silk clung to her body, outlining her like some of the erotic statues he'd seen in Miklagaard. He drew off his cloak. "Here. This will help you stay warm until the sun dries you." He took her hand and pulled her to her feet, wrapping the cloak about her shoulders. "And move away from the rail." He led her over to the bulkhead where Anatoly and Inga had found seats. He wanted to gaze at her enticing body, but at the same time he wanted to cover her, to keep the sight of her for him alone.

It was the first time he'd ever heard her laugh, except for the fluting, flirty laughter at the luncheon of Sextus Demetrios. Had he ever done anything to make her laugh? He'd seen her smile at Sextus Demetrios, and the sight of it had driven him half crazy with anger and desire. He wanted to have her smile at him that way, but he had to admit that ever since he'd captured her, the situation between them had been serious. Or dangerous. Only when she was at the house of the Greek had she been pampered and complimented and given some reason to smile. Now Anatoly and Inga had made her laugh at being splashed by a wave. Or was it the wine?

She held out the empty wine bowl to him and smiled, her face lighting up in the morning sunshine. "Andrei, join us," she said. "You can have some of the wine. It's Anatoly's, but I'm sure he'll be willing to share. And Inga is sharing her clothes with me."

He wanted to say that he'd leased the ship and seen to loading their cargo, that he was responsible for all three of them, but that would only make him look surly. As he poured the wine, a bit splashed onto Talia's fingers, She touched his lip s she'd done with Sextus Demetrios, as Bysas had taught her to do.

Andrei drew her finger into his mouth and sucked off the drop of wine. Their gazes met and held, and Andrei sensed only the sweet tang of the wine, and the golden glints in Talia's eyes. Neither noticed that the shallow bowl was tipped and wine spilled onto the deck.

Anatoly broke the spell. "That's good wine! Drink it or leave it, but don't waste it."

Andrei wanted to pull Talia into his arms and kiss her, to take her to the cabin below and make love to her. He dared not, not when Anatoly and Inga were staring at the two of them. He could have taken her last night or could any time, by force. But he didn't want it that way. He wanted not just her submission or even her willingness, but her passion. He wanted to feel her hands against his bare back, clasping him to her. He wanted to taste her mouth, and hear words of love from her lips.

He thrust the wine bowl to Talia and turned away. "I have work to do," he announced, and strode away down the deck.

"Why is he leaving?" Talia asked. "Did I do something wrong?"

Anatoly laughed. "No, he did. He let his feelings show, and a warrior of Prince Vladimir isn't supposed to do that. Enjoy the wine, ladies. I managed to rescue only the two bottles, and I think it's fitting that we drink it to celebrate our safe departure from the amazing Miklagaard."

Talia stared after Andrei. She'd felt so close to him, looking into his eyes, touching his lips with her fingertips, oblivious to what Inga or Anatoly must think of her.

Andrei walked with long, commanding strides. The breeze whipped his shirt and loose trousers against his body, emphasizing his fitness as much as his uniform did. The sunlight on his hair haloed him in gold. *Look back. Look back at me*, she willed him silently, but he did not.

She turned back to listen to what Anatoly was saying, something about Andrei's being a warrior. He'd shown his feelings to her, just for a moment, without words, and someday he would again. She'd make sure of it.

Chapter 29

The day dragged. Inga and Anatoly obviously wanted to be alone, and after they finished the bottle of wine, they left Talia to her own devices. She found the goat and fed it. As she tied it to the rail, she saw Andrei farther down the deck and smiled at him, but he didn't seem to see her. How could he not? she wondered. But maybe he was ignoring her purposely, and if that was the case, then she could ignore him. They had to share a cabin at night, but they didn't have to spend time together in the daytime. She turned away from him and nuzzled her face against the soft side of the goat.

Andrei watched her go, angry without knowing why. She was still his slave, though he had promised to free her, and he could by rights have commanded her to stay by his side and do his bidding. It rankled that she preferred the company of a stinking goat to him. He should have had the animal killed earlier and turned into a feast for the crew. That at least would have won him some good will. Letting the creature live just because Talia wanted it was a mistake.

He watched her hands gentle the animal's quivering muscles, her cheek rubbing against the goat's soft nose. Andrei wanted her hands on his thighs, her cheek against his chest, and—

Without thinking, he called out, "All right! I'll free you!"

Talia ran to him and threw her arms around him. "Thank you, Andrei. Can it be now? Right this moment?"

Half stunned at his decision and at her reaction, he nodded. "Anatoly and Inga can witness my words. If we can find them." He sent crewmen in search of them. Soon the pair appeared on deck beside him, flushed and disheveled.

"The wine," Anatoly apologized.

Andrei doubted the excuse, but then recalled the wine's effect on Talia and shrugged off the apology. "No matter. We want you to witness that I am this day freeing Talia Militskaya. She is no longer my slave."

Inga smiled in delight and hugged Talia. "Now you can be one of the witnesses to our marriage—tomorrow, when we land at Kherson."

As the two women walked away chatting, Andrei asked, "What have I done? If she's not my slave, what is she? What position does she have in my household?"

"She could be your wife," Anatoly suggested. "You need to marry again and produce sons for the prince."

"Marry her? No, I couldn't. She's no longer a slave, but she's still a Slav."

"Andrei, you're a pig-headed fool! What difference does it make that she's a Slav?"

"Slavs are inferior."

"Do you think Talia is inferior? Sextus Demetrios didn't think so. He was willing to pay the exorbitant price you asked for her, and still would. He would have married her and had her at his side among the highest society. And our high and mighty prince doesn't mind who his wives are—or were. Now that he's become a Christian the princess will force him to put aside all the others."

"It's hard to change the beliefs of a lifetime," Andrei said. "I must think about it."

"Don't think too long," Anatoly advised. "Or Talia may leave you and make her way without you. Or find someone else."

"Then I may have made a mistake in freeing her."

"No, she's proud and fierce and might have left you anyway, now that she's had other people treat her as an equal. Inga is a chieftain's daughter and will have power over many, and she sees Talia as her equal, and so do I. Someday you will too, but it may be too late." Anatoly too turned and left.

Andrei walked toward the tethered goat, which bleated piteously. He untied the animal, talking to it as he led it from the rail. "They've forgotten all about you. You're fortunate that I didn't slaughter you, and I may yet, but for now I'll at least take you to the shady side of the ship and get you some water to drink."

Talia was already in the cabin when Andrei came in to bed. The night was clear, so he left the hatch open for fresh air. The moon was almost full, and threw silvery light and strong shadows over the floor, the bunks, and Talia.

Andrei stood a moment taking in her naked beauty, haloed in silver blue. She lay so still that he thought for a moment she was asleep. Should he awaken her? He lusted for her so much that his mouth felt dry and his heart pounded in anticipation. With slow, steady movements he removed his shoes and set them one after the other onto the floor at the end of the bunk, careful to make no noise. He untied the drawstring of his trousers and drew them off, then pulled his shirt over his head and dropped the clothing atop the shoes. He eased onto the bunk and lay back staring through the open hatch at the moon, and then turned to look again at Talia.

She reached her hand across to take his.

"I thought you were asleep. I didn't want to disturb you."

"I was waiting for you."

Her voice, low and husky, almost a whisper, besotted him. He had to have her, and she was willing. He hesitated. His own words today had changed the way he would treat her from now on. He had to please her, or she might leave him. He'd sworn in front of two witnesses—powerful, believable witnesses—that she was now free. When they landed at Kherson, she might find someone with a ship who'd take her back to Miklagaard, back to Demetrios or some other man who would treat her well.

Damn! He had put himself into a bad position where Talia was concerned, and he knew her well enough by now to know that she would take advantage of her freedom.

If she left him, what would he do? And if she didn't, if she stayed, what then? She was no longer his slave, but what was she? A servant? He'd have to pay her wages, and have her stay in the women's quarters, off limits to him.

Considering everything, he almost lost his desire for her.

Then she turned and in the moonlight he saw her smile. She still held his hand, and drew it toward her, kissing his palm.

Andrei forgot his qualms as his desire for her coursed back in a rush. He slid into the bunk beside her and gathered her warm, naked body against his. He trailed kisses up the length of her neck to her ear and to the spot where her hair had been shorn away, telling her in this way that all of her was beautiful.

Talia held his face between her hands and brought his mouth down on hers. Andrei kissed her, loving the taste of her, warm, still bearing a hint of the wine from Byzantium. As he claimed her mouth, Talia moved her hands to his bare back, caressing him down his spine to his buttocks, her fingernails digging into his flesh, pulling him closer to her than he'd thought possible.

Talia wanted him! he realized joyously. He didn't need to ravish her or seduce her. She wanted him as much as he wanted her. And he wanted to please her, to satisfy her, to hear her moan in ecstasy. He lifted his mouth from her lips and moved down to the soft hollow of her throat, then slowly, tantalizingly, down the curve of her right breast. Knowing the power his touch had over her body exhilarated him.

Talia was moving beneath him, opening her thighs to clasp his. Her breath came in short gasps.

"No," he said. "Wait." He held himself back, intent on making her want him almost beyond bearing. His lips trailed kisses across her abdomen and to the soft furry mound that he sought.

"Not there.

"Shhh!" He couldn't hold off much longer, and he didn't have to. Talia pulled him down against her, into her, matching her movements to his thrusts.

"Oh, oh, oh," she whimpered.

Afterward she lay curled against him, soft and damp. Andrei was finally aware once more of the moonlight, the cool breeze coming through the open hatch, the possibility that someone walking past might have heard and spied on them. At the time he'd been past all caring.

"Tonight with you was wonderful," he said. "You were passionate."

"It was different. I'm free now. I could choose."

"What if you'd rejected me and I'd overcome you?"

"Then I wouldn't have been passionate. Obedience you can command, but passion has to be given freely."

He laughed lightly. "If I'd known you'd react so passionately, I might have freed you long ago."

She didn't answer, and after a while he said, "We land tomorrow. It will be a busy day, unloading all our cargo, finding river boats or porters and starting our journey upriver."

"And there's the wedding," she said.

"Yes, there is. I hope the prince hasn't taken all the priests away with him." He slid off the bunk. "With all that's happening tomorrow, we'll need to be rested. Good night, Talia."

"Good night, Andrei."

"Not 'master' anymore."

The bump and lurch of the ship being pulled up to the pier awoke her. She sat up, realized she was still naked, and grabbed for her clothes. Then she lay back, remembering Andrei's lovemaking from the night before. She'd partaken, had encouraged him, and he'd enjoyed it. She closed her eyes, relishing her sense of power over him. She'd make him care for her, desire her, be so dependent on her that he would love her and want to marry her and keep her with him always.

A kernel of doubt troubled her. Was what she had done a sin? She must ask Inga. But Inga would be busy with the wedding today.

Anatoly and Inga were already ashore, standing together on a small point of land that thrust into the river delta. A curious group of people was gathering around them, and a man in black with his back to the ship stood in front of them. Talia waved and called out, and Inga looked up and returned the wave.

Where was Andrei? Wasn't he going to join in the wedding ceremony? She saw him off to the side, directing the unloading of the ship. She must go ashore! She poured water into the small basin in the corner and sponged her body. She reveled in Andrei's smell that clung to her, not wanting to scrub it away.

Her bath finished, she, slipped her feet into her sandals and draped the new gown about her, clasping it at the shoulder with the medallion from Miklagaard.

Ashore she joined Inga and Anatoly. Their faces shone with such happiness Talia could scarcely bare to look at them. She was glad for their sake, but envious. Would such joy, such loving security, ever come to her?

The man in black wore a silver cross set with colored stones on a chain around his neck, and a small, close-fitting hat on his long dark hair. He asked Anatoly and Inga for their names, and if they were Christian. They answered.

"Who are the witnesses?"

"I am," Talia said.

"And are you a free person, not a slave?"

"I am!" Her voice rang out proudly.

"Are you a Christian?"

"I'm not sure," Talia admitted.

"Perhaps we can talk afterward," he said. "Who else is to witness?"

Andrei stepped forward. "I will."

"Are you a free man? It seems an unnecessary question, since you appear to own the trade goods."

"I am free, and a warrior of my lord Vladimir," Andrei answered.

"And are you Christian?"

"No, but I am loyal to Prince Vladimir, who is now a Christian and will vouch for me if necessary."

"That won't be necessary. We can go on with the ceremony." He turned to Inga and Anatoly. "Do you swear that you are not wed to any other? As a Christian you may have only one husband and one wife as long as you both live." When they answered, he went on, "I confess I am new at performing wedding ceremonies. Prince Vladimir had many of us consecrated as priests who were just learning the scripture and rules of the church, so bear with me. The church will bless your union whether I say the words exactly right or not, and the presence of these witnesses will insure that it is a legal marriage. Do you both swear to love and honor each other and to live together under God's rules?"

"We do."

"Then you are now married. In the name of the Father, the Son, and the Holy Ghost." He lifted his cross and added, "Amen."

Just as he finished, one of the crew ran forward, pulling Talia's goat by a rope. "Here's a goat for the wedding feast!"

"No! He's mine!" Talia cried, throwing herself on her goat.

The priest held up his hand. "We don't need to kill this animal."

"He lives," Andrei announced. "Find something else to feast on."

As the disgruntled crewman walked away and Andrei went back to work, Talia said to the priest, "Thank you for saving my pet."

"I could see that he is special to you. Every creature is special to someone, and to God. The church calls Jesus Christ the Lamb of God who was slain for our sins, but we don't need any other sacrifices today." He put his arm about Talia's shoulder. "We can go to the shade of that tree and talk about Christ if you wish, while the work goes on."

His lined face told her he'd lived long and seen much of the world and perhaps would not be judgmental. His voice soothed away some of her anxiety at talking with a stranger about something so personal, so frightening and so important to her future.

Would he understand her fear, and her need for forgiveness? Perun and Svarog were gods of wrath, demanding sacrifices and sending down thunder and lightning to destroy unbelievers. Inga had said the Christian god was different, and from what she had seen in the great church in Byzantium, Talia thought of it as a beautiful religion, where prayers and songs soared to heaven in breathtaking swells.

She followed the priest, uncertain how to tell him what she was thinking. The prince had found a priest for this settlement who at least spoke her language, so she didn't need a translator, as she had with nearly every conversation in Byzantium. It would have been doubly embarrassing to have a third person hear her worries and sins, especially if that person happened to be Andrei.

The priest sat on a heap of tanned skins and patted a space beside him for Talia to sit.

She shook her head. She had to remain standing, ready to bolt if she lost her nerve and couldn't tell him the whole story.

"All right, my child, what troubles you?" His voice was calming and even, and though his words were serious, he smiled, inviting her to confide in him.

"I think I have sinned by lying with a man, by having—"

"Carnal knowledge? That's how the church describes what I think you mean. Is he wed to another?"

"No." Talia didn't know what to call the priest, so she settled on using no title.

"Are you?"

"No."

"Then it is not as serious a sin as it might be. The Commandments say that we shall not commit adultery. What you have done is fornication. Has this happened before?"

"Yes, but in a different way. Before, I was a slave and he was therefore entitled to take me as his property."

"I disagree with that. It is a sin to misuse another human being, and especially to have taken advantage of a slave. Under God, slave and master are equal in His sight."

"But I'm not a slave now," Talia said. "My master Andrei freed me."

"That is to his credit. So he has less to confess."

"He won't confess. He's not a Christian. He still believes in the power of Perun and Svarog. And he sometimes says he believes in nothing except the power of his sword and the strength of his arm."

"And you? What do you believe?"

"I don't know anymore. I'm not sure if I am a Christian." Resolutely, she went back to what she really wanted to discuss. "When I was a slave, I could not object to anything he did, so submitting couldn't be considered a sin, could it?" Without waiting for his answer, she went on, "Now I'm free, I can choose, and I went to him willingly."

"Do you repent?"

"Repent? What is that?"

"Are you sorry for your sin?"

Talia hesitated. Was she sorry she'd enjoyed sharing her body with Andrei? She couldn't honestly say she was.

The priest laughed at her hesitation. "Yours is not a mortal sin, and you have not yet professed yourself a Christian, so I can't absolve you of your sin. Perhaps after you have thought more carefully about your beliefs and have been baptized, we can talk again and I'll hear your confession. Or some other priest can."

Talia was startled. "Not you?"

He shook his head. "Your prince has raided the coast, rounding up all the priests he could inveigle into going with him to the northland. For most it was an easy choice. They are bound by their vows to go forth to the whole world, preaching the good news of Christ and bringing converts into the church. A country such as the prince's with few Christians is fertile field for priests and missionaries. The prince's aim is to replace the old pagan beliefs with Christianity, of the special kind that we in the East practice. Someone needs to stay to look after the needs of Christians here. I have family here, so I chose to stay."

"Is there more than one kind of Christianity?" Talia asked, surprised.

"Alas, yes. There is the Roman church. We differ on few details, but it's enough to cause a break. Do you know any Christians?"

"Yes. Inga is a Christian, and her new husband Anatoly was just baptized." Talia thought a moment, remembering her mother's death and the cross she'd placed over the grave. "My mother was a believer. Even in our remote village she had somehow been converted."

The priest's eyes widened in surprise. "And why did you not follow in her ways?"

"It seemed weak," Talia admitted. "And without benefit to her."

"And what has made you begin to consider this weak religion?"

"In Miklagaard I was taken to a church service. The music and the words and the church building were all beautiful."

"But those are superficial things. I admit that I too like the beauty of the big churches, but God is not in gold and gemstones and silk tapestries. He is everywhere in his Creation: in the sea and sky, the animals and birds, and in all human beings who will accept him as Lord."

"Even people who sin, as I did."

"Especially sinners. Christ died on the cross for our sins."

"It's too much for me to understand," Talia said.

"It's too much for anyone to understand, or to deserve. We must accept the great gift and try to live our lives according to His words."

"What can I do about Andrei?"

"Do you want to be wed to him?"

"Yes, but it may never be."

"Pray, my child. If it is meant to be, God will make it happen."

"I prayed when I was captured, and Andrei came to save me."

"Perhaps God hastened Andrei's footsteps, because he cares for you."

"Thank you," Talia said, and turned to go.

He stood. "Wait. Will you kneel, please?"

Talia did, puzzled at the request. He placed his hands on her head and said, "Bless this child, Lord Jesus, and do what is best for her. In the name of the Father, the Son, and the Holy Spirit." He lifted one hand and made an up and down, sideways and down motion that seemed to draw the shape of a cross in the air before her.

Talia rose, said "Thank you," again, and walked away, scarcely watching where she went. There was much to think of. This Christian God was supposed to be loving and caring, and to consider each person the equal to every other one, and yet nothing seemed to change here on earth. There were still slaves and masters and people still died in battle or drowned in the rapids, or died of the wasting, coughing disease as her mother had done. This god decided what was right, and sometimes gave people what they prayed for and sometimes not. That was a lot like Perun.

"Talia," Andrei called. "I've got you a horse for the journey. Do you want to get on and try riding it?"

So they weren't going by boat. That made sense. Coming down river they had moved with the flow of the current and avoided the rapids. Going back it would mean hard rowing all the time, against the current, and they'd still have to avoid the rapids.

Andrei stood holding the reins and when Talia came up beside the horse, Andrei said, "Put your foot in my hand."

Talia did, and felt herself boosted up and onto the broad back of the horse. She gripped the horse's mane to keep from falling off the opposite side, and reached for the reins. She rode slowly around the grassy area near the water, feeling the strange sensation of the horse's warm flesh beneath her thighs and the sun heating her back. Birds wheeled overhead in the cloudless sky, and in the distance, she could hear the surf lapping against the land. She knew Andrei was watching her. It was the first time she'd ridden since the day at the home of Sextus Demetrios, and she remembered the panic she'd felt then when the horse reared. This one was sturdier and less sleek and fleet. Even if she felt uncomfortable, she wouldn't let Andrei see her concern.

This horse was a symbol Andrei cared for her. Otherwise, he would have let her walk and carry a load back to Kiev. Instead, she would ride. And she could tie her goat behind the horse, she decided. Riding instead of walking, they'd soon be back in Kiev.

The thought of seeing Olga and the other villagers excited her. It would be good to be back in the north country, among friends, with no worry about Rognol or Marya. She hadn't wished them dead, especially Marya, even though Marya had tried to kill her. At the last she'd chosen Talia's side, and had died for it. How would God treat Marya? What if someone was a good person without believing in Jesus Christ? There was much she needed to sort about the new faith and the old, and about what was to become of her. What would Andrei do back in Kiev?

Chapter 30

Within a day, Andrei had rounded up horses and found warriors ready to return northward. The cargo was much lighter on the return trip. There were no stacks of hides and furs, no resin or lumber, no urns of honey, no animals for sale, no ships to be guided and then broken up and sold. This time they carried bolts of silk fabric, small vials of perfume, gold jewelry set with precious stones. It was valuable, but weighed far less than the bulky down-river trade items. They did have to carry food and cooking equipment, but no livestock feed. The horses and Talia's goat could forage on the abundant grass that was now at its summer peak.

Following a well-trod trail, they moved steadily northward. The days were long and they could travel until well into the night before darkness came. Talia felt easier after they passed the great rapids. A lump formed in her throat at the memory of the wrecked boats and lost travelers who had been taken by the river. There were still other rapids, but they could look down on them from the trail.

And there were the Pechenegs. Several times Talia thought she saw men moving along beyond the ridge, parallel to their route, and she rode up next to Andrei to tell him.

"I've seen them," he said quietly. "We keep riding. As long as they leave us alone, we'll leave them alone. I have warriors riding out among them who will give us enough warning in case of trouble."

Of course Andrei would have made provisions for their protection, she realized. It was his expedition and the trade goods were his. Anatoly and Inga rode with them, armed to fight and guarding their own property.

The Pechenegs appeared at mid-morning on the third day of following. A group blocked the trail, standing with shields touching so there was no passing between them.

Andrei raised his hand as he had the first day she'd seen him, the day she'd been captured, and the group behind him halted. For a few seconds she was conscious of the clinking of horses' harnesses, and felt her horse shiver beneath her. Should she spur her horse and flee? Was Andrei giving a signal that she didn't understand?

Andrei spoke quickly in a language she only half-understood. "We don't seek battle, but we will fight if we must, and kill you if we have to."

A grizzled man with gapped, broken teeth spit before he spoke. "We too seek no battle, but we will fight if we must."

"Then move aside and let us pass," Andrei said. Behind him his warriors on horseback moved up close, and Talia could hear the swish of swords being drawn. Facing them she saw the Pecheneg leaders drawing knives and lances. Who would back down first? Or would there be a battle despite what both leaders said?

"Pay us tribute."

"What do you demand? We have few goods that your people would want: spices, silk, jewelry."

"You have food, and horses. Your prince took our best animals and scattered our people and our livestock to the plains beyond the great river."

"We have scarcely enough food to last the remainder of our journey," Andrei argued, "and we need the horses to carry us and our goods. You seized part of our cargo on our way southward. That should have been sufficient tribute."

"Pay us or you can't pass."

"We'll fight, and there are more of us," Andrei countered.

"But many of you are women. They are good for slavery and bearing babies, not fighting."

Inga spurred her horse to the front of the group, close to the Pecheneg leader. "I will fight any of your men," she declared. "Anatoly, give me your sword."

"No, Inga," Anatoly protested. "I don't want to lose you. I'll fight him. I'm strong enough for both of us."

She jerked his sword from its scabbard.

The Pecheneg backed off. "We don't fight women. If we kill you, what have we accomplished?"

"You are sure you will kill me?" Inga asked.

"I'll join you," Talia said, moving her horse forward beside Inga. "Let's see if they consider it worthwhile to kill two of us."

The Pecheneg kept is his hand on his sword. "Two of you may be able to kill one of my men, and the man would die in shame, killed by women." He spat on the ground. "We will fight one of your men, and whoever wins will get food, the dead man's horse, and that animal." He pointed to the goat. "It will be good to eat."

"No!" Talia protested.

"I will fight you," Andrei said, "to defend our women, our horses and our trade goods, as well as my lady's goat."

Talia gazed at him with shining eyes. Not only was he willing to fight to protect her and her pet, but he'd called her his lady! She closed her eyes and said a quick silent prayer that God would guide Andrei's sword and strengthen his arm to defeat the Pecheneg.

Andrei slid to the ground and handed the reins of his horse to Anatoly. "If the worst happens, look after my lady Talia. She is free and must not be sold for my debts, but she is still my responsibility."

Talia reached down to touch him and speak her gratitude, but Andrei's attention was on the Pecheneg.

The two rival leaders faced each other, swords drawn. Both were bare from the waist up, and their bodies glistened with sweat from the heat of the summer morning. Both had hair that fell to their shoulders, Andrei's golden, the Pecheneg's tangled and dark.

Andrei was taller, but the Pecheneg was sturdy and thickly muscled.

They edged around each other, their swords striking and clanging against their shields. They were well matched for battle.

The Pecheneg struck first, lunging at Andrei with a harsh, guttural cry. Andrei parried the blow with his lifted shield, but the tip of the other's sword pierced the hand that held the shield, and Talia saw the gush of Andrei's blood.

She gasped, but Inga assured her, "It's a minor wound, not serious. He'll be all right."

"But he's weakened."

"Don't worry," Inga said. "Pray instead, and God will protect him."

"I have been praying," Talia said. "But I don't know how to say a proper prayer."

"The Lord God will understand however you say it."

Talia was so intent on watching Andrei that she didn't notice the other Pechenegs until she heard the frightened bleat of her goat. She whirled to see a Pecheneg trying to cut the goat loose. She jumped from her horse, dagger drawn, and slashed at the man, slicing into the hand he used to cut the tether.

He screamed, dropped his knife, and clutched his bleeding arm. Talia grabbed the goat's tether and turned to strike at the Pecheneg again, but he hobbled off, howling with pain, humiliated.

Talia pulled the frightened goat against her, heedless of its smell and shedding hair. Its eyes were wide, but it had stopped bleating, and snuggled against her. She made sure its rope was securely tied before turning her attention back to Andrei.

Andrei and the Pecheneg leader grappled with each other, both bodies so slick with blood and sweat that neither could get a stranglehold. Their shields clanked uselessly together, the sound mingling with the cheers and jeers of the crowd.

Talia watched, spellbound. Jesus Christ didn't seem to be helping Andrei. Should she pray as well to Perun or Svarog?

She watched, horrified, as the Pecheneg threw Andrei to the ground, close to the edge of the cliff overlooking the rapids. She started to run toward him, but Inga grabbed her and held her back. The Pecheneg stepped away for a moment, drawing in gasping breaths, and then advanced on Andrei.

"Oh, no!" Talia cried out.

But Andrei wasn't finished. As the Pecheneg bore down on him, Andrei grabbed the attacker's leg and threw him over the edge into the water. He screamed all the way down, and then there was a splash and silence.

Andrei stood and looked over the cliff's edge into the water before turning back to the crowd. Several of the Pecheneg warriors advanced on him, seeking vengeance for their leader's death, but Anatoly held them back until Andrei could come safely away from the cliff.

"We have won," Andrei announced. "By your leader's agreement, we now will pass and continue our journey homeward. See to your leader. He may not be dead, just injured by his fall onto the rocks below." He swiped his hand across his face, glanced at the bloody result, and wiped his hand on his trousers. "I think I need to rest for a few moments. Anatoly, can you see to distributing some food to our people and to these Pechenegs?"

"They don't deserve anything," Anatoly objected. "We agreed to their terms and you won."

"True," Andrei agreed. "But do we always deserve what we get? Perhaps by showing them generosity we can do a little to make things better between the Pechenegs and us."

Anatoly nodded. "I'll do what you say, though I don't agree with you. Still, generosity is God's way." He stalked away, his back stiff, and issued orders to the others in the caravan.

The Pechenegs looked doubtfully at the first food handed them. It might be poisoned, a trick of the victor to kill them all. But after a few tentative bites, they thrust food into their mouths, and ate with wolf-like gulps, despite their suspicions.

Talia approached Andrei where he sat on the ground. She carried a small basin of water, and from it she took a cloth and wiped Andrei's face with gentle strokes.

He winced.

"I'm sorry you're injured, and I don't mean to hurt you further," she said.

"Aye, it stings where the water touches the open cuts, but I'll recover."

"You were so brave," she said. "I was afraid you'd be killed."

"So was I, but it suddenly seemed that I had extra strength from some source. Perun rewarded me for my sacrifices in the past."

"It wasn't Perun, I prayed to the Lord Jesus Christ, as Inga and the priest told me to do, and they are right. I could feel that you would win. It was the Christ's will."

Andrei studied her face. Whether right or wrong, she believed. He nodded. "Whatever god helped me, or if it was just fate, we are free to continue our journey." He stood and gave orders for the cargo to be repacked and within a few minutes the caravan was winding its way northward beside the river.

Talia looked back at the rapids that still frightened her. She breathed easier when the caravan had passed beyond sound of the roaring mighty falls.

In the following days Andrei distributed the food so that each person had a little less than they might have had before feeding the Pechenegs, but Talia didn't want even the small amount allotted to her. She had little appetite, and felt queasy.

When she confided in Inga, Inga smiled with delight. "Talia, you may be with child, as I am. This is wonderful news for both of us, isn't it?"

"No. You and Anatoly are married, and your child will become a chieftain of your tribe someday. I have nothing to offer a child."

"But Andrei will marry you. He must."

"I don't want him to marry me just because of the child—if that is indeed what ails me. I only want him if he loves me."

"He may come to love you after you're married," Inga said. "Or he may love you and just not realize it, or not be able to express it."

"He can certainly express himself on everything else," Talia retorted. "I'm not going to tell him, and you must not either."

"Sooner or later he's bound to notice," Inga said. "It's not something you can hide forever. What are you going to do?"

"I don't know," Talia said. "Will God help me?"

"It's God's will that you are with child," Inga said. "Otherwise it wouldn't have happened. It didn't happen before, did it? There is some purpose for everything, Talia. God will show you what to do."

Talia nodded doubtfully and edged her horse away from Inga's. If this was truly the will of God, why had it happened just after she was freed? If it had happened back in Kiev, Andrei would never have taken her on the journey to Byzantium, and she'd never have seen the beautiful church or the city. She would still be his slave, and so would her coming child. He had called her his "lady," but what did that signify? And even though she was free, having a child all alone would take away that freedom. Babies needed care and attention. She could go with Inga and Anatoly to their home on the northern sea, but then what? How could she support herself and a child?

Chapter 31

Runners had seen their approach, and by the time the caravan arrived at Kiev, the great gates of the city were flung open and crowds poured out to greet them, eager to see the wares brought from Byzantium.

Andrei dismounted and Talia slid down from her horse, untied her goat, and stood beside Andrei. Someone took the reins of both horses and led them away as people swarmed around the bundles.

Anatoly and Inga stayed on their horses, waiting for an invitation to stay until they could arrange their onward journey. Andrei noticed and called a servant to take the couple to his home.

Talia stood alone, uncertain where she was to go. Inga motioned for her to follow, but Talia dared not without Andrei's permission. She no longer belonged to him as a slave or a servant, but she had no other place in his life or his home either.

Andrei was quickly surrounded by buyers of the precious goods, and by the rest of the caravan, awaiting his instructions for where to store his cargo.

"Talia!"

Talia turned at a familiar voice and saw Olga running toward her, arms outstretched in welcome. Nicolai followed his wife, carrying the baby.

Talia clasped her friend close. "Olga, you've changed. You look beautiful. I left a gaunt, sick woman and return to find a plump rosy maiden."

"Not a maiden," Olga protested, turning to Nicolai. "A contented wife with a good husband."

Nicolai too had changed. Talia had thought him scarred and ugly, but his smile lighted up his face, and Talia could tell that he cared for Olga and her child. Kindness and gentleness shone from him, making him almost handsome. He was still reserved and quiet, standing a few steps back. His limp was less noticeable. Marriage had been good for both of them, and Talia envied her friend whom she'd once pitied.

Nicolai squatted beside the goat and let the infant touch it. "What have we here, Talia?" he asked. "Is this all you brought back from Miklagaard?"

"It's a long story," Talia said. "When we sheltered under an upturned boat during an attack, the goat joined us, eager to save its own life. I persuaded Andrei to let me keep it."

Nicolai stood and grinned. "I think you made a good choice. It's a female, and unless I'm mistaken in the signs, it's soon to have young. So you'll have the beginning of a flock and milk to make cheese like the Byzantines do."

"Oh, Talia, we have so many questions, and there's so much I want to hear about your trip!" Olga said, uninterested in the goat. "I'm so glad you came back. I thought Andrei would sell you to some rich man."

"I thought so too," Talia said, "but he didn't."

"So, you're still his slave."

"No, he freed me. I don't know what I am now, or where to go."

"There's always a place here for you," Olga assured her. "And we can look after your goat until you decide." She took the baby from Nicolai, who led the goat away. "Let's walk up the hill, Talia. You must see what Prince Vladimir is doing to Kiev."

Olga walked rapidly, even encumbered by the baby. Talia paused to rest, and when she caught up, Olga asked, "What's wrong? You used to have so much energy I could never keep up with you."

"I think I am with child," Talia said.

Olga's reaction was the opposite of Inga's. "Oh, Talia, I was afraid this would happen, but it was inevitable if Andrei continued to use you. It is his child, isn't it?"

"Of course, but, I went to him willingly. He never forced me, except at first," Talia confessed.

"He must marry you and accept the child, Nicolai will speak to him."

Talia gripped her friend's arm. "No! I don't want him to be forced to marry me."

Olga laughed lightly. "He may not have a choice, even without the child. Nicolai says the prince is planning to have all his warriors marry the women they have been living with. It's part of the new religion, Nicolai said. Rognol will have to marry Marya, whether she wants him or not. Where are they? Are they coming later?"

"They are both dead," Talia said, shuddering at the memory.

"How?"

"Rognol tried to kill me, and he killed Marya. When Andrei and Anatoly came to save me, they fought and Rognold was killed. We all had to flee from Byzantium before the crime was discovered."

Olga's eyes were wide with horror. "How terrible! But why wasn't Andrei protecting you?"

"Inga and I were put in the slave quarters and groomed to be sold to rich Byzantine men. The Kievan warriors were staying at another part of the city."

"Who is Inga?"

"A chieftain's daughter who was captured by Prince Vladimir and enslaved. Anatoly took her as his reward for killing Pechenegs."

"None of this makes sense, Talia," Olga said. "So much has happened to you I can't comprehend it all. We must spend a lot of time together over the next few weeks while you tell me everything, a little bit at the time. For now, I'm just glad you are alive and back here with me, and that your enemies are dead. I know as a

Christian I'm not supposed to rejoice in the death of enemies. We're supposed to forgive them, many times over, but that's hard to do."

"You have become a Christian?"

"Yes. Because of Nicolai. He didn't try to convert me, but the way he lives persuaded me."

"You're fortunate," Talia said.

"No, I'm blessed. I had no real choice, being a widow with a baby, as well as a brother who is sometimes hard to get along with. Nicolai never forced me. He's been kind and gentle, and he rescued me from being separated from my baby and sold as a slave. What began as gratitude has become a deep love for him. I want to bear him children and spend the rest of my life with him."

"I might have come to love Sextus Demetrios," Talia mused. "I thought I could. He treated me well and even introduced me at the court in Byzantium, and he said he would marry me."

"Why didn't you marry this man?"

"At the last moment, when his money for my purchase was on the table, Andrei refused to sell me."

"Then he cares for you!" Olga declared. Her baby had begun to fuss and she patted it gently against her shoulder. "Let's move on to a shady spot. Little Nicolai doesn't do well in the hot sun."

"You named him Nicolai?"

"Nicolai said it would be all right to name him Oleg after his father, but I thought it best to call him after the only father he'll ever know. Naming him Oleg would have meant a lot of explanations as he grows up, and it would stir memories of things we must put behind us."

As they reached the crest of the hill, Talia could only stare at the building being constructed there. Trees had been cleared away and the steep slope flattened to a broad, grassy area. On a stone cross-shaped foundation walls were rising for what was clearly a church. She turned to Olga in wonderment.

Olga nodded in answer to her unspoken question. "Whether you like the prince or fear him, you must admire his leadership and persistence. He returned with his new wife, the Princess Anna, and announced that henceforth his domain will be Christian, beginning with this church. He's pulled men from military duty to help build the church, and brought with him stonemasons from the south. It's almost complete."

Talia stared up at the walls where men were spreading mortar on stones and pushing them into place, then reaching for more. Others on the ground were mixing mortar, hauling stones up the hillside, and hoisting both up to the masons by a series of pulleys. She had stood on this spot only a few months before, sorrowful, lost, staring down at the silvery river.

Now it was all changed. From the church she could look down on the city and the river spread below. She vowed silently that when the church building was completed, she'd profess her belief and be baptized a Christian. Both Olga and Inga believed, and they were happily married to men they loved. Men who loved them, she reminded herself. She didn't have that.

"How long do you think it will be before the church is finished?" she asked.

"I don't know. After the outside is completed, different men will work on the inside," Olga said. "The prince comes often with drawings of how he wants his church to look. Nicolai says there will be paintings done in gold, and carvings and fine tapestries. Imagine that!"

Talia recalled the splendor of the Hagia Sofia of Miklagaard, the way the light shone through the colored glass of the windows, the soaring music. This church wasn't like that, but it had a certain majesty about it, and the priest had prayed with her in the outdoors, by the sea, with no church at all. The church at Byzantium was wonderful, but it wasn't the only place to worship.

Out in front of the church stood the statues of Perun and Svarog, glowering at all who passed. Some of the workers stared at the evil faces, some made what Talia had come to know as the sign of the Cross, and still others looked away, uncertain if the gods still had power, unwilling to test their wrath.

Talia had once thought of the totems as frightening gods that must be appeased. Now she considered them merely ugly, wooden carvings. She had seen the sculptures in Miklagaard, horses so lifelike she could almost have ridden one away, beautiful serene figures of saints and — most moving of all — the mosaics of the face of Jesus Christ, gold halo above His head.

Nearby stood a zigzag piece of metal topped by a huge medallion, almost like the shield Andrei carried. This was supposed to represent the protection as well as the destruction Svarog could dispense.

"I once feared them," Olga said, giving voice to Talia's thoughts as well.

"So did I, but no more. Why does Prince Vladimir allow them to remain beside his church? Don't the priests and the princess object?"

A trumpet sounded, its notes echoing throughout the city.

"We're being summoned for something," Olga said. "It's probably another gathering to pray. The prince has held them fairly often ever since he got back from Byzantium with his new wife. We'd better go."

They made their way down the hill to join the swelling crowd near the riverbank. The prince and princess, both dressed in white, stood with their backs to the water, facing the crowd. Beside them were two priests, robed in black, their long hair tied back and topped by a small black cap. Each man wore a heavy jeweled cross around his neck, a contrast to the prince and princess who wore no jewels.

Nicolai stood near the royal couple, his hand on the shoulder of a youth that Talia realized with a start was Grigor. He'd grown taller and put on weight during the time she'd been away. Nicolai edged people aside to make space for Olga and Talia.

Talia looked around for Andrei. Where was he? She longed to see him, yet perversely wanted to avoid him.

The prince, too, was looking over the crowd as if he knew well who was missing. The gathering was silent, waiting the prince's message.

Andrei was among the last few stragglers, and Talia realized that Inga and Anatoly were missing. Had they already left Kiev to go north? Inga would surely have said goodbye. But after all the prince had done to Inga, she'd want to avoid him. Besides, both Inga and Anatoly were already Christians, so they had no need of the prince's public prayers. They could pray directly to the Christ whenever they wished.

The prince raised his hands and began speaking in a deep, serious voice. "My subjects! Most of you have become accustomed to my public prayers, and I have waited for the arrival of the warriors from Miklagaard for the next step. I have been baptized and some of you have as well. Today the remainder of you will be baptized and become Christian."

Some of the newcomers murmured in puzzlement. How were they to be suddenly made Christians? And why?

"It is time for us to set aside our pagan ways and join the civilized nations around us. We will no longer worship angry gods who pull our ships into the watery deep or who want us to kill each other or to put our weakened parents and grandparents on ice floes to die. From now on we will all worship Jesus Christ, the son of God the Creator. He is your Father in Heaven and I here on earth will be your Little Father. As you have been told, I have searched diligently to find the best religion for you, my children. Emissaries went to the Kazars to talk with the Jews. That faith has much to recommend it, and indeed Jesus Christ himself was born of a Jewish mother, and He is the promised Savior, though the Jews do not accept him as such. We decided against Islam for several reasons. We examined the Catholicism of both Germany and Rome, which are quite different, but once we saw and heard the marvelous church services in Byzantium, we felt sure that this was best for us."

He indicated the beautiful woman who stood serenely by his side. "In addition to choosing a religion that will encompass my empire, I found the best wife to help me spread this new faith to our whole realm."

Talia listened raptly. She had no experience with any of the other religions he mentioned, but the quiet, serene way her mother had lived showed the goodness of Christianity, and what Prince Vladimir described was the very way she had felt in the Hagia Sofia in Miklagaard. Talking with the priest had made her more certain. She was ready to accept the new religion, faith in the Lord Jesus Christ.

"I have been blessed by my faith," the prince continued, "and I want to share this faith with all of you, my children. I have brought you here by the river so that you may be baptized by the living water. Who wants to be the first to be baptized today?"

"I do!" Talia cried.

The prince looked startled. "I had thought one of my brave warriors would come first to be an example to the others." He glanced around at his troops, and seemed to recover his thoughts. "But perhaps our women are becoming warriors, strengthened by their newfound faith."

Olga and Nicolai were both smiling as they nudged Talia toward the prince and the priests. She moved forward almost in a trance, telling herself that she would not fear the water. There were no rapids here, and the spot the prince had chosen for the baptisms was a still pool, dappled by the sunlight.

"I'll go first!" Andrei called out, pushing his way through the crowd.

The prince smiled. "That position is taken, Andrei Ivanovich, by the woman you chose as your slave. You may take second place, or forbid her to be baptized, as is your right as master."

"I am no longer her master, nor is she my slave. I freed her before we returned from Miklagaard, and she chooses baptism of her own free will."

"That does surprise me," the prince said. "And you chose not to sell her. That is commendable."

Talia looked from Andrei to the prince. *Commendable, the way Andrei had treated me?* The prince had enslaved Inga, and only released her when Anatoly won her for bravery. Had the prince freed all his slaves? Perhaps his new wife and Christianity were working miracles on him.

Deep in thought, Talia didn't realize she was being led to the water's edge, and when she became aware of what was about to happen, it was too late to change her mind. She was lifted off her feet and dunked into the water, three times. Each time, as she surfaced, sputtering and terrified, remembering her near-death at the falls, more water was poured over her head from the priest's hand, while he said, "In the name of the Father, and of the Son and of the Holy Ghost, Amen."

The assembled crowd repeated "Amen," and made the sign of the Cross. Then, as she was set onto her feet, she felt as if a weight had been lifted from her. It was more than relief at being out of the water. She felt freer than before, clean and rinsed of her cares. Hardly watching where she walked, and unaware of how she looked with her wet clothing clinging to her body, she stumbled and fell into Andrei's arms.

She wanted to tell him how she felt, to ask him what he was thinking, but there was no time to talk. It was Andrei's turn to be baptized. As she watched, it seemed as if a special shaft of sunlight was shed on Andrei, setting his red-gold hair aflame, almost like the halo above the head of the Christ in the Miklagaard church.

"Do you accept the Lord Jesus Christ as your Savior?" the priest asked Andrei. He had not asked her. Perhaps he doubted Andrei's sincerity.

Talia too wondered if Andrei really believed, or if he only stepped forward to be baptized to impress the prince. *I mustn't doubt*, she thought. *He may be wondering the same about me. Something will happen to make him believe, as I do. I know it was the Christ who sent Andrei to save me from Rognold. Perun and Svarog only do violent things.*

Andrei stepped from the water, his clothing clinging to his body, his hair hanging in damp tendrils. His appearance was changed, and Talia knew that she too looked different. He came toward her, arms outstretched, and gathered her against him.

Talia reveled in the warmth of his body, and laughed at the water dropping from their hair onto their shoulders. She shook her head, sending tiny droplets flying into the air.

"Where were you?" he asked, setting her back from him so he could look into her face. "I didn't see you until you stepped forward to be baptized."

"I was with Olga."

"I looked for you. Why didn't you come home?"

"Home?"

"My house. That's still your home."

"As what? Your servant? Your mistress?"

"As my wife."

She waited, hardly breathing, for his next words, a proposal and a declaration of love, but before he could say more, the prince was speaking again. "When all have been baptized, we will go to the hilltop and destroy the images of Perun and Svarog. We have no further need of these so-called gods from our ignorant, pagan past."

There were gasps of disbelief from some listeners. How could they destroy what they had believed in all their lives? Surely it was possible to worship the new God along with the old. After all, they had worshiped many gods in the past.

Hearing their dismay, the prince went on, even as the baptisms continued, "The Christian God is more powerful than Perun or Svarog or any other of our gods. They don't control our world. We do, by our faith in Jesus Christ and by our own actions. We may not always have our prayers answered as we would wish, but in the long run what God decides is what is best for us. We may continue to suffer in this world, but if we believe, and repent of our sins and try to lead a good life, then we will have eternal life hereafter."

How is it possible?

Talia heard the murmured question that she herself had asked in the past.

"You may not understand the immensity of God. I do not understand it myself. No man does, but I accept it, as you must."

Talia knew that she must not talk while the prince was speaking, or while the priests were performing baptisms, but she waited impatiently for Andrei's proposal.

But he didn't seem to feel it was necessary, she decided. He had said he wanted her to be his wife and come back to live at his home. Once, that would have been enough, but not now. Now Talia wanted love, and a Christian wedding.

As they made their way up the hill along with the crowd, Talia felt faint, but she bit her lip to hold back the nausea. Andrei mustn't know about the baby, not yet.

The crowd stood back from the images of Perun and Svarog, still half fearful of the dreaded power of the pagan gods. The prince could decree, could force them to be baptized, but it would take time to wipe out the teaching of generations. They gathered in clusters, standing close but not looking at each other, drawing courage from their fellows to follow the prince's orders.

The prince strode into the center of the clearing, close beside the feared icons. His wife, the empress Anna, now princess, walked triumphantly beside him, not trailing steps behind as his previous wives had done.

Two servants followed, each carrying an ax. The royal couple stopped before the church door, and the prince held up his hands for silence, needlessly, as the crowd was cowed into silence.

"Who will strike the first blow against these evil statues?" he asked.

For a moment there was an even deeper silence, tinged with fear. Who would dare to strike the powerful figures, images of power that had in the past struck at the people?

Andrei stepped forward. "I will." He took the ax.

"Will you destroy Perun or Svarog?" the prince asked.

"Whichever my Lord Prince chooses."

"Svarog, then. Do you wish to destroy both statues, or is there someone else brave enough to strike down the evil past?"

"I will do so, Prince Vladimir," Anatoly said, stepping from the back of the crowd. Inga moved up to stand near him.

"You are a Christian? I did not see you baptized today."

"I was baptized in Miklagaard, and my wife has been long a Christian, long before you defiled her and made her your slave."

The prince's hand reached for his sword, ready to strike down anyone who dared speak thus to him, but he realized he carried no sword today. His hand halted and he looked steadily at Inga and Anatoly. "You earned your wife's freedom in bravery for me, and in truth, she would not have been a suitable wife for me."

Anatoly nodded, and Talia saw a smile, the beginning of laughter, cross his face and Inga's.

To her surprise, the prince said, "Inga, daughter of Regnald, wife of Anatoly, forgive me."

There was a gasp from the crowd. Their all-powerful prince was asking forgiveness of a woman. Before today, they would not have thought such a thing possible. He would have beheaded anyone who dared speak against him.

Inga nodded, made the sign of the Cross, and went to stand beside Talia, taking her hand. Talia could feel the tremor in Inga's hand. She and Anatoly had been brave, had trusted that Christianity had transformed the prince, but still had some fear of him.

Anatoly accepted the proffered ax and stood beside Andrei. "You first," he said.

Sparks shot out where the ax struck metal, and chips of wood flew into the air to fall at the prince's feet. Andrei paused, stripped off his shirt, and tossed it to the ground. The muscles of his damp torso moved with powerful rhythm as he struck again and again, with almost supernatural strength.

Talia thought she saw precious, glittering stones drop from the eyes of the god, to roll on the ground and stop at the feet of the prince. He signaled a servant to pick up the stones. They might be only glass, or they might indeed be valuable and have some secret power. In either case, the god Svarog had no more use for them.

With a thud the statue broke from its pedestal and fell to the ground, bounced slightly and lay still.

Anatoly swung his ax like a pendulum, then approached the image of Perun and struck it a mighty blow. The sound rang out in the silence as he struck repeated blows without stopping.

Talia remembered the feel of the ax in her own hands, first cutting down trees for firewood and then striking at Rognol.

When the second statue fell, the sky was lit with a faint shiver of lightning, followed by a far-off rumble of thunder. Several in the crowd shrieked in terror, but the prince showed no emotion as he held up his hands. "The power of these gods to do you harm has departed. They accept that Jesus Christ is more powerful. You have no reason to fear." To Talia's astonishment, he quoted something the priest had said at Byzantium, "Fear not, for I am with you."

"Now," the prince ordered, "chop these logs of wood into pieces. They are no longer gods, merely wood. Then anyone of you who needs firewood is free to take as much as you can carry. Nothing should remain here of the statues to besmirch the entry to our church. There will be no more sacrificial offerings made here, and the blood of animals and fowl shed for these pagan gods will help to fertilize the soil. We shall plant flowers and grass, perhaps vines to make wine grapes for our Holy Eucharist services. We will set up a cross here, but it would not be appropriate to make it from such wood. We will have a stone cross carved just for our church."

No one stepped forward to claim the wood. It was unthinkable, burning a portion of a god to cook beans or heat water to wash clothing or one's body.

Andrei and Anatoly continued to chop, turning the pagan carvings into wood no longer than a man's forearm. Both warriors completed the destruction and stood leaning on the handles of their axes, breathing heavily from their exertion.

Then Nicolai walked to the heap of wood nearest him. "I'll take wood. Grigor, can you carry an armful?" His stepson picked up so much wood he staggered with its weight, proud to be singled out before the prince for a task.

The spell was broken. Others gathered up wood. It was, after all, seasoned wood that would catch fire easily and burn well. It should not be left out to rot and go to waste. And too, the prince had said it must be burned to make space for growing plants. There was a quick scrabble for firewood, and within a few moments the hilltop was cleared of all remnants of the feared gods.

Talia stared at the torn up earth where the icons had stood, where their fall had dug indentations in the earth, where the feet of the crowd had ripped away the vegetation. Only slivers of wood remained. Some people, she thought, had probably taken pieces of the gods not for firewood but as relics to be treasured. They had believed in the evil gods too long to change in the course of a single morning. Had Andrei changed? When had his conversion begun?

Chapter 32

Talia saw something glittering in the torn-up earth, half-covered.
She bent and picked it up, wiping it on her skirt. It was one of the
stones from the images. She closed her fingers around it before
anyone noticed.

Andrei had seen. "What did you find? Are you taking splinters
of the gods to worship?"

"No, I believe in the Lord Jesus Christ. I 'm not one who longs
for the old gods and the old ways. I saw in Miklagaard what the
new life could be like."

"Then what do you have in your hand?"

She opened her fingers to display the stone. In the sunlight it
shone with red fire. "It may be nothing more than glass like the
church windows, but I want to keep it."

"I'll have it set into a silver necklace for you, unless you want to
return it to the prince."

"No," she said. "I found it, and I may need it. The prince and
his wife have more than enough valuable things. I have nothing."

He didn't deny her statement, but neither did he take away the
stone. Talia held it tightly. Unless Andrei married her, she would
go north with Inga and Anatoly. She couldn't bear the shame of
living here with Andrei's child and not as his wife, the torture of
seeing him but not being with him.

The others had left the hillside, and the workmen had returned
to their tasks, pulling at ropes to bring stones up the slope and then
to move them into place in the wall of the church.

Talia turned in a circle, looking at the church, the river, the
great wooden gates, the city. Then she felt faint and dizzy and

collapsed. Everything went black. When she opened her eyes, she was looking into Andrei's face as he bent to lift her head.

"What's wrong? Turning shouldn't make you faint. Have you been starving yourself? Let's get you home where I can see that you are fed."

"I'm with child," she blurted. She hadn't meant to tell him like this, when she was helpless and without the support of Olga or Inga. But unless she left Kiev, he would soon know anyway.

"Then that's another reason why we must marry. I can't have my child born a bastard. He must have my name and my protection."

"He? It may be a girl, and it is my child too. I have some say-so about what happens to it."

"But don't you want to marry me?"

"Yes, but not just to give a child its father's name. What is your other reason?" She felt ashamed to push him into declaring love, but she would not marry without love, even to Andrei.

"The prince has decreed that all of his subjects must marry the women they have been consorting with. That is his word. I consider what we have done more than consorting, so I will abide by his decree."

"The prince has no control over me, and neither do you. You said that to the prince before hundreds of witnesses. I am free. I can marry or not and stay here or not." She wanted him to say that he couldn't bear it if she went away, that he loved her and couldn't live without her, but he didn't. He was only concerned with what the prince said and with what people thought. She longed for him to kiss her, to make love to her, but that wasn't going to happen, not here anyway. What if she went with him to his home as she had so often in the past, and went to his bed? Could she resist him? She forced herself to stand, to put space between herself and him

She looked at her empty hand. "Where is my stone?"

He handed it to her. "I wouldn't keep it from you. And it will pass to our daughter, or our son's wife, along with the other jewels I still have from my other wife."

"Your other wife?"

"She died. I told you."

"Oh." She had forgotten, but it didn't change her need. He had loved the wife who had died in childbirth while he was away. That could be part of the reason he wanted to marry, to make sure he had an heir, safely born while he was present. But he had said that he wanted her to be his wife, before he knew about the child. She waited for him to say more.

"So, will you marry me? I can give you a good life, though perhaps not as good as the life Sextus Demetrios offered you." Andrei was looking at her with those blue eyes that could convince her of almost anything. Almost.

"No." She made herself say the word, holding out for the words she wanted to hear.

"Why not?"

"Because you don't love me."

"Of course I love you." He sounded puzzled that she didn't know.

"Then say it. Say that you love me."

"Talia Militskaya, I love you. Now, will you marry me?"

"Yes, Andrei Ivanovich, I will," she said, no longer feeling faint. Her heart was singing with happiness. She threw her arms around him and lifted her face for his kiss. She was careful to hold onto the stone. That was her talisman, her insurance in case something happened to him before they married. Or even after.

Together, arm in arm, they started walking down the hill. "We can have our wedding in the new church, and I'll have a dress made for you of the finest silk we brought from Byzantium," he said.

"No," Talia said. "By the time the church is finished, I'll begin to show I'm with child and everyone will think you married me only because of that. Or the child may even have been born. There is still much to be done to the church." Now that she had secured Andrei's declaration of love, there was no reason to delay marriage, and every reason to marry quickly. "We can be married today, as soon as the priests finish the baptisms, and I don't need a special dress." She looked down at the garment that had worn thin and ragged from the journey. She remembered Andrei's discarding her clothing, sending it to be burned, when he'd first brought her to Kiev. If he too were remembering, maybe she should wait at least long enough for a suitable dress to be made. How quickly could Olga or Inga stitch her a wedding gown?

"You are right, my dearest," he said, the first time she remembered his calling her by any affectionate term. "I will love you and marry you in what you are wearing, with the promise of more beautiful garments as soon as they can be made. I will love you in whatever you wear, or in nothing at all."

It seemed to Talia that a dam had broken. Once Andrei had admitted that he loved her, the stream of loving words could flow freely.

Had he only said he loved her because she had pushed him into saying it? She had to know, even if it hurt. She knew she should be satisfied that he was saying the words she wanted now, and not question the past, but she asked anyway. "When did you first love me? Just today?"

"I think I fell in love with you the first moment I saw you, standing in the snow with your hair streaming out from your fur hood and your face red from the cold. You were so fierce, like a warrior. Then you defended yourself. I hated that Rognol attacked you, but he was my warrior and I had to allow him to capture you. But I was glad you didn't let him defile you. I knew even then that I wanted you for myself. I wanted to be the one to claim your virginity."

"Why didn't you tell me this long ago? Why did you make me tend Rognol? And why did you take me to Miklagaard to sell? I almost died at the falls."

"I was a proud fool. At first, I was still grieving the loss of my wife and child, and I thought you were inferior, not worthy to marry one of the prince's special warriors, not worthy to replace my wife."

Talia felt her face growing hot with anger as she remembered his allowing her to wear the clothes that had belonged to his wife, how she'd enjoyed the feeling of fine garments against her skin. All along he had thought of her as inferior, no better than to be his slave. She pulled away from him.

"I was wrong," he protested. "I said I was a fool. Can you accept that I have changed? At first I couldn't admit even to myself that you are worthy of me, worthy of any man, even the prince. I could only see your beauty that tempted me. I thought I could sell you and remove you from my temptation, even when I saw how brave you were, how you tended wounds without cringing. You did your share of the heavy work and managed to cheer up Inga, and save her. I loved touching your body, joining it with mine, but it was not until Miklagaard that I knew I wanted you for more than physical loving. I want you for your spirit, your intelligence, your courage, and your companionship. You are everything I want in a wife."

"What made you change your mind in Miklagaard?" she asked, though she thought she knew. She wanted to hear him declare over and over that he loved her and wanted her.

"When I saw how you could ornament the home and life of Sextus Demetrios, I knew I wanted you for myself. I could hardly endure seeing you smile at him and touch him. And when money was actually on the table and I realized that I would be letting you go for a handful of besants, I couldn't sell you. You were worth much more than that."

"But you didn't say that," she said, still rankled that he had for so long considered her inferior, not allowing himself to love her. "You left me at the slave quarters."

"And I regretted it the moment I left you. I started making arrangements immediately to leave Miklagaard, knowing I wanted to bring you back here to Kiev. Anatoly can attest to that. And you remember I did have the ship loaded and ready to leave," he went on, defending himself.

"But you didn't tell me that. I thought when Byzas said you had sent for me that you were ready to go, or that you wanted me to stay in better quarters. You know I would never have gone to Rognol willingly."

He stopped walking, and Talia saw with surprise that they had reached the door of his house, now to be hers as well. "Would you have gone if Sextus Demetrios had sent for you?" he asked.

"Probably. I would have thought you had changed your mind and sold me after all. He had treated me well and would have been a good husband. But I might have doubted. I'd told Byzas I wasn't marrying Sextus Demetrios, and he was furious at me. He would have been happier if I were to marry and stay in Miklagaard. I came close to dying," she reminded him.

"Yes, I was really a fool then, and frightened as well."

"Why didn't you tell me then that you loved me — if you did?"

"I took it for granted that you knew, that women always know. I thought my freeing you, giving up a lot of money, would tell you."

She shook her head. "Inga said you loved me, but I needed to hear it from you."

"I said I was a fool. I love you. Can you accept that? If Inga can forgive the prince, can you forgive me for misusing you?"

Talia nodded, feeling tears spring to her eyes. Andrei was a proud man, unused to asking anyone for forgiveness, unwilling to admit that he had been wrong or acted foolishly. But for her he had changed.

He opened the front door and stepped back to let her enter. Before she'd followed him.

Inga and Anatoly met them just inside, dressed and packed ready for their northward journey. "Where have you been?" Inga asked. "Anatoly has found boats for us and loaded our cargo. We didn't want to leave without saying goodbye."

"Can you stay a few hours longer for our wedding?" Andrei asked.

Inga threw her arms around Talia. "Of course! This makes me almost as happy as you are, my wonderful friend." She stepped back, rummaged in her pack, and brought out a silk shawl, red with threads of gold. Draping it around Talia's shoulders, she said, "You can't be married in just that rag. This is my wedding gift to you. Now, when and where is the wedding to be?"

"Right here," Andrei decided. "I'll go for a priest."

"I'll go," Anatoly said. "You stay right here."

Andrei laughed. "I accept, but you needn't think I'd try to escape. It was difficult enough to persuade Talia to marry me. She put up all kinds of objections."

Inga took charge, calling for servants to put their bags away and to cook a dinner suitable for a bridal feast. To Andrei she said, "Don't just stand there. Go to the sauna and get yourself cleaned up, then put on some decent clothing. No, on second thought, don't go to the sauna. You've been dipped and cleansed already today, at the river. Just change, while I prepare Talia. We can't do anything about the clothing except cover it with the shawl, but I can brush the tangles from your hair and add a bit of color to your face."

Talia laughed and followed Inga, who talked as she led the way. "You'll make a fine chieftain," she said. "I'm just sorry you won't be here."

"I belong in my own country, and it's time I took charge. I'll share responsibility and power with Anatoly, of course. And you'll share power with Andrei, of course."

The two women laughed together, knowing what power they had over their men. "And perhaps we can return to Kiev to have our children baptized together in the prince's grand church."

As she sat on a bench for Inga to smooth her hair and cover the stubbled spot with another shawl, Talia suddenly remembered her mother's carved chest with its special meaning. "Today is my wedding day, the day I'm supposed to open the box."

Inga looked puzzled. "What box?"

"You wouldn't know about it. It's all I have from my mother. Olga has it, and I want her to be at my wedding. And her husband Nicolai and her brother and the baby."

Inga sent another servant scurrying off to find Olga.

Within a short time, the group gathered and Anatoly returned with a priest. Talia took the box from Olga and broke the seal. What would she find? She peered down into the box, and lying on a bit of fur was a jeweled cross on a silver chain. She touched it with her fingertip, as if checking to see if it was real. It had been her mother's, had touched her skin, been held in her hands. Talia closed her eyes, remembering her mother's face, her voice, her gentleness. Then she slipped the chain around her neck, and Andrei fastened it.

"It's as if she knew I'd be a Christian, and would want to wear a cross for my wedding."

"Are you ready for the marriage ceremony?" the priest asked.

"Now we are," Talia and Andrei answered together.